BOOK
HOUSE
布可屋

— 1天10分鐘，輕鬆考高分 —

NEW TOEIC

多益最新
應考策略

突破900分必考
單字‧聽力‧閱讀

附QR碼線上音檔
行動學習‧即刷即聽

張小怡‧Johnson Mo◎合著

BOOK
HOUSE
布可屋

高速循環速記，輕鬆考高分

NEW TOEIC測驗，主要是測驗應試者，針對目前和未來，能夠更了解實際職場、生活、社交，所需具備的英語溝通和使用技巧。試題內容分兩大部分：聽力、閱讀。

NEW TOEIC測驗，採用全世界近10多年來，職場和社交場合，使用頻率比較高的英語，讓考生進入職場時，能馬上派上用場。

◆高速循環速記單字，1 分鐘反覆背誦，記憶最強，突破最高分

單字、閱讀和聽力是學英文最重要的關鍵，也是最難的關卡，一下要打通這任督三脈，想要參加NEW TOEIC考試的人中，都很想知道「要如何提升自己的單字、聽力、閱讀？」答案都在本書中。

要有好的分數，必須要針對NEW TOEIC的出題方向來考慮策略。第一要先分析在NEW TOEIC考試要具備多少的單字力，將出題可能性較高的重要單字，集中學習；而且自己的單字能力，到底達到什麼程度，了解哪個領域，是自己的弱點，也是很重要的。

◆事半功倍，效率提高100%

NEW TOEIC測驗的重點，擺在「聽懂英語，讀懂英語」的能力，本書是為了有效率地，提升NEW TOEIC應試者的英語的運用能力，以及綜合能力企劃而成。

本書針對NEW TOEIC的解題、答題、猜題，做綜合整理，不僅教您在短期內準備好考試，而且對於想要擁有應付自如的「英語聽讀、溝通能力」的讀者，更會為您帶來意想不到的效果。

即使不考多益，相信您的英語溝通能力，也會因為本書而突飛猛進，可以輕鬆應付平常英文業務，成為人人稱羨的「國際人」。只要確實讀完本書，我們保證您在極短的時間內，輕取證明國際業務處理的能力，並奠下您邁向獲取更高分的基礎。

◆閱讀和聽力，快速大躍進

NEW TOEIC測驗偏向：企業、商務、金融、科技、製造業、辦公室、人事採購、房地產、保健、外食、娛樂、旅遊等12大主題，不論聽力或閱讀測驗，考題都是來自這些情境。

◆提高聽力測驗分數的方法

老師歸納3個方法：1.跟聽、跟讀；2.跟聽、跟說；3.跟聽、跟寫。練習聽力時，要全心注意聽外籍老師的發音、速度和語調。先別看內容，而是先依照所聽到的速度，跟著大聲唸出來，再來對照內容文字。

◆提高閱讀測驗分數的方法

也有3招。1.掌握關鍵單字；2.掌握閱讀；3.掌握閱讀測驗出題文章的主題和領域。閱讀測驗的關鍵，是在「單字片語」和「文法句型」，單字片語記得多、文法句型能力好，閱讀能力就跟著水漲船高。

有關聽力，最好是：聽什麼就能聽懂什麼；如果不行的話，那麼就多做練習，也就是聽外師錄音「洗英語澡」，即使聽100遍，也不嫌多。在此同時，要全力注意聽外籍老師的發音、速度和語調，如果能夠這樣長期練習，你的聽力和口說能力，會快速大躍進。

考試的勝負，往往決定於困難部份的分數，像閱讀測驗中的單篇文章、多篇文章的理解；聽力測驗中的簡短對話、簡短獨白部份。閱讀測驗的單句填空、和短文填空部份，是大家比較容易掌握的部份。

閱讀測驗是大家學習英文時最常接觸的題型，在校考試時常會有練習的機會，準備方向也較易掌握，不外乎就是字彙的累積、句型文法的掌握。然而，礙於國內英語環境的欠缺，聽力顯然是國人一直無法突破的瓶頸，常常不知從何處著手加強。

若想脫穎而出拿高分，一次突破900分，就要在別人不會的方面下功夫。所以本書特別加強聽力、長篇文章的練習，讓你上考場前，不但有萬全的準備，還擁有比別人有更深厚的基礎，和拿分的技巧，精讀本書後，臨上考場，你已經贏人家一大步，輕鬆得高分沒問題。

高分速記
循環流程圖

P Plan（計畫）

1. 預計考試時間
2. 擬定閱讀計劃
3. 收集考試教材

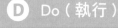

D Do（執行）

1. 每天背多少單字
2. 每天記多少文法
4. 每天練多少聽力
5. 每天做多少模擬測驗

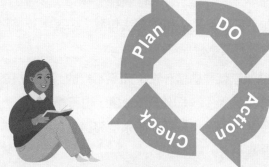

A Action（行動）

1. 重新啟動導航
2. 修正閱讀進度
3. 調整準備方法

C Check（校驗）

1. 單字文法都記住嗎？
2. 聽力測驗有問題嗎？
3. 閱讀測驗有問題嗎？
4. 模擬測驗成績驗收

- 多益最新，應考策略，不管怎麼考，都不怕！
- 百萬考生都推薦的 NEW TOEIC 考試書。

同義字　　詞性　　MP3 曲目　　必考單字　　中文字義　　考試頻率

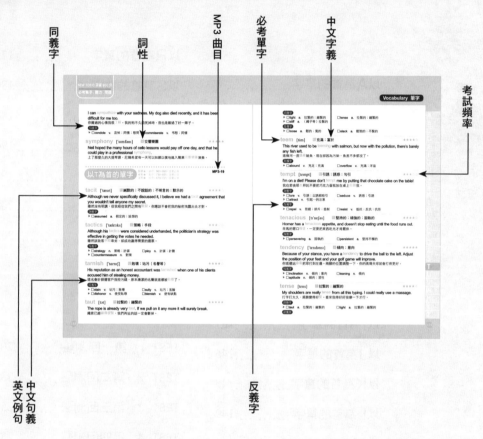

英文例句　中文句義　　　　　　　　　　反義字

符號說明

v. 動詞　　　　　　　adv. 副詞

a. 形容詞　　　　　　n. 名詞

動 動詞　　　　　　　形 形容詞

▶ 英文例句　　　　　▶ 中文句義

副 副詞　　　　　　　名 名詞

Contents

Part 1

突破900分，必考單字

Part 2

突破900分，L&R特訓

Part 3

突破900分，聽力&閱讀

Part 1

Vocabulary 單字

突破900分
必考單字

以A為首的單字

5 顆★：金色（860~990）證書必背
4 顆★：藍色（730~855）證書必背
3 顆★：綠色（470~725）證書必背

abandon [ə'bændən] 動 丟棄；拋棄；遺棄 ★★★★☆

Jason gave up trying to fix the car, and abandoned it on the side of the road.
傑森放棄修車，把車子丟棄在路邊。

同義字
▶ □desert v. 拋棄；遺棄；離棄 　　□forsake v. 拋棄；遺棄；背棄
▶ □discard v. 拋棄；摒棄；丟棄

反義字
▶ □maintain v. 維持；保持 　　□retain v. 保留；保持
▶ □conserve v. 保存；保護；節省

abbot ['æbət] 名 修道院院長；方丈 ★★★★☆

In this monastery, the abbot makes all major decisions.
這所修道院是由修道院院長負責一切重大決定。

同義字
▶ □monk n. 修道士；僧侶 　　□friar n. （天主教的）化緣修士

反義字
▶ □abbess n. 女修道院院長

abet [ə'bɛt] 動 1. 幫助；支持 2. 教唆；唆使；煽動 ★★★★☆

He abetted the thief to rob the bank by driving the getaway car.
他負責開車逃亡來幫助那個賊搶銀行。

同義字
▶ □help v. 幫助；援助；助長 　　□support v. 支持；擁護；資助
▶ □bolster v. 援助；支持

反義字
▶ □back v. 威懾住；嚇住；使斷念 　　□prohibit v. 妨礙；阻止
▶ □repress v. 抑制；壓制；約束

able-bodied ['ebḷ'bɑdɪd] 形 1. 強壯的；健全的 2. 熟練的 ★★★★★

The government encouraged all able-bodied people to join the military during the war. Those who were sick or hurt would not be accepted.
戰爭期間，只要沒有生病或受傷，凡是身強體健者政府都鼓勵從軍。

同義字
▶ □muscular a. 肌肉發達的 　　□athletic a. 行動敏捷的
▶ □sinewy a. 肌肉發達的；有力的 □brawny a. 頑強的
▶ □strapping a. 魁梧的

反義字
▶ □weak a. 虛弱的；衰弱的 　　□feeble a. 虛弱的；無力的
▶ □faint a. 虛弱的；衰弱的

A

abrupt [əˋbrʌpt]　形 1. 突然的；意外的 2. 唐突的；魯莽的；陡峭的
★★★☆☆

The abrupt change in weather caught the hiker off-guard, so he quickly put on his raingear.
天氣驟變讓登山客猝不及防，趕緊把雨衣穿上。

同義字
▶ □sudden　a.　突然的；意外的　　□unexpected　a.　意外的
▶ □hasty　a.　倉促的；輕率的　　□curt　a.　簡慢的；唐突草率的

反義字
▶ □usual　a.　通常的；平常的　　□regular　a.　經常的；習慣性的

absent [ˋæbsnt]　形 缺席的；不在場的（+from）
★★★★☆

Susan was absent from school today because she had a very high fever.
蘇珊今天發高燒，沒去上學。

同義字
▶ □away　adv.　不在；外出　　□missing　a.　不在的；缺席的
▶ □truant　a.　逃學的；懶散的

反義字
▶ □present　a.　出席的；在場的　　□on the scene　出現

absorb [əbˋsɔrb]　動 汲取；理解（知識等）
★★★★★

It's too difficult to absorb all the information presented in class, so I record it and review it at home.
要把上課講的東西全部吸收太難了，所以我錄下來準備回家複習。

同義字
▶ □incorporate　v.　包含；吸收　　□assimilate　v.　吸收（知識等）
▶ □suck up　吸收

反義字
▶ □extract　v.　抽出；榨取　　□withdraw　v.　抽回；取回

abstain [əbˋsten]　動 戒；避免；避開
★★★★★

Although all of his friends smoked, Mark decided to abstain to remain healthy.
雖然馬克所有的朋友都有抽煙，為了健康，他還是決定戒煙。

同義字
▶ □refrain　v.　忍住；抑制；節制　　□withhold　v.　克制；自制
▶ □do without　戒絕；摒棄　　□forbear　v.　克制；忍耐；避免

反義字
▶ □indulge　v.　沈迷；放縱自己　　□wallow　v.　沈迷；縱樂
▶ □revel　v.　著迷；陶醉

abuse [əˋbjuz]　動 濫用；妄用
★★★★★

Ken abused alcohol for years before finally seeking help for his problem.
肯酗酒多年，終於尋求協助解決問題。

▶ □maltreat　v.　誤用；濫用　　　□misuse　v.　誤用；濫用
▶ □pervert　v.　誤用；濫用　　　　□misapply　v.　誤用；濫用

academic　[ˌækəˈdɛmɪk]　形 學術的　　★★★★☆

After a distinguished academic career as a professor and a researcher, Margot left the university and began working in a company.
馬爾蓋特離開大學，開始去一家公司上班之前，是學術界頗負盛名的教授和研究員。

同義字
▶ □theoretical　a.　理論的；非應用的　　　□learned　a.　學問上的

accessory　[ækˈsɛsərɪ]　名 附件；配件；附加物件　　★★★☆☆

Along with the new suit and tie, Alex bought several accessories: a belt, tie clip, and some cuff links.
為了搭配新西裝和新領帶，艾力克斯買了幾樣配件，包括皮帶、領夾和一些鏈扣。

同義字
▶ □fixture　n.　（房屋等的）固定裝置　　　□accompaniment　n.　伴隨物
▶ □annex　n.　附加物；附件；附錄

acclaim　[əˈklem]　動 向…歡呼；為…喝采；稱讚　　★★★☆☆

The audience gave Justine a standing ovation when she was acclaimed the athlete of the year.
觀眾起立鼓掌，為賈斯汀當選年度最佳運動員喝采。

同義字
▶ □applaud　v.　向…鼓掌；向…喝采　　　□extol　v.　讚美；頌揚
▶ □praise　v.　讚美；表揚；歌頌　　　　□cheer　v.　歡呼；高呼
▶ □applause　n.　鼓掌歡迎；喝采

反義字
▶ □blame　v.　責備；歸咎　　　□criticize　v.　批評；苛求；非難
▶ □censure　v.　責備；譴責

accommodation　[əˌkɑməˈdeʃən]　名 住處；膳宿　　★★★★★

What are the accommodations like at the summer camp? Do we sleep in dormitories, private rooms, or tents?
夏令營要住什麼樣的地方？我們要睡大寢室、小房間還是帳篷？

同義字
▶ □facility　n.　（供特定用途的）場所　　　□convenience　n.　便利設施

accompany　[əˈkʌmpənɪ]　動 陪同；伴隨　　★★★★★

Would you like to accompany me to the store? I hate shopping alone.
你可以陪我去店裡嗎？我不喜歡一個人買東西。

同義字
▶ □escort　v.　護送；為…護航　　　□chaperon　v.　陪伴；護送

▶ □attend　v.　陪同；護送

反義字
▶ □leave　v.　離開（某人）的身邊　　□depart　v.　離開；離去
▶ □quit　v.　離開；退出

accomplish　[əˈkɑmplɪʃ]　動 完成；實現；達到　★★★★☆

If you are persistent, you can accomplish anything.
只要肯堅持，沒有完成不了的事情。

同義字
▶ □realize　v.　實現；使成為事實　　□do　v.　做；實行；完成
▶ □complete　v.　完成；結束　　　　□perform　v.　履行；執行；完成

反義字
▶ □frustrate　v.　挫敗；阻撓　　　　□obstruct　v.　妨礙；阻擾
▶ □thwart　v.　反對；阻撓；受挫折　□hinder　v.　妨礙；阻礙

according　[əˈkɔrdɪŋ]　形 相符的；和諧的；相應的　★★★★★

Students should conduct themselves according to the rules established by the school.
學生的操行必須符合學校所制訂的校規。

同義字
▶ □accordance　n.　一致；和諧　　□conformity　n.　相似；一致

accumulate　[əˈkjumjəˌlet]　動 累積；積聚；積攢　★★★☆☆

Diana couldn't believe how many pairs of shoes she had accumulated. They now filled up an entire closet!
戴安娜不敢相信自己居然積了那麼多雙鞋子在衣櫥裡，把整個衣櫥都給塞滿了！

同義字
▶ □gather　v.　收集；召集；使聚集　□amass　v.　積聚（財富）；積累
▶ □compile　v.　收集（資料等）

反義字
▶ □dissipate　v.　驅散；使消散　　□waste　v.　浪費；濫用
▶ □squander　v.　浪費；揮霍

accurate　[ˈækjərɪt]　形 準確的；精確的；正確的　★★★★☆

Is this information accurate? Some of these numbers don't look quite right to me.
這項數據正確嗎？有些數字我看起來好像不太對。

同義字
▶ □perfect　a.　完美的；理想的　　□correct　a.　正確的；對的
▶ □O.K.　a.　可以的；不錯的　　　　□all right　正確的

反義字
▶ □inaccurate　a.　不正確的　　　　□ incorrect　a.　不正確的；錯誤的

accuse　[əˈkjuz]　動 指控；控告；譴責　★★★★☆

A
B
C
D
E
F
G
H
I
J
K
L
M
N
O
P
Q
R
S
T
U
V
W
X
Y
Z

Not only did she accuse her neighbor of stealing her car, but she also claimed he has been harassing her.
她不僅控告鄰居偷她的車，還聲稱他一直在騷擾她。

同義字
▶ □denounce　v.　指責；譴責　　　□impeach　v.　控告；檢舉
▶ □blame　v.　責備；指責

反義字
▶ □defend　v.　防禦；保衛；保護　　□absolve　v.　寬恕；使免受罰

accustomed　[əˋkʌstəmd]　形習慣的；適應的　★★★☆☆

I'm not accustomed to the culture in this country, so please forgive me if I do something inappropriate.
我還不太適應這個國家的文化，如果有什麼不得體的地方，還請多多包涵。

同義字
▶ □habitual　a.　習慣的；習以為常的　　□adapted　a.　適應的；適宜的
▶ □familiar　a.　熟悉的；通曉的

反義字
▶ □unaccustomed　a.　不習慣的　　　□unfamiliar　a.　不熟悉的
▶ □unused to　不習慣

achievement　[əˋtʃivmənt]　名成就；成績　★★★★★

The writer's greatest achievement was winning the Pulitzer Prize for Literature.
該作家最大的成就，就是贏得普立茲文學獎。

同義字
▶ □accomplishment　n.　成就；成績　　□ feat　n.　功績；業績；英勇事跡
▶ □exploit　n.　功績；功勳　　　　　　□performance　n.　成績；成果

反義字
▶ □failure　n.　失敗　　　　　　　　　□ downfall　n.　墜落；垮臺；沒落
▶ □crash　n.　失敗；垮臺；破產

acquaintance　[əˋkwentəns]　名相識的人；熟人　★★★★☆

Iris is just an acquaintance whom I met through a friend, so I wouldn't feel right asking her such a big favor.
艾莉斯只是朋友介紹認識的，不太好意思請她幫這麼大的忙。

同義字
▶ □friend　n.　朋友；同伴　□companion　n.　同伴；伴侶
▶ □chum　n.　好友

反義字
▶ □stranger　n.　陌生人　□outsider　n.　外人

acquisition　[͵ækwəˋzɪʃən]　名獲得物；增添的　★★★☆☆

This computer company has been growing by buying smaller companies. Their latest acquisition is a manufacturer of laptops.

這家電腦公司利用併購小公司來擴大公司規模。最近一次併購對象是一家筆記型電腦製造商。

同義字
▶ □obtainment　n.　獲得；得到　　　□acquirement　n.　取得；學得
▶ □procurement　n.　獲得；取得　　　□annexation　n.　附加；合併

反義字
▶ □forfeit　n.　喪失的東西　□ sacrifice　n.　虧本出售；大賤賣

---

acquit [əˈkwɪt] 動 宣告…無罪；無罪釋放　　★★★★★

The man was acquitted of all charges, and left the courthouse a free man.
法官宣告這名男子一切罪名不成立，並當庭釋放恢復他自由之身。

同義字
▶ □discharge　v.　允許…離開；釋放　　　□absolve　v.　寬恕；使免受罰
▶ □exonerate　v.　證明…無罪　　　□exculpate　v.　開脫；使無罪

反義字
▶ □arrest　v.　逮捕；拘留　　　□catch　v.　逮住；捕獲
▶ □capture　v.　捕獲；俘虜

---

acrid [ˈækrɪd] 形 （味道等）刺激的；辣的；苦的　　★★★★☆

The acrid smell of burning rubber made me pinch my nose and walk away quickly.
聞到燃燒橡膠那種刺激味道，我邊捏著鼻子邊快速走開。

同義字
▶ □harsh　a.　刺耳的；澀口的　　　□sharp　a.　（感覺、味道）強烈的
▶ □nasty　a.　齷齪的；令人作嘔的　　　□stinging　a.　尖酸的；刺痛的

反義字
▶ □smooth　a.　溫和的；可口的　　　□mild　a.　味淡的；不濃烈的

---

actuary [ˈæktʃʊˌɛrɪ] 名 （保險）精算師；（保險公司）會計　　★★★★★

After receiving his mathematics degree, William went on to work as an actuary for an insurance company.
威廉拿到數學學位後，便到一家保險公司從事保險精算師的工作。

同義字
▶ □accountant　n.　會計師；會計人員

---

acupuncture [ˈækjʊˌpʌŋktʃɚ] 名 針灸；針刺療法　　★★★☆☆

Jamie didn't want to treat his illness with acupuncture because the idea of sticking needles into his skin made him nervous.
傑米不想用針灸治病，因為他一想到把針刺進皮膚裡就會緊張。

---

acute [əˈkjut] 形 尖銳的；敏銳的　　★★★★☆

If you lose the sense of sight, your other senses will become more acute.
如果你失去視覺，身體其他感官會變得更加敏銳。

同義字

▶ □keen　a.　敏銳的；敏捷的　　□smart　a.　伶俐的；機警的
▶ □astute　a.　敏銳的；精明的　　□shrewd　a.　機靈的；敏銳的

反義字
▶ □dull　a.　愚鈍的；笨的；遲鈍的　□blunt　a.　（感覺等）遲鈍的
▶ □obtuse　a.　愚鈍的

addendum　[ə'dɛndəm]　名補遺；追加；補篇；附錄　★★★★★

The addendum to the report was added a week after I originally wrote it, and clarifies some of the facts and figures in the proposal.
我寫完這篇報告一個禮拜後，又加上一些附錄，以釐清提案中的一些事實和數字部分。

同義字
▶ □addition　n.　附加；增加的　　□appendix　n.　附錄；附件

adhere　[əd'hɪr]　動黏附；緊黏　★★★★☆

The poster is adhered to the wall with glue.
海報用膠水黏在牆上。

同義字
▶ □cling　v.　黏著；纏著；緊握不放　　□cohere　v.　黏合；附著；凝聚
▶ □stick　v.　黏貼；張貼

反義字
▶ □part　v.　使分開；使分離　　□sever　v.　把…分隔開；使分離
▶ □divide　v.　使分開；使隔開

adjacent　[ə'dʒɛsənt]　形毗連的；鄰接的　★★★☆☆

Residents of the apartment building were very upset when workers began constructing a new building in the adjacent lot.
工人開始在鄰近空地蓋新房子，讓公寓住戶覺得很生氣。

同義字
▶ □neighboring　a.　鄰近的　　□adjoining　a.　鄰接的
▶ □contiguous　a.　接觸的；鄰近的　　□surrounding　a.　周圍的

反義字
▶ □remote　a.　相隔很遠的；偏僻的　　□far　a.　遙遠的；那一邊的
▶ □distant　a.　遙遠的；遠離的

administration　[əd,mɪnə'streʃən]　名1. 行政；施政 2. 管理；經營　★★★☆☆

After graduating from clerical college, Judy worked as a secretary and managed all the company's administration.
神學院畢業後，茱蒂便擔任秘書，負責公司一切行政事務。

同義字
▶ □disposition　n.　配置；排列　　□regulation　n.　管理；調整
▶ □direction　n.　指導；指揮；管理

admittance　[əd'mɪtəns]　名進入；入場許可　★★★★★

Only those with clearance passes can gain admittance into the classified areas of the building.

要進入這棟建築物的各個分區，得持有許可證才行。

同義字
▶ □admission n. 進入許可　　　　　□entry n. 進入；入場
▶ □passport n. 護照；通行證；執照

反義字
▶ □prohibition n. 禁止；禁令　　　　□forbiddance n. 禁止
▶ □ban n. 禁止；禁令

admonish [əd'mɑnɪʃ] 動 告誡；警告　　★★★★☆

Dad admonished her for being so naughty, but didn't go as far as to punish her in any way.

父親只是警告她不要那麼調皮，並未給她任何具體的懲罰。

同義字
▶ □caution v. 警告；告誡　　　　　□advise v. 勸告；忠告
▶ □warn v. 警告；告誡；提醒

advent ['ædvɛnt] 名 出現；到來　　★★★★★

Before the advent of computers, these calculations were difficult.

電腦出現以前，要計算這些東西可是不容易。

同義字
▶ □appearance n. 出現；顯露　　□approach n. 接近；靠近
▶ □coming n. 來到；臨近；到達　□emergence n. 出現；浮現

反義字
▶ □disappearance n. 消失；失蹤　□dispersal n. 消散；消失
▶ □vanishment n. 消失

adverse [əd'vɝs] 形 1. 不利的；有害的　2. 逆向的；相反的　★★★★☆

Despite the adverse circumstances, Ken overcame his challenges and became very successful in his field.

儘管遭遇逆境，肯依然克服所有難關，在該領域上出類拔萃。

同義字
▶ □harmful a. 有害的　　　　　　□unfavorable a. 不利的
▶ □unfriendly a. 不相宜的；不利的　□detrimental a. 有害的

反義字
▶ □favorable a. 有利的；適合的　□beneficial a. 有益的
▶ □helpful a. 有幫助的；有益的　□salutary a. 有益的；有利的

advocate ['ædvəkɪt] 名 提倡者；擁護者　　★★★★☆

Penny is an advocate of animal rights, and is currently petitioning the government to stop whale hunting.

佩妮是動物權的擁護者，目前正在向政府請願，要求停止獵鯨。

同義字
▶ □supporter n. 支持者；擁護者　□proponent n. 提議人；擁護者
反義字
▶ □opposite n. 對立面；對立物　□counter n. 相反之事物

aerial [ˈɛrɪəl] 形 1. 航空的；飛機的；由飛機進行的 2. 高聳的；巍峨的 ★★★★★

Please take some aerial photographs of the farm when you're up in the plane.
請你坐飛機時，從上空拍些農場照片。

同義字
▶ □aloft adv. 在上面；在高處　□high a. 高的
▶ □lofty a. 高聳的；極高的　□elevated a. 升高的；提高的
反義字
▶ □underground a. 地下的　□subterranean a. 地下的

affable [ˈæfəbl̩] 形 和藹可親的；容易親近的；友善的；慈祥的 ★★★★☆

My supervisor is very affable, so I never feel nervous approaching him with complaints or questions.
我主管為人相當友善，有什麼抱怨或問題去找他時，我從來不覺得緊張。

同義字
▶ □pleasant a. 討人喜歡的　□gracious a. 親切的；和藹的
▶ □approachable a. 可接近的　□amiable a. 和藹可親的
反義字
▶ □vicious a. 惡意的；惡毒的　□malicious a. 惡意的；懷恨的
▶ □venomous a. 惡意的；惡毒的

affection [əˈfɛkʃən] 名 情愛；鍾愛；感情 ★★★☆☆

More than anything, the child wanted love and affection from his mother.
孩子最想要的，便是媽媽的疼愛和關心。

同義字
▶ □attachment n. 情感；愛慕　□adoration n. 崇拜；敬愛
反義字
▶ □dislike n. 不喜愛；厭惡　□hatred n. 憎恨；增惡；敵意

affiliate [əˈfɪlɪˌet] 動 接納…為成員（或分支機構）；使隸屬於（+to/with） ★★★★★

I'm no longer affiliated with that company. I quit over a year ago.
我已離職一年多，不再是那家公司的員工。

同義字
▶ □subordinate a. 次要的；隸屬的　□belong to 是…的成員
反義字
▶ □dominant a. 支配的；統治的　□leading a. 領導的；帶領的

affirmative [əˈfɝmətɪv] 形 肯定的；表示贊成的 ★★★★☆

When asked whether or not they would go to university, 80% of the students gave an affirmative response. The other 20% would look for jobs or go traveling.
被問及是否要上大學時，80% 的學生都持肯定態度，其他 20% 則要找工作或旅行。

同義字
▶ □assertive　a.　斷言的；肯定的　　□affirmatory　a.　表示肯定的
▶ □favorable　a.　贊同的　　□positive　a.　肯定的；確實的

反義字
▶ □negative　a.　否定的；否認的　　□disapproving　a.　不滿的
▶ □opposing　a.　反對的

affix　[əˈfɪks]　　📖貼上；把⋯固定　　★★★★★

Don't forget to affix a label onto the package, otherwise it may not get sent to the right address.
別忘了在包裹上貼上標籤，否則可能無法送達正確地址。

同義字
▶ □paste　v.　黏貼　　□stick　v.　黏貼；張貼

反義字
▶ □part　v.　使分開；使分離　　□sever　v.　把⋯分隔開；使分離

affluent　[ˈæflʊənt]　　📖富裕的；豐富的　　★★★★☆

This is an affluent neighborhood, as apparent by all the Jaguars and Rolls Royce in the driveways.
從停車道上停滿積架和勞斯萊斯，可以明顯看出附近住的都是有錢人家。

同義字
▶ □wealthy　a.　富裕的；豐富的　　□abundant　a.　豐富的；富裕的
▶ □ample　a.　大量的；豐富的　　□rich　a.　有錢的；富有的

反義字
▶ □poor　a.　貧窮的；貧乏的　　□penniless　a.　身無分文的
▶ □needy　a.　貧窮的　　□destitute　a.　窮困的；貧困的

affront　[əˈfrʌnt]　　📖公然侮辱；輕蔑　　★★★★☆

Stop that! Such rude behavior is an affront to the hosts of the party!
住手！如此無禮的舉動等於是公然冒犯宴會主人！

同義字
▶ □offense　n.　冒犯；觸怒　　□aggress　n.　侵略；挑釁；攻擊
▶ □insult　n.　侮辱；羞辱　　□indignity　n.　輕蔑；無禮舉動

反義字
▶ □respect　v.　尊敬；敬重　　□esteem　v.　尊重；尊敬；珍重
▶ □honor　v.　尊敬

aggravate　[ˈæɡrəˌvet]　　📖1. 加重；增劇；使惡化 2. 激怒；使惱火　★★★★★

Please turn down the stereo. The loud music is aggravating my headache.
請把音響關掉，音樂開那麼大聲讓我的頭痛得更厲害了。

同義字
▶ □sharpen　v.　加重；加劇　　　□compound　v.　增加；加重
▶ □irritate　v.　使惱怒；使難受　　□vex　v.　使生氣；使痛苦

反義字
▶ □mitigate　v.　使緩和；減輕　　　□alleviate　v.　減輕；緩和

aggressive [əˋgrɛsɪv]　形 侵略的；侵犯的；好鬥的；挑釁的；有幹勁的　★★★☆☆

He's an aggressive hockey player who starts many fights.
他是個很愛挑釁的曲棍球員，老是找人打架。

同義字
▶ □combative　a.　好戰的；好鬥的　□belligerent　a.　好戰的；好鬥的
▶ □offensive　a.　冒犯的；唐突的　□provocative　a.　氣人的

反義字
▶ □defensive　a.　防禦的；保護的　□safeguard　n.　保護；防衛

aghast [əˋgæst]　形 嚇呆的；驚駭的　★★★★☆

He was aghast when he saw a ghost outside his window.
他看到窗外有鬼，簡直被嚇壞了。

同義字
▶ □astonished　a.　驚訝的；驚愕的　　□astounded　a.　被震驚的
▶ □amazed　a.　吃驚的　　□surprised　a.　感到驚訝的
▶ □thunderstruck　a.　嚇壞了的

反義字
▶ □unafraid　a.　無畏的；不恐懼的　□fearless　a.　不怕的；無畏的
▶ □intrepid　a.　勇敢的；大膽的　□dauntless　a.　無畏的；勇敢的

agile [æˋdʒaɪl]　形 1. 輕快的；敏捷的　2. 機敏的；靈敏的　★★★☆☆

Megan is very agile, and was the first competitor to make it through the obstacle course.
梅根身手相當敏捷，領先所有對手第一個通過障礙超越訓練場。

同義字
▶ □athletic　a.　體格健壯的　□nimble　a.　靈活的；靈巧的
▶ □spry　a.　活潑的；敏捷的　□swift　a.　快速的；快捷的

反義字
▶ □dull　a.　遲鈍的；不活躍的　□slow　a.　緩慢的；遲鈍的
▶ □torpid　a.　不活潑的；懶散的　□sleepy　a.　想睡的；不活躍的

agitate [ˋædʒəˌtet]　動 1. 使激動；使焦慮　2. 鼓動；煽動　★★★★☆

Mr. Brown was agitated by the alarming news of his friend's car accident.
布朗先生得知他朋友發生車禍的驚人消息時，顯得很激動。

同義字
▶ □disturb　v.　攪亂；使心神不寧　□excite　v.　刺激；使激動
▶ □inflame　v.　使極度激動；使憤怒

反義字

▶ □compose　v.　使安定；使平靜　　　□quiet　v.　使安靜；使平息
▶ □calm　v.　使鎮定；使平靜　　　　　□soothe　v.　安慰；撫慰

agrarian [ə'grɛrɪən] 　　　形農業的；土地的；耕地的　　　★★★★★

This is primarily an agrarian society, but now more and more young people are moving to the cities.
雖然這裡原本是農業社會，但現在已有越來越多年輕人搬到城裡去。

同義字

▶ □agricultural　a.　農業的　　　　□cultivation　n.　耕作；耕種
▶ □farming　n.　農業；養殖　　　　□husbandry　n.　農事；耕種

ailment ['elmənt] 　　　名病痛；（尤指輕微的）疾病　　　★★★★★

You should see the doctor about your ailment. It's probably nothing, but you don't want it to get worse.
有病痛就應該去看醫生才對，或許沒什麼大不了，但你也不想讓病情惡化吧。

同義字

▶ □illness　n.　患病；身體不適　　　□sickness　n.　疾病；噁心
▶ □indisposition　n.　不舒服；微恙　□malady　n.　疾病

反義字

▶ □health　n.　健康　　　□well　a.　健康的；健全的

albeit [ɔl'biɪt] conj. 儘管；雖然　　　★★★★☆

This city is known for its sunny, albeit cold weather.
儘管天氣寒冷，這座城市仍以其陽光普照而聞名。

同義字

▶ □although　conj.　儘管；雖然　　　□notwithstanding　conj.　儘管
▶ □even though　即使；雖然　　　　　□in spite of　儘管

alcoholism ['ælkəhɔl,ɪzəm] 　　　名酗酒；酒精中毒　　　★★★★☆

This group helps people suffering from alcoholism, so you should see them if you think you have a drinking problem.
這個團體專門幫助那些受酗酒之苦的人，所以你如果有酗酒問題，就應該去找他們。

同義字

▶ □intemperance　n.　酗酒

alias ['elɪəs] 　　　名化名；別名　　　★★★☆☆

Her real name is Sydney Jones, but she goes by the alias Alice Johnson.
她的真名是雪梨・瓊斯，不過一直都用愛麗絲・詹森這個化名。

同義字

▶ □pseudonym　n.　假名；筆名；雅號

alien ['elɪən] 　　　名外國人；僑民　　　★★★★☆

He's an alien in this country, and is unfamiliar with our laws and customs.
他是這個國家的僑民，並不熟悉我們的法律和習俗。

【同義字】
▶ □stranger　n.　外地人；外國人　　□foreigner　n.　外國人

【反義字】
▶ □native　n.　本地人；本國人　　□local　n.　當地居民；本地人

alienate　[ˈeljənˌet]　　囫 使疏遠；離間　　★★★★★

The politician alienated many of his supporters when he changed his views.
該名政治人物改變觀點後，便疏遠了許多原本的支持者。

【同義字】
▶ □estrange　v.　使疏遠　　□rupture　v.　破裂；不和
▶ □disunite　v.　使分離；分裂　　□disjoin　v.　分開

【反義字】
▶ □conciliate　v.　把…爭取過來　　□ harmonize　v.　使協調；使和諧

allege　[əˈlɛdʒ]　　囫 斷言；宣稱　　★★★☆☆

The defendant pleads innocent, and alleges that he was not at the scene of the crime.
被告辯稱無罪，並宣稱自己當時並未出現在犯罪現場。

【同義字】
▶ □declare　v.　斷言；宣稱　　□claim　v.　主張；斷言；聲稱
▶ □profess　v.　公開宣稱；表示　　□assert　v.　斷言；聲稱

【反義字】
▶ □disclaim　v.　放棄；否認　　□repudiate　v.　否認；駁斥
▶ □renounce　v.　聲明放棄；拋棄

alleviate　[əˈlivɪˌet]　　囫 減輕；緩和　　★★★☆☆

Why don't you take some medicine to alleviate the pain?
你何不吃點藥讓痛苦減輕一點？

【同義字】
▶ □mitigate　v.　使緩和；減輕　　□abate　v.　減少；減弱；減輕
▶ □remit　v.　緩和；減輕；減退　　□relax　v.　緩和；放寬；減輕
▶ □assuage　v.　緩和；減輕（病痛等）

【反義字】
▶ □sharpen　v.　加重；加劇　　□compound　v.　增加；加重

alliance　[əˈlaɪəns]　　囵 結盟；聯盟；同盟；聯姻　　★★★★☆

The three countries formed an alliance to defend themselves against enemy attack.
這三個國家建立同盟，一起對抗敵人的攻擊。

【同義字】
▶ □union　n.　結合；合併；聯盟　　□alignment　n.　結盟；組合

▶ □association　n.　聯合；結合　　□league　n.　同盟；聯盟

反義字
▶ □enemy　n.　敵人；仇敵　　□opponent　n.　對手；敵手
▶ □rival　n.　競爭者；對手；敵手　□foe　n.　敵人；仇敵

• allot [ə'lɑt]　動 分配；撥出　　★★★★☆

The MC allotted ten minutes for each speaker to make their presentation.
司儀限定每個發言者發言十分鐘。

同義字
▶ □distribute　v.　分發；分配　　□assign　v.　分配；分派
▶ □render　v.　給予；提供　　□dispense　v.　分配；分發

反義字
▶ □withhold　v.　抑制；阻擋；不給　□monopolize　v.　獨佔

• allude [ə'lud]　動 暗示；間接提到；轉彎抹角地說到 (+to)　★★★★★

In your speech, you alluded to Case 114. Can you provide us with more detail?
你演講中曾提到第 114 號案例，可以再講清楚一點嗎？

同義字
▶ □hint　v.　暗示；示意　□intimate　v.　提示；暗示
▶ □suggest　v.　提議；暗示　□imply　v.　暗指；暗示；意味著
▶ □refer　v.　論及；談到；提及

ally [ə'laɪ]　名 同盟國；同盟者　　★★★★☆

The two countries were allies in the war, and their soldiers fought alongside each other for over three years.
這兩個國家戰時建立同盟，雙方士兵因而並肩作戰了三年多。

同義字
▶ □consociate　n.　聯合；聯盟　□helpmate　n.　合作者；夥伴
▶ □copartner　n.　合作者；合夥人

反義字
▶ □enemy　n.　敵人；仇敵　　□opponent　n.　對手；敵手

• aloof [ə'luf]　形 冷漠的；冷淡的；疏遠的；遠離的　★★★★★

Chad is very aloof, and tends not to go out on Friday nights.
查德超然離群，禮拜五晚上傾向不出門。

同義字
▶ □distant　a.　冷淡的；疏遠的　□standoffish　a.　冷淡的
▶ □unsociable　a.　不愛交際的　□reserved　a.　沈默寡言的
▶ □remote　a.　冷淡的；孤高的

反義字
▶ □familiar　a.　親近的；親密的　□close　a.　密切的；親密的
▶ □eager　a.　熱心的；熱切的　□intimate　a.　親密的；熟悉的

A
B
C
D
E
F
G
H
I
J
K
L
M
N
O
P
Q
R
S
T
U
V
W
X
Y
Z

altar [ˈɔltɚ] 名聖壇；祭壇 ★★★★☆

The nun put offerings on the altar and bowed.

尼姑把祭品放到祭壇上然後鞠躬。

同義字
▶ □chancel　n.　聖壇　　　□sanctuary　n.　聖殿；祭坊
▶ □shrine　n.　聖壇；神龕；聖祠

alter [ˈɔltɚ] 動改變；修改 ★★★★★

This suit jacket is a little tight around the chest. Could you take it to the tailor and alter it?

這件西裝外套胸部附近有點緊，你可以拿到裁縫師那裡改一改嗎？

同義字
▶ □change　v.　改變；更改　　　□vary　v.　變更；修改
▶ □modify　v.　更改；修改　　　□revise　v.　修改；修正
▶ □adjust　v.　調整；適應

反義字
▶ □preserve　v.　維持；維護　　　□fix　v.　使固定；確定
▶ □uniform　v.　使成一樣；使一律化

altercation [ˌɔltɚˈkeʃən] 名爭論；爭吵 ★★★★☆

The police were called to break up the altercation between two drunken sports fans.

兩邊的運動迷酒後爭吵不休，只好報警加以擺平。

同義字
▶ □disagreement　n.　爭吵；爭論　　　□jangle　n.　爭吵；爭論；吵嚷
▶ □quarrel　n.　爭吵；不和；吵鬧　　　□contention　n.　爭論；爭吵

反義字
▶ □agreement　n.　同意；一致　　　□accord　n.　一致；符合；調和
▶ □assent　n.　同意；贊成

alternate [ˈɔltɚnɪt] 形供選擇的；供替換的 ★★★★★

If it rains, our alternate plan is to rent movies.

下雨的話，我們就改成租影片回來看。

同義字
▶ □replaceable　a.　可替換的　　　□substitutive　a.　代理的
▶ □exchangeable　a.　可兌換的　　　□interchangeable　a.　可交換的

反義字
▶ □unchangeable　a.　不變的　　　□constant　a.　固定的；不變的
▶ □fixed　a.　固定的；不變的

alternative [ɔlˈtɝnətɪv] 名選擇；二擇一；供選擇的東西（或辦法等） ★★★★☆

We have no money left. We have no alternative except to sell the car.

我們沒錢了，除了賣車別無他法。

同義字
▶ □choice n. 選擇 □ option n. 選擇；可選擇的東西
▶ □substitute n. 代替人；代替物 □replacement n. 代替者

altitude [ˈæltəˌtjud] 名高度；海拔 ★★★☆☆

The altitude of the tallest mountain on earth is 8,848 meters above sea level.
全世界最高山海拔 8848 公尺。

同義字
▶ □height n. 高度；海拔 □elevation n. 高度；海拔

amateur [ˈæməˌtʃʊr] 名業餘愛好者；外行 ★★★★☆

I'm an amateur photographer, and have no interest in turning my hobby into a profession.
我只是名業餘攝影師，沒有興趣把嗜好變成職業。

同義字
▶ □dilettante n. 美術的愛好者 □dabbler n. 涉獵者；淺嘗者
▶ □nonprofessional n. 非專家

反義字
▶ □professional n. 職業選手；內行 □ expert n. 專家；能手；熟練者
▶ □specialist n. 專家

ambiguous [æmˈbɪgjʊəs] 形含糊不清的；引起歧義的 ★★★★★

The wording of this sentence is so ambiguous. I can't understand if he's for or against the issue.
這句話措辭過於含糊，我不明白他是支持還是反對該議題。

同義字
▶ □equivocal a. 有歧義的 □two-edged a. 有雙重含義的
▶ □vague a. （想法等）不明確的 □indefinite a. 不明確的
▶ □weasel-worded a. 模稜兩可的

反義字
▶ □clear a. 清楚的；清晰的 □distinct a. 明顯的；清楚的
▶ □definite a. 明確的；確切的 □explicit a. 詳盡的；清楚的

ambitious [æmˈbɪʃəs] 形有雄心的；野心勃勃的 ★★★★☆

Mark is an ambitious young businessman who wants to make a million dollars before aged thirty.
馬克是個野心勃勃的年輕生意人，希望在三十歲前賺到一百萬。

同義字
▶ □aspiring a. 有志氣的 □enterprising a. 有事業心的
▶ □avid a. 渴望的；熱心的 □pushing a. 有企業心的
▶ □driving a. 強勁的

反義字
▶ □lazy a. 懶散的；怠惰的 □indolent a. 懶惰的
▶ □idle a. 不工作的；無所事事的

ambush ['æmbʊʃ] 動 埋伏；伏擊 ★★★★★

The soldiers hid in the bushes and ambushed the unsuspecting enemy.
士兵們躲在灌木叢中，用敵人料想不到的方式發動伏擊。

同義字
- □waylay　v.　（為搶劫等）伏擊　　□lie in wait for　埋伏以待

amicable ['æmɪkəbḷ] 形 友善的；友好的；溫和的 ★★★★☆

Despite all their previous disagreements, their latest meeting was very amicable.
雖然他們先前意見不合，但最近一次碰面大家態度都很友好。

同義字
- □friendly　a.　友好的；親切的　　□neighborly　a.　像鄰居的
- □fraternal　a.　友好的；友愛的　　□affable　a.　友善的；慈祥的

反義字
- □inimical　a.　敵意的；不友好的　　□quarrelsome　a.　喜歡爭吵的
- □hostile　a.　懷敵意的；不友善的

amphibious [æm'fɪbɪəs] 形 兩棲（類）的 ★★★☆☆

An amphibious animal, like a frog, can live on both land and in water.
像青蛙這類兩棲動物，能同時在陸上和水中生活。

amphitheater [ˌæmfɪ'θɪətɚ] 名 圓形露天劇場；競技場 ★★★☆☆

There is a large amphitheater in the park where concerts and plays are held.
公園裡有座供音樂會和各項表演之用的大型露天劇場。

同義字
- □theater　n.　劇場；電影院　　□stadium　n.　體育場；運動場

amplify ['æmplə,faɪ] 動 1. 放大（聲音等）；增強　2. 擴大；擴展 ★★★★☆

These speakers should amplify your voice enough so that the audience in the back can hear you.
這些擴音器可以把你聲音放大，讓後面的聽眾也聽得到你在講什麼。

同義字
- □expand　v.　擴大；擴充；發展　　□increase　v.　增大；增加
- □swell　v.　（聲音、音樂等）增強　　□aggrandize　v.　加大；強化

反義字
- □reduce　v.　減少；縮小；降低　　□lessen　v.　變小；變少；減輕
- □drop　v.　下降；變弱

amputate ['æmpjə,tet] 動 切斷；鋸掉；截（肢） ★★★★★

The doctor amputated his leg to prevent the poison from spreading to the rest of his body.
醫生把他的腿鋸掉，以免毒素擴散到身體其他部位。

同義字

▶ □dismember　v.　肢解；分割　　□mutilate　v.　切斷（手足等）

amusement [əˈmjuzmənt]　图 樂趣；娛樂；消遣　★★★★☆

I like to swim, paint, and collect stamps. What do you do for amusement?
我喜歡游泳、畫畫和收集郵票；那你喜歡做何消遣？

同義字
▶ □entertainment　n.　娛樂；消遣　□ pleasure　n.　樂趣；娛樂；消遣
▶ □recreation　n.　消遣；娛樂　　□diversion　n.　娛樂；消遣
▶ □enjoyment　n.　樂趣；享受

反義字
▶ □boredom　n.　無聊；厭倦　　□work　n.　工作；勞動；作業
▶ □drudgery　n.　苦工；沈悶的工作

analyze [ˈænḷˌaɪz]　動 分析；解析　★★★★★

There is a lot of data here. It will take me a long time to analyze it.
手上資料很多，要分析得花很多時間。

同義字
▶ □dissect　v.　仔細分析　□scrutinize　v.　詳細檢查；細看

反義字
▶ □synthesize　v.　綜合；合成　　□ compound　v.　使混合；使化合

anatomy [əˈnætəmɪ]　图 解剖學；解剖；（植物的）解剖結構　★★★★★

In biology class today, we studied the anatomy of amphibians by dissecting a frog.
為研究兩棲動物的解剖結構，我們今天上生物課時解剖了青蛙。

同義字
▶ □dissection　n.　切開；解剖

anesthetic [ˌænəsˈθɛtɪk]　图 麻醉劑　★★★★☆

The dentist gave me some anesthetic so that it wouldn't hurt so much when he pulled out my tooth.
牙醫幫我打了些麻醉劑，拔牙時就不會那麼痛了。

同義字
▶ □drug　n.　麻醉藥品；毒品　　□narcotic　n.　麻醉劑；毒品

animation [ˌænəˈmeʃən]　图 1. 卡通片；卡通片繪製 2. 生氣；活潑；熱烈　★★★★★

The animation in this cartoon is amazing. The characters look so lifelike!
這部卡通畫得太棒了，每個人物看起來都栩栩如生！

同義字
▶ □life　n.　元氣；活力　　□pep　n.　活力；銳氣；勁頭
▶ □kick　n.　精力；力氣

反義字
▶ □inanimation　n.　無生命；無活動

animosity [ˌænəˈmasətɪ] 图仇恨；敵意；憎惡 ★★★★★

There is much animosity between the two men, as one stole the other's girlfriend.
這兩個男人彼此嫌隙很深，因為其中一個搶了另一個的女朋友。

同義字
▶ □hatred n. 憎恨；憎惡；敵意　　□dislike n. 不喜愛；厭惡
▶ □rancor n. 仇恨；激烈的憎惡　　□hostility n. 敵意；敵視
▶ □ill will 惡意；敵意；憎惡

反義字
▶ □favor n. 善意的行為；恩惠　　□goodwill n. 善意；好心；友好
▶ □amity n. 和睦；親善　　　　　□benevolence n. 仁慈；善心

annual [ˈænjʊəl] 图一年的；一年一次的；每年的；全年的 ★★★☆☆

The company's annual staff barbecue is held the first Saturday of every June.
公司年度員工烤肉在每年六月的第一個禮拜六舉辦。

同義字
▶ □yearly a. 每年的；一年一次的　□anniversary a. 週年的

反義字
▶ □perennial a. 終年的；常年的　□daily a. 每日的；日常的

anonymous [əˈnɑnəməs] 图匿名的；姓氏不明的 ★★★★★

The police received an anonymous phone call that revealed the location of the criminals. The identity of the caller may never be known.
警方接到檢舉罪犯藏身之處的匿名電話，而通報者的身分可能永遠查不出來。

同義字
▶ □nameless a. 匿名的　　　　□unnamed a. 未命名的
▶ □innominate a. 無名的　　　□unknown a. 不知道的
▶ □unidentified a. 未辨別出的

反義字
▶ □famous a. 著名的；出名的　　□renowned a. 有名的
▶ □distinguished a. 卓越的；著名的　□well-known a. 出名的

antidote [ˈæntɪˌdot] 图解毒藥；解毒劑 ★★★★☆

Quick! She's been bitten by a poisonous rattlesnake! Get the antidote from the medicine cabinet.
快！她被有毒的響尾蛇咬了！快去藥櫃裡拿解毒劑。

同義字
▶ □alexipharmic n. 解毒藥

antique [ænˈtik] 图1. 古代的；古老的；年代久遠的 2. 古式的；古董的 ★★★★★

This antique vase dates back to the time of Napoleon.
這支古董花瓶可以追溯到拿破崙時代。

同義字

▶ □ancient　a.　古代的；古老的　　□archaic　a.　古式的
▶ □curiosa　n.　古董

反義字

▶ □modern　a.　現代的；時髦的　　□new　a.　新的；新鮮的

appall [əˋpɔl]　動使驚恐；使膽寒　　★★★★☆

He was appalled to discover that his house had burned down while he was on vacation.
發現度假時家裡被燒毀，讓他大為震驚。

同義字

▶ □horrify　v.　使恐懼；使驚懼　　□shock　v.　使震驚
▶ □dismay　v.　使驚慌；使沮喪　　□terrify　v.　使害怕；使恐怖
▶ □scare　v.　驚嚇；使恐懼

反義字

▶ □cheer　v.　使振奮；使高興　　□calm　v.　使鎮定；使平靜
▶ □quiet　v.　使安靜；使平息　　□soothe　v.　安慰；撫慰

apparent [əˋpærənt]　形明顯的；顯而易見的　　★★★★★

The truth should be apparent. I shouldn't have to explain it to you.
真相應該很明顯，不用我再跟你解釋了吧。

同義字

▶ □clear　a.　顯然的；明顯的　　□obvious　a.　明顯的；顯著的
▶ □evident　a.　明顯的；明白的　　□visible　a.　顯而易見的

反義字

▶ □obscure　a.　含糊不清的　　□abstruse　a.　深奧的；難懂的
▶ □indefinite　a.　不明確的　　□vague　a.　（想法等）不明確的

appease [əˋpiz]　動平息；緩和；撫慰　　★★★☆☆

I tried to appease the angry customer by offering 10% off the merchandise.
該項商品我打了九折，希望能平息顧客的憤怒。

同義字

▶ □ease　v.　減輕；緩和；放鬆　　□quiet　v.　使安靜；使平息
▶ □allay　v.　使平靜；使緩和　　□relieve　v.　使寬慰；使放心
▶ □pacify　v.　使平靜；撫慰

反義字

▶ □provoke　v.　對…挑釁；煽動　　□offend　v.　冒犯；觸怒
▶ □irritate　v.　使惱怒

appraise [əˋprez]　動估計；估量；估價　　★★★★☆

I don't know how much this diamond ring costs. Let's take it to the jewelry store and get it appraised.
我不曉得這只鑽石戒指值多少錢，不如拿到珠寶店估個價。

同義字

▶ □evaluate　v.　估價　　□valuate　v.　估價

▶ ☐assess v. 對…進行估價　　☐rate v. 對…估價；對…評價

apprehend [ˌæprɪˈhɛnd]　🔊逮捕　★★★★★

The policemen chased the criminal down the alley and apprehended him when he had no where else to run.
警方沿著小巷追捕該名罪犯，最後他無路可逃，只好乖乖束手就擒。

同義字
▶ ☐seize v. 逮捕；擄獲 ☐arrest v. 逮捕；拘留
▶ ☐catch v. 逮住；捕獲 ☐capture v. 捕獲；俘虜

反義字
▶ ☐loose v. 釋放；把…放開　　☐discharge v. 允許…離開
▶ ☐release v. 釋放；解放　　☐liberate v. 解放；使獲自由

appropriate [əˈproprɪˌet]　🔊適當的；恰當的；相稱的　★★★★★

Jeans and an old t-shirt is not appropriate dress for a job interview.
牛仔褲和舊運動衫並不適合工作面試時穿。

同義字
▶ ☐suitable a. 適當的；合適的　　☐becoming a. 合適的
▶ ☐fitting a. 適當的；合適的　　☐proper a. 適合的；適當的

反義字
▶ ☐inappropriate a. 不適當的　　☐unsuitable a. 不合適的
▶ ☐unfit a. 不相宜的；不勝任的　　☐improper a. 不合適的

arbitrary [ˈɑrbəˌtrɛrɪ]　🔊隨便的；隨心所欲的　★★★★☆

We just ate at the first restaurant we saw, an arbitrary choice.
我們先看到哪一家餐廳就吃那一家，隨便挑而已。

同義字
▶ ☐casual a. 漫不經心的　　☐random a. 胡亂的；隨便的
▶ ☐at will 任意；隨心所欲地

反義字
▶ ☐deliberate a. 故意的；蓄意的　　☐willful a. 故意的；存心的
▶ ☐voluntary a. 有意的；故意的　　☐ intentional a. 有意的；故意的

aristocratic [əˌrɪstəˈkrætɪk]　🔊貴族的；有貴族氣派的；儀態高貴的　★★★★★

They are an aristocratic family descended from royalty.
他們是貴族之家，乃皇室後裔。

同義字
▶ ☐patrician a. 貴族的；高貴的　　☐blue-blooded a. 貴族的
▶ ☐noble a. 貴族的；顯貴的　　☐well-born a. 出身名門的

反義字
▶ ☐humble a. （身分、地位）低下的　　☐lowly a. （地位等）低下的
▶ ☐simple n. 出身（或地位）低下者

armful ['ɑrm͵fəl] 名 （雙臂或單臂的）一抱 （之量）（+of） ★★★★☆

The camper carried an armful of wood from the shed to the campfire.
露營成員從庫房抱了一堆木材到營火那裡。

arrangement [ə'rendʒmənt] 名 安排；準備工作 ★★★☆☆

My travel agent makes the necessary arrangements for my business trips, such as applying for visas, buying plane tickets, and booking hotels.
這趟出差旅行所有必要的準備工作，如申請簽證、買機票和旅館訂房等等，旅行社職員都替我安排好了。

同義字
- ▶ □preparation n. 準備　　　□provision n. 預備；防備
- ▶ □disposition n. 處理；解決　□fix up （為…）作出安排

反義字
- ▶ □disorder n. 混亂；無秩序　□confusion n. 混亂；混亂狀況
- ▶ □disturbance n. 擾亂；打擾

arrive [ə'raɪv] 動 到達；到來 ★★★★★

The plane is scheduled to arrive at 2:00, but because of the bad weather it won't get here until nearly 3:00.
飛機本預定下午兩點抵達，但由於天候不佳，遲至三點左右才到。

同義字
- ▶ □come v. 來；來到　　□reach v. 抵達；到達；達到
- ▶ □get in 到達

反義字
- ▶ □go v. 去；離去　　　□depart v. 起程；出發；離開
- ▶ □leave v. 離開

arrogant ['ærəgənt] 形 傲慢的；自大的；自負的 ★★★☆☆

Dan's a very arrogant person, and likes to show off in his fancy red sports car.
丹這個人很自大，很愛炫耀他那輛名貴的紅色跑車。

同義字
- ▶ □cavalier a. 傲慢的　　□insolent a. 傲慢的；無禮的
- ▶ □haughty a. 高傲的；傲慢的　□pompous a. 愛炫耀的
- ▶ □conceited a. 驕傲自滿的

反義字
- ▶ □modest a. 謙虛的；審慎的　□humble a. 謙遜的；謙恭的
- ▶ □unassuming a. 謙虛的　　□unpretentious a. 不矯飾的

aspiration [͵æspə'reʃən] 名 熱望；志向；抱負 ★★★★☆

Your aspiration of becoming a millionaire won't be reached if you keep working at this low-paying job.
如果你繼續做這份低薪工作，想變成百萬富翁的抱負就會落空。

同義字

▶ □ambition　n.　雄心；抱負　　□craving　n.　渴望；熱望
▶ □enterprise　n.　冒險精神；進取心

反義字
▶ □laziness　n.　怠惰；懶散；徐緩　□indolence　n.　懶散；懶惰
▶ □idleness　n.　懶惰；閒散；安逸

assassinate [ə'sæsɪnˌet]　勔1. 暗殺；對…行刺　2. 詆毀；糟蹋（名譽等）　★★★★★

American President John F. Kennedy was assassinated while riding in a car. His killer may never be known.
美國總統約翰·甘乃迺坐車時不幸遇刺，而兇手身分可能永遠石沈大海。

同義字
▶ □murder　v.　謀殺；兇殺　　□slander　v.　誹謗；詆毀
▶ □defame　v.　誹謗；破壞…的名譽

反義字
▶ □praise　v.　讚美；表揚；歌頌　　□compliment　v.　讚美

assess [ə'sɛs]　勔確定（稅、罰款、賠償金等）的金額；（為徵稅）估定（財產）的價值 ★★★★☆

After the fire, the tenant returned to his apartment to assess the damage.
火災過後，住戶回到公寓估算損失程度。

同義字
▶ □estimate　v.　估計；估量；估價　　□appraise　v.　估計；估量；估價
▶ □measure　v.　測量；估量

assimilate [ə'sɪmlˌet]　勔吸收（知識等）；理解；消化；同化 ★★★★★

At first, it was difficult for Sven to adapt to the new culture, but eventually he assimilated quite well.
雖然斯文一開始很不能適應這裡的新文化，最後卻被同化得很徹底。

同義字
▶ □absorb　v.　吸收；汲取　　□digest　v.　消化；領悟

反義字
▶ □dissimilate　v.　不同

audible ['ɔdəbl]　勔可聽見的；聽得見的 ★★★★☆

Speak up. This is a bad phone line. Your voice is barely audible.
大聲一點。現在通話品質不佳，幾乎聽不到你的聲音。

反義字
▶ □Inaudible　a.　聽不見的；無法聽懂的

audition [ɔ'dɪʃən]　勔（演員等發聲的）試聽 ★★★★★

Many actresses audition for the role of "Susan", but only one will get it.
為「蘇珊」一角前來參加發聲試聽的女演員不少，但只有一人能爭取到該角色。

同義字

▶ □hearing n. 聽取；被傾聽的機會

authentic [ɔ'θɛntɪk] 🔣真正的；非假冒的 ★★★☆☆

These are not authentic Levi's jeans. They're just cheap imitations.
這些不是真正的李維斯牛仔褲，不過是些便宜的仿冒品。

同義字
▶ □true a. 真實的；確實的   □real a. 真的；真正的
▶ □genuine a. 真的；非偽造的   □ substantial a. 真實的；實在的
反義字
▶ □spurious a. 假的；偽造的   □ fictitious a. 虛構的；非真實的
▶ □false a. 假的；偽造的；人造的

autobiography [ˌɔtəbaɪ'ɑgrəfɪ] 🔣自傳 ★★★★☆

When I retire, I'll write an autobiography telling the world about who I am.
我退休時要寫一本自傳向世人介紹我自己。

同義字
▶ □memoir n. 回憶錄；自傳

autopsy ['ɔtɑpsɪ] 🔣屍體解剖；驗屍 ★★★★★

The coroner performed an autopsy on the dead body to determine the cause of death.
驗屍官對屍體進行驗屍工作以確認死因。

avalanche ['ævl̩ˌæntʃ] 🔣雪崩；山崩 ★★★☆☆

Skiers should be careful. A loud noise in these mountains can cause an avalanche.
到這幾座山滑雪的人要小心不要發出太大的聲音，否則可能造成雪崩。

同義字
▶ □snowslide n. 雪崩   □landslide n. 山崩

avert [ə'vɝt] 🔣避開；防止；避免 ★★★★☆

Dennis averted an accident by turning sharply and slamming on the brakes.
為了避免發生車禍，丹尼斯猛地一轉，然後急踩煞車。

同義字
▶ □prevent v. 防止；預防；阻止   □avoid v. 避開；躲開；避免
▶ □dodge v. 巧妙地迴避   □ward v. 避開；擋開；避免
反義字
▶ □confront v. 迎面遇到；面臨   □meet v. 遇見；碰上；遭遇
▶ □encounter v. 遭遇；遇到

awaken [ə'wekən] 🔣1. 喚醒；使覺醒 2. 喚起；激起 ★★★★★

Mother was awakened by the sound of her baby crying.
媽媽被嬰兒的哭聲給弄醒。

同義字
▶ □waken　v.　喚醒；弄醒　　　□rouse　v.　弄醒；叫醒
▶ □revive　v.　甦醒；復甦　　　□arouse　v.　喚起；激
反義字
▶ □sleep　v.　睡　　　　　　　□nap　v.　打盹；小睡
▶ □slumber　v.　用睡眠打發　　□drowse　v.　使昏昏欲睡

以B為首的單字

5 顆★：金色（860~990）證書必背
4 顆★：藍色（730~855）證書必背
3 顆★：綠色（470~725）證書必背

MP3-03

bacteria [bæk'tɪrɪə] 名細菌（bacterium 的複數） ★★★★☆

Please wash your hands with disinfectant to kill the bacteria.

為了殺菌，請用消毒劑洗手。

同義字
▶ □germ　n.　微生物；細菌；病菌

badger ['bædʒɚ] 動困擾；糾纏 ★★★☆☆

Stop badgering me with all these useless questions! I'm trying to get some work done.

不要再拿這些沒用的問題來煩我！不然我什麼事都做不成了。

同義字
▶ □bother　v.　煩擾；打擾　　　□upset　v.　打亂；攪亂
▶ □pester　v.　煩擾；糾纏　　　□harass　v.　使煩惱；煩擾
▶ □annoy　v.　打擾；困擾；惹惱
反義字
▶ □gratify　v.　使高興；使滿意　□please　v.　使高興；使喜歡
▶ □amuse　v.　使歡樂；使發笑

baffle ['bæfl] 動 1. 使困惑；難住　2. 使受挫折；阻撓 ★★★★★

Marcia was baffled by the poorly written instructions, and in the end was unable to put together her new bookshelf.

說明書寫得很差，把瑪西亞給難倒了，新書架最後還是組裝不起來。

同義字
▶ □puzzle　v.　使迷惑；使為難　□perplex　v.　使困惑；使費解
▶ □confound　v.　使混亂；使困惑　□bewilder　v.　使迷惑；使糊塗
反義字
▶ □clarify　v.　澄清；闡明　　　□illustrate　v.　說明；闡明
▶ □expound　v.　解釋；詳細述說

bailiff ['belɪf] 名法警 ★★★☆☆

The judge asked the bailiff to escort the defendant out of the courtroom.

法官要求法警護送被告離開法庭。

ballad ['bæləd]　名民謠；民歌；敘事歌謠　★★★★★

"Imagine", by John Lennon, is a popular ballad sung all around the world.

約翰・藍儂寫的「想像」，是紅遍全球的流行民歌。

同義字
▶ □ditty　n.　歌謠；小調　□folk song　民謠

barring ['barɪŋ]　介除…以外　★★★★☆

Barring bad weather, our plans for the company picnic will remain unchanged.

除非天候不佳，否則公司野餐計畫照常進行。

同義字
▶ □but　prep.　除…以外　□except　prep.　除…之外
▶ □save　prep.　除…之外

bask [bæsk]　動取暖；曬太陽　★★★★★

Beachgoers basked in the warmth of the morning sun, and sought shade when it became too strong around noon.

海灘遊客會先沐浴在早晨陽光的溫暖當中，等到接近中午太陽太大時，再找地方遮蔭。

同義字
▶ □sun　v.　曬太陽

batter ['bætɚ]　名麵糊（用雞蛋、牛奶、麵粉等 調成的糊狀物）；麵糰　★★★★★

The batter for the cake is too thick. Maybe you should add some water.

做蛋糕用的麵糊太黏稠了，可能加點水會比較好。

同義字
▶ □paste　n.　（做糕點用的）麵糰　□dough　n.　生麵糰

bawl [bɔl]　動大喊；大叫；放聲痛哭　★★★★☆

The child bawled loudly when his brother took away his toy.

那個孩子的玩具被他哥哥拿走了，便放聲大哭起來。

同義字
▶ □shout　v.　叫喊；大聲說　□yell　v.　叫喊著說；大聲嚷道
▶ □wail　v.　慟哭；嚎啕　□howl　v.　噑叫；怒吼
▶ □scream　v.　尖叫；放聲大哭

反義字
▶ □convulsion　n.　大笑；狂笑　□roar　n.　呼叫；大笑聲

befriend [bɪ'frɛnd]　動對…以朋友相待；和…交朋友　★★★★★

I befriended the poor homeless man, and gave him a warm meal and a place to stay the night.

我把那名又窮又無家可歸的人當朋友看，不僅拿新鮮食物給他吃，還讓他有溫暖地方可以過夜。

▶ ☐make friends with　交朋友

belated　[bɪˈletɪd]　形誤期的；太遲的　★★★☆☆

Happy belated birthday! I'm sorry I forgot the exact date, but better late than never, right?

過期生日快樂！很抱歉我忘了正確日期，不過遲了總比沒有好，對吧？

同義字

▶ ☐tardy　a.　遲延的；遲到的　　☐late　a.　遲的
▶ ☐overdue　a.　過期的；遲到的

反義字

▶ ☐early　a.　提早的；早產的　　☐premature　a.　比預期早的

belittle　[bɪˈlɪtl]　動輕視；貶低　★★★★★

You shouldn't belittle people when they make mistakes. Instead, encourage them to try harder.

人們犯錯時不該加以貶低，反而更應該鼓勵他們再努力試試看。

同義字

▶ ☐cheapen　v.　使受人輕視　　☐depreciate　v.　輕視；貶低
▶ ☐disparage　v.　貶低；輕視　　☐disdain　v.　輕蔑；鄙視
▶ ☐look down on　輕視

反義字

▶ ☐value　v.　尊重；重視；珍視　　☐respect　v.　尊重；重視
▶ ☐make much of　重視

belligerent　[bəˈlɪdʒərənt]　形好戰的；好鬥的　★★★★☆

He is a very belligerent president, and sends his troops into war without any regard for life.

他是個相當好戰的總統，不顧士兵性命，只會拼命將部隊送上戰場。

同義字

▶ ☐combative　a.　好戰的；好鬥的　　☐bellicose　a.　好鬥的；好戰的
▶ ☐pugnacious　a.　好鬥的　　☐warlike　a.　好戰的；尚武的
▶ ☐militant　a.　好戰的；激進的

反義字

▶ ☐kind　a.　富於同情心的；仁慈的　　☐benevolent　a.　仁慈的
▶ ☐merciful　a.　仁慈的；慈悲的

benefactor　[ˈbɛnəˌfæktə]　名捐助人；施主；恩人　★★★☆☆

Mr. Winspear is a rich and generous man. He is the benefactor of several charities in the community.

溫斯比爾先生既有錢又慷慨，捐助了該社區好幾個慈善團體。

同義字

▶ ☐contributor　n.　捐贈者；捐款人　☐angel　n.　贊助人；後臺老板
▶ ☐supporter　n.　支持者；擁護者　☐patron　n.　贊助者；資助者

beneficial [ˌbɛnəˈfɪʃəl] 形 有益的;有利的;有幫助的 ★★★★★

The new drugs have been very beneficial to grandmother's health. Her condition has improved a lot since she began taking them.
這些新藥對祖母的健康助益很大,服用以來,身體情況已大為改善。

同義字
▶ □useful　a.　有用的;有益的　　□helpful　a.　有幫助的;有益的
▶ □profitable　a.　有益的;有用的　□favorable　a.　有利的;順利的

反義字
▶ □harmful　a.　有害的　　　　　□hazardous　a.　有害的
▶ □useless　a.　無效的;無益的　□futile　a.　無益的;無用的

berth [bɜθ] 名（火車、船等的）舖位;坐位 ★★★★☆

I like to sleep in the top berth when taking overnight trains.
坐夜班火車時,我喜歡睡在上舖。

同義字
▶ □bunk　n.　架式床舖;舖位

bewilder [bɪˈwɪldɚ] 動 1. 使迷惑;使糊塗;難住　2. 使迷路 ★★★★☆

The endless twists and turns in the cave bewildered us, and soon we were lost.
洞穴裡無止盡的蜿蜒曲折把我們搞得一頭霧水,很快就迷路了。

同義字
▶ □baffle　v.　使困惑;難住　　□puzzle　v.　使迷惑;使為難
▶ □perplex　v.　使困惑;使費解　□confound　v.　使混亂;使困惑

反義字
▶ □clarify　v.　澄清;闡明　　　□illustrate　v.　說明;闡明
▶ □expound　v.　解釋;詳細述說

bibliography [ˌbɪblɪˈɑgrəfɪ] 名 參考書目;書誌學;目錄學 ★★★★★

At the end of the essay there is a bibliography listing all the books and articles that were researched for this paper.
論文最後有附上參考書目,將這篇研究報告用到的所有書籍和文章都列在裡面。

同義字
▶ □list　n.　表;名冊;目錄　　□catalogue　n.　目錄;目錄冊

bide [baɪd] 動 等待;停留 ★★★★★

Having lost my house keys, I bided my time on the front steps until my wife came home.
我因為弄丟了家裡的鑰匙,只好在前階那裡等我太太回來。

同義字
▶ □wait　v.　等待　　　　　□tarry　v.　逗留;停留;等待

反義字
▶ □despair　v.　絕望;喪失信心　□give up　放棄

bilateral [baɪˈlætərəl] 形 雙方的；雙邊的 ★★★★☆

The two countries signed a bilateral trade agreement that would increase agricultural trade.

兩國簽訂了增進農業貿易的雙邊貿易協定。

同義字
- ▶ □bipartite　a.　雙方的；雙邊的

bilingual [baɪˈlɪŋwəl] 形 （能說）兩種語言的；雙語的 ★★★☆☆

Having grown up with English-speaking parents and a French-speaking nanny, Peggy was bilingual before age eight.

佩姬的父母講英語，保姆講法語，在這樣的成長環境下，她不到八歲就會講兩種語言。

bitter [ˈbɪtɚ] 形 有苦味的；苦的 ★★★★☆

This coffee is too bitter for me. Do you have any cream and sugar?

這種咖啡對我來說太苦了。有奶精和糖嗎？

同義字
- ▶ □acrid　a.　刺激的；辣的　　□distasteful　a.　不合口味的

反義字
- ▶ □sweet　a.　甜的　　□sugary　a.　含糖的；甘的

blatant [ˈbletn̩t] 形 公然的；露骨的 ★★★★★

This is a blatant disregard for school rules. You will certainly be punished, if not expelled.

這樣公然藐視校規，就算不被開除，也一定會受到處罰。

同義字
- ▶ □openly　a.　公開地；公然地　　□flagrant　a.　明目張膽的
- ▶ □aboveboard　a.　率直地　　□barefaced　a.　拋頭露面的

反義字
- ▶ □secret　a.　秘密的；機密的　　□private　a.　私下的；非公開的
- ▶ □covert　a.　隱蔽的；暗地的　　□confidential　a.　秘密的

blaze [blez] 名 火焰；火災；熊熊燃燒 ★★★★☆

The firefighters raced to put out the huge blaze.

消防人員火速前來撲滅熊熊大火。

同義字
- ▶ □fire　n.　火；火災　　□flame　n.　火焰；火舌
- ▶ □flare　n.　（瞬間的）閃耀的火光

bleak [blik] 形 無希望的；渺茫的；淒涼的；陰暗的 ★★★☆☆

Our future looks quite bleak. We have no money, no jobs, and will soon be kicked out of this apartment.

我們看起來前途茫茫。不僅沒錢沒工作，而且很快就要被趕出這棟公寓。

A

同義字
- ▶ □hopeless　a.　不抱希望的　　　　　　□slim　a.　渺茫的
- ▶ □forlorn　a.　幾乎無望的；凄涼的

反義字
- ▶ □hopeful　a.　有希望的；有前途的　　□promising　a.　有希望的
- ▶ □probable　a.　很有希望的

blemish　[ˈblɛmɪʃ]　🔲 傷疤；（身體的）疤；粉刺　　★★★★★

She covered up the blemish on her chin with a little make-up.
她化了點妝，把下巴上的傷疤給蓋住。

同義字
- ▶ □scar　n.　疤；傷痕　　　　　　□spot　n.　疤；痣；丘疹；瘡
- ▶ □wound　n.　創傷；傷口；傷疤

blockade　[blɑˈked]　🔲 封鎖；道路阻塞；障礙物；阻礙物　　★★★☆☆

The military set up a blockade around the city, shutting off the insurgents from supplies.
軍方將城市周邊道路加以封鎖，以阻斷暴動者的貨品供應。

同義字
- ▶ □fortification　n.　設防；築城　　□obstruction　n.　阻塞物；障礙
- ▶ □barrier　n　障礙物；路障

bodily　[ˈbɑdɪlɪ]　🔲 肉體的；身體的　　★★★★☆

She suffered bodily harm from the attack, and is now in a wheelchair.
她遭受攻擊而身體受傷，現在坐在輪椅上。

同義字
- ▶ □physical　a.　身體的；肉體的　　□corporal　a.　肉體的；身體的
- ▶ □fleshly　a.　肉體的

反義字
- ▶ □mental　a.　精神的；心理的　　□spiritual　a.　精神（上）的
- ▶ □psychological　a.　心理的

boisterous　[ˈbɔɪstərəs]　🔲 喧鬧的；愛鬧的；狂歡的　　★★★★★

The audience was very boisterous while waiting for the band to come out on stage.
等待樂團上台表演前，觀眾在底下嘰哩呱啦，非常吵鬧。

同義字
- ▶ □noisy　a.　喧鬧的；嘈雜的　　□tumultuous　a.　吵鬧的
- ▶ □loud　a.　大聲的；喧噪的　　□vociferous　a.　喊叫的；喧嚷的

反義字
- ▶ □quiet　a.　安靜的；輕聲的　　□silent　a.　寂靜無聲的；沈默的
- ▶ □still　a.　寂靜的；靜默的；平靜的

bolster　[ˈbolstɚ]　🔲 援助；支持；撐；加固　　★★★★☆

Hiring a new bookkeeper for the company should bolster the accounting department during the busy season.

公司旺季時請了個新簿記員來支援會計部門。

同義字
▶ ☐help　v.　幫助；援助；助長　　☐back　v.　支持；援助；贊助
▶ ☐support　v.　支持；資助　　☐abet　v.　幫助；支持

反義字
▶ ☐deter　v.　威懾住；嚇住　　☐prohibit　v.　妨礙；阻止
▶ ☐repress　v.　抑制；壓制

bombard [bɑmˋbɑrd]　1. 不斷攻擊；向…連續提出問題 2. 砲擊；轟炸 ★★★★☆

He was bombarded with criticisms and insults when he announced the bad news.

他宣佈這些壞消息時，各種批評和羞辱排山倒海而來。

同義字
▶ ☐attack　v.　進攻；抨擊；責難　　☐assault　v.　攻擊；襲擊；譴責
▶ ☐lash　v.　抨擊；斥責　　☐tilt　v.　攻擊；抨擊

反義字
▶ ☐defend　v.　防禦；保衛；保護　　☐protect　v.　保護；防護
▶ ☐guard　v.　保衛；守衛；警衛

botanical [boˋtænɪkl]　☒植物學的；植物的；來自植物的　★★★★☆

If you want to learn about plants, you can register for the tour at the botanical gardens.

如果你想學習植物的相關知識，可以去登記參觀植物園。

同義字
▶ ☐plant　n.　植物；農作物　　☐vegetative　a.　植物的

反義字
▶ ☐animal　a.　動物的；獸類的

bountiful [ˋbaʊntəfəl]　☒充足的；豐富的　★★★★★

The farmers celebrated their bountiful harvest.

農夫們慶祝豐收。

同義字
▶ ☐abundant　a.　大量的；充足的　　☐plentiful　a.　豐富的；充足的
▶ ☐bounteous　a.　充足的；豐富的　　☐generous　a.　大量的；豐富的
▶ ☐affluent　a.　豐富的；富饒的

反義字
▶ ☐scarce　a.　缺乏的；不足的　　☐scant　a.　不足的；貧乏的
▶ ☐meager　a.　粗劣的；不足的　　☐deficient　a.　不足的；缺乏的

boycott [ˋbɔɪˏkɑt]　☒聯合抵制；拒絕參加（或 買等）；一致與…絕交
★★★★☆

We should boycott this company's products to protest their poor environmental policies.

為了抗議這家公司對環保的漠視，我們必須聯合抵制他們的產品才行。

同義字
- ▶ □resist　v.　抵抗；反抗；抗拒　　□react　v.　抗拒；反抗
- ▶ □blackball　v.　投反對票；排斥

反義字
- ▶ □obey　v.　服從；聽從；執行　　□submit　v.　使服從；使屈服
- ▶ □succumb　v.　屈服；委棄

brandish　[ˈbrændɪʃ]　　v. 揮動；揮舞　　★★★★☆

The knight brandished his sword and challenged his enemy to a dual.

這名騎士揮舞著劍，準備和敵人決一死戰。

同義字
- ▶ □wave　v.　對…揮（手、旗等）　　□wield　v.　揮舞（劍等）

bravo　[ˈbrɑˈvo]　　int.　好極了　　★★★★★

At the end of the classical music concert, the audience shouted "Bravo!".

這場古典音樂會終場時，觀眾大喊「好極了！」。

同義字
- ▶ □wonderful　a.　極好的；精彩的　　□fantastic　a.　極好的；了不起的
- ▶ □fabulous　a.　極好的　　□gorgeous　a.　令人十分愉快的
- ▶ □magnificent　a.　極好的

反義字
- ▶ □terrible　a.　極糟糕的；極差的　　□awful　a.　極壞的；極糟的
- ▶ □horrible　a.　極討厭的；糟透的　　□gross　a.　令人噁心的

breach　[britʃ]　　v.（對法律等的）破壞、違反；（對他人權利的）侵害　　★★★☆☆

You've breached your contract with the company, and may be fined for giving away company secrets.

你違反了和公司簽訂的合約，將因洩露公司機密而遭罰款。

同義字
- ▶ □violate　v.　違犯；違背；違反　　□break　v.　破壞
- ▶ □trespass　v.　侵害；違背　　□infringe　v.　違犯；侵犯；違反

反義字
- ▶ □observe　v.　遵守；奉行　　□obey　v.　服從；聽從；執行
- ▶ □follow　v.　聽從；採用；仿傚　　□comply　v.　依從；順從；遵從

brittle　[ˈbrɪtḷ]　　a. 脆的；易碎的；易損壞的　　★★★☆☆

At age 96, Mr. Davis's bones are very brittle. He must take care not to fall.

96 歲的戴維斯骨頭很脆弱，得小心不要跌倒才好。

同義字
- ▶ □fragile　a.　易碎的；易損壞的　　□frail　a.　易損壞的；不堅實的
- ▶ □breakable　a.　會破的；脆的　　□frangible　a.　脆弱的；易破的

反義字
- ▶ □sturdy　a.　堅固的；經久耐用的　　□strong　a.　堅固的；牢固的
- ▶ □solid　a.　結實的；堅固的　　□firm　a.　穩固的；牢固的

broach [brotʃ] 動 開始提及；引入；提出；開始討論 ★★★★☆

I don't want to put this off any longer. I'm going to broach the subject of marriage with James tonight.

這件事我不想再拖了，今晚就要和詹姆斯討論結婚事宜。

同義字
- ▶ □propose   v.   提議；建議；提出   □advance   v.   提出
- ▶ □discuss   v.   討論；商談；論述   □ventilate   v.   討論問題

反義字
- ▶ □reject   v.   駁回；否決 □overrule   v.   否決…的意見
- ▶ □veto   v.   否決；禁止；反對

broadcast ['brɔd͵kæst] 動 廣播；播送 ★★★★☆

The concert was broadcast around the world on TV and the Internet.

這場音樂會利用電視和網際網路在全球播放。

同義字
- ▶ □air   v.   廣播；播送   □televise   v.   電視播送
- ▶ □telecast   v.   電視廣播 □radio   v.   用無線電發送
- ▶ □transmit   v.   發射；播送

brokerage ['brokərɪdʒ] 名 1. 經紀業；掮客業務 2. 佣金；經紀費 ★★★★★

This brokerage firm buys and sells technology stocks.

這家經紀公司買賣科技類股。

同義字
- ▶ □agency   n.   代辦處；經銷處   □commission   n.   佣金

bronchitis [brɑn'kaɪtɪs] 名 支氣管炎 ★★★★☆

Your cough sounds terrible! It might be bronchitis, in which case you should see the doctor and get some antibiotics.

你咳嗽聽起來蠻嚴重的！萬一得的是支氣管炎，你就得看醫生並服用一些抗生素才行。

brooch [brotʃ] 名 女用胸針（或領針） ★★★★★

Auntie Ann likes to wear a brooch of a butterfly on her sweater.

安姑姑喜歡在毛衣上別個蝴蝶胸針。

bullock ['bulək] 名 閹牛 ★★★★☆

Farmers in this country still plow their fields with a bullock.

這個國家的農夫仍然用閹牛耕田。

同義字
- ▶ □ox   n.   去勢公牛；閹牛   □steer   n.   小公牛；閹牛

反義字
- ▶ □cow   n.   母牛；奶牛

bumper [ˈbʌmpɚ]　图 緩衝器；減震物；（汽車前後的）保險槓　★★★☆☆

The dent in the back bumper is from when I got hit from behind while waiting at a red light.

汽車後保險槓的凹痕，是我在等紅燈時被別人從後面撞到的。

同義字
▶ □buffer　n.　緩衝器；減震器　　□shock absorber　減震器

buoyant [ˈbɔɪənt]　图 有浮力的；能浮起的　★★★★★

Should you fall into the water, hang on to anything buoyant, like a log.

如果掉進水裡，要緊緊抓住任何像圓木這類會浮的東西。

同義字
▶ □floating　a.　漂浮的　　□afloat　a.　飄浮著的

反義字
▶ □submerged　a.　在水中的　　□sunken　a.　沈沒的

bureau [ˈbjʊro]　图 五斗櫃；衣櫥；梳妝臺　★★★★☆

My folded shirts are put into the bureau, and my pants and dress shirts are hung up in the closet.

我摺好的襯衫都放進五斗櫃裡，褲子和西裝襯衫則掛在衣櫥裡。

同義字
▶ □chest　n.　五斗櫃；衣櫃　　□dresser　n.　衣櫥；梳妝臺
▶ □wardrobe　n.　衣櫥；衣櫃　　□chiffonier　n.　帶鏡高五斗櫥
▶ □chifforobe　n.　帶抽屜之衣櫥

bureaucracy [bjʊˈrɑkrəsɪ]　图 官僚體制；繁文褥節；形式主義　★★★☆☆

The bureaucracy in this country is very slow. It takes months to get anything from the government.

這個國家的官僚體制效率不彰，往往耗廢數月才等到政府下文。

bustle [ˈbʌsl]　图 忙亂；喧囂　★★★★☆

Do you enjoy the hustle and bustle of the city, or do you prefer the peace and quiet of the country?

你喜歡熙來攘往的城市生活，還是偏愛鄉下的安詳和寧靜？

同義字
▶ □commotion　n.　騷動；喧鬧　　□hubbub　n.　吵鬧聲；騷動
▶ □noise　n.　聲響；喧鬧聲　　□to-do　嚷鬧；騷亂；忙亂

反義字
▶ □quietness　n.　安靜；肅靜　　□calmness　n.　平靜；安寧
▶ □peace　n.　和平；和睦；安詳　　□tranquility　n.　平靜；安靜

butt [bʌt]　動 用頭（或角）猛撞；角力　★★★★☆

The two of them have very different opinions, and butt heads whenever there is a

political discussion.
他們兩個意見相當分歧，一討論起政治就會針鋒相對。

同義字
▶ □contest　v.　競爭；角逐；爭辯　　□argue　v.　爭論；辯論；爭吵
▶ □quarrel　v.　爭吵；不和

反義字
▶ □agree　v.　同意；意見一致　　□consent　v.　同意；贊成；答應
▶ □assent　v.　同意；贊成　　□see eye to eye　看法一致

by-law ['baɪˌlɔ] 🔲地方法則；內部章程；細則 ★★★★☆

Because of the new city by-law, smokers are no longer able to light up inside public buildings.
新設立的城市地方法規定，癮君子不准繼續在公共場所內吸煙。

同義字
▶ □regulation　n.　規章；規則　　□constitution　n.　憲法；章程
▶ □ordinance　n.　法令；條令　　□prescription　n.　命令；指示

以C為首的單字

5 顆★：金色（860~990）證書必背
4 顆★：藍色（730~855）證書必背
3 顆★：綠色（470~725）證書必背

MP3-04,05

cabinet ['kæbənɪt] 🔲內閣；全體閣員 ★★★★★

The Prime Minister consulted his cabinet before making the decision.
首相和內閣商量後再做決定。

同義字
▶ □ministry　n.　內閣；全體閣員　　□government　n.　政府

calculate ['kælkjəˌlet] 🔲計算 ★★★★☆

This is a very difficult mathematical problem that requires a supercomputer to calculate.
這道數學問題很難，得用超級電腦才算得出來。

同義字
▶ □count　v.　計算；數　　□figure　v.　計算
▶ □compute　v.　計算；估算　　□reckon　v.　計算；數

calorie ['kælərɪ] 🔲卡路里；大卡 ★★★☆☆

You should watch the amount of calories you intake if you want to lose weight.
如果你想減重，便要注意吸收了多少卡路里。

campaign [kæm'pen] 🔲競選運動；運動 ★★★★★

One year before the election, the two candidates began their campaign by touring different parts of the country.
離選舉還有一年，兩位候選人便開始到全國各地巡迴，為競選活動造勢。

同義字
- ▶ □drive　n.　運動；宣傳活動　　□movement　n.　運動；活動
- ▶ □crusade　n.　運動

---

candid　['kændɪd]　形 坦率的；直言的；公正的；公平的

It was a difficult question, but he gave me a candid, honest answer.
雖然問題不好回答，他還是給了我一個坦率誠實的答案。

同義字
- ▶ □sincere　a.　忠實的；誠實的　　□outspoken　a.　坦率的
- ▶ □straightforward　a.　正直的　　□frank　a.　坦白的；直率的
- ▶ □righteous　a.　公正的；正當的

反義字
- ▶ □partial　a.　不公平的；偏袒的　　□unfair　a.　不公平的；不正當的
- ▶ □unjust　a.　不公平的；不正當的　□false　a.　不忠實的；無信義的
- ▶ □insincere　a.　無誠意的

---

captivate　['kæptə,vet]　動 使著迷；打動；蠱惑　　★★★★★

The audience was captivated by the movie stars' beauty and eloquence.
該電影明星的美貌和雄辯，深深打動了觀眾。

同義字
- ▶ □charm　v.　使陶醉；吸引　　□fascinate　v.　迷住
- ▶ □bewitch　v.　使陶醉；使銷魂　　□enchant　v.　使陶醉；使入迷
- ▶ □spellbind　v.　迷住；以咒語壓住

反義字
- ▶ □disenchant　v.　使醒悟　　□disillusion　v.　使醒悟
- ▶ □undeceive　v.　使不受迷惑

---

carcass　['kɑrkəs]　名（動物的）屍體；（人的）屍首　　★★★★☆

The carcass of the cow is being fought over by vultures.
禿鷹爭食該母牛的屍體。

同義字
- ▶ □body　n.　（人、動物等的）屍體　□corpse　n.　屍體

---

cardiac　['kɑrdɪ,æk]　形 心臟的；心臟病的　　★★★☆☆

These French fries are terrible for your heart. If you don't stop you'll have a cardiac arrest soon.
這些炸薯條對心臟很不好，如果你再不停止食用，很快就會罹患心臟停跳。

---

caricature　['kærɪkətʃə]　名 漫畫；諷刺畫；漫畫藝術；漫畫手法　　★★★☆☆

The street artist drew a caricature of me flying like Superman.
街頭藝術家幫我畫了一幅像超人一樣在天上飛的漫畫。

同義字
- ▶ □cartoon　n.　連環漫畫；卡通　　□comic　n.　連環漫畫
- ▶ □burlesque　n.　諷刺 的模仿

carnivorous [kɑrˈnɪvərəs]　形肉食性的　★★★★☆

Carnivorous animals, like lions and wolves, eat meat.
獅子和狼這類肉食動物會吃肉。

同義字
▶ □predator　n.　食肉性物；掠奪者

反義字
▶ □herbivore　n.　食草性物

cartridge [ˈkɑrtrɪdʒ]　名墨水匣；墨水筒；筆芯　★★★★★

My printer is almost out of ink. Could you pick up a cartridge from the computer store?
我的印表機墨水用完了，你可以到電腦店買個墨水匣回來嗎？

casually [ˈkæʒjʊəlɪ]　副隨便地；隨意地；偶然地；碰巧地　★★★☆☆

This is just an informal dinner, so please dress casually.
這只是非正式晚宴，所以請隨便穿就好。

同義字
▶ □randomly　adv.　胡亂地；隨便地　　□informally　adv.　非正式地
▶ □haphazard　adv.　無計劃地　　□arbitrarily　adv.　任意地

反義字
▶ □formally　adv.　正式地；正規地　　□regularly　adv.　正規地
▶ □solemnly　adv.　正式地；神聖地

casualty [ˈkæʒjʊəltɪ]　名1. 死者；受害人 2. 意外事故；不幸事故　★★★★☆

Over one hundred people were injured during the earthquake, but luckily there were no casualties.
地震受傷人數超過一百人，但幸好沒有發生任何死亡事故。

同義字
▶ □sufferer　n.　受害者；受難者　　□mishap　n.　不幸事故；災難
▶ □accident　n.　事故；災禍　　□ misfortune　n.　不幸的事；災難

反義字
▶ □survivor　n.　倖存者；生還者　　□happiness　n.　幸福；快樂
▶ □fortune　n.　好運；幸運

catastrophe [kəˈtæstrəfɪ]　名大敗；慘敗；大災難；翻天覆地的事件　★★★★★

This dinner is a catastrophe! The chicken is burnt, the wine is sour, and the soup is bland. No wonder the guests are leaving!
這次晚宴簡直慘不忍睹！雞肉焦了、酒酸了，連湯也淡而無味。難怪客人都跑光了！

同義字
▶ □calamity　n.　災難；大禍　　□tragedy　n.　悲劇性事件；慘案
▶ □disaster　n.　災害；災難；不幸

反義字
▶ □comedy　n.　喜劇

A
B
C
D
E
F
G
H
I
J
K
L
M
N
O
P
Q
R
S
T
U
V
W
X
Y
Z

cease [sis] 勔停止；終止；結束 ★★★★☆

Everyone celebrated when the fighting between the two countries ceased.
大家都在慶祝兩國停戰。

同義字
▶ □stop　v.　停止；中止；止住　　□end　v.　結束；終止；了結
▶ □halt　v.　停止行進；停止；終止　□discontinue　v.　停止；中斷

反義字
▶ □begin　v.　開始；著手；動手　□continue　v.　繼續；持續；延伸
▶ □endure　v.　持久；持續　　□last　v.　持續；持久

cede [sid] 勔1. 割讓；讓與；交出　2. 轉讓；過戶 ★★★☆☆

After one hundred years of British rule, Hong Kong was ceded to China.
香港被英國統治了一 年後，終於交回中國手上。

同義字
▶ □relinquish　v.　交出；讓與　　□surrender　v.　交出；放棄
▶ □give up　放棄

censor [ˈsɛnsɚ] 勔檢查（出版物等）；審查 ★★★★★

The newspaper article was censored because the information was morally objectionable.
報紙上刊出的這篇文章，因內容有違善良風俗而遭到審查。

同義字
▶ □examine　v.　檢查；細查；診察　□inspect　v.　檢查；審查
▶ □check　v.　檢查；檢驗；核對　　□look over　仔細檢查

census [ˈsɛnsəs] 名人口普查；人口調查 ★★★☆☆

The last census found that sixty percent of people living in this neighborhood own at least one car.
最近一次人口調查發現，鄰近地區的居民當中，至少擁有一輛車的人口比例占了百分之六十。

同義字
▶ □head count　點人數；人口統計

cereal [ˈsɪrɪəl] 名穀類植物；穀類加工食品；麥片 ★★★★☆

Cereals, like wheat and oats, are grown throughout the prairies.
像小麥和燕麥這類穀類食物，都是種滿整片大草原。

同義字
▶ □grain　n.　穀粒；穀物；穀類

ceremony [ˈsɛrəˌmonɪ] 名儀式；典禮；禮儀；禮節 ★★★★★

A traditional Chinese wedding ceremony consists of the bride and groom offering tea to their parents and grandparents.
新娘和新郎奉茶給父母和祖父母，是傳統中國婚禮的一部分。

同義字
▶ □rite　n.　儀式；慣例　　□ritual　n.　儀式；典禮
▶ □function　n.　盛大的集會　　□observance　n.　禮儀；儀式

chagrin [ʃəˈgrɪn]　图懊惱；悔恨；苦惱　　★★★★☆

Much to his chagrin, the party ended when he arrived.
他因為派對結束才抵達，感到非常懊惱。

同義字
▶ □remorse　n.　痛悔；自責　　　□regret　n.　懊悔；悔恨；抱歉
▶ □rue　n.　後悔；悔恨；悲嘆　　　□repentance　n.　悔悟；悔改

chaos [ˈkeɑs]　图混亂；雜亂的一團（或一堆等）　　★★★★★

During the blackout, there was chaos and confusion all over the city.
停電期間，整座城騷動不安、亂成一團。

同義字
▶ □muddle　n.　糊塗；混亂狀態　　□disorder　n.　混亂；無秩序
▶ □confusion　n.　混亂；混亂狀況　　□anarchy　n.　無秩序；混亂

反義字
▶ □cosmos　n.　秩序；和諧　　　□system　n.　秩序；規律
▶ □order　n.　整齊；有條理；秩序

characteristic [ˌkærəktəˈrɪstɪk]　图特性；特徵；特色　　★★★★☆

Her most noticeable characteristic is her ability to be cheerful at all times.
她最明顯的特色就是能隨時保持愉快的心境。

同義字
▶ □feature　n.　特徵；特色　　　□attribute　n.　屬性；特性；特質
▶ □property　n.　特性；性能　　　□trait　n.　特徵；特點；特性

check [tʃɛk]　動檢查；查對；查核　　★★★★★

Please check your coats and bags before entering the auditorium.
進觀眾席前，請先檢查你的外套和袋子。

同義字
▶ □examine　v.　檢查；細查；診察　□inspect　v.　檢查；審查
▶ □censor　v.　檢查（出版物等）

chronological [ˌkrɑnəˈlɑdʒɪkl]　形依時間前後排列而記載的　　★★★☆☆

Please list your work history in chronological order, starting with your most recent employer.
請從最近的雇主開始，依時間先後列出你的工作經歷。

circulate [ˈsɜkjəˌlet]　動流通；循環；傳播；流傳　　★★★★★

This room is so stuffy. Please open the window so that the air can circulate.
這間房間很悶，請打開窗戶讓空氣流通一下。

同義字
▶ □distribute　v.　散佈；分佈　　　□spread　v.　散佈；傳播
▶ □scatter　v.　使消散；使分散
反義字
▶ □gather　v.　聚集；積聚　　　□collect　v.　聚集；堆積

circumference [səˈkʌmfərəns]　图 圓周；周長　★★★★☆

The distance around the earth at the equator, or its circumference, is 40,075.16 kilometers.
地球繞赤道一周的距離，也就是它的圓周，為 40,075.16 公里。

同義字
▶ □circuit　n.　環道；一圈；一周

circumnavigate [ˌsɝkəmˈnævəˌget]　图 繞一周；環航　★★★☆☆

This is a really big island. We can either circumnavigate it, or pick up our canoe and carry it overland.
這座島可真大。我們可以環航一周，或是收起獨木舟，背著它走陸路探險。

同義字
▶ □circle　v.　環繞…移；環行

citadel [ˈsɪtəd!]　图 （護城）城堡；堡壘　★★★★☆

The guard watched for enemy troops from the citadel on top of the hill.
衛兵從山丘最頂端的堡壘，監視著敵方部隊。

同義字
▶ □fortress　n.　要塞；堡壘　　　□stronghold　n.　堡壘；要塞
▶ □bastion　n.　堡壘　　□fastness　n.　據點；堡壘

cite [saɪt]　图 引用；引…為證；舉出　★★★★★

In his speech, Professor Jenkins cited a poem by Robert Frost.
詹金斯教授在其演說中，引用了一首羅伯特‧佛洛斯特的詩。

同義字
▶ □quote　v.　引用；引述 □extract　v.　摘錄；選用（例子）

claim [klem]　图 1.（根據權利）要求；認領；索取 2. 自稱；聲稱；主張　★★★★☆

If nobody returns to claim this lost cell phone, I'm going to keep it.
這支遺失的手機如果沒人回來認領，我就把它拿走了。

同義字
▶ □demand　v.　要求；請求　　　□profess　v.　公開宣稱；承認
▶ □proclaim　v.　宣告；公佈；聲明 □assert　v.　斷言；聲稱
▶ □ask for　要求
反義字
▶ □disclaim　v.　放棄；否認　　　□renounce　v.　聲明放棄；拋棄

clairvoyant [klɛr'vɔɪənt] 形 千里眼；有超人之目力或洞察力的 ★★★★☆

Charlene claims she's clairvoyant, but I don't think she has any psychic powers at all.

雖然查琳自稱有千里眼，但我覺得她一點超自然力量都沒有。

clandestine [klæn'dɛstɪn] 形 秘密的；暗中的；偷偷摸摸的 ★★★★★

The CIA fought a clandestine war in Laos, unknown to the American public.

中情局背著美國人民，暗中在寮國發 一場戰爭。

同義字
- □secret a. 秘密的；機密的　□private a. 私下的
- □closet a. 私下的；秘密的　□confidential a. 秘密的

反義字
- □openly a. 公開地；公然地　□flagrant a. 明目張膽的
- □aboveboard a. 率直地　□blatant a. 公然的；露骨的

clarify ['klærə,faɪ] 動 澄清；闡明；使清楚 ★★★★☆

I'm sorry, but I didn't understand your last point. Could you please clarify?

對不起，你最後的論點我沒有弄懂。可以再說清楚一點嗎？

同義字
- □explain v. 解釋；說明；闡明　□ interpret v. 解釋；說明；詮釋
- □illustrate v. 說明；闡明　□expound v. 解釋；詳細述說
- □clear up 澄清

反義字
- □confuse v. 把…弄糊塗；使困惑　□muddle v. 使糊塗
- □jumble v. 使混亂；使雜亂　□bewilder v. 使迷惑；使糊塗

classify ['klæsə,faɪ] 動 將…分類；將…分等級 ★★★☆☆

The books are classified according to subject matter, not according to the author.

這些書是按照內容，而非按照作者來分類的。

同義字
- □bracket v. 把…歸入同類　□group v. 把…分組
- □categorize v. 使列入…的範疇　□sort v. 把…分類

反義字
- □blend v. 混和；混雜；交融　□mix v. 使混和；攪和
- □combine v. 使結合；使聯合　□mingle v. 使混合；使相混

clearance ['klɪrəns] 名 （船隻）結關；出入港許可證 ★★★★★

You need high level clearance to enter this restricted area.

你需要有高等許可證才可以進入此一限制區。

同義字
- □permit n. 許可證；執照　□licence n. 許可證；執照

coalition [,koə'lɪʃən] 名 （政黨、國家等）臨時結成的聯盟；結合；聯合 ★★★☆☆

The two opposition parties formed a coalition to bring down the ruling government.
兩個反對黨建立聯盟，想要讓執政的政府垮臺。

同義字
▶ □alliance n. 結盟；聯盟；聯姻 □league n. 同盟；聯盟
▶ □confederacy n. 聯盟；同盟 □association n. 聯盟；聯合

反義字
▶ □enemy n. 敵人；仇敵 □opponent n. 對手；敵手
▶ □rival n. 競爭者；對手；敵手 □foe n. 敵人；仇敵

coddle [ˈkɑdḷ] **勔**嬌養；當嬰兒對待； 悉心照料（病人、嬰兒等） ★★★★★

Please don't coddle me. I'm not a kid anymore.
請不要再對我那麼溺愛，我已經不是小孩了。

同義字
▶ □pamper v. 縱容；姑息；嬌養 □spoil v. 溺愛；寵壞
▶ □indulge v. 縱容；遷就 □humor v. 迎合；遷就
▶ □baby v. 把…當嬰兒般對待

反義字
▶ □nurture v. 養育；培育；教養 □breed v. 養育；培育；教養
▶ □educate v. 教育；培養；訓練

coerce [koˈɝs] **勔**強制；迫使 ★★★★☆

Vince didn't want to retire as President of the company, but was coerced by the Board of Directors who wanted someone younger to run the company.
凡斯不想從公司董事長的位子退下來，不過董事會希望讓年輕一輩來管理公司，便強制他退休。

同義字
▶ □compel v. 強迫；使不得不 □force v. 強迫；迫使
▶ □impel v. 激勵；驅使；迫使 □constrain v. 強迫；迫使

反義字
▶ □volunteer v. 自願；自願服務 □come forward 自告奮勇
▶ □willing to 樂意；願意

cognizant [ˈkɑgnɪzənt] **形**認知的；認識的 ★★★★☆

He's been unconscious since the accident, and isn't cognizant of what's going on around him.
意外發生後他就一直不省人事，周遭發生什麼事一概不知。

同義字
▶ □aware a. 知道的；察覺的 □conscious a. 神志清醒的
▶ □sensible a. 意識到的

反義字
▶ □ignorant a. 不知道的 □unaware a. 不知道的
▶ □unconscious a. 未發覺的

cohesion [koˈhiʒən] **名**結合；凝聚；團結力；附著 ★★★★☆

There was little cohesion in the student group, went their own way after university.
學生團體的凝聚力不夠，所以大學畢業後，大家就各奔東西了。

同義字
- ▶ □coherence　n.　黏著；凝聚　　　□union　n.　結合；合併
- ▶ □solidification　n.　團結　□consolidation　n.　聯合；統一

反義字
- ▶ □division　n.　分開；分割　　　□severance　n.　分離；分開
- ▶ □separation　n.　分開；分離

coincide　[ˌkoɪnˈsaɪd]　　**動**1. 同時發生 2. 相符；巧合；一致　　★★★☆☆

Oh no! My business trip coincides with our wedding anniversary. We'll have to change our plans.
哎呀，完蛋了！我的出差旅行和我們的結婚週年紀念撞在一塊，原本的計畫得更改一下才行。

同義字
- ▶ □synchronize　v.　同時發生　　　□concur　v.　同時發生
- ▶ □accord　v.　（與…）一致；符合　□jibe　v.　相一致；符合

反義字
- ▶ □disaccord　v.　不一致；相爭　　　□disagree　v.　不符；不一致
- ▶ □discord　n.　不一致；不協調

collaborate　[kəˈlæbəˌret]　　**動**共同工作；合作　　★★★★☆

Scientists from around the world are collaborating on a cure for AIDS.
世界各地的科學家正合作研究如何治療愛滋病。

同義字
- ▶ □cooperate　v.　合作；同心協力　□conspire　v.　協力；共同促成
- ▶ □coordinate　v.　協調一致　　　□concert　v.　協力；協調

collapse　[kəˈlæps]　　**動**倒塌；崩潰；瓦解；暴跌；（計劃等）突然失敗
★★★★★

The house of cards collapsed when a gust of wind came in through the window.
一陣強風從窗戶吹進來，把紙牌屋給吹倒了。

同義字
- ▶ □topple　v.　倒塌；倒下　　　□ tumble　v.　（房屋）倒塌
- ▶ □crumble　v.　摧毀；破碎；崩潰　□come down　倒塌

colleague　[kɑˈlig]　　**名**同事；同僚；同行　　★★★☆☆

This is my colleague Tina. We work in the human resources department together.
這是我同事蒂納，我們一起在人事部門工作。

同義字
- ▶ □coworker　n.　共同工作者；幫手　□associate　n.　夥伴；同事
- ▶ □comrade　n.　夥伴；同事

collective　[kəˈlɛktɪv]　　**形**集體的；共同的　　★★★★☆

Keeping the house clean is a collective responsibility. Everyone must pitch in.
維持屋子的整潔是大家共同的責任，每個人都要貢獻一分心力才對。

同義字
▶ □common　a.　共同的；共有的　　□mutual　a.　共有的；共同的
▶ □corporate　a.　共同的；全體的

反義字
▶ □particular　a.　特殊的；特定的　　□special　a.　專門的
▶ □peculiar　a.　特有的

collide　[kə'laɪd]　v. 碰撞；相撞　★★★★★

There was a huge explosion when the truck collided with a train.
卡車和火車相撞時，發出一陣很大的爆炸聲。

同義字
▶ □bump　v.　碰；撞　　□clash　v.　砰地相碰撞
▶ □bang　v.　猛擊；猛撞；撞傷　　□hurtle　v.　猛烈碰撞；猛衝
▶ □smash　v.　猛撞；猛衝

colloquial　[kə'lokwɪəl]　adj. 口語的；會話的；用於口語的　★★★★★

When you listen to native speakers converse, you may find that their colloquial language differs from the English you've learned in school.
注意聽當地人講話你就會發現，很多口語都和學校教的英語不同。

同義字
▶ □informal　a.　口語的；通俗的　　□vernacular　a.　用本國語的
▶ □conversational　a.　會話的

反義字
▶ □literary　a.　文言的

collude　[kə'lud]　v. 共謀；串通　★★★★★

The shopkeepers in town colluded to keep the price of fruits and vegetables high, despite having an overabundance of produce.
雖然生產過剩，但鎮上的店家一起串通好，要讓蔬果的價格居高不下。

同義字
▶ □conspire　v.　同謀；密謀　　□complot　v.　共謀
▶ □connive　v.　共謀

comical　['kɑmɪkl]　adj. 滑稽的；詼諧的；古怪的　★★★★☆

That's quite a comical photo of you. I can't help but laugh when I see it.
你這張照片真滑稽，叫人看了不想笑都很難。

同義字
▶ □funny　a.　有趣的；滑稽可笑的　　□humorous　a.　幽默的；詼諧的
▶ □ludicrous　a.　滑稽的　□zany　a.　荒唐可笑的

反義字
▶ □serious　a.　嚴肅的；莊嚴的　　□severe　a.　嚴肅的；正經的

▶ □solemn　a.　嚴肅的；莊重的

commemorate [kə'mɛmə,ret] 　動 紀念；慶祝　★★★☆☆

This statue was erected to commemorate the firefighters who died trying to save people trapped in burning buildings.
這群救火英雄為解救困於火場建築物的人而不幸喪生，故豎立這座雕像來紀念他們。

同義字
▶ □remember　v.　記住；牢記；不忘　　　　□celebrate　v.　慶祝；頌揚
▶ □observe　v.　慶祝（節日等）

commentary ['kɑmən,tɛrɪ] 　名 實況報導；評論　★★★☆☆

The volume was turned down, so I couldn't hear the commentary for the baseball game.
因為音量被關小了，我聽不到棒球賽的實況報導。

同義字
▶ □outside broadcast　實況轉播
反義字
▶ □rebroadcast　v.　轉播；重播

commission [kə'mɪʃən] 　名 委任；委託　★★★★☆

The government commissioned the artist to paint a mural in the lobby of City Hall.
政府委託該名畫家在市政廳的大廳牆壁上作畫。

同義字
▶ □entrust　v.　信託；委託；託管　　　□depute　v.　把⋯交託給
▶ □consign　v.　把⋯交付給　　　　　　□authorize　v.　授權給

commitment [kə'mɪtmənt] 　名 承諾；保證；承擔的義務　★★★★☆

If you want to join the basketball team, you must make a commitment to come to every practice and game during the season.
如果你想加入棒球隊，必須保證球季的每場練習和比賽都能到場才行。

同義字
▶ □promise　n.　承諾；諾言　　　　　□undertaking　n.　保證；許諾
▶ □pledge　n.　保證；誓言　　　　　　□guarantee　n.　保證；擔保

commodity [kə'mɑdətɪ] 　名 1. 商品；日用品　2. 有用的東西；有價值之物　★★★☆☆

During difficult times, gold is a commodity that is extensively traded.
經濟蕭條期間，黃金是被人廣泛交易的一項商品。

同義字
▶ □product　n.　產品；產物；產量　　　□ware　n.　商品；貨物
▶ □merchandise　n.　商品；貨物　　　　□goods　n.　商品；貨物
▶ □article　n.　一件；商品

commotion [kə'moʃən] 　名 騷動；喧鬧　★★★★☆

What's all the commotion about? I heard the noise from down the street.
這陣騷動是怎麼回事？我聽到街尾那邊傳來喧鬧聲。

同義字
▶ □bustle   n. 忙亂；喧囂   □hubbub   n.   吵鬧聲；騷動
▶ □noise   n. 聲響；喧鬧聲   □to-do   嚷鬧；騷亂；忙亂

反義字
▶ □quietness n. 安靜；肅靜   □calmness   n.   平靜；安寧
▶ □peace   n. 和平；和睦；安詳   □tranquility n.   平靜；安靜

commute [kə'mjut]   🔧1.通勤；2.減輕；交換   ★★★★☆

Wendall lives in the suburbs, so he must commute one hour to work downtown.
萬達爾住在郊區，必須通勤一小時才能進城工作。

comparable ['kɑmpərəbl]   📝可比較的；比得上的   ★★★★★

Although this cough medicine is much cheaper than the rest, its effectiveness is comparable to the most expensive brands.
雖然這種咳嗽藥比其他藥便宜很多，其藥效卻比得上最昂貴的商標製藥。

同義字
▶ □condescending a. 對應的   □analogous   a.   類似的
▶ □corresponding a. 相當的   □proportionate a.   相稱的
▶ □matching   a. 相配的；相稱的

反義字
▶ □incomparable a. 不能比較的   □peerless   a.   無與倫比的
▶ □unrivaled   a. 無可比擬的

compensate ['kɑmpən,set]   🔧補償；賠償；抵銷   ★★★☆☆

He was compensated one million dollars for the loss of his legs in the accident.
他因為意外事故失去雙腿而獲賠一百萬。

同義字
▶ □recompense v. 賠償；補償   □redeem   v.   補救；彌補
▶ □indemnify   v. 賠償；補償   □atone   v.   補償；彌補；贖回

competent ['kɑmpətənt]   📝有能力的；能幹的；能勝任的；稱職的   ★★★★☆

Irena is a very competent employee who knows her job inside out. I think she deserves a promotion.
艾莉娜是名非常能幹的員工，工作裡裡外外各項細節都很清楚。我覺得她獲得升遷是實至名歸。

同義字
▶ □able   a. 有能力的；能幹的   □adequate   a.   勝任的
▶ □capable   a. 有才華的   □qualified   a.   具備必要條件的

反義字
▶ □incompetent a. 無能力的   □unable   a.   無能力的
▶ □inadequate   a. 不充分的   □incapable a.   不能勝任的

▶ □unqualified　a.　不夠資格的

competitive　[kəm'pɛtətɪv]　形 競爭的；競爭性的；好競爭的　★★★★★

We have a very competitive hockey team this year. I think we have a chance to win the championship.
我們今年的曲棍球隊競爭心很強，我想應該有機會贏得總冠軍。

同義字
▶ □rival　a.　競爭的　　　□vying　a.　競爭的；競賽的
▶ □emulous　a.　好勝的

反義字
▶ □allied　a.　結盟的；聯姻的　　□unitable　a.　可聯合的
▶ □joint　a.　聯合的；共同的

complacent　[kəm'plesṇt]　形 滿足的；自滿的　★★★★★

Bill has become complacent after years of success in business.
比爾因多年的事業成功而變得自滿。

同義字
▶ □contented　a.　滿足的；知足的　□self-satisfied　a.　自滿的
▶ □fulfilled　a.　滿足的

反義字
▶ □dissatisfied　a.　不滿的　　　□discontented　a.　不滿的
▶ □unfulfilled　a.　未實現的

complement　['kɑmpləmənt]　動 補充；補足；與…相配　★★★☆☆

His experience and strength really complement the speed and energy we already have on our hockey team.
他在曲棍球方面的經驗和長處，大大補足了球隊原有的速度與活力。

同義字
▶ □supply　v.　供給；供應；補充　□supplement　v.　增補；補充
▶ □recruit　v.　補充　　　□match up　相配

反義字
▶ □exhaust　v.　用完；耗盡　　　□drain　v.　耗盡
▶ □spend　v.　耗盡；用盡

complex　['kɑmplɛks]　形 複雜的；難懂的　★★★★☆

This is a complex problem that will take many people months to solve.
這是很多人都要花好幾個月時間才能解決的複雜問題。

同義字
▶ □complicated　a.　複雜的；難懂的　　□elaborate　a.　複雜的
▶ □perplexed　a.　複雜的

反義字
▶ □easy　a.　容易的；不費力的　　□simple　a.　簡單的；簡易的
▶ □uncomplicated　a.　不複雜的

compliant [kəmˈplaɪənt]　形 順從的；應允的　★★★★★

He was very compliant when he was arrested, and answered all of the police officers questions cooperatively.
他乖乖束手就擒，並且很合作地回答了警方所提出的所有問題。

同義字
▶ □yielding　a.　聽從的；柔順的　　□obedient　a.　服從的；順從的
▶ □passive　a.　順從的；順服的

反義字
▶ □incompliant　a.　不順從的　　□disobedient　a.　不服從的
▶ □forward　a.　難駕馭的；剛愎的

complicated [ˈkɑmpləˌketɪd]　形 複雜的；難懂的　★★★★☆

Life was so simple when I was young. Now, with a job, a wife, and a mortgage, life is quite complicated.
年輕時生活很單純，不像現在有工作有老婆又有貸款，生活變得複雜多了。

同義字
▶ □complex　a.　複雜的；難懂的
▶ □perplexed　a.　糾纏不清的；複雜的

反義字
▶ □easy　a.　容易的；不費力的　　□simple　a.　簡單的；簡易的
▶ □uncomplicated　a.　不複雜的

complicity [kəmˈplɪsətɪ]　名 共謀；串通關係　★★★★★

He did not deny his complicity with the burglars, so he was charged as an accomplice to the robbery.
他不否認和竊賊串通，便被人指控為搶案共犯。

同義字
▶ □collusion　n.　共謀；勾結　　□conspiracy　n.　陰謀；謀叛
▶ □complot　n.　共謀

compliment [ˈkɑmpləmənt]　動 讚美；恭維；祝賀　★★★★☆

Vera blushed when Tom complimented her on her eyes.
湯姆讚美薇拉眼睛好看時，薇拉臉紅了。

同義字
▶ □praise　v.　讚美；表揚；歌頌　　□extol　v.　讚美；頌揚
▶ □admire　v.　稱讚；誇獎

反義字
▶ □blame　v.　責備；歸咎　　□criticize　v.　批評；苛求；非難
▶ □censure　v.　責備；譴責

component [kəmˈponənt]　名（機器、設備等的）構成要素；零件；成分　★★★★☆

The machinery broke down because one of its many components was broken.
因為眾多零件當中壞了一個，所以整台機器就故障了。

同義字

▶ □part　n.　部件；零件　□constituent　n.　成分
▶ □element　n.　要素；成分　　□ingredient　n.　（構成）要素

composure [kəmˈpoʒɚ] 名平靜；鎮靜；沈著 ★★★★☆

I can't believe you were able to keep your composure during that crisis! I was so angry.
真不敢相信遇到那種危機你還能保持鎮靜！我簡直氣炸了。

同義字
▶ □composedness　n.　鎮靜；沈著　□calmness　n.　冷靜；沈著
▶ □poise　n.　鎮定；鎮靜；自信　□sedateness　n.　安詳；鎮靜
▶ □imperturbability　n.　沈著；冷靜

反義字
▶ □haste　n.　慌忙；性急　□hurry　n.　急忙；倉促；忙亂
▶ □rush　n.　匆忙；緊急　□fluster　n.　慌亂；激動

comprehension [ˌkɑmprɪˈhɛnʃən] 名理解；理解力 ★★★☆☆

Roberto only recently started studying English, so his comprehension of spoken English is quite low.
羅伯托最近才開始讀英文，所以對英文口語的理解力還很低。

同義字
▶ □understanding　n.　了解；理解　□apprehension　n.　理解；領悟
▶ □realization　n.　領悟；認識　□grasp　n.　理解；領會

反義字
▶ □misunderstanding　n.　誤解　□misconstruction　n.　誤解
▶ □misapprehension　n.　誤解　□misconception　n.　誤解

comprehensive [ˌkɑmprɪˈhɛnsɪv] 形廣泛的；綜合的 ★★★★☆

Our insurance company offers a comprehensive package that will cover all of your insurance needs.
我們公司推出了一種含蓋一切個人保險需求的綜合型套裝式保單。

同義字
▶ □all-inclusive　a.　包括一切的　　□all-round　a.　綜合性的
▶ □extensive　a.　廣大的；大規模的　□ broad　a.　廣泛的；各式各樣的
▶ □sweeping　a.　全面的；徹底的

反義字
▶ □incomprehensive　a.　範圍狹小的　□narrow　a.　狹窄的
▶ □limited　a.　有限的　　□confining　a.　受限的；狹窄的

compress [kəmˈprɛs] 動壓；壓緊；壓縮 ★★★★☆

The sleeping bag is filled with down, so it compresses into this little carrying case.
這個睡袋裡頭塞滿了絨毛，所以可以可以壓進小提箱裡。

同義字
▶ □squeeze　v.　榨；擠；壓；擰　□press　v.　按；壓；擠
▶ □constrict　v.　壓縮；束緊　□impact　v.　壓緊；擠滿

反義字
- ▶ □loosen　v.　鬆開；解開　　　□unbind　v.　鬆開；解開
- ▶ □untie　v.　鬆開；解開

---

comprise　[kəmˈpraɪz]　**動**包含；包括；由…組成　★★★★★

A paragraph is comprised of three parts: the opening, the body, and the conclusion.
一段落是由開頭、本文和結論三部分所組成。

同義字
- ▶ □include　v.　包括；包含　　　□contain　v.　包含；容納
- ▶ □embrace　v.　包括；包含　　　□consist　v.　組成；構成

反義字
- ▶ □exclude　v.　把…排除在外　　　□except　v.　把…除外；不計

---

compulsory　[kəmˈpʌlsərɪ]　**形**1. 必須做的；義務的 2. 強制的；強迫的
★★★★☆

School is compulsory up to age 16. After that, you can do what you want with your life.
十六歲前要接受義務教育，之後便可安排自己的人生。

同義字
- ▶ □obligated　a.　責無旁貸的　　　□required　a.　必須的
- ▶ □forced　a.　強迫的　　　□constrained　a.　被迫的；
- ▶ □impellent　a.　驅使的；強迫的

反義字
- ▶ □volunteer　a.　自願的　□willing　a.　樂意的
- ▶ □volitient　a.　願意的

---

compute　[kəmˈpjut]　**動**計算；估算；推斷　★★★★★

I can't compute the square root of 13 in my head. Please hand me the calculator.
我無法在腦中計算 13 的平方根，請把計算機拿給我。

同義字
- ▶ □calculate　v.　計算；估計　　　□count　v.　計算；數
- ▶ □figure　v.　計算　　　□reckon　v.　計算；數

---

concede　[kənˈsid]　**動**（勉強）承認；承認失敗　★★★☆☆

They fought a hard battle, but had to concede defeat when most of their men were captured.
他們艱苦作戰，但是當大部分人都被俘虜時，只好承認失敗。

同義字
- ▶ □admit　v.　承認　　　□confess　v.　承認；坦白
- ▶ □acknowledge　v.　承認　　　□own　v.　承認

反義字
- ▶ □deny　v.　否定；否認　　　□disclaim　v.　否認；放棄
- ▶ □repudiate　v.　否認；駁斥　　　□negate　v.　否定；否認

conceited [kənˈsitɪd]　　　🈺自負的；驕傲自滿的；自誇的　★★★★☆

Valerie is very conceited, and won't associate with us because we're not rich or glamorous.
瓦萊麗很自負，因為我們沒什麼錢又長得不迷人便不和我們交往。

同義字
- ▶ □arrogant　a.　傲慢的；自負的　　□cavalier　a.　傲慢的
- ▶ □insolent　a.　傲慢的；無禮的　　□haughty　a.　高傲的；自大的
- ▶ □pompous　a.　愛炫耀的

反義字
- ▶ □modest　a.　謙虛的；審慎的　　□humble　a.　謙遜的；謙恭的
- ▶ □unassuming　a.　不出風頭的　　□unpretentious　a.　不矯飾的

conceive [kənˈsiv]　　　🈺構想出；想像；設想　★★★★☆

While walking to the bus, I conceived of a new business idea.
我邊走向公車邊想出一個新的生意點子。

同義字
- ▶ □think　v.　想；思索；理解　　□envisage　v.　想像；設想
- ▶ □devise　v.　策劃；想出；設計　　□excogitate　v.　想出

conclusive [kənˈklusɪv]　　　🈺決定性的；確實的；最終的　★★★☆☆

After years of research, scientists have finally found conclusive evidence linking high fat foods to heart disease.
經過多年研究，科學家終於發現決定性的證據，可以證明高脂肪食物和心臟病有關。

同義字
- ▶ □decisive　a.　決定性的；決定的　　□definitive　a.　決定性的
- ▶ □final　a.　最後的；決定性的　　□ultimate　a.　最後的；最終的

反義字
- ▶ □inconclusive　a.　非決定性的　　□indefinite　a.　不確定的
- ▶ □questionable　a.　可疑的　　□uncertain　a.　不明確的

concur [kənˈkɝ]　　　🈺同意；一致；贊成　★★★☆☆

I concur with the committee's decision, but there are many who feel otherwise.
雖然我贊成委員會員的決定，但仍有很多人持反對意見。

同義字
- ▶ □agree　v.　同意；意見一致　　□consent　v.　同意；贊成；答應
- ▶ □assent　v.　同意；贊成　　□see eye to eye　看法一致

反義字
- ▶ □disagree　v.　意見不合；有分歧　　□differ　v.　意見不同
- ▶ □dispute　v.　爭論；爭執　　□argue　v.　爭論；辯論；爭吵

concussion [kənˈkʌʃən]　　　🈺腦震盪　★★★★★

He suffered a concussion from the car accident, when he hit his head on the steering wheel.

車禍發生時，他的頭因為撞到方向盤而導致腦震盪。

condensation [ˌkɑndɛnˈseʃən] 名 凝聚；凝結；凝結物；冷凝 ★★★★☆

The bartender took out the can of beer from the refrigerator, wiped off the condensation, and served it to the customer.

酒保從冰箱裡拿出啤酒罐，把凝結的冰去掉，然後拿給客人。

同義字
▶ □congealment n. 凍結；凝結　□coagulation n. 凝結；凝結物
▶ □freeze n. 結冰；凝固

condense [kənˈdɛns] 動 1. 縮短；減縮（文章等）2. 壓縮；濃縮 ★★☆☆☆

Simms, your ten page report is much too long. Please condense it into three or four pages.

席姆斯，你的報告寫十頁太長了，請把它縮成三到四頁。

同義字
▶ □shorten v. 縮短；減少　□curtail v. 縮減；削減；省略
▶ □abbreviate v. 縮短；使簡短　□compress v. 壓；壓緊；壓縮
反義字
▶ □lengthen v. 使加長；使延長　□extend v. 延長；延伸；擴展
▶ □expand v. 擴大；擴充；發展

condescending [ˌkɑndɪˈsɛndɪŋ] 形 高傲的 ★★★★☆

Jamie thinks he's better than everyone and talks in a condescending way to me.

傑米覺得自己比任何人都要優秀，連和我講話的方式都顯得很高傲。

同義字
▶ □supercilious a. 高傲的　□toffee-nosed a. 勢利的
▶ □contemptuous a. 表示輕蔑的　□haughty a. 高傲的；傲慢的
▶ □disdainful a. 輕蔑的；驕傲的
反義字
▶ □modest a. 謙虛的；審慎的　□humble a. 謙遜的；謙恭的
▶ □self-effacing a. 謙遜的　□unassuming a. 謙虛的

condolence [kənˈdoləns] 名（常複數）弔辭；弔唁；慰問 ★★★☆☆

I'm very sorry to hear that your aunt passed away. Please send my condolences to your uncle.

得知你伯母去世，深感遺憾。請代我慰問你伯父。

同義字
▶ □comfort n. 安慰；慰問　□consolation n. 安慰；慰藉
▶ □sympathy n. 慰問；弔唁　□commiseration n. 弔慰；同情

conducive [kənˈdjusɪv] 形 有助的；有益的；促成的 ★★★★☆

This working conditions in this dimly lit factory are not conducive to productivity.

這間工廠光線昏暗，這種工作環境對提高生產力沒有幫助。

同義字
▶ ☐good a. 有益的；有效的　　☐profitable a. 有利的
▶ ☐favorable a. 有利的；順利的　☐beneficial a. 有幫助的

反義字
▶ ☐harmful a. 有害的　　　☐unfavorable a. 不利的
▶ ☐unfriendly a. 不相宜的　☐detrimental a. 有害的

conduit [ˈkɑndʊɪt] 　 名導水管；導管 ★★★☆☆

This pipe serves as a conduit to bring water to each of the apartment units.
這條水管是用來將水送到公寓各戶的導管。

同義字
▶ ☐duct n. 輸送管；導管

反義字
▶ ☐drain n. 排水管

confectionery [kənˈfɛkʃənˌɛrɪ] 　 名糕點糖果；糖果糕點店 ★★★★☆

I'm sorry, we don't sell candy. But there's a confectionery stand over there.
對不起，我們不賣糖果。不過那邊有個糕點糖果攤。

同義字
▶ ☐candy n. 糖果　　　☐pastry n. 酥皮點心 (如餡餅)
▶ ☐sweet shop 糖果店

confer [kənˈfɝ] 　 動授予；給予；賦予 ★★★★★

The mayor conferred a medal to the brave police officers who put away the mafia.
市長將勳章授予讓黑手黨鋃鐺入獄的英勇警察。

同義字
▶ ☐grant v. 給予；授予　☐award v. 授予；給予

confidant [ˌkɑnfɪˈdænt] 　 名知己；密友 ★★★☆☆

I tell Glen all of my secrets because he's my best friend and confidant.
因為葛蘭是我最要好的朋友和知己，我就把自己所有秘密都告訴了他。

同義字
▶ ☐intimate n. 至交；密友　　☐bosom friend 知心朋友

反義字
▶ ☐confidante n. 知己女友

confidence [ˈkɑnfədəns] 　 名信心；自信；信賴；信任 ★★★★☆

I have every confidence in your ability to do the job. You have both the skills and experience.
我對你做好這分工作的能力很有信心，因為不管是技術或經驗方面你都沒有問題。

同義字
▶ ☐faith n. 信念；完全信賴　　☐reliance n. 信賴；信心
▶ ☐assurance n. 把握；信心

〔反義字〕
▶ □diffidence　n.　缺乏自信；懦怯　　□distrust　n.　不信任；懷疑

confine　[kənˈfaɪn]　　動 禁閉；幽禁　　★★★★☆

As punishment for his crimes, he was placed under house arrest. He will be confined in his home two more years.
軟禁是他所犯罪行的懲罰，他要被禁閉在家中達兩年以上。

〔同義字〕
▶ □imprison　v.　關押；禁錮　　□immure　v.　監禁；禁閉
▶ □coop up　將…禁錮在狹小空間

〔反義字〕
▶ □free　v.　使自由；解放　　□liberate　v.　釋放；解放
▶ □release　v.　釋放；解放　　□affranchise　v.　恢復自由；釋放

confiscate　[ˈkɑnfɪsˌket]　　動 沒收；將…充公；徵收　　★★★☆☆

My math teacher confiscated my Gameboy because I was playing with it during class.
因為我在上課時玩掌上型電玩遊戲機，數學老師就把它給沒收了。

〔同義字〕
▶ □seize　v.　沒收；扣押；查封　　□expropriate　v.　沒收；徵用
▶ □sequestrate　v.　扣押；沒收　　□dispossess　v.　沒收；奪取

confluence　[ˈkɑnfluəns]　　名 （河流的）匯合；匯流點　　★★★★★

This is the confluence of the two rivers. From here, they flow as one all the way to the sea.
兩條河在這裡匯合成一條後，便一路流向大海。

〔同義字〕
▶ □convergence　n.　會合；聚合　　□meeting　n.　匯合點；交叉點
▶ □concourse　n.　匯合；集合；合流

〔反義字〕
▶ □divergence　n.　分歧；背離；分離　　□discrepance　n.　不一致；分歧

conform　[kənˈfɔrm]　　動 符合；相一致　　★★★★☆

Your product does not conform to your advertising claims. I want my money back!
你這項產品和廣告所宣稱的不符。我要退錢！

〔同義字〕
▶ □agree　v.　相符；一致

〔反義字〕
▶ □disagree　v.　不一致；不符　　□disaccord　v.　不一致；相爭
▶ □discord　v.　不一致；不協調

confront　[kənˈfrʌnt]　　動 1. 迎面遇到；遭遇　2. 使面對；使對質　　★★★☆☆

I've suspected my roommate of stealing from me for a long time, and finally confronted him last night.

我懷疑室友偷我東西已經很久了，昨晚終於被我當場逮到。

同義字
▶ □encounter　v.　遭遇（敵人）　　□face　v.　面向；正對；使面對
▶ □run up against　碰見

congregate [ˈkɑŋɡrɪˌget]　**勔**聚集；集合　　★★★★☆

Fans congregated in front of the concert hall hours before the start of the performance.
離節目開演還有好幾個小時，樂迷便已聚集在音樂廳前面。

同義字
▶ □gather　v.　召集；使聚集；收集　□assemble　v.　集合；召集
▶ □aggregate　v.　聚集

反義字
▶ □dismiss　v.　解散；遣散　　　□disband　v.　解散；遣散
▶ □disperse　v.　解散；疏散

conjecture [kənˈdʒɛktʃɚ]　**图**推測；猜測；推測的結果　　★★★☆☆

Do you know that for sure, or is it just conjecture?
你是真的知道，還是說只是推測？

同義字
▶ □guess　n.　猜測；推測　　　□inference　n.　推論；推斷
▶ □presumption　n.　推測；假定　□ surmise　n.　推測；猜測；臆測

反義字
▶ □proof　n.　證明；論證　　　□verification　n.　確認；證明
▶ □authentication　n.　確證；證明

conjoin [kənˈdʒɔɪn]　**勔**結合；聯合　　★★★★☆

Rebecca and Theresa are conjoined twins who have been joined at the hip since birth.
麗蓓嘉和特麗莎是連體雙胞胎，她們出生時臀部就連在一起。

同義字
▶ □join　v.　連結；使結合　　　□combine　v.　使結合；使聯合
▶ □connect　v.　連接；連結

反義字
▶ □disjoin　v.　分開　　　　　□divide　v.　使分開；使隔開
▶ □separate　v.　分隔；使分離

connive [kəˈnaɪv]　**勔**1. 共謀　2. 假裝不見；默許；縱容　　★★★★☆

The warden suspected the guards of conniving with the prisoners in their escape.
典獄長懷疑警衛和犯人共謀，幫助他們逃走。

同義字
▶ □collude　v.　共謀；串通　　　□complot　v.　共謀
▶ □conspire　v.　同謀；密謀

connoisseur [ˌkanəˈsɝ] 名（尤指藝術品的）鑑賞家；行家 ★★★☆☆

Francois is a connoisseur of fine wines, and is often asked to taste new wines.
法蘭西斯是美酒行家，經常受邀品嘗新酒。

同義字
▶ □expert　n.　專家；熟練者　　□specialist　n.　專家
▶ □professional　n.　專家；內行　　□judge　n.　鑑定人；鑑賞家

反義字
▶ □amateur　n.　外行；業餘從事者　□laity　n.　外行人
▶ □stranger　n.　外行；生手

conquer [ˈkaŋkɚ] 動征服；克服；戰勝；成功地登上 ★★★★☆

At the peak of his empire, Genghis Khan had conquered most of Asia.
成吉思汗帝國最強盛時期，一度征服大部分亞洲地區。

同義字
▶ □overwhelm　v.　戰勝；征服　　□subdue　v.　制服；征服；鎮壓
▶ □subjugate　v.　征服；制服　　□vanquish　v.　征服；擊敗

反義字
▶ □submit　v.　屈從；忍受；甘受　　□surrender　v.　投降；屈服

conscience [ˈkanʃəns] 名良心；道義心；善惡觀念 ★★★★☆

I know everyone is downloading free music, but my conscience tells me it's wrong so I refuse to do it.
我知道大家都在下載免費音樂，但是我的良心告訴我這樣是錯的，所以我拒絕同流合污。

同義字
▶ □principle　n.　道義；節操　　□morality　n.　道德觀
▶ □ethics　n.　倫理觀；道德標準

conscious [ˈkanʃəs] 形神志清醒的；有知覺的 ★★★★★

This patient isn't conscious, but the doctor hopes that with the proper medication he will be feeling and thinking soon.
這名病患失去知覺，醫生希望透過適當的藥物治療，他能很快恢復知覺和思考能力。

同義字
▶ □sensible　a.　有知覺的

反義字
▶ □unconscious　a.　不省人事的　　□senseless　a.　失去知覺的
▶ □insensible　a.　昏迷的

conscript [ˈkanskrɪpt] 動徵召 ★★★★☆

If there is a shortage of soldiers, the government will conscript people into the military.
如果兵源短，政府就會徵兵。

同義字
▶ □enlist　v.　徵募；徵（兵）　　□draft　v.　徵兵；徵集

▶ □conscribe v. 徵召…入伍 □impress v. 強迫…服役
▶ □recruit v. 徵募；吸收

consecutive [kənˋsɛkjʊtɪv] 形 連續不斷的 ★★★☆☆

Lance Armstrong has won 7 consecutive Tour de France titles, and looks like he'll continue his winning streak this year.
蘭斯‧阿姆斯壯連續七年獲得環法錦鏢賽冠軍，看來今年冠軍又是他的囊中物了。

同義字
▶ □continuous a. 連續的；不斷的 □successive a. 連續的
▶ □serial a. 連續的；一連串的

反義字
▶ □discontinuous a. 間斷的 □interrupted a. 中斷的
▶ □alternate a. 間隔的

consensus [kənˋsɛnsəs] 名 一致 ★★★☆☆

The Board reached a consensus, and has given its full support to our plans to expand into China.
董事會取得共識，將全力支持我們擴展中國市場的計劃。

同義字
▶ □agreement n. 同意；一致 □consistency n. 一貫；一致
▶ □accordance n. 和諧；符合 □coincidence n. 符合；一致

反義字
▶ □disagreement n. 不一致 □disaccord n. 不一致；不和
▶ □discord n. 爭吵；不一致

conservative [kənˋsɝvətɪv] 形 保守的；守舊的；傳統的；老式的 ★★★☆☆

He's so conservative he still thinks women should stay at home to cook and clean.
他真是老古板，還認為女人應該待在家裡煮飯做家事。

同義字
▶ □old-fashioned a. 守舊的 □ antiquated a. 陳舊的；過時的
▶ □outdated a. 舊式的；過時的 □obsolete a. 過時的；老式的
▶ □hidebound a. 保守的

反義字
▶ □radical a. 極端的；激進的 □progressive a. 進步的
▶ □new-fashioned a. 時髦的

conservatory [kənˋsɝvəˌtorɪ] 名 音樂學校 ★★★★☆

The students of this music conservatory will play in a concert this Friday.
這所音樂學校的學生本週五將在音樂會上演出。

consistency [kənˋsɪstənsɪ] 名 一貫；一致；符合；協調 ★★★☆☆

Robert's work has really been up and down. There's been no consistency in his performance at all.

羅伯特的工作表現好壞起伏很大，完全看不到一致。

同義字
- □agreement　n.　同意；一致　　□accordance　n.　一致；和諧
- □coincidence　n.　符合；一致　　□consensus　n.　一致

反義字
- □disagreement　n.　不一致　　□disaccord　n.　不一致；不和
- □discord　n.　不和；爭吵

console [kən'sol]　動安慰；撫慰；慰問　★★★☆☆

May's cat died, so we should console her. Let's take her out to a movie or something.

梅的貓死了，我們應該安慰她一下，不如帶她去看場電影什麼的。

同義字
- □condole　v.　哀悼；同情；慰問　　□comfort　v.　安慰；慰問
- □sympathize　v.　同情；憐憫　　□commiserate　v.　弔慰；同情

consolidate [kən'salə,det]　動鞏固；加強；合併；聯合；統一　★★★★☆

The politician consolidated his power by uniting both parties under his leadership.

該名政治人物聯合兩個政黨統一領導，藉以鞏固自身權力。

同義字
- □strengthen　v.　加強；增強　　□solidify　v.　使堅固；使團結
- □cement　v.　鞏固；加強；凝成

反義字
- □weaken　v.　削弱；減弱　　□abate　v.　減少；減弱；減輕
- □wear down　削弱

conspicuous [kən'spɪkjʊəs]　形明顯的；易看見的；顯著的　★★★★★

Penny tried to cover up the bruise with makeup, but it was still very conspicuous so everyone asked her how she got it.

雖然佩妮想要用化妝把傷痕蓋住，但還是很明顯，大家都在問是怎麼弄傷的。

同義字
- □noticeable　a.　顯而易見的　　□distinct　a.　明顯的
- □clear　a.　顯然的；明顯的　　□obvious　a.　明顯的；顯著的
- □prominent　a.　突出的

反義字
- □unnoticeable　a.　未被注意的　　□inconspicuous　a.　不顯著的
- □unapparent　a.　不明顯的　　□invisible　a.　微小得覺察不出的

conspire [kən'spaɪr]　動同謀；密謀　abel　★★★★☆

The bank teller conspired with the burglars to rob the bank by telling them the password to the safe.

銀行出納員告訴竊賊保險密碼，串通要一起搶銀行。

同義字
- □collude　v.　共謀；串通　　□complot　v.　共謀
- □connive　v.　共謀

constellation [ˌkɑnstəˈlɛʃən]　名星座；星座區域　★★★☆☆

Tonight, if you look at the northern part of the sky, you will see the constellation of Orion.
今晚往天空北邊看，你會看到獵戶星座。

同義字
▶ □star sign　星座

constituency [kənˈstɪtʃʊənsɪ]　名選區；選區的全體選民　★★★☆☆

The political candidate campaigned by going door to door in his constituency asking for support.
為了勝選，該政黨候選人在選區內挨家挨戶拜訪請選民支持。

constrict [kənˈstrɪkt]　動壓縮；束緊　★★★★☆

This snake isn't poisonous. It wraps itself around its prey and constricts it to death.
這條蛇沒有毒，它會先纏住獵物再把獵物壓迫致死。

同義字
▶ □compress　v.　壓緊；壓縮　　□tighten　v.　使變緊；使繃緊
▶ □press　v.　壓；重壓

反義字
▶ □loosen　v.　鬆開；解開　　□unbind　v.　鬆開；解開
▶ □untie　v.　鬆開；解開

consulate [ˈkɑnslɪt]　名領事館　★★★☆☆

If you want to visit the United States, you must get a visa from the American consulate.
如果你想去美國，得去美國領事館申請簽證才行。

同義字
▶ □embassy　n.　大使館　　□chancellery　n.　大使館

consumption [kənˈsʌmpʃən]　名消耗；消費　★★★☆☆

Mankind's consumption of oil is causing changes in the Earth's climate.
人類對於石油的消耗正導致地球氣候不斷改變當中。

同義字
▶ □depletion　n.　消耗；用盡　　□waste　n.　消耗；損耗；毀壞
▶ □exhaustion　n.　耗盡；枯竭

反義字
▶ □production　n.　生產　　□output　n.　出產；生產

contagious [kənˈtedʒəs]　形接觸傳染性的　★★★★☆

Since SARS is a contagious disease, people wore masks to avoid catching it or spreading it to others.
由於 SARS 是傳染性疾病，大家都戴口罩以免自己被人傳染或傳染給別人。

同義字

▶ □infectious　a.　傳染的；傳染性的　□epidemic　a.　傳染的；流行的
▶ □catching　a.　傳染性的　□communicable　a.　會傳染的

contaminate [kən'tæmə,net]　📖污染；毒害；弄髒　★★★★★

The oil spill contaminated the lake and killed many animals.
石油溢出污染了這座湖，造成很多動物死亡。

同義字

▶ □pollute　v.　污染；弄髒　　　□defile　v.　污染；弄髒；損污
▶ □infect　v.　污染

contemplate ['kɑntɛm,plet]　📖思量；沈思；深思熟慮　★★★☆☆

Justine sat beside the river and contemplated the meaning of life.
賈斯汀坐在河邊，沈思著生命的意義。

同義字

▶ □consider　v.　考慮；細想　　　□meditate　v.　沈思；深思熟慮
▶ □ponder　v.　沈思；仔細考慮　　□deliberate　v.　仔細考慮
▶ □speculate　v.　思索；沈思

contemptible [kən'tɛmptəbḷ]　📖無恥的；可鄙的；卑劣的；不屑一顧的　★★★☆☆

He is a contemptible criminal who preyed on the sick and elderly.
他是個連病人和老人都搶的無恥罪犯。

同義字

▶ □mean　a.　卑鄙的；卑劣的　　　□base　a.　卑鄙的；惡劣的
▶ □despicable　a.　可鄙的　　　　□vile　a.　卑鄙的；可恥的
▶ □pitiful　a.　可鄙的

反義字

▶ □noble　a.　高貴的；高尚的　　　□respectable　a.　可敬的

contender [kən'tɛndɚ]　📖爭奪者；競爭者　★★★★☆

He has been the heavyweight boxing champion for over twenty months, and has defeated every contender who has challenged him.
他連續二十幾個月蟬聯重量級拳擊手冠軍，任何競爭對手向他挑戰都被他打敗了。

同義字

▶ □ opponent　n.　對手；敵手　　　□antagonist　n.　敵手；對手
▶ □competitor　n.　競爭者；對手　　□match　n.　對手；敵手

continuation [kən,tɪnjʊ'eʃən]　📖繼續；延續　★★★☆☆

The TV network wanted to cancel the show, but fans called in and begged for its continuation.
電視台想要停播該節目，但熱情的觀眾打電話進去要求繼續播出。

同義字

▶ □extension　n.　延長；延期　　　□prolongation　n.　延長；延期
▶ □proceeding　n.　繼續進行　　　□pursuit　n.　繼續進行

反義字
▶ □discontinuity　n.　中斷　　　　□suspension　n.　暫停；中止
▶ □halt　n.　暫停；停止；終止　　□standstill　n.　停止；停滯不前

contort [kənˋtɔrt]　　圖 扭曲；曲解　　★★★☆☆

The circus performer contorted her body to fit inside a little box.
馬戲團演員扭曲身體，把自己擠進一個小箱子裡。

同義字
▶ □bend　v.　彎曲；折彎　□flex　v.　使（肌肉）收縮
▶ □curve　v.　使彎曲；使成曲線　　□twist　v.　扭轉；扭彎；旋轉

反義字
▶ □stretch　v.　伸直；拉直　　　　□string　v.　伸展；拉直

contraband [ˋkɑntrəˏbænd]　　图（總稱）走私貨；違禁品　★★★★☆

These pirated CDs are contraband. They must have been smuggled into the country.
這些盜版光碟是違禁品，一定是走私進來的。

同義字
▶ □smuggling　n.　走私；偷運

contradiction [ˏkɑntrəˋdɪkʃən]　　图矛盾；抵觸　　★★★★★

That assertion is a contradiction to what you said earlier. How do you explain this inconsistency?
那分聲明和你先前所說的互相抵觸。你要怎麼解釋這種前後矛盾？

同義字
▶ □conflict　n.　衝突；抵觸；矛盾　　□incompatibility　n.　矛盾
▶ □discrepancy　n.　不一致；不符　　□repugnance　n.　矛盾；抵觸

contravene [ˏkɑntrəˋvin]　　圖與…相抵觸；違反（法律等）　★★★☆☆

If you leave the country, you will contravene the court order and may get charged.
你出國的話就會因違反法院命令而遭到指控。

同義字
▶ □transgress　v.　違反；違背　　□violate　v.　違犯；違背；違反
▶ □infringe　v.　違犯；侵犯；違反　　□disobey　v.　不服從；違抗

反義字
▶ □legitimate　v.　使合法

contribute [kənˋtrɪbjut]　　圖1. 貢獻；出力2. 捐（款）；捐獻；捐助★★★☆☆

I don't work for the Red Cross for money or fame. I do it to contribute to a great cause.
我替紅十字會工作不是為了名利，而是基於一分偉大的理想，希望自己有所貢獻。

同義字
▶ □subscribe　v.　認捐；捐款　　　□donate　v.　捐獻；捐贈

contrive [kənˈtraɪv]　　動 1. 設法做到；以計謀達成　2. 發明；設計；策劃
★★★★☆

The kindergarten teachers contrived ways to amuse the children during recess.
幼稚園老師設法在下課時逗孩童開心。

同義字
▶ □scheme　v.　計劃；設計　　　□compass　v.　圖謀；計劃
▶ □devise　v.　設計；發明；策劃

control [kənˈtrol]　　名 控制；支配；調節；抑制
★★★☆☆

The President lost control of the country when citizens began rioting and the military refused to follow his orders.
當人民開始暴，軍隊也不接受指揮時，總統便失去了國家的控制權。

同義字
▶ □bridle　v.　約束；控制　　　□dominate　v.　支配；統治
▶ □rule　v.　統治；管轄；支配　　□govern　v.　控制（感情等）

contusion [kənˈtjuʒən]　　名 挫傷
★★★☆☆

She has a slight contusion on her cheek from being struck by the mugger.
她臉頰因為被強盜攻擊，有輕微挫傷。

同義字
▶ □bruise　n.　擦傷；碰傷；挫傷

convene [kənˈvin]　　動 集會；聚集；召集 （會議）
★★★☆☆

The annual meeting of the National Association of Graphic Designers will convene on July 1st, in Chicago.
平面造型設計師協會的年度會議，將於七月一號在芝加哥舉行。

同義字
▶ □assemble　v.　集合；召集　　□rally　v.　集合；召集
▶ □congregate　v.　聚集；集合　　□convoke　v.　召集
反義字
▶ □adjourn　v.　休會；中止活動　　□recess　v.　使（會議等）暫停

convenience [kənˈvinjəns]　　名 方便；合宜
★★★★☆

For your convenience, the hotel swimming pool will now be open 24 hours a day.
為方便房客，旅館游泳池現在開始 24 小時開放。

同義字
▶ □expediency　n.　適宜；方便　　□handiness　n.　便利
▶ □facility　n.　便利；方便
反義字
▶ □inconvenience　n.　不便；麻煩

converge [kənˈvɝdʒ]　　動 會合
★★★★★

The four streets converge at the town square.
四條街道在市中心廣場會合。

同義字
▶ □meet　v.　交會　　　□join　v.　與…會合；與…交接

反義字
▶ □diverge　v.　（道路等）分叉　　□fork　v.　分歧；分叉

convert [kən'vɝt]　轉變；變換　★★★☆☆

How do you convert 20 degrees Celsius into degrees Fahrenheit?
攝氏 20 度要怎麼變成華氏？

同義字
▶ □change　v.　改變；更改；變化　□transform　v.　改變；變換
▶ □alter　v.　改變；變樣

convoy [kən'vɔɪ]　受護送的船隊（或車隊等）；（互相護送的）同行船隊（或車隊等）　★★★★★

While traveling through the city, the Minister of Foreign Affairs was protected by a convoy of five police cars.
外交部長行經該城時，受到五輛警車組成的車隊加以保護。

同義字
▶ □escort　n.　護衛隊；護航隊

copious ['kopɪəs]　豐富的；大量的；多產的　★★★★☆

There were copious amounts of food and drink at the feast.
宴會上有豐盛的菜餚和美酒可以享用。

同義字
▶ □rich　a.　豐富的　　　□plentiful　a.　豐富的；充足的
▶ □abundant　a.　充足的；豐富的　□ample　a.　豐富的；充裕的
▶ □affluent　a.　豐富的；富饒的

反義字
▶ □poor　a.　貧乏的；缺少的　　□lean　a.　貧瘠的；貧乏的
▶ □barren　a.　沒有的；缺乏的　　□meager　a.　貧乏的；不足的

cornucopia [ˌkɔrnə'kopɪə]　裝滿花果及穀穗表豐饒的羊角狀物（豐饒角）　★★★☆☆

German schoolchildren are given a cornucopia filled with fruits and gifts to celebrate their first day of school.
德國學童第一天上學時，都會拿到一個裝滿水果和禮物的角形裝飾物作為慶祝。

coronation [ˌkɔrə'neʃən]　加冕典禮　★★★☆☆

The coronation of the new king is a ceremony not to be missed.
新任國王的加冕典禮可不能錯過。

同義字
▶ □crowning　n.　加冕（典禮）

corporate [ˈkɔrpərɪt] 形 團體的；公司的；法人的 ★★★★★

No longer happy as a civil servant, Mindy found a job as a corporate accountant in an insurance company.

敏蒂無法繼續當個快樂的公務員，便在一家保險公司找到公司會計的工作。

同義字
- ▶ □collective a. 集體所有（或經營）的

corpse [kɔrps] 名 屍體 ★★★★☆

Police officers examined the corpse that had floated to shore. They suspect the victim had been dead nearly a week.

警方檢查了漂到岸邊的屍體後，懷疑死者已經死了快一個禮拜。

同義字
- ▶ □carcass n. 屍體　　□body n. 屍體

correlate [ˈkɔrəˌlet] 動 關聯 ★★★☆☆

My assumptions correlate with the data that I've collected. You will find no discrepancies.

我的假設和我收集到的資料有關，兩者之間並無矛盾之處。

同義字
- ▶ □relate v. 使有聯繫　　□connect v. 聯繫；結合
- ▶ □link v. 連接；結合；聯繫

反義字
- ▶ □have nothing to do with 與…無關

corroborate [kəˈrɑbəˌret] 動 證實；確證 ★★★☆☆

The witness corroborated the defendant's alibi, and so he was found innocent.

目擊證人證實了被告的不在場證明，總算還他清白。

同義字
- ▶ □verify v. 證明；證實　　□confirm v. 證實；確定
- ▶ □prove v. 證明；證實　　□testify v. 證實；表明；證明
- ▶ □corroborate v. 證實；確證

反義字
- ▶ □guess v. 猜測；推測　　□infer v. 推斷；推論；猜想
- ▶ □presume v. 假定；假設　　□surmise v. 推測；猜測

corrode [kəˈrod] 動 侵蝕；損害 ★★★☆☆

The sea breeze has corroded my metal bicycle, and now it's just a useless pile of rust.

我的金屬製腳踏車被海風給侵蝕了，如今成了一堆沒用的鏽鐵。

同義字
- ▶ □erode v. 腐蝕；侵蝕；磨損　　□corrade v. 刻蝕；力侵蝕

corrupt [kəˈrʌpt] 形 腐敗的；貪污的；墮落的 ★★★★☆

Don't worry; the cops in this country are corrupt. If they stop you, just slip them a few dollars and you'll be on your way.

不用擔心，這個國家的警察都很腐敗；他們如果制止你，塞一點錢給他們就沒事了。

同義字
▶ ☐rotten　a.　腐敗的；卑劣的　　☐degenerate　a.　衰退的
▶ ☐depraved　a.　頹廢的；邪惡的

反義字
▶ ☐incorruptible　a.　不腐敗的　　☐clean-handed　a.　清廉的

cosmetic　[kɑzˈmɛtɪk]　🈂化妝品；裝飾品　★★★★★

If you're looking for lipstick or eyeliner, the cosmetic counter is on the second floor.

如果你在找口紅或眼筆，二樓有化妝品專櫃。

同義字
▶ ☐lotion　n.　化妝水　　☐cream　n.　化妝用乳霜

cosmic　[ˈkɑzmɪk]　🈂宇宙的　★★★☆☆

The space shuttle was launched to explore the universe, and answer many of our cosmic questions.

發射太空梭是為了探索宇宙，解答人類對宇宙的種種疑問。

同義字
▶ ☐universal　a.　宇宙的；全世界的

cosmopolitan　[ˌkɑzməˈpɑlətn̩]　🈂世界性的；國際性的　🈂世界各地都有的東西

★★★☆☆

These products are cosmopolitan. I've seen them in every country I've traveled to.

這些產品世界各地都有，每個我去過的國家我都看過。

同義字
▶ ☐international　a.　國際性的　　☐global　a.　全世界的
▶ ☐world-wide　a.　遍及全世界的

反義字
▶ ☐regional　a.　地區的；局部的　　☐localized　a.　地區的
▶ ☐territorial　a.　地區的；區域的

counteract　[ˌkɑʊntɚˈækt]　🈂對…起反作用；抵消；中和；消解　★★★★☆

The antidote should counteract the effects of the poison within two minutes.

解毒劑會在兩分鐘內把毒素中和掉。

同義字
▶ ☐neutralize　v.　中和　　☐counterbalance　v.　使平衡
▶ ☐kill　v.　中和；抵消

counterfeit　[ˈkɑʊntɚˌfɪt]　🈂偽造的；假冒的　★★★★★

The crooks made counterfeit money by photocopying real money.

這些騙子影印真鈔來製造偽鈔。

同義字
▶ □imitative　a.　模仿的；偽造的　　□fake　a.　假的；冒充的
▶ □artificial　a.　假的；人工的　　□factitious　a.　人工的；虛假的

反義字
▶ □genuine　a.　非偽造的 □authentic　a.　真正的

counterpart　['kaʊntɚ͵pɑrt]　圖對應的人（或物）；配對物；互為補充的人 ★★★☆☆

Their Prime Minister is the counterpart of our President.
他們的首相等於是我們的總統。

同義字
▶ □equivalent　n.　相等物；等價物　　□correspondent　n.　對應物

courage　['kɝɪdʒ]　圖膽量；勇氣；英勇 ★★★☆☆

In the Wizard of Oz, the Cowardly Lion was searching for courage, but discovered
that he was brave all along.
「綠野仙蹤」裡的膽小獅要尋找勇氣，結果卻發現自己其實一直都很勇敢。

同義字
▶ □bravery　n.　勇敢；勇氣　　□boldness　n.　勇敢；大膽
▶ □nerve　n.　勇敢；膽量　　□valor　n.　英勇；勇氣；勇猛
▶ □spunk　n.　精神；勇氣

反義字
▶ □timidity　n.　膽怯；羞怯　　□cowardice　n.　膽小；懦弱

course　[kors]　圖路線；方向 ★★★☆☆

The wind pushed the boat ten degrees off course, causing it to run into some
rocks.
風把船吹離航線十度，讓船撞到了一些岩石。

同義字
▶ □way　n.　路途；路線　　□route　n.　路；路線；路程
▶ □line　n.　交通線；航線；鐵路線

courtesy　['kɝtəsɪ]　圖禮貌；殷勤；好意；謙恭有禮的言辭（或舉動） ★★★★☆

The front desk staff of this hotel are known for their courtesy. They are always kind
and polite, no matter what your demands are.
這家旅館的接待人員以禮貌聞名，無論你有什麼要求，他們總是那麼親切有禮。

同義字
▶ □politeness　n.　有禮貌；客氣　　□civility　n.　禮貌；客氣；謙恭
▶ □ceremony　n.　虛禮；客套　　□manners　n.　禮貌；規矩
▶ □complaisance　n.　彬彬有禮；殷勤

反義字
▶ □rudeness　n.　無禮貌；粗野　　□impudence　n.　厚臉皮；無禮
▶ □insolence　n.　傲慢；無禮；厚顏 □impertinence　n.　傲慢；莽撞

covert [ˈkʌvɚt] 形 隱蔽的；隱藏的；暗地的 ★★★★★

The CIA led a covert operation to topple another country's government. Only people in the highest levels of the White House know about it.
中情局暗地展開推翻他國政府的行 ，只有最高層級的白宮官員知道這件事。

同義字
▶ □secret a. 隱蔽的；暗藏的   □hidden a. 隱藏的；隱秘的
▶ □covered a. 隱蔽著的
反義字
▶ □visible a. 可看見的；引人注目的   □ exposed a. 暴露的；無遮蔽的

cower [ˈkauɚ] 動 抖縮；畏縮；蜷縮 ★★★☆☆

The little boy cowered in the corner as the monster neared.
怪物接近時，那個小男孩蜷縮在角落裡。

同義字
▶ □crouch v. 蹲伏；彎腰；蜷伏   □cringe v. 畏縮；蜷縮
▶ □squat v. 蹲伏；蜷伏   □huddle v. 使蜷縮

crass [kræs] 形 粗魯的；愚鈍的 ★★★☆☆

He's always cursing and spitting in public. I've never met a crasser individual.
他老是當眾咒罵和吐痰。我從沒看過有人那麼粗魯。

同義字
▶ □rough a. 粗暴的；粗俗的   □rude a. 粗野的；無禮的
▶ □vulgar a. 下流的   □uncouth a. 粗野的
反義字
▶ □civilized a. 有教養的   □refined a. 文雅的
▶ □decent a. 合乎禮儀的

crave [krev] 動 渴望獲得；迫切需要 ★★★★☆

Every morning, I crave a cup a coffee. I can't do anything else before satisfying this desire.
我每天早上都很需要來杯咖啡，沒有滿足前什麼事都做不了。

同義字
▶ □covet v. 垂涎；貪圖   □desire v. 渴望；要求
▶ □lust v. 貪求；渴望   □long v. 渴望
▶ □pine v. 渴望

creak [krik] 動 發出咯吱咯吱聲；嘎嘎作響 ★★★★★

The floorboards in the old house creak whenever someone walks across the kitchen.
只要有人走過廚房，這間舊屋的地板就會嘎嘎作響。

creamy [ˈkrimɪ] 形 含乳脂的；多乳脂的 ★★★☆☆

There's not enough milk in my latte. I like my coffee very creamy.
我的拿鐵牛奶放得不夠，我喜歡喝乳脂很多的咖啡。

同義字
▶ □milky　　a.　產乳的；含乳的

credible [ˈkrɛdəb!]　 形 可信的；可靠的　　★★★★☆

This man isn't very credible. He's known as a liar and a thief.
這個人不太可靠，他可是有名的騙子和小偷。

同義字
▶ □reliable　a.　可信賴的　　　　□dependable　a.　可靠的
▶ □trustworthy　a　值得信賴的　　□trusty　a.　可信的

反義字
▶ □incredible　a.　不能相信的　　□unreliable　a.　不可信任的
▶ □untrustworthy　a.　不可信賴的　□untrusty　a.　不可靠的

crevasse [krəˈvæs]　 名 （地球表面的）裂縫；裂隙　　★★★★★

The ice climber descended down the deep crevasse.
冰攀者沿者深邃的裂縫往下走。

同義字
▶ □fissure　n.　裂縫；裂隙　　　　□crevice　n.　裂縫；裂隙
▶ □cleft　n.　裂縫；裂口

crevice [ˈkrɛvɪs]　 名 裂縫；裂隙；破口　　★★★★☆

How do you get the crumbs out from the crevice in the kitchen counter?
你是怎麼把碎屑從廚房流理台的裂縫中弄出來的？

同義字
▶ □crevasse　n.　（地球表面的）裂縫　　□fissure　n.　裂縫；裂隙
▶ □cleft　n.　裂縫；裂口

criteria [kraɪˈtɪrɪə]　 名 （判斷、批評的）標準；準則；尺度（criterion 的複數）
★★★☆☆

Students are admitted into this school based on certain criteria. You must fulfill them all in order to get accepted.
學生要進這間學校有一定標準，你得全部達成才能獲准入學。

同義字
▶ □standard　n.　標準；水準；規格　□yardstick　n.　衡量標準

critique [krɪˈtik]　 名 批評；評論　　★★★★☆

The movie received terrible critiques in the newspapers, but the fans still loved it.
這部電影雖然被各方報紙批評得很兇，但影迷依然很喜歡它。

同義字
▶ □review　n.　批評；評論　　　　□comment　n.　註釋；解釋
▶ □animadversion　n.　責難；批評

▶ □praise　n.　讚揚；稱讚　　　　□admiration　n.　欽佩
▶ □compliment　n.　恭維　　　　　□laud　n.　讚美

culinary [ˈkjulɪˌnɛrɪ] 形烹飪的；廚房的 ★★★★★

You're such a fabulous cook! Did you go to culinary school?

你這個廚子真不是蓋的！你有上過烹飪學校嗎？

cull [kʌl] 動挑出；選出；揀選 ★★★★☆

The farmer culled the sick chickens and slaughtered them.

農夫挑出病雞加以屠宰。

同義字
▶ □pick　v.　挑選；選擇　　　　　□choose　v.　選擇；挑選
▶ □select　v.　選擇；挑選

culprit [ˈkʌlprɪt] 名罪犯 ★★★☆☆

The police found the culprit counting the money he had stolen from the old lady.

警方發現該名罪犯正在數他從老婦人那裡偷來的錢。

同義字
▶ □criminal　n.　罪犯　　　□wrongdoer　n.　做壞事的人
▶ □felon　n.　罪犯　　　　　□lawbreaker　n.　犯法者
▶ □malefactor　n.　罪人；壞人

curator [kjʊˈretɚ] 名館長 ★★★★☆

Adam studied museum sciences, and is now the curator of the art museum.

亞當唸的是博物館相關科系，如今成了美術館館長。

cursory [ˈkɝsərɪ] 形匆忙的；粗略的 ★★★☆☆

Dad makes a cursory glance at the newspaper headlines before hurrying off to work.

爸大概看了一下報紙標題，便趕去上班。

同義字
▶ □hasty　a.　匆忙的；倉促的　　　□hurried　a.　倉促的；草率的
▶ □sketchy　a.　概略的；不完全的　□ superficial　a.　粗略的；草率的
反義字
▶ □deliberate　a.　從容的　　　　□unhurried　a.　不慌不忙的

curt [kɝt] 形簡明的；簡要的；簡慢的；唐突草率的 ★★★★☆

Instead of introducing himself properly to the group, Kyle made a few curt comments and sat down quickly.

凱爾沒有對其他團體成員適當自我介紹，只是簡慢地說了兩句便很快坐下。

同義字
▶ □short　a.　簡短的；簡慢的　　　□negligent　a.　簡慢的

▶ □laconic　a.　簡潔的；簡明的　　□concise　a.　簡明的；簡潔的

反義字
▶ □assiduous　a.　一絲不苟的　　□scrupulous　a.　一絲不苟的
▶ □meticulous　a.　嚴密的

curtail [kɚ'tel] 　 縮減；縮短 　★★★★★

The hockey season was curtailed because of the players' strike.
曲棍球季因為球員罷工事件而變短了。

同義字
▶ □shorten　v.　使變短；減少　　□cut　v.　削減；縮短
▶ □abridge　v.　縮短　　□reduce　v.　減少；降低

反義字
▶ □lengthen　v.　使加長；使延長　　□ increase　v.　增大；增加；增強

curtsy ['kɚtsɪ] 　 行屈膝禮 　★★★☆☆

After the performance, the boys bowed and the girls curtsied.
表演完後，男孩鞠躬，女孩則行屈膝禮。

cynical ['sɪnɪkl̩] 　 1. 憤世嫉俗的；悲觀的　　2. 挖苦的；冷嘲的 ★★★☆☆

Grandpa is cynical of the politician's promises. He says he's heard these lies before.
葛蘭達不相信該名政治人物的承諾，他説這些謊言以前就聽過了。

同義字
▶ □skeptical　a.　懷疑的；多疑的　　□resentful　a.　忿恨的；怨恨的
▶ □distrustful　a.　不信任的；懷疑的　　□ironic　a.　冷嘲的；挖苦的

以D為首的單字

5 顆★：金色（860~990）證書必背
4 顆★：藍色（730~855）證書必背
3 顆★：綠色（470~725）證書必背

MP3-06

dare [dɛr] 　 挑逗；激；膽敢 　★★★★☆

I dare you to dive off that cliff. I don't think you've got the guts.
我諒你不敢從那座懸崖上跳下去，我覺得你沒那個膽。

data ['detə] 　 資料；數據（datum 的複數） 　★★★★★

The scientist based his theory on the data from his research.
這名科學家以其研究資料為基礎，建立了他的理論。

同義字
▶ □information　n.　報導；情報資料　　□papers　n.　資料；證件；文件
▶ □dead-heat　n.　無勝負；平手

dead-heat ['dɛd'hit] 　 無勝負；平手；並列名次 　★★★☆☆

The race ended in a dead-heat, so both runners received a gold medal.
比賽最後以平手收場，兩位跑者都得到了金牌。

同義字
▶ □draw　n.　平局；平手　　　　□deuce　n.　平手
▶ □tie　n.　得分相等；平手

debatable [dɪˈbetəbl̩] 可爭辯的；可爭論的；有問題的；有爭議的；未決的 ★★★★★

Your claim that this car never breaks down is certainly debatable. I own this model, and it breaks down all the time.
你說這種車從不故障顯然有問題。我也開這種車，結果老是故障。

同義字
▶ □questionable　a.　不確定的　　　□disputable　a.　有討論餘地的
▶ □controvertible　a.　可爭論的

反義字
▶ □undebatable　a.　無辯論餘地　　□ unquestionable　a.　毫無疑問的
▶ □indisputable　a.　無爭論餘地　　□incontrovertible　a.　無疑的

debut [dɪˈbju] 初次登台；首次亮相 ★★★★☆

Tonight is Don's debut as a theater actor. Before this, he's only done some TV commercials.
今晚是唐以電影演員身分首次亮相，之前他只拍過一些電視廣告。

deceive [dɪˈsiv] 欺騙；蒙蔽 ★★★☆☆

Appearances can deceive. You should get to know a person before making any judgments.
外表是會騙人的，評斷一個人之前應該先了解他。

同義字
▶ □cheat　v.　欺騙；騙取；詐取　　　□hoax　v.　欺騙；愚弄
▶ □delude　v.　欺騙；哄騙；迷惑　　　□fool　v.　愚弄；欺騙
▶ □beguile　v.　欺騙；誆騙

反義字
▶ □undeceive　v.　使醒悟　　　　　　□disenchant　v.　使醒悟
▶ □disillusion　v.　使…的理想破滅

decent [ˈdisn̩t] 1. 正派的；合乎禮儀的　2. 體面的；像樣的；還不錯的 ★★★★★

Gary was brought up in a good family, and is now a decent young man with excellent manners.
蓋瑞在一個好家庭中長大，如今是個彬彬有禮的正派青年。

同義字
▶ □respectable　a.　名聲好的　　　□proper　a.　循規蹈矩的
▶ □chaste　a.　正派的；高尚的

反義字
▶ □indecent　a.　下流的；猥褻的　　□vulgar　a.　粗俗的；下流的

▶ □rough　a.　粗暴的；粗野的

decimal　[ˈdɛsɪml̩]　形十進位的；小數的　★★★☆☆

The number pi to five decimal places is 3.14159.
圓周率計算到小數點第五位是 3.14159。

decimate　[ˈdɛsəˌmet]　動大量毀滅；成批殺死　★★★★☆

Deforestation has decimated many animal and plant populations. If it's not stopped, they may become extinct.
許多動植物都因砍伐森林而大量滅絕，如果再不停止，可能就要絕種了。

同義字
▶ □butcher　v.　屠殺；殘殺　　　□massacre　v.　屠殺；殘殺
▶ □slaughter　v.　殺戮；屠殺

decipher　[dɪˈsaɪfɚ]　動辨認（潦草的字跡等）；解釋（古代文字等）　★★★★★

Your handwriting is barely legible. I can't decipher the message at all.
你的筆跡很潦草，無法辨認你寫的是什麼。

同義字
▶ □identify　v.　確認；識別　　　□recognize　v.　認出；識別
▶ □discern　v.　辨明；分清

declare　[dɪˈklɛr]　動宣佈；宣告；聲明　★★★☆☆

The President declared a state of emergency immediately after the huge earthquake.
總統在大地震後立刻宣佈進入緊急狀態。

同義字
▶ □announce　v.　宣佈；發佈　　　□ proclaim　v.　宣告；公佈；聲明
▶ □herald　v.　宣佈；通報　　　□advertise　v.　公佈；通知
反義字
▶ □conceal　v.　隱蔽；隱藏　　　□hide　v.　隱瞞；隱藏
▶ □suppress　v.　隱瞞；藏匿　　　□withhold　v.　不吐露；隱瞞

decorate　[ˈdɛkəˌret]　動裝飾；修飾；佈置　★★★★☆

This room is so bland. Let's decorate it with some flowers and paintings.
這間房間很單調，我們拿些花和畫來裝飾一下吧。

同義字
▶ □adorn　v.　裝飾；使生色　　　□trim　v.　裝點；佈置
▶ □embellish　v.　美化；裝飾　　　□ornament　v.　裝飾；美化
▶ □deck　v.　裝飾；打扮
反義字
▶ □disfigure　v.　損毀⋯的外形　　　□deform　v.　使變醜陋
▶ □deface　v.　損壞　　　□mar　v.　毀損；損傷；玷污

decoy [dɪˋkɔɪ] 图 （捕鳥獸的）假鳥、假獸；誘餌動物 ★★★☆☆

The hunter used a decoy to lure the ducks to within shooting range.
這個獵人用假鳥來引誘鴨子進入射程。

同義字
▶ □bait　n.　引誘物；誘餌；圈套　　□lure　n.　（捕鳥獸的）誘餌

decrepit [dɪˋkrɛpɪt] 图 衰老的；東倒西歪的；破舊的 ★★★★★

The decrepit old man is suffering from cancer, and is on the verge of death.
這名老人已是風中殘燭，又飽受癌症之苦，生命危在旦夕。

同義字
▶ □aged　a.　年老的；舊的　　　□elderly　a.　年長的；
▶ □senile　a.　老邁的；老態龍鍾的　□ senescent　a.　老邁的；衰老的

反義字
▶ □young　a.　年輕的；幼小的　　□youthful　a.　年輕的；青年的
▶ □juvenile　a.　少年的；幼年的　□adolescent　a.　幼稚的

dedicate [ˋdɛdə͵ket] 1. 奉獻（著作）　2. 把（時間、精力等）用於 ★★★★☆

The author dedicated his book to his late father.
作者把他的書獻給已故的父親。

同義字
▶ □inscribe　v.　題獻；題贈　　　□devote　v.　將…奉獻（給）
▶ □consecrate　v.　獻身於；致力於

deduce [dɪˋdjus] 圗 演繹；推論 ★★★☆☆

Using the clues found at the crime scene, the detective deduced that the intruder had come in through the window and went out the front door.
這名偵探利用犯罪現場找到的線索，推論闖入者是從窗戶進來，然後從前門出去。

同義字
▶ □conclude　v.　推斷出；斷定　　□infer　v.　推斷；推論；猜想
▶ □reason　v.　推論；推理；思考

反義字
▶ □induce　v.　歸納　　　□generalize　v.　歸納；概括

deface [dɪˋfes] 圗 毀壞…的外貌；塗污（使難辨認） ★★★☆☆

The side of the bus was defaced with graffiti.
公車這一側因為塗鴉而變得面目全非。

同義字
▶ □disfigure　v.　損毀…的外形　　□deform　v.　使變醜陋
▶ □mar　v.　毀損；損傷；玷污

反義字
▶ □adorn　v.　裝飾；使生色　　　□trim　v.　裝點；佈置
▶ □embellish　v.　美化；裝飾　　□ornament　v.　裝飾；美化

defame [dɪˋfem]　　🔊 誹謗；破壞…的名譽　　★★★★☆

You shouldn't defame your ex-employers. When you need a reference, you'll regret all the nasty things you've said.

你不應誹謗過去的雇主，哪天需要找人推薦時，你就會後悔自己說過那些難聽話。

同義字
▶ □malign　v.　誹謗；中傷　　　□slur　v.　污辱；毀謗
▶ □slander　v.　詆毀；造謠中傷　　□disparage　v.　毀謗
▶ □abuse　v.　辱罵；毀謗

反義字
▶ □eulogize　v.　頌揚　　□extol　v.　讚美；頌揚
▶ □celebrate　v.　頌揚；讚美　　□praise　v.　讚美；表揚；歌頌

default [dɪˋfɔlt]　　🔊 不參加（比賽）；（中途）棄權　　★★★★★

Since your opponent has failed to show up, you win by default.

既然對手未到，你便因其棄權而獲勝。

同義字
▶ □abstention　n.　棄權

defendant [dɪˋfɛndənt]　　🔊 被告　　★★★☆☆

In this trial, the defendant has pleaded innocent on all charges of fraud and theft.

在這場審判中，被告辯稱所有關於詐騙和竊盜的指控都是不實的。

同義字
▶ □accused　n.　被告　　　□respondent　n.　被告

反義字
▶ □complainant　n.　原告　　□plaintiff　n.　起訴人；原告
▶ □demandant　n.　原告　　　□prosecutor　n.　原告；起訴人
▶ □accuser　n.　原告；控告者

defense [dɪˋfɛns]　　🔊 防禦；保衛；防護　　★★★☆☆

The porcupine has an excellent defense mechanism. When it's in danger, it shoots quills to protect itself.

豪豬的防禦機制很強，一旦遇到危險，它就會射出身上的刺來保護自己。

同義字
▶ □protection　n.　保護；防護　　□shelter　n.　掩蔽；遮蔽；庇護
▶ □security　n.　防備；保安；防護

反義字
▶ □attack　n.　進攻；抨擊　　　□assault　n.　攻擊；襲擊；譴責
▶ □lash　n.　抨擊；斥責　　　　□tilt　n.　攻擊；譴責

defer [dɪˋfɝ]　　🔊 推遲；延期　　★★★★☆

Since not even half the members have shown up to this meeting, we'll defer all major decisions until next week.

既然這次開會連一半人數都不到，只好將所有重大決議延至下週。

同義字
- ▶ □postpone　v.　使延期；延遲　　　□delay　v.　延緩；使延期
- ▶ □hold over　延期　　　□stand over　延期

反義字
- ▶ □advance　v.　將…提前

defiance　[dɪ'faɪəns]　🔊反抗；蔑視；藐視　★★★☆☆

Although the insurgents were surrounded, they refused to surrender and fought on in defiance.
雖然暴動分子已被包圍，卻無視這一切而不願投降、繼續奮戰。

同義字
- ▶ □scorn　n.　輕蔑；藐視　□contempt　n.　輕視；蔑視
- ▶ □disrespect　n.　輕蔑；蔑視

反義字
- ▶ □respect　n.　尊敬；敬重　　　□deference　n.　敬意；尊敬
- ▶ □homage　n.　尊敬；敬意　　　□reverence　n.　敬畏

deficient　[dɪ'fɪʃənt]　🔊不足的；缺乏的　★★★★★

Our water supply is deficient. We should stock up before driving across the desert.
我們的供水不足。要開車橫越沙漠前，得貯存足夠的水才行。

同義字
- ▶ □insufficient　a.　不充分的　　　□scarce　a.　缺乏的；不足的
- ▶ □scant　a.　不足的；貧乏的　　　□meager　a.　粗劣的；不足的

反義字
- ▶ □abundant　a.　大量的；充足的　□plentiful　a.　豐富的；充足的
- ▶ □bounteous　a.　充足的；豐富的　□generous　a.　大量的；豐富的
- ▶ □affluent　a.　豐富的；富饒的

definite　['dɛfənɪt]　🔊明確的；確切的　★★★☆☆

My stay in Vancouver isn't definite. It could be three months or three years, depending on how long my contract for work is.
我要在溫哥華待多久並不確定，可能是三個月也可能是三年，一切依工作契約簽多久而定。

同義字
- ▶ □explicit　a.　詳盡的；清楚的　　□unequivocal　a.　毫不含糊的
- ▶ □decided　a.　明確的；顯然的　　□positive　a.　確定的；確實的

反義字
- ▶ □indeterminate　a.　不確定的　　□indefinite　a.　不確定的
- ▶ □undefined　a.　不明確的

deforest　[dɪ'fɔrɪst]　🔊採伐…的森林；清除…上的樹林　★★★★☆

Large areas of the rainforest have been deforested to create farmland.
為了建造農田，大片雨林已遭砍伐。

反義字

▶ □afforest　v.　造林於…

defraud　[dɪˈfrɔd]　⬛詐取；詐騙　★★★★☆

Ed is an unethical accountant, and has defrauded his company of thousands of dollars.

艾德是個不道德的會計師，已經詐騙了公司很多錢。

[同義字]
▶ □cheat　v.　欺騙；騙取；詐取　　　□swindle　v.　詐騙；騙取
▶ □gyp　v.　詐欺　　　　　　□cozen　v.　騙取；哄騙；詐騙
▶ □shark　v.　詐騙；行騙

degenerate　[dɪˈdʒɛnəˌret]　⬛衰退；墮落；變壞　★★★☆☆

She was once a great writer, but her work degenerated as she began to drink.

她曾是名大作家，但自從開始喝酒後，作品就變差了。

[同義字]
▶ □corrupt　v.　墮落；腐化　　　□deprave　v.　使墮落；使惡化
▶ □deteriorate　v.　惡化　□worsen　v.　（使）更壞

[反義字]
▶ □improve　v.　改進；增進　　　□develop　v.　進步；進化
▶ □ameliorate　v.　改善；改良　　□better　v.　改善；提高

deity　[ˈdiətɪ]　⬛神；女神　★★★★☆

She kept pictures and statues of deities on her altar, and prayed to them morning and night.

她把神明的畫像和雕像擺在祭壇上，早晚祈求。

[同義字]
▶ □divinity　n.　神；女神　□god　n.　男神；上帝

deject　[dɪˈdʒɛkt]　⬛沮喪的；情緒低落的；氣餒的　★★★★★

He felt dejected after being turned down by all ten universities that he applied to.

他因為申請十所大學都沒有獲准入學，心情變得很沮喪。

[同義字]
▶ □depressed　a.　憂鬱的　　　□discouraged　a.　灰心的
▶ □downcast　a.　垂頭喪氣的　　□disheartened　a.　沮喪的
▶ □damp　a.　消沈的；沮喪的

[反義字]
▶ □spirited　a.　生氣勃勃的　　　□vivacious　a.　活潑的
▶ □encouraged　a.　受到鼓舞的　　□heartening　a.　鼓舞人心的

delectable　[dɪˈlɛktəbl]　⬛好吃的；甘美的　★★★☆☆

This delectable Thai papaya salad is sour, spicy, and sweet. It's a real treat for the senses.

這種好吃的泰國番木 沙拉又酸又辣又甜，可真是感官的一大享受。

同義字
▶ □tasty　a.　美味的；可口的　　□delicious　a.　美味的
▶ □yummy　a.　好吃的；美味的　　□palatable　a.　美味的
▶ □luscious　a.　甘美多汁的

反義字
▶ □unpalatable　a.　味道差的　　□distasteful　a.　不合口味的
▶ □unsavory　a.　難吃的　　□tasteless　a.　沒味道的

delicacy　[ˈdɛləkəsɪ]　🔲美味；佳餚　　★★★☆☆

In some countries, cockroaches are a delicacy. But I guess my tastes are not refined enough to appreciate them.
有些國家把蟑螂當做一道美味佳餚，不過我想我的味覺還沒有精緻到可以品味這道菜。

同義字
▶ □dainty　n.　美味；精美的食品　　□morsel　n.　（美味）小吃
▶ □goody　n.　好吃的東西

delirious　[dɪˈlɪrɪəs]　🔲精神錯亂的；狂喜的　　★★★★☆

The high fever must be making Jan delirious. She's yelling and screaming gibberish.
詹恩一定是因為發高燒導致精神錯亂，才會胡言亂語地又叫又喊。

同義字
▶ □insane　a.　（患）精神病的　　□deranged　a.　精神錯亂的
▶ □raving　a.　胡言亂語的　　□lunatic　a.　瘋的；精神錯亂的
▶ □demented　a.　精神錯亂狀態的

反義字
▶ □sane　a.　神智正常的；頭腦清楚的

delude　[dɪˈlud]　🔲欺騙；哄騙；迷惑　　★★★★★

You must be deluded if you think that salesman is only concerned about giving you the best deal.
如果你覺得推銷員只關心你買得划不划算，那你一定是被騙了。

同義字
▶ □deceive　v.　欺騙；蒙蔽　　□cheat　v.　欺騙；騙取；詐取
▶ □hoax　v.　欺騙；愚弄　　□fool　v.　愚弄；欺騙
▶ □beguile　v.　欺騙；誆騙

反義字
▶ □undeceive　v.　使不受迷惑　　□disenchant　v.　使醒悟
▶ □disillusion　v.　使醒悟

deluge　[ˈdɛljudʒ]　🔲（洪水般）湧至；大量泛濫　　★★★☆☆

He got a deluge of fan mail when his song went to number one on the charts.
他的歌擠進排行榜第一名時，大批歌迷的信立刻蜂擁而至。

同義字
▶ □overflow　n.　溢出；過剩；泛濫　□inundation　n.　淹沒；泛濫
▶ □flooding　n.　泛濫

demeanor [dɪˈminɚ]　图舉動；行為；風度　★★★☆☆

During a job interview, your demeanor will determine whether or not the boss thinks you have the right personality to fit into his company.
參加工作面試時，會不會讓老闆覺得你的個 適合他們公司，關鍵就在你的行為舉止。

同義字
▶ □behavior　n.　行為；舉止；態度　□deportment　n.　舉止；風度
▶ □bearing　n.　舉止；風度；體態　□manner　n.　態度；舉止
▶ □conduct　n.　行為；品行；舉動

demented [dɪˈmɛntɪd]　图精神錯亂狀態的；瘋狂的　★★★★☆

That guy is demented and should be placed in an asylum for the insane.
那傢伙精神錯亂，應該當做精神病患送到精神病院才對。

同義字
▶ □delirious　a.　精神錯亂的　　□insane　a.　（患）精神病的
▶ □deranged　a.　瘋狂的　　　　□raving　a.　胡言亂語的
▶ □lunatic　a.　瘋的；精神錯亂的

反義字
▶ □sane　a.　神智正常的；頭腦清楚的

demerit [diˈmɛrɪt]　图缺點；過失；罪過　★★★★★

I got two demerits on my driving record for speeding and running a red light.
我過去的駕駛記錄只有兩次過失，一次是超速，一次是闖紅燈。

同義字
▶ □fault　n.　錯誤；毛病；缺陷　　□error　n.　錯誤；過失；罪過
▶ □mistake　n.　錯誤；過失

反義字
▶ □merit　n.　長處；優點；功績　　□credit　n.　榮譽；讚揚；功勞

demolish [dɪˈmɑlɪʃ]　囫毀壞；破壞；拆除　★★★☆☆

The old warehouse will be demolished to make room for a parking lot.
舊倉庫即將拆除，並改建成停車場。

同義字
▶ □destroy　v.　毀壞；破壞　　□dismantle　v.　去掉…的覆蓋物
▶ □tear down　拆除；扯下　　　□pull down　拆毀（房屋等）

反義字
▶ □establish　v.　建立；創辦　　□build　v.　建築；造；建立
▶ □construct　v.　建造；構成

demonstrate [ˈdɛmənˌstret]　囫示範操作；展示　★★★☆☆

Ladies and gentleman, I am going to demonstrate how well this revolutionary mop works.
各位先生，各位女士，我即將展示這種革命性的拖把工作起來是多麼有效率。

同義字
▶ □display　v.　顯示；表現；展示　　□unfold　v.　顯露；表露；呈現

▶ □show　v.　展示；露出

denizen　[ˈdɛnəzn̩]　　名居民；居住者　★★★★☆

Denizens of Hawaii get excellent weather year round. Why would anyone move away?

住在夏威夷一年到頭都是好天氣，誰會想搬走？

同義字
▶ □resident　n.　居民；僑民　　　□liver　n.　居住者；居民
▶ □inhabitant　n.　居民；居住者　　□dweller　n.　居民；居住者

denomination　[dɪ͵nɑməˈneʃən]　　名面額；（度量衡等的）單位　★★★★★

The Canadian dollar comes in denominations of 5, 10, 20, 50, 100, and 1000.

加幣面額分5、10、20、50、100 和 1000。

denominator　[dɪˈnɑmə͵netə]　　名分母　★★★☆☆

In the fraction 2/3, two is the numerator and three is the denominator.

在 2/3 這個分數中，2 是分子，3 是分母。

denote　[dɪˈnot]　　動表示；預示；（符號等）代表　★★★☆☆

A flag at half mast denotes mourning.

降半旗表哀掉之意。

同義字
▶ □indicate　v.　表明；象徵；指示　□mean　v.　意指；意謂
▶ □signify　v.　表示；表明；意味著

denouement　[deˈnumɑŋ]　　名（小說、戲劇等的）結局、收場　★★★★☆

I can't wait for the denouement of the mystery novel. It's unbearable not knowing who the murderer is.

我迫不及待想知道這本推理小說的結局，不知道兇手是誰實在叫人難以忍受。

同義字
▶ □conclusion　n.　結尾；結局　　□ outcome　n.　結果；結局；後果
▶ □ending　n.　（故事等的）結局　□upshot　n.　結果；結局

denounce　[dɪˈnauns]　　動指責；譴責　★★★★★

Leaders around the world denounced the hijacking as an act of terrorism.

全世界的領導人同聲譴責這次劫機事件為恐怖主義的行徑。

同義字
▶ □blame　v.　責備；指責　　　□censure　v.　責備；譴責
▶ □reproach　v.　責備；斥責　　□condemn　v.　責難；譴責
▶ □reprimand　v.　訓斥；斥責

反義字
▶ □praise　v.　讚美；表揚；歌頌　□compliment　v.　讚美；恭維
▶ □extol　v.　讚美；頌揚　□admire　v.　稱讚；誇獎

deplete [dɪˈplit]　**動**用盡；耗盡…的資源（精力等）　★★★☆☆

Our reserve of money will soon be depleted if you don't go out and get a job.

如果你再不出門找工作，我們剩下的錢很快就會用光了。

同義字
▶ □exhaust　v.　用完；耗盡　　　□drain　v.　耗盡
▶ □spend　v.　耗盡；用盡

反義字
▶ □complement　v.　補充；補足　　□supply　v.　供給；供應；補充
▶ □supplement　v.　增補；補充　　□recruit　v.　補充

deplorable [dɪˈplorəbl]　1. 悲慘的；糟糕的；骯髒的　2. 可嘆的；可悲的；可憐的　★★★☆☆

The Mayor promises to improve the deplorable housing conditions in the inner city.

市長答應改善內城骯髒的居住環境。

同義字
▶ □terrible　a.　極糟糕的；極差的　　□awful　a.　極壞的；極糟的
▶ □vile　a.　骯髒的；污穢的　　　　□ghastly　a.　極壞的

反義字
▶ □superb　a.　極好的；上乘的　　□splendid　a.　極好的
▶ □fabulous　a.　極好的　　　　　□magnificent　a.　極好的

deport [dɪˈport]　**動**驅逐（出境）；放逐　★★★★☆

Landed immigrants are deported back to their home country if they commit a serious crime.

擁有不動產的僑民如果犯了重罪，便會被驅逐出境，趕回故國。

同義字
▶ □expel　v.　驅逐；趕走　　　　　□transport　v.　放逐；流放
▶ □exile　v.　流放；放逐；使離鄉背井　□banish　v.　流放；放逐

deposit [dɪˈpazɪt]　**動**把（錢）儲存；存放（銀行等）　★★★★★

After receiving her paycheck, Sandy immediately deposited it into her bank account so that she couldn't spend it.

珊蒂一收到薪資支票，立刻存入銀行帳戶以免亂花。

同義字
▶ □save　v.　儲蓄；積蓄　□pay in　把…存入銀行

反義字
▶ □withdraw　v.　提款

depreciate [dɪˈpriʃɪˌet]　**動**降價；跌價；貶值；折舊　★★★☆☆

The vaue of my car has depreciated a lot since I bought it. It is only worth 10% of its initial value.

我這輛車買來以後折舊率很高，目前的價值只剩原價的一成。

同義字
▶ □devaluate　v.　降低…的價值　　□cheapen　v.　跌價；減價
▶ □mark down　減價

▶ □appreciate　v.　增值　□mark up　加價

depress　[dɪ'prɛs]　**動**壓下；壓低　★★★☆☆

To turn your computer off, depress the power button for three seconds.
電腦要關機，只要壓下電源鈕三秒鐘即可。

同義字
▶ □press　v.　按；壓；擠

反義字
▶ □loosen　v.　鬆開；解開

depression　[dɪ'prɛʃən]　**名**沮喪；意氣消沈　★★★★☆

After losing his job and his wife, John fell into depression.
約翰因為失去工作又失去老婆而變得意氣消沈。

同義字
▶ □discouragement　n.　沮喪　　　□disheartenment　n.　氣餒
▶ □damp　n.　消沈；沮喪 □despondency　n.　失去勇氣

反義字
▶ □spiritedness　n.　有精神；活潑　□vivacity　n.　活潑；快活

depth　[dɛpθ]　**名**深度；厚度　★★★☆☆

The depth of this swimming pool is only two meters. It's not deep enough for diving.
這座游泳池的深度只有兩公尺，要潛水的話還不夠深。

同義字
▶ □deepness　n.　深；深度　　　　□profundity　n.　深度；深淵

derelict　['dɛrə,lɪkt]　**形**被拋棄了的；無主的　★★★☆☆

The derelict building will soon be torn down to build a new condominium.
這棟廢棄的建築物即將拆除，以重建新的公寓大廈。

同義字
▶ □outcast　a.　被拋棄的　□abandoned　a.　被放棄的
▶ □uninhabited　a.　杳無人跡的

deride　[dɪ'raɪd]　**動**嘲笑；嘲弄　★★★☆☆

The bully derided Samantha on her outdated clothes.
這個惡霸嘲笑莎曼莎穿過時的衣服。

同義字
▶ □ridicule　v.　嘲笑；戲弄　　　□mock　v.　嘲弄；嘲笑
▶ □taunt　v.　辱罵；嘲笑　　　　□laugh at　嘲笑

反義字
▶ □respect　v.　尊敬；敬重　　　□esteem　v.　尊重；珍重
▶ □honor　v.　尊敬

derive [dɪˈraɪv] 🔳 取得；得到 ★★★★☆

She derives many of her ideas from the books she reads.
她從讀過的書當中得到很多點子。

同義字
▶ □get　v.　獲得；得到　　　　□obtain　v.　得到；獲得
▶ □acquire　v.　取得；獲得

dermatologist [ˌdɜməˈtɑlədʒɪst] 🔳 皮膚科醫生 ★★★★★

You should see a dermatologist about the spots on your skin.
你應該去找皮膚科醫生，看看皮膚上那塊斑是怎麼回事。

descendant [dɪˈsɛndənt] 🔳 子孫；後裔 ★★★☆☆

Many descendants of the Incas still live in the Andes Mountains, and try to carry on some of the traditions of their forefathers.
許多印加人後裔仍然住在安地斯山脈當中，設法將一些祖先留傳下來的傳統繼續傳承下去。

同義字
▶ □offspring　n.　子女；後代　　　□ progeny　n.　（動、植物）的後代
▶ □posterity　n.　後裔；子孫　　　□child　n.　子孫；後代

反義字
▶ □ascendant　n.　祖先　　　　　　□ancestor　n.　祖宗；祖先
▶ □forefather　n.　祖先；前輩

descend [dɪˈsɛnd] 🔳 下來；下降 ★★★★☆

The elevator takes ten seconds to descend from the top floor to the lobby.
這部電梯從頂樓降到一樓大廳只需十秒鐘。

同義字
▶ □fall　v.　落下；降落　　　　　□drop　v.　滴下；落下；掉下

反義字
▶ □ascend　v.　登高；上升　　　　□rise　v.　上升；升起；增加

desert [dɛˈzɚt] 🔳 拋棄；遺棄；離棄 ★★★☆☆

The owner gave up trying to fix his old car and deserted it on the side of the road.
車主放棄修理他的舊車，便把車子丟棄在路邊。

同義字
▶ □abandon　v.　丟棄；拋棄；遺棄　□forsake　v.　拋棄；遺棄；背棄
▶ □discard　v.　拋棄；摒棄；丟棄

反義字
▶ □maintain　v.　維持；保持　　　□retain　v.　保留；保持
▶ □conserve　v.　保存；節省

desiccant [ˈdɛsəkənt] 🔳 乾燥劑 ★★★★★

When shipping things by sea, be sure to put desiccant into the package to keep the contents dry and free of mildew.

A B C **D** E F G H I J K L M N O P Q R S T U V W X Y Z

包裹如果用海運，記得裡面要放乾燥劑，東西才能保持乾燥、不會長霉。

同義字
▶ □exsiccator　n.　乾燥劑；除濕劑　□dryer　n.　乾燥劑

designate [ˈdɛzɪɡˌnet]　　動委任；指派　　★★★☆☆

The President designated John the Attorney General.
總統委任約翰為首席檢察官。

同義字
▶ □nominate　v.　任命；指定　　□appoint　v.　任命；指派
▶ □assign　v.　派定；指定；選派

despair [dɪˈspɛr]　　名絕望；喪失信心　　★★★★☆

After countless failed attempts to win Jessica's heart, Mitchell finally gave up in despair.
為了贏得傑西嘉的芳心，米歇爾經過無數次的努力還是沒有成功，終於絕望地放棄了。

同義字
▶ □hopelessness　n.　不抱希望

反義字
▶ □hope　n.　希望；期望　　□wish　n.　希望；願望
▶ □promise　n.　希望；前途

desperate [ˈdɛspərɪt]　　形極度渴望的；情急拼命的；挺而走險的　　★★★☆☆

I've got no money in my bank account. I'm desperate for a job, any job!
我的銀行帳戶裡沒有半毛錢，我很想要一份工作，什麼工作都行！

同義字
▶ □thirsty　a.　渴望的；渴求的　　□yearning　a.　渴望的；思念的
▶ □anxious　a.　渴望的　　□longing　a.　渴望的

despicable [ˈdɛspɪkəbl̩]　　形可鄙的；卑劣的　　★★★☆☆

He's a despicable scam artist who even ripped off the Red Cross.
他是一個卑鄙的詐騙專家，連紅十字會都騙。

同義字
▶ □contemptible　a.　無恥的　　□mean　a.　卑鄙的；卑劣的
▶ □base　a.　卑鄙的；惡劣的　　□vile　a.　卑鄙的；可恥的
▶ □pitiful　a.　可鄙的

反義字
▶ □noble　a.　高貴的；高尚的
▶ □respectable　a.　可敬的

despite [dɪˈspaɪt]　　介儘管；雖然；任憑　　★★★★☆

Despite not being able to see, Jacob succeeded in summiting Mount Everest.
雖然看不到，雅各還是成功登頂聖母峰。

同義字
▶ □though　conj.　雖然；儘管　　□although　conj.　雖然；儘管

▶ □notwithstanding prep. 雖然 □even if / though 即使;雖然
▶ □in spite of 儘管

despot ['dɛspɑt] 名專制君主;暴君 ★★★★★

The despot took the throne by violence, and now rules with equal disregard for life.
這名專制君主是用暴力即位的,如今在他的統治下,依然漠視生命的價值。

同義字
▶ □tyrant n. 暴君;專制君主 □dictator n. 獨裁者
▶ □autocrat n. 獨裁者;專制君主

destitute ['dɛstə,tjut] 形窮困的;貧困的 ★★★☆☆

This non-profit helps destitute families who live in rundown shacks in the inner city.
這個非營利組織專門協助那些住在內城破落小屋內的窮困家庭。

同義字
▶ □poor a. 貧窮的;貧困的 □penniless a. 身無分文的
▶ □needy a. 貧窮的 □impoverished a. 窮困的
▶ □down-and-out a. 窮困潦倒的

反義字
▶ □rich a. 有錢的;富有的 □wealthy a. 富裕的;豐富的
▶ □affluent a. 富裕的 □well-off a. 富裕的
▶ □forehanded a. 富裕的

deter [dɪ'tɝ] 動威懾住;嚇住;使斷念 ★★★★☆

Do you think this scarecrow will deter the crows from my field?
你覺得這個稻草人能夠嚇住農場上的烏鴉嗎?

同義字
▶ □terrorize v. 使恐怖;恐嚇 □intimidate v. 威嚇;脅迫
▶ □frighten v. 使驚恐;使駭怕 □scare v. 驚嚇;使恐懼

反義字
▶ □calm v. 使鎮定;使平靜 □compose v. 使安定;使平靜
▶ □quiet v. 使安靜;使平息 □soothe v. 安慰;撫慰

deteriorate [dɪ'tɪrɪə,ret] 動惡化;退化;下降;墮落 ★★★★★

Eli's memory deteriorated as he grew in age.
隨著年紀漸長,艾里的記憶力也開始退化。

同義字
▶ □worsen v. (使)更壞;(使)惡化 □aggravate v. 加重;增劇

反義字
▶ □improve v. 改進;改善;增進 □develop v. 進步;進化
▶ □ameliorate v. 改善;改良 □better v. 改善;改進;提高

determined [dɪ'tɝmɪnd] 形已下決心的;果斷的; 決然的;堅定的 ★★★☆☆

When Tanya is determined to do something, she does it no matter what the obstacles.
坦雅一旦下定決心,就會排除任何阻礙,全力完成目標。

91

同義字
▶ ☐firm　a.　堅定的；堅決的　　　☐resolved　a.　下定決心的
▶ ☐decided　a.　果斷的；堅決的　　☐bent　a.　決心的；決意的

反義字
▶ ☐double-minded　a.　三心二意的　☐undecided　a.　優柔寡斷的

deterrent [dɪˈtɝrənt] ☑制止物；威懾力量 ★★★★☆

I wonder if this "Beware of Dog" sign is enough deterrent against burglars.
我懷疑這塊「注意惡犬」的牌子真的會嚇住竊賊。

同義字
▶ ☐restraint　n.　抑制；克制；阻止　☐prevention　n.　阻止；妨礙
▶ ☐determent　n.　威懾物；制止物

detest [dɪˈtɛst] 動厭惡；憎惡 ★★★☆☆

I detest this apartment. The plumbing doesn't work, the neighbors are loud, and the rent is high.
我恨死這棟公寓了。馬桶壞掉、鄰居吵吵鬧鬧，租金又貴得要命。

同義字
▶ ☐hate　v.　仇恨；憎恨；嫌惡　　☐dislike　v.　不喜愛；厭惡
▶ ☐loathe　v.　厭惡；憎恨　　　　☐abhor　v.　厭惡；憎惡
▶ ☐abominate　v.　厭惡；痛恨

反義字
▶ ☐love　v.　愛戴；疼愛　　　　　☐adore　v.　愛慕；熱愛
▶ ☐like　v.　喜歡

detract [dɪˈtrækt] 動減損；降低 ★★★★★

Too much information on an advertisement will detract from its overall effectiveness.
廣告上訊息太多會降低其整體效果。

同義字
▶ ☐lower　v.　減低；減弱　☐reduce　v.　減少；使變弱
▶ ☐weaken　v.　削弱；減弱；減少

反義字
▶ ☐strengthen　v.　加強；增強；鞏固　　☐increase　v.　增大；增加；增強
▶ ☐heighten　v.　增強；增加；提高

deviate [ˈdivɪˌet] 動脫離；越軌 ★★★★☆

Once we've decided on a course of action, we shouldn't deviate from it too much.
一旦我們決定行動方針，就不應偏離太多。

同義字
▶ ☐deflect　v.　使偏斜；使轉向　　☐vary　v.　偏離；違反
▶ ☐diverge　v.　偏離；背離　　　　☐depart　v.　背離；違反

devise [dɪˈvaɪz] 動策劃；想出；設計；發明 ★★★☆☆

As a structural engineer, my job is to devise ways to solve architectural problems.
身為建築工程師，我的工作就是設法解決和建築有關的各項問題。

同義字
- ▶ □conceive v. 構想出；想像　　□think v. 思索；想像；理解
- ▶ □envisage v. 想像；設想　　　□excogitate v. 想出

devout [dɪˈvaʊt]　　形 虔誠的；虔敬的　　　★★★★★

Margot is a devout Buddhist who goes to the temple daily.
瑪爾蓋特是個每天上寺廟的虔誠佛教徒。

同義字
- ▶ □pious a. 虔誠的；篤信的　　　□devout a. 虔誠的；虔敬的
- ▶ □religious a. 篤信宗教的　　　□reverent a. 恭敬的；虔誠的
- ▶ □pietistic a. 虔信派的；虔誠的

反義字
- ▶ □impious a. 不敬神的；不虔誠的　　　□blasphemous a. 褻瀆的
- ▶ □profane a. 褻瀆的；好咒罵的

dexterity [dɛksˈtɛrətɪ]　　名 （手等）靈巧；熟練；敏捷　　★★★★☆

I'm right-handed, and have absolutely no dexterity in my left hand. I can't do anything with it.
我是右撇子，左手自然不可能一樣靈巧，光用左手是辦不了什麼事的。

同義字
- ▶ □cleverness n. 靈巧；機敏　　　□adroitness n. 靈巧；機敏
- ▶ □nimbleness n. 靈活；敏捷　　　□agileness n. 靈活；敏捷

反義字
- ▶ □phlegm n. 遲鈍；冷淡　　　□ inertia n. 遲鈍；不活動；懶惰
- ▶ □dilatoriness n. 遲緩；拖延　　　□ sluggishness n. 不活潑；遲緩

diagnose [ˈdaɪəgnoz]　　動 診斷　　　★★★☆☆

After analyzing the test results, the doctor diagnosed him with tuberculosis.
檢查結果經過分析後，醫生診斷他得了結核病。

dialect [ˈdaɪəlɛkt]　　名 方言；土話

Cantonese is a dialect of Chinese that is spoken in the southwest region of China and the Chinatowns of the west.
廣東話是一種流傳於中國西南地區和外國唐人街的方言。

同義字
- ▶ □speech n. 民族語言；方言　　　□idiom n. 方言；土話
- ▶ □patois n. 方言；土語　　　□vernacular n. 本國語；方言

dialogue [ˈdaɪəˌlɔg]　　名 對話、對白　　　★★★★★

Can you rewind the movie? I didn't understand the dialogue between the two characters.

你可以把影片倒帶嗎？那兩個角色之間的對話我不太明白。

dictate [ˈdɪktet]　　動 口授；口述；命令　　★★★★☆

The manager dictated the memo as the secretary wrote it down.
經理口述備忘事項讓秘書記下來。

同義字
▶ □narrate　v.　講述；敘述

difference [ˈdɪfərəns]　　名 差別；差異　　★★★☆☆

The differences between the two products are slight, but one is much more expensive than the other.
這兩種產品之間的差別很小，只不過其中一種比另外一種貴多了。

同義字
▶ □distinction　n.　區別；差別　　□diversity　n.　差異；不同點
▶ □odds　n.　區別；差異；差額　　□variation　n.　差別；差異
▶ □dissimilarity　n.　不同；相異

反義字
▶ □sameness　n.　相同　　□equality　n.　相等；平等；均等

dignitary [ˈdɪgnəˌtɛrɪ]　　名 顯貴；重要人物　　★★★★★

The White House is hosting various dignitaries from around the world, including ambassadors and heads of state.
來自世界各地不同的重要人物，包括各國大使和國家元首在內，都會在白宮內接受招待。

digress [daɪˈgrɛs]　　動 走向岔道；脫離主題

Half way through his speech on banking, Vincent began to digress and talked about his childhood in London.
文森的銀行專題演講講到一半開始脫離主題，談起他在倫敦的童年生活。

dilate [daɪˈlet]　　動 擴大；使膨脹　　★★★★☆

When there is little light, your pupils will dilate to let in more light.
光線不足時，瞳孔就會放大讓更多光線進來。

同義字
▶ □expand　v.　使膨脹；使擴張　　□enlarge　v.　擴大；擴展；放大
▶ □magnify　v.　放大；擴大

反義字
▶ □reduce　v.　減少；縮小；降低　　□narrow　v.　變窄；收縮；減少

dilemma [dəˈlɛmə]　　名 困境；進退兩難　　★★★★★

I have a dilemma; should I stay here to be with my girlfriend, or go abroad to take my dream job?
我現在進退兩難：是應該留下來陪我女朋友，還是出國從事我夢想中的工作？

同義字

▶ ☐predicament　n.　尷尬的處境　　☐fix　n.　困境；窘境

diligent [ˈdɪlədʒənt]　勤勉的；勤奮的　★★★☆☆

Mandy is a diligent worker who finishes all projects she starts.
曼蒂工作勤奮，完成了所有她負責的案子。

同義字
▶ ☐industrious　a.　勤勉的　　　☐assiduous　a.　勤勉的
▶ ☐sedulous　a.　勤勉的　　　　　☐hard-working　a.　努力工作的

反義字
▶ ☐idle　a.　懶惰的；無所事事的　　☐lazy　a.　懶散的；怠惰的
▶ ☐indolent　a.　好逸惡勞的

dilute [daɪˈlut]　稀釋　★★★☆☆

Yuck! This soup is way too salty. You should dilute it with some hot water.
唉！這湯太鹹了。你應該加點熱水把它沖淡一點。

同義字
▶ ☐water　v.　攙水沖淡；加水稀釋

dimly [ˈdɪmlɪ]　昏暗地；朦朧地；模糊地　★★★★☆

It was hard to make out who was in the dimly lit room.
房間裡光線昏暗，看不太出來是誰在裡面。

同義字
▶ ☐duskily　adv.　昏暗地；微黑地　　☐ hazily　adv.　有薄霧地；模糊地
▶ ☐mistily　adv.　朦朧地；含糊地

反義字
▶ ☐clearly　adv.　明亮地；清楚地　　☐ distinctly　adv.　清楚地；清晰地

diplomat [ˈdɪpləmæt]　外交官　★★★★★

The ambassador is the highest diplomat in a foreign country, and can make statements for his government.
大使是外國境內最高級的外交官，可以代表政府發表聲明。

同義字
▶ ☐envoy　n.　使者；外交使節

disapprove [ˌdɪsəˈpruv]　不贊成；不同意；不喜歡　★★★☆☆

My supervisor disapproves of staff sending personal emails while at work.
我主管不贊成員工上班時收發私人電子郵件。

同義字
▶ ☐disfavor　v.　不贊成　　☐oppose　v.　反對
▶ ☐object　v.　反對

反義字
▶ ☐approve　v.　贊成；同意　　☐agree　v.　同意；贊同
▶ ☐assent　v.　同意；贊成

disarm [dɪsˈɑrm] 　動 繳…的械；解除…的武裝 　★★★☆☆

The police officer quickly disarmed the culprit and handcuffed him.
警方迅速解除該名罪犯的武裝，並給他戴上手銬。

discard [dɪsˈkɑrd] 　動 拋棄；摒棄；丟棄 　★★★☆☆

If you don't keep your receipt, please don't throw it onto the floor. Discard it in that bin over there.
就算你不保留收據，也不要丟在地板上。請丟到那邊的箱子裡。

同義字
▶ □abandon　v.　丟棄；拋棄；遺棄　□desert　v.　拋棄；遺棄；離棄
▶ □forsake　v.　拋棄；遺棄；背棄

反義字
▶ □maintain　v.　維持；使繼續　　□retain　v.　保留；保持
▶ □conserve　v.　保存；節省

disciple [dɪˈsaɪpl] 　名 信徒；門徒；追隨者 　★★★★☆

The kung-fu master taught his disciples everything he knew.
功夫大師把一身絕學傾囊相授給自己的門徒。

同義字
▶ □believer　n.　信徒；信教者　　□adherent　n.　追隨者；擁護者
▶ □follower　n.　追隨者；擁護者

discipline [ˈdɪsəplɪn] 　名 紀律；風紀；教養 　★★★★★

This school believes in very strict discipline. If you show up late for class, you must write a one thousand word essay.
這間學校採取非常嚴格的風紀管理，如果你上課遲到，就得寫篇一千字的文章。

discolor [dɪsˈkʌlə] 　動 使變色；使褪色；玷污 　★★★★★

My new rug was discolored from people walking in and out with their dirty shoes on.
我的新地毯因為大家穿著髒鞋進進出出，已經褪色了。

同義字
▶ □fade　v.　（顏色）褪去　　□weather　v.　風化；褪色

discomfort [dɪsˈkʌmfət] 　名 不舒服；不適；不安 　★★★★☆

The discomfort of taking a hot, crowded bus was too much to bear, so Lola got off and hailed down a taxi.
蘿拉受不了搭乘又熱又擠的公車那種不舒服的感覺，於是下車招了輛計程車。

同義字
▶ □disorder　n.　紊亂；不適；小病　□indisposition　n.　不舒服；微恙

反義字
▶ □comfort　n.　安逸；舒適　　□ease　n.　舒適；悠閒

discord [ˈdɪskɔrd] 名不和；爭吵；不一致 ★★★☆☆

The discord between the two nations began when the President of one country insulted the Prime Minister of the other.

兩國之間的不和肇因於，其中一國的總統羞辱了另一國的首相。

同義字
▶ □disagreement n. 爭吵；爭論 □disaccord n. 不和；不一致
▶ □quarrel n. 爭吵；不和；吵鬧

反義字
▶ □harmony n. 和睦；融洽；一致 □concord n. （國際的）和睦
▶ □amicability n. 友善；親善

discredit [dɪsˈkrɛdɪt] 動 使不足信；使丟臉；敗壞⋯的名聲 ★★★★★

The lawyer tried to discredit the witness's testimony by questioning his reputation.

律師想要藉由質疑證人聲望的方式，讓證人的證詞變得不足採信。

同義字
▶ □disgrace v. 使丟臉；使蒙受恥辱 □dishonor v. 使丟臉；使受恥辱
▶ □shame v. 使蒙受羞辱；使丟臉 □humiliate v. 羞辱；使丟臉

反義字
▶ □honor v. 使增光；給⋯以榮譽 □grace v. 使增光

discreet [dɪˈskrit] 形 樸素的；不引人注意的 ★★★★☆

Young lady! That sweater is too revealing! Put on something more discreet.

小姑娘！那件毛衣太露了！加件樸素一點的衣服吧。

同義字
▶ □plain a. 簡樸的；不攙雜的 □severe a. 純潔的；樸素的
▶ □austere a. 樸素的；無裝飾的

反義字
▶ □showy a. 豔麗的 □fancy a. 別緻的；花俏的
▶ □loud a. （衣服顏色等）鮮豔的

discrepancy [dɪˈskrɛpənsɪ] 名不一致；不符；差異；不一致之處 ★★★★★

There was a discrepancy between the price on the tag and the price the cashier charged me, so they had to check to see which was correct.

出納員的索價和標籤上的價格不符，所以必須查一查哪邊才是對的。

同義字
▶ □conflict n. 衝突；抵觸；矛盾 □incompatibility n. 矛盾
▶ □discrepancy n. 不一致；不符 □repugnance n. 矛盾；抵觸

discriminate [dɪˈskrɪməˌnet] 動區別；辨別 ★★★☆☆

You should discriminate among the options available, and choose the best one.

你必須辨別各個選項的差異，然後選出一個最好的。

同義字

▶ □separate　v.　區分；識別　　　□distinguish　v.　區別；識別
▶ □differentiate　v.　區別；區分

反義字
▶ □confuse　v.　把…混同；混淆

discussion [dɪ'skʌʃən]　　名討論；商討；談論　★★★★☆

Mom and dad are having a serious discussion on whether to move to Florida or not.
爸媽正在認真討論究竟要不要搬到佛羅里達州。

同義字
▶ □canvass　n.　討論　　　□talking　n.　講話；談話；討論

disinfect [ˌdɪsɪn'fɛkt]　　動將…消毒（或殺菌）　★★★☆☆

This soap will disinfect your hands, killing all harmful bacteria.
這塊肥皂會消毒你的手，把所有有害的細菌都給殺死。

同義字
▶ □sterilize　v.　使無菌；消毒　　　□asepticize　v.　使無菌；消毒

dismiss [dɪs'mɪs]　　動免…的職；解雇；開除　★★★★★

He was dismissed from his job for swearing at customers.
他因為對客人罵髒話而遭解雇。

同義字
▶ □fire　v.　解雇；開除　□sack　v.　開除；解雇
▶ □lay off　解雇 □kick out　解雇

反義字
▶ □employ　v.　雇用　　　□hire　v.　雇用；租用
▶ □engage　v.　雇；聘

dismount [dɪs'maʊnt]　　動下車；下馬　★★★☆☆

Please be careful when you dismount the horse. Just call me and I'll help you down.
下馬時請小心。乾脆打電話給我，我就來幫你下馬。

反義字
▶ □mount　v.　使上馬（或車）

disobedient [ˌdɪsə'bidɪənt]　　形不服從的；違抗命令的；違反（規則等）的 ★★★★☆

Jimmy is a disobedient student who disobeys every rule the teacher sets.
吉米是個不聽話的學生，老師規定的每件事都不遵從。

同義字
▶ □incompliant　a.　不順從的　　　□defiant　a.　違抗的；蔑視的
▶ □indocile　a.　不聽話的　　　□forward　a.　難駕馭的；剛愎的

反義字
▶ □compliant　a.　順從的　　　□obedient　a.　服從的；順從的

▶ □submissive　a.　柔順的　　　　□passive　a.　順從的；順服的

disparity [dɪsˈpærətɪ]　🔲不同；不等　　★★★☆☆

There is tremendous disparity between the rich and the poor. The rich own several mansions, while the poor sleep on the street.
貧富之間的差距相當懸殊。富人房子好幾棟，窮人則是睡在馬路上。

同義字
▶ □difference　n.　差別；差異　　　□distinction　n.　區別；差別
▶ □diversity　n.　差異；不同點　　　□variation　n.　差別；差異
▶ □dissimilarity　n.　不同；相異

反義字
▶ □sameness　n.　相同　　□equality　n.　相等；平等；均等

disqualify [dɪsˈkwɑləˌfaɪ]　🔲取消⋯的資格　　★★★★★

This scholarship is for people under 18. Being over 20 disqualifies you from it.
未滿 18 歲才能申請這項獎學金，你已超過 20 歲，資格不符。

反義字
▶ □qualify　v.　使具有資格；使合格

disrupt [dɪsˈrʌpt]　🔲使中斷；使混亂　　★★★★☆

A loud knock at the door disrupted our meeting.
有人大聲敲門，把我們的會議給打斷。

同義字
▶ □interrupt　v.　打斷；中斷　　　□break into　打斷
▶ □cut short　打斷

dissect [dɪˈsɛkt]　🔲解剖；切開　　★★★☆☆

In biology class, we dissected a frog to study its organs.
上生物課時，我們解剖青蛙研究它的器官。

同義字
▶ □anatomize　v.　解剖；分解

disseminate [dɪˈsɛməˌnet]　🔲散播；宣傳　　★★★★★

This TV station is owned by the government, and disseminates government propaganda.
這家電視台是政府經營的，會播放政府各項宣傳活 。

同義字
▶ □air　v.　廣播；播送　　□propagate　v.　傳播；使普及
▶ □propagandize　v.　進行宣傳

dissent [dɪˈsɛnt]　🔲不同意；異議　　★★★★★

Dissent among the crew soon led to a mutiny against the ship's captain.

船員之間缺乏共識的結果，很快導致船員對船長發動叛變。

同義字
- ▶ □division　n.　（意見等的）不一致　　　　□disagreement　n.　意見不一
- ▶ □objection　n.　反對；異議

反義字
- ▶ □agreement　n.　同意；一致　　　　□approval　n.　贊成；同意
- ▶ □assent　n.　同意；贊成

dissertation　[ˌdɪsəˈteʃən]　图博士論文；專題論文；學術演講　★★★★☆

After two years writing his Master's dissertation, Clark must defend it in front of a panel.
克拉克在耗時兩年撰寫他的碩士論文之後，必須在委員會面前接受口試。

同義字
- ▶ □thesis　n.　論文；畢業論文　　　□paper　n.　論文；報告

dissipate　[ˈdɪsəˌpet]　勔消散；消失　★★★★★

The crowd began to dissipate when the lights went out, signaling the end of the show.
燈光熄滅、人群散去，代表表演結束了。

同義字
- ▶ □scatter　v.　消散；分散　　　□disperse　v.　驅散；疏散

反義字
- ▶ □assemble　v.　集合；聚集　　　□gather　v.　收集；召集

dissolve　[dɪˈzɑlv]　勔溶解；融化；液化　★★★☆☆

Stir your coffee so that the sugar can dissolve faster.
咖啡要攪拌一下，糖才會融化得更快。

同義字
- ▶ □melt　v.　融化；熔化　　□liquefy　v.　（使）液化

distinction　[dɪˈstɪŋkʃən]　图優秀；卓越；區別　★★★★★

Nadia got 86% and graduated with honors, but Jeff received honors with distinction for his mark of 98%.
娜迪亞拿到 86 分，以優秀成績畢業，但傑夫拿到 98 分，以優異成績畢業。

同義字
- ▶ □excellence　n.　優秀；傑出　　　□superiority　n.　優越；優勢

反義字
- ▶ □inferiority　n.　劣勢；劣等；下等

distort　[dɪsˈtɔrt]　勔扭曲；扭歪　★★★★☆

The unethical used car salesman distorted information on the vehicle just to make a sale.
這名不道德的二手車推銷員，為了賣車不惜歪曲車訊。

同義字
- ▶ □twist　v.　歪曲；曲解　　　　□contort　v.　扭曲；曲解
- ▶ □misrepresent　v.　誤傳；歪曲　□falsify　v.　竄改；偽造

diversity [daɪˈvɝsətɪ] 图 1. 多樣性　2. 差異；不同點　★★★☆☆

Canada is a country known for its diversity. It accepts people from around the world, regardless of skin color or language.
加拿大是個以多樣性著稱的國家，世界各地的人不分膚色或語言，都可以在那裡定居。

同義字
- ▶ □variety　n.　多樣化；變化　　□multiplicity　n.　多樣性

反義字
- ▶ □monotony　n.　（聲音等的）單調　□dullness　n.　乏味；單調

divert [daɪˈvɝt] 勔 使轉向；使改道　★★★★☆

The police are diverting traffic to Highway 2 because of the huge collision on Highway 1.
由於一號公路發生大車禍，警方便讓車輛改道二號公路。

同義字
- ▶ □veer　v.　改變方向；轉向

divisible [dəˈvɪzəbḷ] 形 可除盡的　★★★☆☆

Thirteen is a prime number because it is only divisible by the number 1 and itself.
13 是質數，因為它只能被數字 1 和本身除盡。

divulge [dəˈvʌldʒ] 勔 洩露；暴露　★★★★☆

Steve had kept the secret hidden for years, until finally divulging it all while under hypnosis.
史蒂夫埋藏這個秘密已經很多年，最後是在催眠狀態下才全盤吐露。

同義字
- ▶ □reveal　v.　揭露；洩露　　　　□disclose　v.　揭發；公開
- ▶ □betray　v.　洩漏；透露　　　　□let out　洩漏

反義字
- ▶ □conceal　v.　隱蔽；隱瞞　　　□hide　v.　隱瞞；隱藏
- ▶ □suppress　v.　隱瞞；藏匿　　　□withhold　v.　不吐露

docile [ˈdɑsḷ] 形 馴服的；易駕御的　★★★★★

A bear may look cute and docile, but it can kill you if it wants to.
熊或許看起來既可愛又溫馴，但它想殺你可是輕而易舉。

同義字
- ▶ □tame　a.　溫順的；聽使喚的　□ tractable　a.　馴良的；易處理的
- ▶ □meek　a.　溫順的；柔順的

反義字
- ▶ □wild　a.　野的；難駕馭的　　　□untamed　a.　未馴服的

dominance [ˈdɑmənəns] 　　n. 優勢；支配（地位）；統治（地位）
★★★☆☆

The company sells 98% of all cell phones in the country, but its dominance is now being challenged by several smaller companies.
這家公司的手機在國內有 98% 的市占率，但這種優勢如今受到好幾家小型公司的挑戰。

同義字
▶ □ascendancy　n.　優勢；優越　　□supremacy　n.　優勢
▶ □superiority　n.　優越；優勢

反義字
▶ □inferiority　n.　劣勢；劣等；次級

donate [ˈdonet] 　　v. 捐獻；捐贈
★★★☆☆

Would you like to donate some money to help families in need?
你想捐點錢幫助窮困家庭嗎？

同義字
▶ □contribute　v.　捐（款）；捐獻；捐助　　□subscribe　v.　認捐；捐款

drain [dren] 　　n. 排水管
★★★★☆

The soup isn't good anymore. Throw out the vegetables and pour the rest down the drain.
湯已經不好喝了。先把裡面的蔬菜丟掉，再把剩下的湯倒到排水管。

同義字
▶ □sewer　n.　污水管；下水道；陰溝

反義字
▶ □conduit　n.　導水管；導管　　□duct　n.　輸送管；導管

drought [draʊt] 　　n. 乾旱；旱災
★★★★★

The drought dried up most of the farmland, causing widespread famine.
大部分農田都因旱災而乾涸，結果造成大饑荒。

同義字
▶ □aridity　n.　乾旱；乾燥

反義字
▶ □flood　n.　洪水；水災

drowsy [ˈdraʊzɪ] 　　a. 昏昏欲睡的；困倦的
★★★☆☆

That cold medicine made me really drowsy. I want to take a nap before driving home.
吃了那個感冒藥讓我覺得好睏，我要先小睡一下再開車回家。

同義字
▶ □sleepy　a.　想睡的；瞌睡的　　□dozy　a.　想睡的
▶ □nodding　a.　昏昏欲睡的　　□somnolent　a.　想睡的

反義字
▶ □awake　a.　醒著的；清醒的　　□conscious　a.　神智清醒的

▶ □wakeful　a.　不眠的；失眠的

drudgery　[ˈdrʌdʒərɪ]　🔲苦工；賤役；單調沈悶的工作　★★★★☆

The drudgery of working 9 to 5 at the factory for 30 years finally led Mickey to quit and go traveling.
米奇做了三十年朝九晚五的工廠單調工作後，終於辭職旅行去了。

【同義字】
▶ □toil　n.　辛苦；勞累；苦工；難事　　　　□sweat　n.　苦差事

dubious　[ˈdjubɪəs]　🔲可疑的；引起懷疑的　★★★★★

Call security. A dubious fellow with a fake moustache and long trench coat just walked in to the store.
快叫警衛過來。剛才有個戴著假鬍、穿著長軍用雨衣的可疑男子走進店裡了。

【同義字】
▶ □suspicious　a.　可疑的　　　　□doubtful　a.　令人生疑的
▶ □suspect　a.　受到懷疑的　　　□questionable　a.　可疑的

【反義字】
▶ □undoubted　a.　無容置疑的　　　□unquestionab　a.　毫無疑問的

dump　[dʌmp]　🔲傾倒；拋棄　★★★☆☆

The garbage truck carried the trash across the city and dumped it at the landfill.
垃圾車把城裡的垃圾運走，再倒到垃圾掩埋場裡。

【同義字】
▶ □abandon　v.　丟棄；拋棄　　　　□discard　v.　拋棄；摒棄
▶ □desert　v.　拋棄；遺棄　　　　　□forsake　v.　拋棄；遺棄；背棄

【反義字】
▶ □maintain　v.　維持；使繼續　　　□retain　v.　保留；保持
▶ □conserve　v.　保存；保護

duration　[djʊˈreʃən]　🔲持續；持久；持續期間　★★★★★

The front doors will be closed for the duration of the performance. If you have to leave during the concert, use the back doors.
音樂會演出期間前門會關閉，中途想離開的話請走後門。

【同義字】
▶ □period　n.　時期；期間　　　　□ length　n.　（時間的）長短
▶ □continuance　n.　繼續；持續

dutiful　[ˈdjutɪfəl]　🔲忠於職守的；盡本分的；恭順的；順從的　★★★☆☆

The dutiful son quit his job in the city to take care of his ailing parents in the country.
這個孝順兒子辭掉了城裡的工作，到鄉下照顧他體弱的雙親。

【同義字】
▶ □submissive　a.　服從的；柔順的　□differential　a.　恭敬的

▶ □obedient　a.　服從的；恭順的　　□filial　a.　孝順的

反義字
▶ □disobedient　a.　違抗命令的　　□defiant　a.　違抗的；挑戰的
▶ □haughty　a.　高傲的；自大的　　□perverse　a.　倔強的

dwindle　[ˈdwɪndl̩]　🔊漸漸減少；變小　★★★★☆

Our vast supply of money has dwindled down to only a few dollars.
我們巨額的生活費漸漸變少，最後只剩幾塊錢。

同義字
▶ □reduce　v.　減少；縮小；降低　　□shrink　v.　變少；變小
▶ □decrease　v.　減少；減小　　□diminish　v.　減少；縮減
▶ □lessen　v.　變小；變少

反義字
▶ □increase　v.　增大；增強　　□add　v.　增加

以E為首的單字

5 顆★：金色（860~990）證書必背
4 顆★：藍色（730~855）證書必背
3 顆★：綠色（470~725）證書必背

MP3-07

eccentric　[ɪkˈsɛntrɪk]　🔊古怪的；反常的　★★★★★

The eccentric old man lives alone on the mountain, and creates art out of broken bottles and bottle caps.
那名古怪老人在山上獨居，並利用破瓶和破瓶蓋創作藝術。

同義字
▶ □freak　a.　反常的；怪異的　　□quaint　a.　古怪的
▶ □odd　a.　奇特的；古怪的　　□queer　a.　奇怪的；古怪的

反義字
▶ □normal　a.　正常的；身心健全的

eclipse　[ɪˈklɪps]　🔊蝕　★★★☆☆

A lunar eclipse occurs when the moon passes into the Earth's shadow.
月亮經過地球的陰影帶時，月蝕就會發生。

economize　[ɪˈkɑnəˌmaɪz]　🔊節約；節省　★★★☆☆

While I'm looking for a job, I try to economize by walking instead of bussing, and cooking instead of eating out.
找工作期間為了多省一點錢，我都走路而不搭公車，三餐也是自己開伙而不吃外食。

同義字
▶ □save　v.　節省；省去　　□retrench　v.　節省；節約
▶ □conserve　v.　節省；保存　　□spare　v.　節約；儉省

反義字
▶ □waste　v.　浪費；濫用　　□squander　v.　浪費；揮霍
▶ □consume　v.　揮霍；浪費

edible [ˈɛdəbl̩]　　形 可食的；食用的　　★★★★★

This plant isn't edible unless first cooked.
這種植物要先煮過才可以吃。

同義字
▶ □eatable　a.　食用的　　　□esculent　a.　適於食用的
▶ □comestible　a.　可食的

反義字
▶ □inedible　a.　不可食的　□uneatable　a.　不能吃的

editor [ˈɛdɪtɚ]　　名 編輯；（報刊專欄的）主筆　　★★★★☆

The newspaper editor changed the reporter's article's first paragraph before publishing it.
報社編輯改了記者文章的第一段後才加以刊登。

反義字
▶ □redactor　n.　編輯者；修訂者　　□compiler　n.　編輯者

effect [ɪˈfɛkt]　　名 效果；效力；作用；影響　　★★★☆☆

The medication had an immediate effect on my headache.
這種藥對我的頭痛有立即的效果。

同義字
▶ □influence　n.　影響；作用　　　□efficacy　n.　效力；功效
▶ □impression　n.　影響；效果

反義字
▶ □ineffectiveness　n.　不起作用　　□invalidation　n.　無效

efficient [ɪˈfɪʃənt]　　形 效率高的；有能力的；能勝任的　　★★★★★

Kim is an efficient worker who accomplishes more in a day than all other workers combined.
金姆工作很有效率，一天之內做完的工作比其他所有員工加起來還要多。

同義字
▶ □competent　a.　稱職的　　　　□qualified　a.　具備必要條件的
▶ □capable　a.　有才華的

反義字
▶ □incompetent　a.　不能勝任的　　□inadequate　a.　不夠格的
▶ □incapable　a.　不能勝任的　　　□unqualified　a.　不夠資格的

effrontery [ɛfˈrʌntərɪ]　　名 厚顏無恥；放肆　　★★★☆☆

I can't believe he would have the effrontery to disrespect the CEO like that.
我不敢相信他會那麼放肆，居然對執行長如此沒禮貌。

同義字
▶ □discourtesy　n.　粗魯的言行　　□rudeness　n.　無禮貌
▶ □impoliteness　n.　無禮；粗魯　　□insolence　n.　傲慢；無禮

▶ □audacity　n.　魯莽；厚顏無恥

反義字
▶ □deference　n.　敬意；尊敬　　□respect　n.　尊敬；敬重
▶ □homage　n.　尊敬；敬意；崇敬　□reverence　n.　敬愛；崇敬

ego [ˈigo]　名 1. 自我；自我意識　2. 自尊心；自負　★★★★☆

He has an enormous ego, so give him plenty of compliments.
他的自尊心很強，所以多給他一點讚美吧。

同義字
▶ □self　n.　自身；自己；自我　　□self-awareness　n.　自我意識
▶ □pride　n.　自尊心　　　　　　　□self-respect　n.　自尊心；自重
▶ □self-esteem　n.　自尊；自負

egregious [ɪˈgridʒəs]　形 極壞的；非常的；震驚的　★★★★★

His attack on the other football player was so egregious that he was not only penalized on the field, but also in the courts.
他對另一名橄欖球選手的攻擊手段過於惡劣，不僅被罰禁賽，還要負法律責任。

同義字
▶ □awful　a.　極壞的；極糟的　　□abominable　a.　糟透的
▶ □dreadful　a.　非常討厭的　　　□odious　a.　可憎的

反義字
▶ □wonderful　a.　極好的；精彩的　□ fantastic　a.　極好的；了不起的
▶ □fabulous　a.　極好的　　　　　　□gorgeous　a.　令人十分愉快的
▶ □magnificent　a.　極好的

eject [ɪˈdʒɛkt]　名 退出鍵　動 驅逐；逐出　★★★☆☆

Your DVD is in the DVD player. Just press eject to get it out.
你的 DVD 放在 DVD 播放機裡，按退出鍵就會看到。

elapse [ɪˈlæps]　動（時間）過去；消逝　★★★☆☆

Not enough time has elapsed for me to forget my ex-girlfriend.
逝去的時光還沒有久到讓我忘了前女友。

同義字
▶ □pass　v.　（時間）推移；流逝　□glide　v.　（時間等）悄悄地消逝

element [ˈɛləmənt]　名 要素；成分　★★★★☆

Key elements in a good player are speed, strength, and the determination to win.
要成為一名好球員，關鍵要素在於：速度、力量，和那分必勝的決心。

同義字
▶ □factor　n.　因素；要素　　□constituent　n.　成分
▶ □ingredient　n.　要素；因素

eligible [ˈɛlɪdʒəbl]　形 有資格的；法律上合格的　★★★☆☆

When you turn 18, you will be eligible to vote.
你只要滿十八歲就有資格投票。

同義字
▶ □qualified　a.　具備必要條件的

反義字
▶ □ineligible　a.　無資格的　　　　□unqualified　a.　不夠資格的

eliminate　[ɪ'lɪmə,net]　　動（比賽中）淘汰　　★★★☆☆

Christine was eliminated from the tournament when she lost in the semi-finals.
克莉斯汀在半準決賽中失利後即慘遭淘汰，無緣再參加錦標賽。

同義字
▶ □knock out　淘汰

反義字
▶ □promote　v.　晉級

eloquent　['ɛləkwənt]　　形雄辯的；有說服力的　　★★★★★

Otis's eloquent speech swayed the audience toward his point of view.
奧提斯的滔滔雄辯讓聽眾開始倒向他的觀點。

同義字
▶ □convincing　a.　有說服力的　　□forceful　a.　有說服力的
▶ □potent　a.　有說服力的　　　　□silver-tongued　a.　雄辯的

反義字
▶ □ineloquent　a.　不善言辭的　　□inconvincible　a.　無法使人信服的

elude　[ɪ'lud]　　動（巧妙地）逃避；躲避　　★★★★☆

The fugitive eluded the police for days after his prison escape, but was finally caught trying to leave town on the train.
該名逃犯越獄後，連續幾天都避開了警方的追捕，但終究在企圖坐火車出城時被抓到。

同義字
▶ □avoid　v.　避開；躲開　　　　□evade　v.　躲避；逃避
▶ □shun　v.　躲開；避開；迴避　　□eschew　v.　避免；避開
▶ □dodge　v.　躲避；巧妙地迴避

反義字
▶ □face　v.　面臨；正視　　　　　□ confront　v.　勇敢地面對；對抗

emaciated　[ɪ'meʃɪ,etɪd]　　形消瘦的；憔悴的；衰弱的　　★★★☆☆

The emaciated little boy had not eaten for days, and was only relying on the charity of others for his survival.
這名憔悴的小男孩幾天沒吃東西了，唯有靠別人施捨才能活下去。

同義字
▶ □gaunt　a.　憔悴的；枯瘦的　　□haggard　a.　憔悴的
▶ □peaky　a.　瘦削的；虛弱的

反義字

▶ □brisk　a.　活潑的；生氣勃勃的　　□spirited　a.　活潑的
▶ □vital　a.　生氣勃勃的

emanate [ˈɛməˌnet]　勔（氣體等）發出、散發；放射　★★★☆☆

The heat emanating from the fireplace warmed up the entire room.
壁爐散發的熱氣讓整個房間溫暖起來。

同義字
▶ □transpire　v.　散發；蒸發；排出

emancipate [ɪˈmænsəˌpet]　勔解放；使不受束縛　★★★★★

Abraham Lincoln emancipated slaves in 1863. From that date on, they were free.
亞伯拉罕‧林肯在 1863 年解放黑奴；從那天起，奴隸便重獲自由。

同義字
▶ □free　v.　使自由；解放　　□liberate　v.　解放；使獲自由
▶ □deliver　v.　解救；解脫；釋放　　□ affranchise　v.　恢復自由；釋放

embargo [ɪmˈbɑrgo]　名禁止（或限制）買賣；港令；禁運　★★★★☆

The United States has an embargo on Cuba, thereby restricting all American companies from doing business in Cuba.
美國對古巴實行禁運，從而限定所有的美國公司不能在古巴做生意。

同義字
▶ □prohibition　n.　禁令　　□ban　n.　禁止；禁令

embark [ɪmˈbɑrk]　勔從事；著手；出發（旅行）　★★★☆☆

Now that my bags are packed, I'm ready to embark on my journey from Istanbul to Katmandu.
既然已打包完畢，我便隨時準備踏上伊斯坦堡到加德滿都的旅程。

同義字
▶ □depart　v.　起程；出發　　□start　v.　出發；起程

embarrass [ɪmˈbærəs]　勔使窘迫；使不好意思；使侷促不安　★★★☆☆

I'm so embarrassed! I just went up on stage with my pant's zipper open!
好糗哦！我登上舞臺後才發現褲子拉鍊沒拉。

同義字
▶ □disconcert　v.　使困窘　　□abash　v.　使不安；使羞愧

embellish [ɪmˈbɛlɪʃ]　勔美化；裝飾　★★★★★

His story isn't a lie, but it sure was embellished to make himself look good.
他的故事不假，只不過一定有經過修飾，讓自己看起來比較過得去。

同義字
▶ □beautify　v.　使更加美麗；美化　　□prettify　v.　美化；修飾
▶ □glorify　v.　美化；使增添光輝　　□adorn　v.　裝飾；使生色

embezzle [ɪmˈbɛzl]　勔盜用；侵佔　★★★★☆

The dirty accountant has embezzled thousands of dollars of the company's money.
這個卑鄙的會計師侵佔了無數的公款。

同義字
▶ □misappropriate　v.　侵佔；盜用

emblem [ˈɛmbləm]　🔳徽章；符號；紋章圖案　★★★☆☆

The emblem on his sleeve signifies that he's with the United States Marines.
他袖子上的徽章代表他是美國海軍陸戰隊的一員。

同義字
▶ □badge　n. 徽章；獎章；紀念章　□insignia　n. 表示階級用的佩章

embody [ɪmˈbɑdɪ]　🔳體現；使具體化　★★★☆☆

The constitution embodies everything the country believes in.
這部憲法體現了該國所相信的一切價值。

同義字
▶ □incarnate　v.　使具體化；體現

embolden [ɪmˈboldn̩]　🔳使大膽；使有勇氣　★★★★☆

Early success in his political career emboldened him to seek for the presidency.
他的政治生涯早年得志，讓他有勇氣參選總統。

同義字
▶ □inspire　v.　鼓舞；激勵；驅使　□animate　v.　激勵；鼓舞

embroil [ɛmˈbrɔɪl]　🔳使混亂；使捲入糾紛　★★★★★

Grant wanted to have a quiet dinner with his ex-wife, but they were embroiled in an argument as soon as he came through the door.
葛蘭特原本想要安靜地和他前妻吃頓晚飯，可是他才一進門，他們就陷入一場爭論當中。

同義字
▶ □involve　v.　使捲入；連累；牽涉

emerge [ɪˈmɝdʒ]　🔳1. 浮現；出現 2.（從困境等中）擺脫；出頭　★★★☆☆

One hundred golfers will start the tournament, but only one will emerge as the champion.
一個高爾夫球選手角逐錦標賽，但能嶄露頭角成為冠軍的只有一人。

同義字
▶ □appear　v.　出現；現露　　　　□occur　v.　發生；出現
▶ □figure　v.　出現；露頭角

反義字
▶ □submerge　v.　潛入水中；淹沒　□lurk　v.　潛伏；埋伏

emigrate [ˈɛməˌgret]　🔳移居外國（或外地區）　★★★☆☆

Every year, millions of people emigrate from one place to another in search of a better life.

為了追求更美好的生活，每年都有成千上萬的人從甲地移居到乙地。

同義字
▶ □migrate　v.　遷移；移居　　　□expatriate　v.　使移居國外
▶ □transmigrate　v.　移居

反義字
▶ □immigrate　v.　遷移；遷入

eminent ［ˈɛmənənt］　形（地位；學識等方面）出眾的；卓越的；著名的　★★★★☆

Dr. Wong is an eminent chemist whose work is followed by people around the world.

王博士是名傑出的化學家，其研究成果深受全球矚目。

同義字
▶ □distinguished　a.　卓越的　　□outstanding　a.　顯著的
▶ □brilliant　a.　傑出的；出色的　□remarkable　a.　值得注意的
▶ □sublime　a.　超群的；出眾的

反義字
▶ □nameless　a.　默默無聞的　　□unknown　a.　不知道的
▶ □recondite　a.　默默無聞的；隱藏的

emit ［ɪˈmɪt］　動散發；放射；發出　★★★★★

This little light bulb doesn't emit enough light. We need something brighter.

這顆小燈泡發出的光不夠亮，我們需要更亮的照明才行。

同義字
▶ □radiate　v.　（光、熱等）散發　□emanate　v.　（氣體等）發出

emphasis ［ˈɛmfəsɪs］　名強調；重視；重點　★★★☆☆

Professor Chou taught many things in writing class, but the emphasis was on research and practice.

周教授的寫作課雖然教了很多東西，但重點擺在研究和練習方面。

同義字
▶ □stress　n.　強調；著重　　　□accent　n.　強調；著重

employee ［ˌɛmplɔɪˈi］　名受僱者；僱工；雇員；從業員工　★★★★☆

There's too much work to do for just the two of us. We need to hire a new employee to help with general office duties.

工作太多了，只有我們兩個一定做不完。我們得雇用一名新員工來幫忙處理一般性的辦公室雜務才行。

同義字
▶ □worker　n.　工人；勞工；勞動者　　　□hired hand　雇工；傭工
▶ □personnel　n.　（總稱）人員

反義字
▶ □employer　n.　雇主；雇用者　　　□boss　n.　老板；上司；主人

▶ □proprietor　n.　所有人；經營者

employer　[ɪmˈplɔɪɚ]　图雇主；雇用者　★★★☆☆

Clint gave his employer two weeks' notice before leaving the job.
克林特離職前兩個禮拜便通知了他的雇主。

同義字
▶ □boss　n.　老板；上司；主人　　□proprietor　n.　所有人；業主

反義字
▶ □employee　n.　受雇者；雇員；　□worker　n.　工人；勞工
▶ □hired hand　雇工；傭工　　□personnel　n.　（總稱）人員

emporium　[ɛmˈpɔrɪəm]　图大百貨店；商店　★★★★★

There's a jade emporium downtown with an excellent collection of jade jewelry and statues.
城裡有家翡翠商店，收藏了很多一流的翡翠首飾和雕像。

同義字
▶ □store　n.　店鋪；大商店　　□outlet　n.　銷路；商店；商行

empower　[ɪmˈpaʊɚ]　勔授權；准許　★★★☆☆

Management empowered all factory workers to do whatever it takes to save time or money.
資方准許所有工廠人員，只要能省時和省錢，怎麼做都行。

同義字
▶ □allow　v.　允許；准許　□permit　v.　允許；許可；准許
▶ □authorize　v.　批准；認可

反義字
▶ □prohibit　v.　禁止　　□forbid　v.　禁止；不許
▶ □ban　v.　禁止

emulate　[ˈɛmjəˌlet]　勔同…競爭；盡力趕上；仿真　★★★★☆

You should try to emulate your elder brother because he's so successful.
你哥哥那麼成功，你應該努力迎頭趕上才對。

同義字
▶ □imitate　v.　以…做為範例　　□compete　v.　競爭；對抗；比賽
▶ □catch up with　趕上

encompass　[ɪnˈkʌmpəs]　勔圍繞；包圍　★★★★★

The field is encompassed on all sides by a wooden fence.
這座農場四面都用木頭籬笆圍了起來。

同義字
▶ □encircle　v.　環繞；包圍　　□surround　v.　圍；圍繞；圈住
▶ □enclose　v.　圍住；圈起

encore ['aŋkor] 名要求加演；加演；加演曲目 ★★★☆☆

After playing a full 20 song set, the band came back for an encore that lasted fifteen minutes.
表演完整整二十首曲目後，該樂團又因為觀眾要求加演而回來多表演了十五分鐘。

encourage [ɪnˈkɝɪdʒ] 動鼓勵；助長；激發；慫恿 ★★★★☆

Coach Kevin encouraged the team to win with an inspirational story.
凱文教練用一個鼓舞人心的故事來激勵球隊取得勝利。

同義字
- ▶ □urge　v.　催促；力勸；激勵　　□inspire　v.　鼓舞；激勵；驅使
- ▶ □hearten　v.　激勵；鼓舞　　□cheer on　鼓勵

反義字
- ▶ □discourage　v.　使洩氣□frustrate　v.　挫敗；阻撓
- ▶ □depress　v.　使沮喪　□deject　v.　使沮喪；使灰心

encroach [ɪnˈkrotʃ] 動侵入；侵佔 ★★★★★

Hunters from the neighboring tribe have been encroaching on our traditional hunting grounds.
鄰近部落的獵人一直在侵佔我們的傳統獵場。

同義字
- ▶ □intrude　v.　侵入；闖入；侵擾　□interfere　v.　干涉；干預
- ▶ □infringe　v.　侵犯；侵害　　□ trespass　v.　侵入；侵害；侵犯
- ▶ □invade　v.　侵入；侵略；侵犯

encyclopedia [ɪnˌsaɪkləˈpidɪə] 名百科全書；大全 ★★★☆☆

The Encyclopedia Britannica is an excellent source of information on any topic.
大英百科全書無所不包，乃查詢資料的最佳工具書。

同義字
- ▶ □cyclopedia　n.　百科全書

endanger [ɪnˈdendʒɚ] 形快要絕種的 ★★★★☆

Panda bears were once endangered animals on the verge of extinction, but now there are many pandas living in the wild.
熊貓一度瀕臨絕種，但現在已有許多熊貓生活在荒野之中。

endemic [ɛnˈdɛmɪk] 形某地特有的 ★★★☆☆

This plant is endemic to this mountain, and can be found nowhere else on earth.
這種植物是這座山特有的，世界上任何其他地方都找不到。

反義字
- ▶ □exotic　a.　外來的；外國產的

endure [ɪnˈdjʊr] 動忍耐；忍受 ★★★★★

The family endured four years of hardship when there was little to eat and nothing to look forward to.
這家人忍受了四年三餐不繼、前途渺茫的艱苦歲月。

同義字
▶ □undergo　v.　經歷；經受；忍受　　　□bear　v.　忍受；承受
▶ □stand　v.　忍受；容忍　　　　　　　□tolerate　v.　忍受；容忍
▶ □put up with　忍受；容忍

energetic　[ˌɛnɚˈdʒɛtɪk]　形精力旺盛的；精神飽滿的　　★★★★☆

Tony is an energetic young man who jogs 10 km each morning, works for 9 hours, and then plays soccer in the evenings.
東尼是個精力旺盛的年輕人，他每天早上慢跑十公里，一天工作九小時，晚上還要踢足球。

同義字
▶ □vigorous　a.　精力充沛的　　　□dynamic　a.　有活力的
▶ □active　a.　活躍的；活潑的　　　□lively　a.　精力充沛的
▶ □vivacious　a.　活潑的

反義字
▶ □inactive　a.　不活動的　　　□slothful　a.　怠惰的；懶散的
▶ □torpid　a.　不活潑的；遲鈍的

engrave　[ɪnˈgrev]　動雕刻；刻　　★★★☆☆

The couple engraved their names on their wedding rings.
這對夫妻把他們的名字刻在結婚戒指上。

同義字
▶ □carve　v.　刻；雕刻　　　□inscribe　v.　刻；雕

engross　[ɪnˈgros]　動使全神貫注（+in）　　★★★☆☆

Pam is totally engrossed in her work, and nothing will distract her until she's finished.
潘全神貫注在工作上，工作沒做完前，任何事都無法讓她分心。

同義字
▶ □concentrate　v.　全神貫注　　　□absorb　v.　使全神貫注
▶ □preoccupy　v.　使入神

反義字
▶ □distract　v.　使分心；使轉向　　　□stray　v.　離題；偏離；分心

enhance　[ɪnˈhæns]　動提高；增加（價值、品質、吸引力等）　　★★★★☆

Red wine enhances your enjoyment of meat dishes, but may not go well with fish.
紅酒配肉會增加肉味，但不適合配魚。

同義字
▶ □improve　v.　改進；改善　　　□better　v.　改善；改進

反義字
▶ □worsen　v.　（使）惡化　　　□impair　v.　削弱；減少
▶ □deteriorate　v.　惡化　　　　□deprave　v.　使墮落；使惡化

enigma [ɪˈnɪgmə] 名謎；難以理解的事物 ★★★★★

This is an enigma that has left detectives baffled for years.
多名偵探都被這個謎困了好幾年。

同義字
- □riddle n. 謎；難題
- □mystery n. 難以理解的事物；謎
- □puzzle n. 難題；謎
- □conundrum n. 謎語；難題

enlist [ɪnˈlɪst] 動從軍；入伍；應募 ★★★★☆

Instead of going to university, Joe enlisted in the military to fight for his country.
喬不繼續唸大學，反而選擇從軍來為國奮戰。

同義字
- □enroll v. 參加；入學
- □join up 入伍

反義字
- □demobiliz v. 退伍

enormous [ɪˈnɔrməs] 形巨大的；龐大的 ★★★☆☆

The Gates live in an enormous mansion rivaling the castles of Europe.
蓋茲一家人住在可媲美歐洲城堡的巨大宅邸裡面。

同義字
- □giant a. 巨人般的；巨大的
- □immense a. 無邊無際的
- □huge a. 龐大的；巨大的
- □vast a. 巨大的；龐大的
- □tremendous a. 巨大的

反義字
- □tiny a. 極小的；微小的
- □wee a. 極小的；很小的

entail [ɪnˈtel] 動需要；使承擔 ★★★☆☆

This job entails a lot of overtime, so be prepared if you're going to take it.
這分工作需要常常加班，要做的話就要先有心理準備。

同義字
- □involve v. 需要；包含；意味著
- □take v. 需要；花費；佔用

entangled [ɪnˈtæŋgld] 形被纏住的；捲入的；陷入的 ★★★★☆

The fly became entangled in the spider web, and could not escape.
蒼蠅被蜘蛛網纏住而無法逃脫。

同義字
- □involved a. 糾纏的；牽扯在內的
- □trapped a. 陷入困境的

enthrall [ɪnˈθrɔl] 動迷住；吸引住 ★★★★★

The magician enthralled the audience with one mesmerizing trick after another.
這名魔術師用一個接一個的催眠戲法吸引觀眾目光。

同義字
- □captivate v. 使著迷；打
- □charm v. 使陶醉；吸引

▶ □fascinate　v.　使神魂顛倒　　□enchant　v.　使陶醉；使喜悅
▶ □spellbind　v.　以咒語壓住

反義字
▶ □disenchant　v.　使不抱幻想　　□disillusion　v.　使醒悟
▶ □undeceive　v.　使醒悟

enthusiastic　[ɪnˌθjuzɪˈæstɪk]　形熱情的；熱烈的；熱心的　★★★☆☆

Eunice is an enthusiastic employee who takes on all tasks with zeal.
尤妮絲是名熱情的員工，對所有工作都充滿熱誠。

同義字
▶ □zealous　a.　熱望的；積極的　　□passionate　a.　熱情的
▶ □ardent　a.　熱心的；忠誠的　　□fervent　a.　熱烈的；熱情的

反義字
▶ □unconcerned　a.　漠不關心的　　□indifferent　a.　不感興趣的
▶ □nonchalant　a.　漠不關心的　　□apathetic　a.　冷淡的

entirety　[ɪnˈtaɪrtɪ]　名全部；全體；完全　★★★★★

I've never watched this movie in its entirety. I've only caught bits and pieces of it on TV.
這部電影我未曾全部看完過，只在電視上看過一些零碎片段而已。

同義字
▶ □all　n.　所有一切　　□whole　n.　全部；全體
▶ □integrity　n.　完整；完全

反義字
▶ □part　n.　部分　　□section　n.　（事物的）部分
▶ □segment　n.　部分；部門；切片　□portion　n.　部分

epic　[ˈɛpɪk]　形史詩的；敘事詩的　名史詩；敘事詩　★★★★☆

This is an epic poem that would take weeks to recite fully.
這一首史詩要花幾個禮拜才能全部吟誦完。

同義字
▶ □Homeric　a.　史詩的；大規模的　□epopee　n.　史詩
▶ □epos　n.　原始敘事詩

反義字
▶ □lyric　n.　抒情詩

epidemic　[ˌɛpɪˈdɛmɪk]　名流行病；時疫　★★★☆☆

Travelers with high fevers were quarantined to stop the SARS epidemic from spreading further.
發高燒的旅客已被隔離，以免流行病 SARS 進一步傳染開來。

同義字
▶ □pestilence　n.　惡性傳染病；瘟疫

epiphany [ɪˈpɪfənɪ] 名頓悟 ★★★☆☆

Patty had an epiphany that the meaning of her life is to help others.
佩蒂頓悟到她的生命意義在於助人。

同義字
▶ □insight   n.   洞悉；深刻的理解

episode [ˈɛpəˌsod] 名連續劇的一齣（或一集）；（文藝作品中的）插曲、片斷 ★★★★☆

In this, the eighth episode in the series, we find out whether the main character will choose love or loyalty.
在這部連續劇的第八集當中，我們會看到主角究竟選擇愛情還是忠誠。

equestrian [ɪˈkwɛstrɪən] 形馬的；騎術的；騎馬者的 ★★★☆☆

Tim loves horses, and is always attending equestrian events.
提姆喜歡馬，任何騎馬活動他都會參加。

反義字
▶ □pedestrian   a.   徒步的；步行的

equivalent [ɪˈkwɪvələnt] 名相等物；等價物 ★★★☆☆

Forty Thai Baht is the equivalent of one US Dollar.
四十泰國銖等於一美元。

同義字
▶ □equal   n.   相等的事物 □sameness   n.   相同
反義字
▶ □unequal   n.   不等同的事物

eradicate [ɪˈrædɪˌket] 動連根拔除；根絕；消滅 ★★★★☆

The new mayor promises to eradicate crime through poverty reduction and a larger police force.
新市長承諾要減少貧窮並擴編警力，以徹底杜絕犯罪。

同義字
▶ □eliminate   v.   排除；消除；消滅 □exterminate   v.   根除；滅絕
▶ □outroot   v.   根絕   □ extirpate   v.   使連根拔起；滅絕

errant [ˈɛrənt] 形走入歧途的；迷路的 ★★★★★

The errant teens should be in school, but are playing video games in the arcade instead.
這群誤入歧途的青少年原本應該待在學校，卻反而在長廊商場打電玩。

同義字
▶ □aberrant   a.   脫離常軌的   □go astray   誤入歧途

erratic [ɪˈrætɪk] 形飄忽不定的；不穩定的；無規律的 ★★★☆☆

The doctor is concerned about Mr. Jones' erratic heartbeat. He has been given medication to try to regulate it.
醫生擔心瓊斯先生心跳不穩定，已經開了讓心跳規律的藥給他吃。

同義字
▶ □irregular　a.　不規則的；不穩定的　　　□unstable　a.　不穩固的

反義字
▶ □regular　a.　規則的；有規律的　　□stable　a.　穩定的；牢固的

erroneous [ɪˈronɪəs] 形 錯誤的；不正確的 ★★★☆☆

The newspaper published some erroneous information for which it had to apologize for in its subsequent issue.
該報刊載了一些不實消息，只好在下一期報紙中公開道歉。

同義字
▶ □wrong　a.　錯誤的；不對的　　□ incorrect　a.　不正確的；錯誤的
▶ □untrue　a.　不真實的；假的　　□false　a.　不正確的；謬誤的
▶ □fallacious　a.　謬誤的

反義字
▶ □right　a.　正確的；準確的　　□correct　a.　正確的；對的
▶ □true　a.　真實的；確實的

erudite [ˈɛrʊˌdaɪt] 形 博學的 ★★★★☆

The erudite professor not only has two degrees, but has also traveled to over fifty countries.
這名博學的教授不僅擁有兩個學位，還去過五十幾個國家。

同義字
▶ □learned　a.　有學問的；精通的　　□scholarly　a.　博學的
▶ □knowledgeable　a.　有知識的　　□well-informed　a.　見多識廣的
▶ □know-it-all　a.　自稱無所不知

反義字
▶ □unlearned　a.　未受教育的　　□ignorant　a.　無知的
▶ □unintelligent　a.　缺乏才智的　　□uninformed　a.　無知的

eschew [ɪsˈtʃu] 動 避免；避開 ★★★☆☆

He taught his children to eschew drugs and alcohol, and to embrace education.
他告誡自己的小孩要避開毒品和酒精的誘惑，並且要全心唸書。

同義字
▶ □avoid　v.　避開；躲開　　□evade　v.　躲避；逃避；迴避
▶ □shun　v.　躲開；避開；迴避　　□dodge　v.　躲避；巧妙地迴避

反義字
▶ □face　v.　面臨；勇敢地對付　　□confront　v.　勇敢地面對；正視

espy [əˈspaɪ] 動 發現（意外的東西） ★★★☆☆

The ship captain espied land through the fog.
船長在霧中窺見了陸地。

同義字
▶ □find　v.　找到；尋得；發現　　□discover　v.　發現
▶ □locate　v.　探出；找出

estimate [ˈɛstəˌmet]　動估計；估量；估價　★★★★☆

I know it's impossible to know for sure, but can you estimate how much it would cost for your company to remodel my house?
我知道不可能有確定數字，但你可以先估算一下，公司如果幫我改建房子要花多少錢嗎？

同義字
▶ □appraise　v.　估計；估量　　□measure　v.　測量；估量

eventually [ɪˈvɛntʃʊəlɪ]　副最後；終於　★★★★☆

Margaret resisted her urge to eat dessert, but eventually gave in to her desires and ate a whole pie.
瑪格麗特雖然抗拒著想吃甜點的衝動，但終究屈服在慾望之下，把整個派吃個精光。

同義字
▶ □finally　adv.　最後；終於　　□ultimately　adv.　最後；最終
▶ □at last　最後；終於

evict [ɪˈvɪkt]　動（房客等）逐出　★★★★★

The landlord evicted his tenant for not paying the rent.
房東因為房客沒付房租而把他趕走。

同義字
▶ □expel　v.　驅逐；趕走 □oust　v.　驅逐；攆走
▶ □eject　v.　逐出；轟出

evolve [ɪˈvɑlv]　動進化　★★★☆☆

Human beings have evolved from ape-like creatures over millions of years.
人類從類猿生物進化而來，已有幾百萬年以上的時間。

exaggerate [ɪgˈzædʒəˌret]　動誇張；誇大；對…言過其實　★★★☆☆

Don't exaggerate! The fish you caught was two feet, not five feet long.
不要誇大其詞！你捕到的魚只有兩英尺，沒有五英尺那麼長。

同義字
▶ □magnify　v.　誇張；誇大　　□overstate　v.　把…講得過分
▶ □amplify　v.　誇大；誇張

反義字
▶ □understate　v.　不充分地陳述；保守地說

excavate [ˈɛkskəˌvet]　動挖掘（穴、洞等）；開鑿　★★★★★

The archeologists excavated the tomb to uncover Inca mummies.
該名考古學家挖掘這座墓，是為了找出印加人的木乃伊。

同義字

▶ □dig　v.　掘（土）；挖（洞、溝）□unearth　v.　（從地下）發掘

反義字

▶ □bury　v.　埋葬；安葬　□inter　v.　埋；葬

excel　[ɪkˈsɛl]　🔲突出；勝過他人；優於　★★★☆☆

Marcia is good at history and science, but she really excels in math. This semester, she got 99%.

雖然瑪莎歷史和自然科學很行，但對數學更是有一套。這學期她拿到 99 分。

同義字

▶ □surpass　v.　勝過；優於；大於　　　□exceed　v.　超過；勝過
▶ □outdo　v.　勝過；超越　　　　　　　□outstrip　v.　超過；勝過

excess　[ɪkˈsɛs]　🔲超越；超過　★★★★☆

Passengers are not allowed to check in baggage in excess of 30kg.

乘客不准帶 30 公斤以上的行李通關。

exclude　[ɪkˈsklud]　🔲拒絕接納；把…排除在外；不包括　★★★☆☆

The older boys excluded little Freddy from the basketball game because he was too short and slow.

這群大孩子不讓小弗瑞迪一起打籃球，因為他太矮，作又太慢。

同義字

▶ □reject　v.　拒絕；抵制　　　　□refuse　v.　拒絕；拒給；不准
▶ □except　v.　把…除外；不計

反義字

▶ □accept　v.　接受；答應　　　　□admit　v.　准許進入
▶ □take in　讓…進入；接受

excursion　[ɪkˈskɝʒən]　🔲遠足；短途旅行　★★★☆☆

We should make an excursion to the mountains this weekend for some hiking and camping.

我們這個週末應該上山遠足，一起走走路、露露營什麼的。

同義字

▶ □outing　n.　遠足；郊遊；短途旅遊　　　□hike　n.　徒步旅行；遠足
▶ □jaunt　n.　遠足；短途旅遊

exemplary　[ɪgˈzɛmplərɪ]　🔲模範的；懲戒性的；示範的　★★★★★

Dawn is an exemplary student. She receives good grades, wins athletic medals, and is in the students' union.

童恩是名模範生，她成績好、得過運動獎牌，還是學生會的一員。

同義字

▶ □laudable　a.　值得讚賞的　　　□commendable　a.　值得讚美的

exert　[ɪgˈzɝt]　🔲運用；行使；用力；盡力　★★★☆☆

You'll have to exert more force than that if you want to move that boulder.
如果你想搬 那顆大圓石，就得更用力才行。

同義字
▶ □use　v.　發揮；行使

exhale [ɛksˈhel]　動呼出；呼（氣）；輕輕發出（聲音等）　★★★☆☆

Take a deep breath and exhale slowly.
深吸一口氣，然後慢慢呼出。

同義字
▶ □expire　v.　呼氣；吐氣　　　　□breathe out　呼氣

反義字
▶ □inhale　v.　吸入

exhaust [ɪgˈzɔst]　名廢氣　★★★★☆

The exhaust from all the cars in the city is contributing to air pollution.
城市裡所有汽車排放的廢氣，讓空氣污染更加嚴重。

同義字
▶ □waste　n.　廢（棄）物；廢料

expand [ɪkˈspænd]　動擴大；擴充；發展　★★★★★

The growing company decided to expand into the Mexican market by opening a branch office in Mexico City.
這家發展中的公司決定在墨西哥城設立分公司，將業務擴展到墨西哥市場。

同義字
▶ □spread　v.　伸展；擴展　　　　□grow　v.　增大；增加；發展
▶ □extend　v.　擴大；擴展

反義字
▶ □reduce　v.　減少；縮小　　　　□narrow　v.　限制；縮小

expect [ɪkˈspɛkt]　動預計…可能發生（或來到）；預料；預期　★★★☆☆

The weatherman said to expect rain, so I took an umbrella when I left the house.
氣象預報員說可能會下雨，所以我出門時便帶了把 。

同義字
▶ □anticipate　v.　預期；預料　　　□foresee　v.　預見；預知

expense [ɪkˈspɛns]　名費用；價錢；開支；經費　★★★☆☆

My monthly expenses include rent, long distance phone calls, and groceries.
我每個月的開銷包括了房租、長途電話費和伙食費。

同義字
▶ □expenditure　n.　消費；支出　　□outgoing　n.　（常複數）開支
▶ □outlay　n.　費用

反義字
▶ □income　n.　收入；收益；所得　□receipt　n.　收入

▶ □earning　n.　收入；工資；利潤

explode　[ɪkˈsplod]　🔢爆炸；爆破　★★★★★

The dynamite exploded, creating a huge hole in the side of the hill.
炸藥爆炸，在山丘的一側炸出了一個大洞。

同義字
▶ □burst　v.　爆炸；破裂　　　□blast　v.　爆炸；炸開
▶ □detonate　v.　爆炸；觸發　　□blow up　炸毀

exposure　[ɪkˈspoʒɚ]　📙暴露；暴曬；揭露　★★★★☆

You should limit your exposure to the sun to decrease chances of skin cancer.
你應該限定自己不要過分暴露在太陽下，以減少罹患皮膚癌的機會。

同義字
▶ □reveal　n.　揭露；暴露　　　□disclosure　n.　揭發；透露

反義字
▶ □hiding　n.　隱匿

extension　[ɪkˈstɛnʃən]　📙延長；延期；緩期　★★★☆☆

One month is not enough time to complete this project. I will need an extension, maybe two more weeks.
要完成這個案子，一個月的時間是不夠的，可能需要再延個兩個多禮拜。

同義字
▶ □prolongation　n.　延長；延期　　□postponement　n.　延期；延緩
▶ □deferment　n.　延期；推遲

反義字
▶ □shortening　n.　縮短；變短　　□curtailment　n.　削減；縮減

exterior　[ɪkˈstɪrɪɚ]　📙外部；外表；表面；外貌　★★★☆☆

The exterior of the house is beautiful, but the inside of the house is very poorly decorated.
這棟屋子外觀很美，但內部的裝潢實在有夠爛。

同義字
▶ □outside　n.　外面；外部；外觀　□outward　n.　外面；外表
▶ □surface　n.　外觀；外表

反義字
▶ □inward　n.　內部；裡面
▶ □interior　n.　內部；內側

extinguish　[ɪkˈstɪŋgwɪʃ]　🔢熄滅（火等）　★★★☆☆

The fireman extinguished the fire with a bucket of water.
消防人員用一桶水把火熄滅。

同義字
▶ □quench　v.　熄滅；撲滅；平息　□go out　熄滅

▶ □snuff out　熄滅

反義字
▶ □burn　v.　燃燒；著火　　　□light　v.　點（火）；點燃
▶ □kindle　v.　點燃；燃起　　□ignite　v.　點燃；使燃燒

以F為首的單字

5 顆★：金色（860~990）證書必背
4 顆★：藍色（730~855）證書必背
3 顆★：綠色（470~725）證書必背

MP3-08

facetious　[fəˈsiʃəs]　形 好開玩笑的；滑稽的　★★★★★

I was only being facetious. Don't take my comments too seriously.
我只是搞笑一下，不要把我說的話太當真。

同義字
▶ □comic　a.　使人發笑的　　□humorous　a.　幽默的；詼諧的
▶ □waggish　a.　淘氣的

反義字
▶ □grave　a.　嚴重的；嚴肅的　□serious　a.　不是開玩笑的
▶ □solemn　a.　嚴肅的；莊重的

famish　[ˈfæmɪʃ]　動 挨餓　★★★★☆

I'm famished! Let's get something to eat before I die of starvation.
好餓哦！我們去吃個東西吧，不然快餓死了。

同義字
▶ □hunger　v.　挨餓　　□starve　v.　使餓死；使挨餓

反義字
▶ □satiate　v.　使飽足　　□sate　v.　充分滿足；使飽享

fastidious　[fæsˈtɪdɪəs]　形 愛挑剔的；難討好的；過分講究的　★★★☆☆

He's a fastidious man, and will notice if you move or rearrange anything on his desk.
他這個人很講究，如果你亂動桌上的東西，或換了位置，他都會注意到。

同義字
▶ □particular　a.　（過於）講究的　□critical　a.　吹毛求疵的
▶ □choosy　a.　難以取悅的　　□finicky　a.　（吃穿）過分講究的
▶ □fussy　a.　挑剔的

反義字
▶ □approbatory　a.　表示讚許的　□uncritical　a.　不加批評的

faulty　[ˈfɔltɪ]　形 有缺點的；不完美的　★★★☆☆

Excuse me. This TV that I bought is faulty. The volume can not be changed.
對不起，我買的這台電視是瑕疵品，沒辦法調整音量。

同義字
▶ □defective　a.　有缺陷的　　□imperfect　a.　不完美的

反義字
▶ □faultless　a.　完美無缺的　　　□perfect　a.　完美的

feasible [ˈfizəbl̩]　形可行的；可實行的　★★★★★

It's a good idea, John, but I don't think it's feasible given our limited resources.
這個點子不錯，約翰。不過我覺得我們資源有限，可能行不通。

同義字
▶ □practicable　a.　行得通的

反義字
▶ □infeasible　a.　不可實行的　　　□impracticable　a.　不能實行的

felon [ˈfɛlən]　名重罪犯　★★★☆☆

The convicted felon has served his ten year sentence, and will be released from prison tomorrow.
這名被判刑的重犯已經吃了十年牢飯，明天就要出獄。

同義字
▶ □criminal　n.　罪犯　　□culprit　n.　罪犯

ferocious [fəˈroʃəs]　形兇猛的；殘忍的　★★★★☆

The ferocious lion devoured the deer in only a few minutes.
那隻兇猛的獅子幾分鐘內就把鹿給吃個精光。

同義字
▶ □fierce　a.　兇猛的；好鬥的　　□savage　a.　野性的；兇猛的
▶ □brutal　a.　殘忍的；粗暴的

反義字
▶ □tame　a.　溫順的；馴良的　　□docile　a.　馴服的；易駕御的
▶ □meek　a.　溫順的；柔順的

fervor [ˈfɝvɚ]　名熱烈；熱情　★★★★★

The priest preached with fervor, and soon began to shake with emotion.
牧師熱情佈道，很快便因過於激動而渾身發抖。

同義字
▶ □passion　n.　熱情；激情　　□enthusiasm　n.　熱心；熱情
▶ □zeal　n.　熱心；熱誠

反義字
▶ □apathy　n.　無感情　　□unconcern　n.　冷漠；不關心

fiasco [fiˈæsko]　名完全失敗；可恥的失敗　★★★☆☆

The last time I had a dinner party everyone got food poisoning. It was a complete fiasco; I'm too embarrassed to try it again.
上回辦晚宴害大家食物中毒，簡直是一次可恥的失敗；我已經糗到沒臉再辦一次了。

同義字
▶ □failure　n.　失敗

反義字

▶ □success　n.　成功；成就；勝利

financial　[faɪˈnænʃəl]　⑱財政的；金融的；財務的　★★★☆☆

After winning over four million dollars in the lottery, Harry's financial troubles were no more.
哈瑞中了四百多萬的彩券，所有財務問題都解決了。

同義字
▶ □pecuniary　a.　金錢的　　　　　□fiscal　a.　財政的；會計的
▶ □monetary　a.　財政的

finite　[ˈfaɪnaɪt]　⑱有限的　★★★★★

The Earth's supply of oil and gas is finite, but when it will run out is anybody's guess.
地球上的石油和天然氣供應量是有限的，不過何時會耗盡，大家也只是各說各話罷了。

同義字
▶ □limited　a.　有限的；不多的
反義字
▶ □infinite　a.　無限的；無邊的　　　□unlimited　a.　無數的；無限的

flexible　[ˈflɛksəbl]　⑱可變通的；靈活的；易適應的　★★★★☆

Lisa is a flexible person who can work in a variety of different environments.
麗莎很懂得變通，可以在各種不同的環境下工作。

同義字
▶ □accommodating　a.　善於適應的　□malleable　a.　可塑的
反義字
▶ □inflexible　a.　不屈不撓的；堅定的　　　□firm　a.　堅定的；堅決的

flimsy　[ˈflɪmzɪ]　⑱脆弱的；易損壞的；輕薄的　★★★★★

The shack's flimsy roof caved in during the first heavy rain.
小木屋的屋頂不太堅固，第一次碰到大雨就坍了。

同義字
▶ □slight　a.　脆弱的；不結實的　　□frail　a.　易損壞的；不堅實的
▶ □fragile　a.　易碎的；易損壞的
反義字
▶ □firm　a.　穩固的；牢固的　　　□strong　a.　堅固的；牢固的

floral　[ˈflorəl]　⑱花的；似花的　★★★☆☆

Sylvia is a florist, and will be in charge of all floral arrangements at my wedding.
西維亞是名花商，我婚禮上的花要怎麼佈置全部交給她安排。

fluctuate　[ˈflʌktʃʊ͵et]　⑲波動；變動；動搖　★★★★☆

The share price has fluctuated wildly this month. It has gone up as many times as

it has gone down.
股價這個月 波動 得很厲害，漲跌的次數都差不多。

同義字
▶ □swing　v.　（利率、物價）漲落

fluent ['fluənt]　形流利的；流暢的　★★★☆☆

After living in Tokyo for five years, Vicky was fluent in Japanese and had no
problems communicating with the locals.
維琪在東 住了五年後，日語變得很流利，和當地人溝通也不再有問題。

同義字
▶ □smooth　a.　流暢的

forecast ['for,kæst]　名預測；預報　★★★☆☆

The weather forecast for the weekend calls for high temperatures with occasional
cloudy periods.
氣象預報説這個週末天氣炎熱，偶而會變陰天。

同義字
▶ □prediction　n.　預言；預報　　□ prognostication　n.　預知；前兆

foreign ['fɔrɪn]　形外國的　★★★★☆

Ben brought home several foreign currencies from his trip to Europe.
班去歐洲旅行時，帶了些外幣回來。

同義字
▶ □alien　a.　外國的；外國人的　　□external　a.　對外的；外國的

反義字
▶ □native　a.　本土的；本國的

foreman ['fɔrmən]　名工頭；領班　★★★★★

The foreman walked around the construction site to ensure that all safety
measures were being followed.
工頭巡視工地，以確保所有的安全設施都沒問題。

同義字
▶ □overseer　n.　督者；工頭　　□taskmaster　n.　工頭
▶ □supervisor　n.　督人；領班

foresee [for'si]　動預見；預知　★★★☆☆

The fortune teller says she foresees me becoming a very successful singer when I
grow up.
算命師説，她預見我長大後會成為一名很成功的歌手。

同義字
▶ □predict　v.　預言；預料　　□forecast　v.　預示；預言
▶ □foretell　v.　預言；預示　　□prophesy　v.　預言；預告

forfeit [ˈfɔrˌfɪt]　　動 喪失（權利、生命、名譽…）　　★★★★☆

The referee informed the coach that they would forfeit the game unless they put the required number of players on the court.
裁判跟教練説除非能補足球員人數，否則就要判他們輸球。

同義字
▶ □lose　v.　失；丟失；喪失

forgery [ˈfɔrdʒərɪ]　　名 偽造物；贗品　　★★★☆☆

The art expert knew right away the painting was a forgery, not the masterpiece the seller claimed it was.
這名藝術品專家立即知道這幅畫是贗品，而不是賣方所聲稱的名作。

同義字
▶ □counterfeit　n.　冒牌貨；仿製品　□fake　n.　冒牌貨；仿造品
▶ □sham　n.　贗品　□mock　n.　仿製品；贗品
▶ □imitation　n.　仿製品；贗品

formidable [ˈfɔrmɪdəbḷ]　　形 難以克服的；難對付的；艱鉅的　　★★★☆☆

Climbing Mount Everest is a formidable task that can only be accomplished by the most physically and mentally fit people.
攀登聖母峰是項艱鉅的任務，只有身心達到最佳狀態的人才有可能完成這項壯舉。

同義字
▶ □arduous　a.　艱鉅的；費力的　□strenuous　a.　艱苦的；繁重的

fracture [ˈfræktʃɚ]　　動 破裂；斷裂；折斷；骨折　　★★★★☆

Steve fractured a few bones in his leg, and will be in a cast for a month.
史蒂夫腿骨斷了幾根，要上一個月的石膏。

同義字
▶ □break　v.　打破；折斷；使碎裂　□rift　v.　開裂；斷裂

fragile [ˈfrædʒəl]　　形 易碎的；脆的；易損壞　　★★★★★

If you are going to send this vase in the mail, make sure you write "FRAGILE" on the package so that the postman handles it gently.
如果你要郵寄這只花瓶，記得包裹要寫上「易碎」字樣，郵差才會小心處理。

同義字
▶ □delicate　a.　脆的；易碎的　□frail　a.　易損壞的；不堅實的
▶ □breakable　a.　會破的；脆的　□flimsy　a.　脆弱的；易損壞的
▶ □brittle　a.　脆的；易損壞的

反義字
▶ □sturdy　a.　堅固的；經久耐用的　□strong　a.　堅固的；牢固的
▶ □solid　a.　結實的；堅牢的　□firm　a.　穩固的；牢固的

frequency [ˈfrikwənsɪ]　　名 頻率；次數　　★★★☆☆

The frequency of his hospital visits increased as his heart trouble got worse.
他上醫院的次數隨著心臟問題日趨惡化而變得越來越頻繁。

frigid ['frɪdʒɪd]　形 寒冷的；嚴寒的　★★★★☆

It was a frigid winter with record low temperatures.
這是一個氣溫創新低的寒冬。

同義字
▶ □cold　a.　冷的；寒冷的　　□frosty　a.　霜凍的；結霜的
▶ □chilly　a.　冷得使人不舒服的

反義字
▶ □hot　a.　熱的　　□torrid　a.　炎熱的；灼熱的
▶ □baking-hot　a.　極熱的；烤人的

frivolous ['frɪvələs]　形 無聊的；瑣碎的　★★★☆☆

This is a frivolous novel that no literary critic will even look at.
這本小說很無聊，沒有任何文學評論家想多看一眼。

同義字
▶ □boring　a.　令人生厭的；乏味的　□dull　a.　乏味的；單調的
▶ □uninteresting　a.　不令人感興趣的

反義字
▶ □interesting　a.　引起興趣的　　□funny　a.　有趣的

frugal ['frugl]　形 節約的；儉樸的　★★★★★

If we want to save money, we'll have to be more frugal with our money.
如果我們要存錢，就得更節儉一點才行。

同義字
▶ □economical　a.　經濟的　　□thrifty　a.　節儉的
▶ □saving　a.　節儉的；節省的　　□prudent　a.　善於經營的

反義字
▶ □wasteful　a.　浪費的；揮霍的　　□extravagant　a.　奢侈的
▶ □prodigal　a.　非常浪費的

fumigate ['fjumə,get]　動（為消毒等）煙燻；燻蒸　★★★★☆

The pest control company fumigated the whole building to rid it of cockroaches.
這家害蟲控制公司為了消滅蟑螂，用煙燻了整棟建築物。

fundamental [,fʌndə'mɛntl]　形 基礎的；根本的；十分重要的　★★★☆☆

All things are subject to change; this is a fundamental law of nature.
自然界的根本法則就是：所有東西都會改變。

同義字
▶ □basic　a.　基礎的；基本的　　□ underlying　a.　基本的；根本的
▶ □radical　a.　根本的；基本的

furnish [ˈfɜnɪʃ]　　**動** 裝潢（傢俱等）；裝備　　★★★☆☆

This luxury apartment building is furnished with the finest appliances money can buy.
這棟豪華公寓裡的裝潢，都是用錢買得到的最高檔貨。

同義字
▶ □dispose　v.　配置；佈置　　　　□configure　v.　安裝；裝配
▶ □outfit　v.　裝備；配備；供給

furtive [ˈfɜtɪv]　　**形** 偷偷的；鬼鬼祟祟的；狡猾的　　★★★★☆

The pickpocket gave a furtive glance at the man's coat pocket before stealing his wallet.
這名扒手先偷偷瞧了一眼那個人的外套口袋，然後才偷他的錢包。

同義字
▶ □secret　a.　秘密的；機密的　　　　□sly　a.　詭祕的
▶ □stealthy　a.　秘密的；鬼鬼祟祟的　　□sneaky　a.　暗中的

反義字
▶ □blatant　a.　公然的；露骨的　　　　□openly　a.　公開地；公然地
▶ □flagrant　a.　明目張膽的　　　　　□aboveboard　a.　率直地
▶ □barefaced　a.　拋頭露面的

futile [ˈfjutl̩]　　**形** 無益的；無效的；無用的；無希望的　　★★★★★

The writer's attempts to start the novel were futile, as he was suffering badly from writer's block.
這名作家因為遇到嚴重的心理阻滯，提筆寫小說的嘗試終告徒勞。

同義字
▶ □useless　a.　無效的；無益的　　　　□vain　a.　徒然的；無益的
▶ □fruitless　a.　無效果的；無益的

反義字
▶ □useful　a.　有用的；有益的　　　　□profitable　a.　有益的；有用的
▶ □beneficial　a.　有益的；有利的

以G為首的單字

5 顆★：金色（860~990）證書必背
4 顆★：藍色（730~855）證書必背
3 顆★：綠色（470~725）證書必背

MP3-09

gauge [gedʒ]　　**名** 測量儀器；規；錶；計　　★★★☆☆

There is a gauge on the dash that measures the amount of gas in the car.
汽車儀表板上有個測量油量的油錶。

gait [get]　　**名** 步伐；步態　　★★★★☆

Her gait changed after she broke her leg; now she walks with a slight limp.
她腿斷掉後，走路的樣子就變得有點跛。

▶ □pace n. 步態；步法   □walk n. 步法；步行姿態
▶ □step n. 步伐；步調

gallant [ˈgælənt] 🔣 英勇的；騎士風度的；豪俠的 ★★★☆☆

The gallant knight overcame all the guards and rescued the princess.
這名英勇騎士戰勝所有的警衛，把公主給救了出來。

同義字
▶ □brave a. 勇敢的；英勇的   □courageous a. 英勇的
▶ □heroic a. 英雄的；英勇的

反義字
▶ □cowardly a. 膽小的；懦怯的   □timid a. 膽小的
▶ □chicken-hearted a. 怯懦的

gamble [ˈgæmbḷ] 🔣 賭博；打賭 ★★★★★

Dean lost all his money gambling at the casino.
狄恩到賭場賭博，把所有錢都輸光了。

同義字
▶ □bet v. 打賭   □ wager v. 押（賭注）

garnish [ˈgɑrnɪʃ] 🔣 為增加色香味而添加的配菜；裝飾物 ★★★★☆

The parsley on the plate is just a garnish, and isn't supposed to be eaten.
盤子上的荷蘭芹只是裝飾用，不是拿來吃的。

同義字
▶ □decoration n. 裝飾物；裝飾品   □embellishment n. 裝飾

generate [ˈdʒɛnəˌret] 🔣 造成；引起；帶來 ★★★☆☆

The salesman generated new business by going door-to-door to meet potential customers.
這名推銷員用挨家挨戶尋找潛在客戶的方式來開創新事業。

同義字
▶ □produce v. 生產；製造   □create v. 引起；產生

generous [ˈdʒɛnərəs] 🔣 慷慨的；大方的 ★★★★☆

Sheila is a generous woman who gives all her time and money to help the homeless.
希拉為人慷慨，把自己所有的時間和金錢都拿來幫助無家可歸的人。

同義字
▶ □big-hearted a. 慷慨的   □free-handed a. 不吝嗇的
▶ □lavish a. 非常慷慨的 □liberal a. 慷慨的；大方的

反義字
▶ □stingy a. 吝嗇的；小氣的   □mean a. 吝嗇的；小氣的
▶ □miserly a. 吝嗇的；貪婪的   □niggardly a. 吝嗇的

gesture [ˈdʒɛstʃɚ] 名姿勢；手勢 ★★★☆☆

The gesture of putting the thumb and index finger together to make a circle means "OK" in North America.

用姆指和食指圍成一個圈圈的手勢，在北美洲代表的意思是「沒問題」。

同義字
- ▶ □posture　n.　姿勢；姿態　　　□pose　n.　（身體呈現的）樣子
- ▶ □sign　n.　手勢；暗號

gigantic [dʒaɪˈɡæntɪk] 形巨大的；龐大的 ★★★★☆

It took eight people holding hands to encircle the gigantic tree.

這棵大樹要八個人合抱才圍得住。

同義字
- ▶ □enormous　a.　巨大的；龐大的　　□vast　a.　巨大的；龐大的
- ▶ □immense　a.　巨大的；廣大的　　□tremendous　a.　巨大的
- ▶ □huge　a.　龐大的；巨大的

反義字
- ▶ □tiny　a.　極小的；微小的　　　□wee　a.　極小的；很小的

glacier [ˈɡleʃɚ] 名冰河 ★★★★★

At the end of the last ice age, glaciers began to retreat, carving out lakes, rivers, and valleys.

上個冰河時期結束時，冰河開始消退，造成了湖泊、河流和山谷。

glimpse [ɡlɪmps] 名瞥見；一瞥 ★★★★☆

I couldn't see much through the crowd, but I think I got a glimpse of Brad Pitt as he got into his limo.

雖然人群中看不太清楚，但我想我有瞥見布萊德‧彼特走進他那台大型豪華轎車裡。

同義字
- ▶ □glance　n.　一瞥；掃視　　　□peep　n.　窺視；偷看；一瞥

反義字
- ▶ □gaze　n.　凝視；注視　　　　□stare　n.　凝視；注視；瞪眼

graceful [ˈɡresfəl] 形優美的；雅緻的；典雅的 ★★★☆☆

Deana is such a graceful dancer. She moves like the wind.

迪安娜舞姿相當優美，作像風一樣飄逸。

同義字
- ▶ □elegant　a.　雅緻的；優美的　　□tasteful　a.　雅緻的；高雅的
- ▶ □refined　a.　優美的；文雅的

反義字
- ▶ □disgraceful　a.　不名譽的　　　□vulgar　a.　粗俗的；下流的
- ▶ □coarse　a.　粗俗的；粗魯的

granary [ˈɡrænərɪ] 名穀倉；糧倉 ★★★★☆

The farmer harvests the grain, and then stores it in the granary until its ready to be sold.
農夫的穀物收成後，便貯藏在穀倉裡等待販售。

同義字
▶ □barn　n.　穀倉；糧倉

granule　[ˈgrænjul]　名細粒　★★★★★

How many little granules of sand are there on this beach?
這座海灘上有多少粒小沙子？

同義字
▶ □particle　n.　微粒；顆粒

gratify　[ˈgrætəˌfaɪ]　動滿足（慾望等）　★★★★☆

Melody always wondered what it would be like to travel, and she finally gratified her curiosity by buying a ticket to Nepal.
梅樂蒂一直想知道旅行的滋味如何，最後終於買了張到尼泊爾的機票來滿足她的好奇心。

同義字
▶ □satisfy　v.　使滿意；使高興　　□content　v.　使滿足
▶ □fulfil　v.　滿足；使滿意　　　　□cater　v.　滿足需要（慾望）

反義字
▶ □dissatisfy　v.　使感覺不滿　　　□discontent　v.　使不滿

gravity　[ˈgrævətɪ]　名重力；地心引力

The apple always falls from the tree because of gravity.
蘋果永遠往下掉，是因為有地心引力存在。

同義字
▶ □gravitation　n.　重力；地心吸力

grease　[gris]　名物脂；油脂；潤滑脂　★★★★☆

After working on his car all afternoon, Harry's hands were covered in grease.
哈瑞整個下午都在弄他的車，弄到兩手都油得要命。

同義字
▶ □oil　n.　油　　□fat　n.　油脂

gregarious　[grɪˈgɛrɪəs]　形群居性的；合群的　★★★☆☆

Carolyn is a gregarious woman who prefers mingling at a party over sitting alone in a park.
卡洛琳喜歡交朋友，和獨自坐在公園裡比起來，她更喜歡在派對上到處交際。

同義字
▶ □companionable　a.　好交往的　　□ sociable　a.　社交性的；交際的

反義字
▶ □solitary　a.　單獨的；獨自的　　□unsociable　a.　不愛交際的

▶ □autistic　a.　孤獨症的

grief [grif]　　图悲痛；悲傷　　★★★★☆

Grief struck the family when they were informed their two sons had died in the war.
這家人得知兩個兒子都戰死沙場時，感到悲痛不已。

同義字
▶ □sorrow　n.　悲痛；悲哀；悲傷　　□sadness　n.　悲哀；悲傷
▶ □anguish　n.　極度的痛苦；苦惱　□ suffering　n.　（身體、精神）痛苦
▶ □heartache　n.　痛心；悲痛

反義字
▶ □joy　n.　歡樂；高興　　　　　□happiness　n.　幸福；快樂
▶ □delight　n.　欣喜；愉快　　　□gladness　n.　高興；喜悅

grimace [grɪ'mes]　　圖作怪相；扮鬼臉　　★★★☆☆

Kai grimaced when the nurse stuck the needle in his arm, but he did not cry.
護士把針刺進凱手臂時，他做了個鬼臉，但沒有哭。

同義字
▶ □make a wry face　做鬼臉

gullible ['gʌləbḷ]　　图易受騙的　　★★★★☆

You're so gullible! I can't believe you fell for that salesman's lies!
你怎麼那麼好騙？真不敢相信你會上那個推銷員的當！

同義字
▶ □deceivable　a.　可欺騙的　　□credulous　a.　輕信的

反義字
▶ □incredulous　a.　不輕信的　　□skeptical　a.　懷疑的；多疑的

gumption ['gʌmpʃən]　　图魄力；精力；進取心　　★★★★★

I can't believe you had the gumption to disagree with your boss at the board meeting.
真不敢相信你有那種魄力，在董事會上和你老闆唱反調。

同義字
▶ □boldness　n.　勇敢；大膽　　□daring　n.　勇敢；膽量

以H為首的單字

5 顆★：金色（860~990）證書必背
4 顆★：藍色（730~855）證書必背
3 顆★：綠色（470~725）證書必背

MP3-10

habitual [hə'bɪtʃʊəl]　　图習慣的；習以為常的　　★★★★☆

He's a habitual liar. He's been doing it since he was young, so it's going to take a miracle to break his habit.

他從年輕時就一直有説謊的習慣，要改變這種習性只能靠奇蹟出現了。

同義字

▶ □regular　a.　經常的；習慣性的　　□customary　a.　習慣上的
▶ □accustomed　a.　通常的

反義字

▶ □casual　a.　偶然的；碰巧的　　　□odd　a.　臨時的；非經常的

happy-go-lucky　[ˈhæpɪgoˌlʌkɪ]　形 逍遙自在的　　★★★★★

The happy-go-lucky youths gather in the park, rain or shine.
這群逍遙自在的小伙子無論晴雨，都會聚集在公園裡。

▶

同義字

▶ □unfettered　a.　自由自在的

harass　[ˈhærəs]　動 使煩惱；煩擾；不斷騷擾　　★★★★☆

Quit harassing me! I told you I don't want to see you again, so leave me alone.
不要再來騷擾我了！我已經説過我不想再見到你，請不要再來煩我。

同義字

▶ □disturb　v.　妨礙；打擾；擾亂　　□molest　v.　妨礙；干擾；騷擾
▶ □annoy　v.　打攪；困擾

反義字

▶ □clam　v.　閉嘴不言；保持沈默

havoc　[ˈhævək]　名 大破壞；浩劫　　★★★☆☆

The typhoon caused tremendous havoc along the east coast. Houses were destroyed, roads flooded, and many people died.
颱風為東海岸帶來了一場浩劫；除了房屋倒塌、道路被水淹沒外，還死了很多人。

同義字

▶ □calamity　n.　災難；大禍；大災害　　　□catastrophe　n.　大災
▶ □disaster　n.　災害；災難；不幸

hazard　[ˈhæzɚd]　名 危險；危害物；危險之源　　★★★★☆

This is a fire hazard. You shouldn't leave candles burning when you're not at home.
不在家時不應該繼續點著蠟燭，否則便有引起火災的危險。

同義字

▶ □danger　n.　危險（物）；威脅　　　□jeopardy　n.　危險；風險；危難
▶ □threat　n.　構成威脅的人

反義字

▶ □safety　n.　安全；平安；安全設施　　□security　n.　安全；防備；保安

heedless　[ˈhidlɪs]　形 不留心的；不注意的　　★★★★★

It was a spur of the moment decision that brought a lot of trouble. I won't be that heedless again.

我因為一時衝 才會惹來那麼多麻煩，以後不會再那麼不小心了。

同義字
- ▶ ☐careless　a.　心的；疏忽的　　☐reckless　a.　魯莽的
- ▶ ☐headlong　a.　欠考慮的　　☐inadvertent　a.　不注意的

反義字
- ▶ ☐thoughtful　a.　細心的；注意的　☐heedful　a.　深切注意的

hemorrhage　['hɛmərɪdʒ]　動出血　★★★★☆

He's cut a major artery! If we don't get him to the hospital, he's going to hemorrhage to death.

他割到大動脈了！不趕緊送醫的話，他就會因失血過多而死。

同義字
- ▶ ☐bleed　v.　出血；流血

hereditary　[hə'rɛdə,tɛrɪ]　形遺傳的　★★★☆☆

There is some evidence that obesity is hereditary; if you're obese, your child has a higher chance of also being obese.

有證據顯示肥胖是會遺傳的。如果你本身過胖，小孩是過重兒的機會也會變高。

同義字
- ▶ ☐inherited　a.　經遺傳而獲得的

反義字
- ▶ ☐acquired　a.　習得的；養成的

hesitate　['hɛzə,tet]　動躊躇；猶豫　★★★★☆

George was determined to ask Wendy out on a date, but hesitated when he actually spoke to her.

喬治下定決心要找溫蒂出來約會，可是真要開口時，卻又變得猶豫不決。

同義字
- ▶ ☐dither　v.　躊躇；猶豫　　☐hover　v.　猶豫；徬徨
- ▶ ☐falter　v.　搖；猶豫；畏縮

反義字
- ▶ ☐dare　v.　敢於面對；敢冒（險）☐determine　v.　使決定

hilarious　[hɪ'lɛrɪəs]　形極可笑的　★★★★★

The hilarious movie made me laugh until my stomach hurt.

這部電影好好笑，害我笑到肚子痛。

同義字
- ▶ ☐laughable　a.　可笑的；有趣的　☐amusing　a.　引人發笑的
- ▶ ☐funny　a.　有趣的；滑稽可笑的　☐ludicrous　a.　荒唐可笑的

反義字
- ▶ ☐boring　a.　令人生厭的；乏味的　☐dull　a.　乏味的；單調的
- ▶ ☐uninteresting　a.　不令人感興趣的

hinder [ˈhɪndɚ] 　動 妨礙；阻礙　　　★★★★☆

Bad weather will hinder our ability to see the road. We might have to turn back.
天候不佳會妨礙到我們的視線而看不清路況，或許掉頭回去比較好。

同義字
▶ □impede　v.　妨礙；阻礙；阻止　　□obstruct　v.　妨礙；阻擾；阻止
▶ □block　v.　阻擋；妨礙；阻止

反義字
▶ □help　v.　幫助；援助　　□assist　v.　幫助；協助

hoard [hord] 　動 貯藏；聚藏；隱藏　　　★★★☆☆

Before the typhoon, the nervous population began to hoard fresh water and instant noodles.
颱風還沒來，大家就緊張得開始貯藏新鮮用水和速食麵。

同義字
▶ □stock　v.　庫存；貯存

hoarse [hors] 　形（嗓音）嘶啞的；啞的　　　★★★★☆

My voice became hoarse from cheering during the football game.
看橄欖球賽時，我嗓子都喊啞了。

同義字
▶ □gruff　a.　（聲音）啞的　　　　□raucous　a.　聲音沙啞的
▶ □cracked　a.　沙啞的；刺耳的　　□husky　a.　（聲音）嘶啞的

hospitable [ˈhɑspɪtəbḷ] 　形 好客的；招待周到的　　　★★★☆☆

Mr. and Mrs. Jones are hospitable, and even open their homes up to complete strangers.
瓊斯先生和瓊斯太太很好客，連完全的陌生人都請進家裡。

同義字
▶ □welcoming　a.　歡迎的；款待的　　　　□cordial　a.　熱忱的；友好的

反義字
▶ □inhospitable　a.　招待不殷勤的

hostility [hɑsˈtɪlətɪ] 　名 敵意；敵視　　　★★★★☆

When they were young, Tom and Dave were sworn enemies. Even today, there is still hostility between the two men.
湯姆和戴夫年輕時是不共戴天的敵人，即使到了今天，兩個人之間仍然彼此懷有敵意。

同義字
▶ □animosity　n.　仇恨；敵意　　　□enmity　n.　敵意；不和
▶ □malice　n.　惡意；敵意；怨恨　　□hatred　n.　憎恨；增惡；敵意

反義字
▶ □amity　n.　友好關係　　　　□ goodwill　n.　善意；好心；友好
▶ □amicability　n.　友善；親善

humanitarian [hju͵mænəˈtɛrɪən]　形人道主義的；博愛的　★★★★★

The Red Cross is a humanitarian organization that helps people regardless of race, color, or nationality.
紅十字會是人道組織，助人不分種族、膚色或國籍。

同義字
▶ □philanthropic　a.　博愛的；仁慈的

反義字
▶ □inhuman　a.　無人性的；野蠻的

humiliate [hjuˈmɪlɪ͵et]　動使蒙恥辱；羞辱；使丟臉　★★★★☆

Joanne was humiliated when audience members began ridiculing her while she was speaking.
瓊安開口時，觀眾開始嘲笑她，讓她覺得很丟臉。

同義字
▶ □discredit　v.　使丟臉　　　　□disgrace　v.　使蒙受羞辱
▶ □dishonor　v.　使受恥辱　　　　□shame　v.　使丟臉

反義字
▶ □honor　v.　使增光；給…以榮譽　□grace　v.　使增光

hustle [ˈhʌsl̩]　名忙碌；奔忙；趕緊　★★★☆☆

I prefer the peace and quiet of the countryside over the hustle and bustle of the city.
我喜歡鄉下的安詳寧靜勝過城市的熙來攘往。

同義字
▶ □rush　n.　匆忙；緊急　　　　□haste　n.　急忙；迅速
▶ □hurry　n.　急忙；倉促；忙亂

反義字
▶ □composedness　n.　鎮靜　　　□calmness　n.　冷靜；沈著
▶ □poise　n.　鎮定；自信　　　　□sedateness　n.　安詳；鎮靜
▶ □imperturbability　n.　冷靜

hygiene [ˈhaɪdʒin]　名衛生　★★★★☆

The kindergarten promotes personal hygiene by making all students wash their hands regularly.
幼稚園叫所有學生經常洗手，以提升個人衛生習慣。

同義字
▶ □sanitation　n.　衛生設備；盥洗設備

hypnosis [hɪpˈnosɪs]　名催眠狀態　★★★☆☆

While under hypnosis, the patient revealed some of his earliest childhood memories.
這名病人在催眠狀態下，透露了早期童年生活的記憶片段。

同義字
▶ □trance　n.　昏睡狀態

hypocrite ['hɪpə,krɪt]　偽善者；偽君子　★★★★☆

You're such a hypocrite! You tell me that it's bad for me to smoke, yet you do it when there's nobody around!

你真是個偽君子！你跟我說抽煙不好，自己卻趁四下無人時偷偷抽。

同義字
▶ □dissembler　n.　偽君子　　　□goody-goody　n.　偽善者
▶ □holier-than-thou　n.　假道學　　□sanctimoniousness　n.　道貌岸然

以I為首的單字

5顆★：金色（860~990）證書必背
4顆★：藍色（730~855）證書必背
3顆★：綠色（470~725）證書必背

MP3-11

icon ['aɪkɑn]　（電腦）圖示　★★★★★

Double click on the Microsoft Word icon on your computer desktop to start the program.

在你的電腦桌面上按兩下 Microsoft Word 圖示，即可開啟程式。

ideal [aɪ'diəl]　理想的；完美的

The ideal job should pay well, be stimulating, offer 8 weeks of holiday, and be close to home. But such a perfect job is hard to find.

理想的工作應該是薪水高、具激勵性、一年有八週假期，還要離家近。要找到這種完美工作實在很難。

同義字
▶ □perfect　a.　完美的；理想的　　□faultless　a.　無缺點的
反義字
▶ □defective　a.　有缺陷的　　　□imperfect　a.　不完美的

idiom ['ɪdɪəm]　慣用語；成語　★★★★☆

The idiom "I'm just pulling your leg" means "I'm only joking."
「我不過鬧著玩的」這句慣用語的意思是「我只是開玩笑而已」。

idolize ['aɪdḷ,aɪz]　把…當偶像崇拜；極度仰慕　★★★★★

Young basketball players idolize Shaquille O'Neil. They wear his jersey and put his poster on their walls.

年輕籃球選手都把俠客歐尼爾當偶像崇拜；他們會穿和他一樣的衣服，還會把他的海報貼在牆上。

同義字
▶ □adore　v.　崇拜；崇敬　　　□worship　v.　崇拜；敬重；愛慕

illicit [ɪ'lɪsɪt]　形 非法的；不法的；違禁的；不正當的　★★★★☆

Unlike drugs in a pharmacy, those pills are illicit, and possession of them could mean time in jail.
和藥房賣的藥不同，這些是非法藥丸，擁有它們意味著等吃牢飯。

同義字
▶ □illegal　a.　不合法的；非法的　　□criminal　a.　犯罪的；犯法的
▶ □unlawful　a.　不合法的；犯法的　□illegitimate　a.　非法的

反義字
▶ □legal　a.　合法的；正當的　　　□lawful　a.　合法的
▶ □rightful　a.　合法的；正當的　　□legitimate　a.　合法的

illuminate [ɪ'lumə,net]　動 照亮；照射　★★★☆☆

The night sky was illuminated by fireworks and spotlights.
煙火和聚光燈照亮了夜空。

同義字
▶ □light　v.　照亮　　　　□brighten　v.　使明亮；使閃亮

imaginary [ɪ'mædʒə,nɛrɪ]　形 想像中的；虛構的；幻想的　★★★★☆

The unicorn is an imaginary animal, and can only be found in stories.
獨角獸這種動物是虛構的，它們只存在於傳說當中。

同義字
▶ □fanciful　a.　富於幻想的；想像的　　□fantastic　a.　想像中的
▶ □unreal　a.　虛構的；幻想的　　　　　□ fictitious　a.　虛構的；非真實的

反義字
▶ □real　a.　真實的；實際的　　　　　　□actual　a.　真實的；實際的
▶ □authentic　a.　真正的　　　　　　　□factual　a.　（根據）事實的

imitation [,ɪmə'teʃən]　名 仿製品；贗品　★★★☆☆

This isn't a real Rolex watch. It's just a cheap imitation.
這不過是便宜的仿冒品，不是真正的勞力士錶。

反義字
▶ □forgery　n.　偽造物；贗品　　□ counterfeit　n.　偽造物；冒牌貨
▶ □fake　n.　冒牌貨；仿造品　　　□sham　n.　贗品
▶ □mock　n.　仿製品；贗品

immaculate [ɪ'mækjəlɪt]　形 潔淨的；無污垢的　★★★★☆

The apartment was immaculate after the housekeeper spent all day cleaning.
女管家打掃了一整天，讓公寓變得一塵不染。

同義字
▶ □pure　a.　純淨的；潔淨的　　□clean　a.　清潔的；乾淨的
▶ □spotless　a.　極其清潔的

反義字
▶ □dirty　a.　髒的；污穢的　　　□filthy　a.　不潔的；污穢的

▶ □unclean　a.　不潔的；骯髒的

immature　[ˌɪməˈtjʊr]　形 幼稚的；不夠成熟的　★★★☆☆

Although he is already 40 years old, Greg is quite immature and acts more like a 10 year old.

葛列格雖然已經 40 歲了，行為還是像十歲小孩一樣幼稚。

同義字
▶ □infantile　a.　幼稚的；嬰兒的　　□adolescent　a.　青少年的
▶ □childish　a.　幼稚的；傻氣的　　□innocent　a.　幼稚的

反義字
▶ □mature　a.　成熟的；穩重的　　□adult　a.　成熟的

immerse　[ɪˈmɝs]　動 使埋首於；使深陷於（+in）　★★★★☆

The researcher is totally immersed in his work, and won't even stop to eat dinner.

該研究員完全埋首於工作之中，連晚餐時間都沒有停下來吃。

同義字
▶ □engross　v.　使全神貫注　　□plunge　v.　陷入
▶ □absorb　v.　吸引　　□preoccupy　v.　使全神貫注

反義字
▶ □distract　v.　使分心；使轉向　　□stray　v.　離題；偏離；分心

immune　[ɪˈmjun]　形 免疫的　★★★★★

After you get this vaccine, you will be immune to polio.

種了牛痘，你對小兒麻痺症就會免疫了。

impair　[ɪmˈpɛr]　動 削弱；減少　★★★★☆

Your ability to react quickly is impaired if you drink alcohol, so please don't drink and drive.

喝酒會降低你快速反應的能力，所以請不要酒後開車。

同義字
▶ □weaken　v.　削弱；減弱　　□abate　v.　減少；減弱；減輕
▶ □wear down　削弱

反義字
▶ □strengthen　v.　加強；鞏固　　□solidify　v.　使堅固；使團結
▶ □cement　v.　鞏固；加強

impartial　[ɪmˈpɑrʃəl]　形 不偏不倚的；公正的；無偏見的　★★★☆☆

The referee is supposed to be impartial, yet it appears that he's favoring the home team.

裁判應該公正才對，可是卻好像在偏袒地主隊。

同義字
▶ □fair　a.　公正的；公平的　　□just　a.　公正的；公平的
▶ □unprejudiced　a.　沒有成見的　　□unbiased　a.　無偏見的

反義字
▶ ☐partial a. 不公平的；偏袒的　☐one-sided a. 片面的
▶ ☐unjust a. 不公平的；不義的　☐prejudiced a. 懷偏見的

impeccable [ɪmˈpɛkəbl] 形無懈可擊的；無缺點的 ★★★★☆

His behavior this semester has been impeccable; he hasn't gotten into trouble once.

他這學期的行為零缺點，沒有半次闖禍記錄。

同義字
▶ ☐flawless a. 無瑕疵的；完美的　☐ unquestionable a. 無懈可擊的
▶ ☐unassailable a. 無爭論餘地　☐ unexceptionable a. 無懈可擊的

反義字
▶ ☐flawed a. 有缺點的　☐vulnerable a. 易受責難的
▶ ☐defective a. 不完美的

impede [ɪmˈpid] 動妨礙；阻礙；阻止 ★★★☆☆

Peter's sprained wrist impeded his ability to work as a waiter.

彼得的手腕扭傷，沒有辦法當服務生。

同義字
▶ ☐hinder v. 妨礙；阻礙　☐obstruct v. 妨礙；阻擾；阻止
▶ ☐block v. 阻擋；妨礙；阻止

反義字
▶ ☐help v. 幫助；援助　☐assist v. 幫助；協助

imperative [ɪmˈpɛrətɪv] 形必要的；緊急的；極重要的 ★★★★★

It's imperative that you pass the final exam. If you don't, you won't graduate.

你期末考非通過不可，否則就不能畢業。

同義字
▶ ☐necessary a. 必要的 ☐crucial a. 決定性的
▶ ☐critical a. 關鍵的 ☐imperious a. 絕對必要的

反義字
▶ ☐unimportant a. 不重要的　☐insignificant a. 無足輕重的
▶ ☐inconsequential a. 不重要的　☐trivial a. 不重要的；無價值的

impersonate [ɪmˈpɝsnˌet] 動扮演；模仿 ★★★★☆

The entertainer put on a hat and boots to impersonate a cowboy.

那名表演者戴上帽子、穿上靴子來模仿牛仔。

同義字
▶ ☐imitate v. 模仿　☐mimic v. 模仿
▶ ☐simulate v. 模仿；模擬　☐portray v. 扮演；表現

imply [ɪmˈplaɪ] 動暗指；暗示；意味著 ★★★☆☆

When you said my work is improving, you implied that my previous projects

weren't very good.
你說我工作有進步，等於暗示我先前的案子沒有做得很好。

同義字
▶ □allude v. 轉彎抹角地說到（+to）　　□hint v. 暗示；示意
▶ □intimate v. 提示；暗示　　　　　　　□suggest v. 提議；暗示

impromptu [ɪm'prɑmptju]　　名即興之作 形即席的　　★★★☆☆

Without warning, Jeannie was called up onto stage to make a speech. Her im-
promptu address was actually very good.
吉妮毫無預警被叫到台上演講，雖然是即席演說，卻仍表現得相當出色。

同義字
▶ □extemporization n. 即席發言

improper [ɪm'prɑpɚ]　　形1. 不合適的；不適當的 2. 不成體統的；不合禮儀的 ★★★★☆

It's improper to ask such a personal question to someone you just met.
向一個你剛認識的人問這種私人問題並不適當。

同義字
▶ □indecent a. 不適當的　　　　□unbecoming a. 不適當的
▶ □unseemly a. 不得體的
▶

反義字
▶ □polite a. 有禮貌的；客氣的　　□courteous a. 殷勤的；謙恭的
▶ □civil a. 彬彬有禮的；客氣的

improvise [ˈɪmprəvaɪz]　　動臨時做事；臨時湊合　　★★★★★

I can't find the installation manual for this shelf. We'll just have to improvise.
我找不到這個架子的安裝手冊，只好臨時做一個。

inadvertently [ˌɪnəd'vɝtṇtlɪ]　　副不慎地；非故意地　　★★★☆☆

I'm so sorry! I inadvertently washed the colored clothing with the whites, and now
everything is pink!
真是抱歉！我不小心把有色衣物和白色衣物放在一起洗，結果把所有東西都變成粉紅色了！

同義字
▶ □mindlessly adv. 不小心地　　□incautiously adv. 不小心地
▶ □remissly adv. 疏忽地　　　　□carelessly adv. 心大意地

反義字
▶ □carefully adv. 警惕地　　　　□cautiously adv. 小心地
▶ □discreetly adv. 慎重地　　　　□punctiliously adv. 小心翼翼地

inanimate [ɪn'ænəmɪt]　　形無生命的　　★★★★☆

This might look like an inanimate object, but it's actually a bug that looks like a twig.
這種東西看似無生物，其實是一種看起來很像細枝的蟲。

▶ ☐lifeless　a.　無生命的；死的　　☐dead　a.　死的；無生命的
▶ ☐exanimate　a.　無生氣的；已死的

▶ ☐animate　a.　有生命的；活的　　☐living　a.　活的；活著的

incentive　[ɪnˈsɛntɪv]　🔲刺激；鼓勵；動機　★★★★★

The incentive for the salesperson to work hard is a 5% commission on all sales.
推銷員努力工作的動機，是為了那 5% 的銷售佣金。

▶ ☐motive　n.　動機；主旨；目的　　☐encouragement　n.　鼓勵的話
▶ ☐inducement　n.　引誘物；誘因

incinerate　[ɪnˈsɪnəˌret]　🔲燒成灰；焚化；灰化　★★★★★

When plastics are burned, many chemicals go into the atmosphere. As a result, the city government chose not to incinerate garbage.
由於燃燒塑膠會釋放許多化學物質到空氣當中，結果市政府決定不焚化垃圾。

▶ ☐cremate　v.　將…燒成灰

incompatible　[ˌɪnkəmˈpætəbḷ]　🔲不能和諧共存的；不相容的；矛盾的
★★★★☆

The two boys are incompatible. They have nothing in common besides arguing and fighting.
那兩個男孩無法和平相處，見了面不是爭吵就是打架。

▶ ☐irreconcilable　a.　不能和解的　　☐opposite　a.　相反的；對立的
▶ ☐irreconcilable　a.　不能和解的

▶ ☐compatible　a.　能共處的　　☐reconcilable　a.　可和解的

inexcusable　[ˌɪnɪkˈskjuzəbḷ]　🔲不可寬恕的；難以原諒的　★★★☆☆

Handing in such a poorly done report is inexcusable. You had plenty of time to do your research.
你的研究時間那麼多，卻交出這樣一分差勁的報告，實在叫人難以原諒。

▶ ☐unpardonable　a.　不可原諒的　　☐unforgivable　a.　不可原諒的

▶ ☐excusable　a.　可辯解的　　☐pardonable　a.　可原諒的
▶ ☐forgivable　a.　可原諒的

infest　[ɪnˈfɛst]　🔲大批出沒於；侵擾；騷擾　★★★☆☆

This place is infested with cockroaches! Let's call the exterminator.

這個地方有大批蟑螂出沒！去找滅蟑的人來吧。

(同義字)
▶ □overrun　v.　蔓延於；侵擾

influence　['ɪnfluəns]　🄽影響；作用；影響力　★★★★☆

Wayne's influence in the company is great. The president always consults with him before making any major decision.
韋恩對公司的影響力很大。總裁制定任何重大決策前，都會先找他商量。

(同義字)
▶ □effect　n.　效果；影響

inherit　[ɪn'hɛrɪt]　🄥繼承（傳統、遺產等）　★★★★★

When her parents died, Janice inherited the family farm and her father's company.
珍妮絲父母過世後，家族的農場和父親的公司便由她繼承。

(同義字)
▶ □accede　v.　就任；繼承　　　□succeed　v.　繼任；繼承

ingredient　[ɪn'gridɪənt]　🄽（構成）要素；因素　★★★☆☆

The key ingredients in this stir-fry recipe are the garlic and soy sauce.
炒這種菜的關鍵要素就在大蒜和醬油。

(同義字)
▶ □factor　n.　因素；要素　　　□constituent　n.　成分
▶ □element　n.　要素；成分

inject　[ɪn'dʒɛkt]　🄥注射（藥液等）（+into）；為（某人）注射（+with）　★★★★☆

The doctor used a large needle to inject the medication into the patient's arm.
醫生用大針筒把藥劑注射到病人手臂裡。

(同義字)
▶ □syringe　v.　注射；洗淨

inland　['ɪnlənd]　🄰在內地；在內陸；向內地；向內陸　★★★★★

If you go inland from this port city, you will cross the plains and eventually reach the mountains.
如果你從這座港口城市往內地方向走，就會經過平原，最後抵達山脈。

(同義字)
▶ □upcountry　adv.　向內地；在內地

inquire　[ɪn'kwaɪr]　🄥詢問；調查　★★★☆☆

Please go to the customer service desk to inquire about refunds.
請至客戶服務臺詢問退費事宜。

(同義字)
▶ □query　v.　詢問　　　□question　v.　詢問；訊問；審問

143

insomnia [ɪnˈsɑmnɪə] 名失眠 ★★★★★

George suffers from insomnia, and spends his sleepless nights reading and watching TV.

喬治為失眠所苦，便趁無眠的夜讀書看電視。

同義字
▶ □insomnolence　n.　失眠　　　□wakefulness　n.　失眠
▶ □sleeplessness　n.　失眠

inspector [ɪnˈspɛktɚ] 名檢查員；視察員；督察員 ★★★★☆

The health inspector surveyed the restaurant's kitchen, and ordered the owner to clean up or be shut down.

衛生稽查員視察了餐廳的廚房，命令店主整理乾淨，否則就讓餐廳關門。

同義字
▶ □censor　n.　審查員　　　□examiner　n.　檢查人；審查員

instigate [ˈɪnstəˌget] 動煽動；挑動 ★★★☆☆

Ben instigated the fight by insulting Mary's mother.

班羞辱瑪麗母親，藉此挑起爭端。

同義字
▶ □incite　v.　激勵；激起；煽動　　□agitate　v.　鼓動；煽動
▶ □ferment　v.　使騷動

反義字
▶ □restrain　v.　抑制；遏制　　　□repress　v.　抑制；壓制；約束

insulate [ˈɪnsəˌlet] 動使絕緣；使隔熱；使隔音 ★★★★★

This winter jacket is very warm. It's insulated with goose down.

這件冬天夾克因為用鵝絨隔熱，所以穿起來很溫暖。

同義字
▶ □isolate　v.　孤立；隔離；脫離　　□separate　v.　分隔；分離；分散

intention [ɪnˈtɛnʃən] 名意圖；意向；目的 ★★★★☆

Frank always has good intentions when he offers to help clean up, but he inevitably ends up breaking something.

法蘭克出於一番好意，自願幫忙整理，但最後總不可避免地會打破一些東西。

同義字
▶ □purpose　n.　目的；意圖　　　□notion　n.　打算；意圖

intercept [ˌɪntɚˈsɛpt] 動攔截；截住；截擊 ★★★☆☆

The message from the General to the soldiers was intercepted by the enemy, and decoded.

將軍要傳達給士兵的訊息遭敵方攔截，而且密碼已被破解。

同義字
▶ □interrupt   v.   中斷；遮斷；阻礙   □hold up   攔截

interim   [ˈɪntərɪm]   形臨時的；暫時的   ★★★★★

After the president resigned, the Treasurer acted as interim president until a new one could be found.
總裁離職後暫時由財務主管擔任總裁，直到新總裁就任為止。

同義字
▶ □provisional   a.   臨時的   □impermanent   a.   不持久的

反義字
▶ □definitive   a.   決定性的；最後的 □determinate   a.   確定的

intermission   [ˌɪntəˈmɪʃən]   名休息時間；幕間休息   ★★★☆☆

The concert will now stop for a fifteen minute intermission so that you can stretch your legs and buy a drink.
音樂會現在中場休息十五分鐘，你可以趁機伸伸懶腰或是喝個飲料。

同義字
▶ □respite   n.   暫時的休息

interpreter   [ɪnˈtɝprɪtɚ]   名口譯員；通譯員   ★★★★☆

I have no idea what they are saying. We should hire an interpreter.
我聽不懂他們在說什麼，看來得請個翻譯員才行。

同義字
▶ □translator   n.   譯者；譯員

interrupt   [ˌɪntəˈrʌpt]   動打斷；中斷   ★★★☆☆

Please don't interrupt us while we're talking. We'll answer your question when we're done our conversation.
請不要打斷我們的談話。我們講完話就會回答你的問題。

同義字
▶ □interject   v.   插話；插嘴   □disrupt   v.   使中斷；使混亂
▶ □break into   打斷   □cut short   打斷

introductory   [ˌɪntrəˈdʌktərɪ]   形介紹的；準備的   ★★★☆☆

This introductory course will teach you the basics of photography. If you want to learn more, you'll have to take a more advanced class.
這堂入門課會教你攝影的基本知識，如果你想學得更多，就要上進階一點的課程。

同義字
▶ □elementary   a.   初級的；基礎的   □preliminary   a.   預備的

反義字
▶ □advanced   a.   高級的；高等的

invalid [ˈɪnvəlɪd]　形 無效的；有病的　★★★★★

Your driver's license is invalid. It expired last month.

你的駕駛執照上個月過期，所以已經失效。

同義字
▶ □void　a.　無效的

investigate [ɪnˈvɛstəˌget]　動 調查；研究　★★★★☆

The police investigated the murder by carefully examining the crime scene, and interviewing eyewitnesses.

為調查該起謀殺案，警方仔細勘察犯罪現場，並和目擊證人進行訪談。

同義字
▶ □search　v.　探究；調查　　　□examine　v.　檢查；調查
▶ □inquire　v.　詢問；調查　　　□probe　v.　徹底調查

investor [ɪnˈvɛstɚ]　名 投資者；出資者　★★★☆☆

He is the largest investor in the company, owning 60% of the shares.

他是公司最大的投資者，擁有 60% 的股權。

同義字
▶ □capitalist　n.　資本家

irrigate [ˈɪrəˌget]　動 灌溉　★★★☆☆

The farmer irrigates his fields by running water through a series of canals.

農夫利用一連串的水道來汲水灌溉自己的農田。

同義字
▶ □water　v.　給…澆水；灌溉

itinerary [aɪˈtɪnəˌrɛrɪ]　名 旅程；路線　★★★★★

The itinerary for our sightseeing trip is as follows: the art museum in the morning, lunch in Chinatown, the zoo in the afternoon, and then back to the hotel for dinner.

我們的觀光旅行路線如下：早上參觀美術館，中午到中國城吃飯，下午參觀動物園，然後回旅館吃晚飯。

同義字
▶ □route　n.　路線；路程

以 J 為首的單字

5 顆★：金色（860~990）證書必背
4 顆★：藍色（730~855）證書必背
3 顆★：綠色（470~725）證書必背

MP3-12

jargon [ˈdʒɑrgən]　名 行話；黑話　★★★★★

When I first started at this computer company, I didn't understand any of the technical jargon spoken by the programmers.

我剛來這家電腦公司時，程式設計師講的那些專業行話我一個都聽不懂。

同義字
- ▶ □cant　n.　行話、術語　□shoptalk　n.　職業用語
- ▶ □buzzword　n.　行話

jeopardize　[ˈdʒɛpəˌdaɪz]　　動 使瀕於危險境地；冒⋯的危險；危及　★★★★☆

Losing two key players to injury will jeopardize our chances of winning the championship.
失去兩個受傷的重要球員讓我們贏球的機會變得岌岌可危。

同義字
- ▶ □risk　v.　冒⋯的風險　□endanger　v.　危及
- ▶ □imperil　v.　危及

judgment　[ˈdʒʌdʒmənt]　　名 判斷力；辨別力　★★★☆☆

Alcohol impaired the driver's judgment of distance, so he crashed into the back of a big truck.
酒精讓司機的距離判斷力變差，所以才會從大卡車後面撞下去。

同義字
- ▶ □discernment　n.　洞察力；識別能力

juggle　[ˈdʒʌɡl̩]　　動 耍（球、盤等）；耍弄　★★★☆☆

The clown juggled five balls while balancing on a unicycle.
這名小丑一邊在單輪腳踏車上保持平衡，一邊耍五個球。

junction　[ˈdʒʌŋkʃən]　　名 接合點；交叉點；（鐵路的）聯軌站；（河流的）匯合處
★★★★★

The two railway lines meet at this junction and continue as one line.
兩條鐵路在這裡會合後變成一條。

同義字
- ▶ □confluence　n.　（河流的）匯合　□convergence　n.　會合；聚合
- ▶ □meeting　n.　匯合點；交叉點　□concourse　n.　匯合；集合

反義字
- ▶ □divergence　n.　分歧；背離　□discrepance　n.　不一致；分歧

junk　[dʒʌŋk]　　名 垃圾；假貨；廢話　★★★★☆

Oh, you can throw out that pile of junk. I don't need any of it anymore.
哦，那堆垃圾你可以丟了，全部的東西都用不到了。

同義字
- ▶ □rubbish　n.　垃圾；廢物　　□trash　n.　廢物；垃圾
- ▶ □scrap　n.　垃圾；破爛　　　□litter　n.　廢棄物；零亂之物
- ▶ □debris　n.　垃圾；碎片

ABCDEFGHIJKLMNOPQRSTUVWXYZ

147

jury [ˈdʒʊrɪ] 名陪審團 ★★★★★

After listening to both sides, the jury found the defendant innocent of all charges.
陪審團聽完兩邊的證詞後，判定被告一切罪名不成立。

同義字
▶ □panel　n.　陪審員名單

juvenile [ˈdʒuvənl̩] 形少年的 ★★★★★

Since he committed the crime when he was under 18, he will be tried in juvenile court.
因為他犯罪時還未滿十八歲，便交由少年法庭審理。

同義字
▶ □adolescent　a.　青少年的

反義字
▶ □adult　a.　成年人的

以 k 為首的單字

5 顆★：金色（860~990）證書必背
4 顆★：藍色（730~855）證書必背
3 顆★：綠色（470~725）證書必背

MP3-12

kernel [ˈkɝnl̩] 名（果核或果殼內）仁；（麥、玉米）粒 ★★★☆☆

At the bottom of every bag of popcorn, there are always a few kernels that don't pop.
每包玉米底下總會有一些沒爆的玉米粒。

同義字
▶ □core　n.　果核；果心

kindhearted [ˈkaɪndˈhɑrtɪd] 形好心腸的；仁慈的；同情的 ★★★★☆

Gill is a kindhearted man who has devoted his life to helping others.
吉爾有付好心腸，把一生都奉獻在助人身上。

同義字
▶ □benevolent　a.　仁慈的　　　　□merciful　a.　慈悲的；寬容的
▶ □compassionate　a.　有同情心的

反義字
▶ □vicious　a.　惡意的；惡毒的　　□malicious　a.　惡意；懷恨的
▶ □venomous　a.　惡意的　　　　　□malevolent　a.　有惡意的

knead [nid] 動揉（麵糰、黏土等）；捏 ★★★★★

The baker kneaded the dough before putting it into the oven.
麵包師傅先把麵糰揉過，再放進烤箱裡。

以L為首的單字

5 顆★：金色（860~990）證書必背
4 顆★：藍色（730~855）證書必背
3 顆★：綠色（470~725）證書必背

---

ladle ['ledl]　图杓子；長柄杓　★★★☆☆

Don't use that tiny spoon to dish out the soup from the pot. Use this ladle instead.

不要用那把小湯匙從鍋子裡舀湯，用這把杓子。

同義字
▶ □dipper　n.　長柄勺；汲器

---

landlord ['lænd,lɔrd]　图房東；（旅館、家庭公寓等的）主人、老板 ★★★★☆

The landlord comes to collect the rent at the beginning of every month.

房東每個月月初會來收房租。

同義字
▶ □proprietor　n.　所有人；經營者　□lessor　n.　出租人

反義字
▶ □tenant　n.　房客；承租人　　□lodger　n.　寄宿人；房客
▶ □roomer　n.　租屋的房客

---

landmark ['lænd,mɑrk]　图地標；陸標　★★★★★

The Eiffel Tower in Paris and the Leaning Tower of Pisa in Italy are two landmarks known all around the world.

巴黎的艾菲爾鐵塔和義大利的比薩斜塔是世界知名的兩處地標。

---

landscape ['lænd,skep]　图風景；景色　★★★★★

The photographer took beautiful landscapes of the rolling hills and streams of the German countryside.

該名攝影師專門拍攝德國鄉間美麗的爬坡和河流景色。

同義字
▶ □scene　n.　景色；景象 □outlook　n.　景色；風光
▶ □prospect　n.　景色；視野

---

laser ['lezɚ]　图雷射　★★★★☆

A laser inside the DVD player will read the information off the disk.

DVD 播放機裡的雷射會去讀碟片上的資訊。

---

laud [lɔd]　勔讚美　★★★☆☆

In his speech, the president lauded Paul on his hard accomplishments.

總裁在他的演說當中，讚美了保羅辛苦得來的成就。

同義字
▶ □praise　v.　讚美；歌頌（+for）　□compliment　v.　讚美；恭維
▶ □extol　v.　讚美；頌揚　　　　　□glorify　v.　讚美

▶ □blame　v.　責備；歸咎　　　　□criticize　v.　批評；苛求；非難
▶ □censure　v.　責備；譴責

laundry [ˈlɔndrɪ]　名送洗的衣服；洗好的衣服　★★★★★

Put all your dirty laundry in the basket, and I'll wash it tomorrow.
把你所有的髒衣服都丟進籃子裡，我明天洗。

同義字
▶ □washing　n.　洗（或待洗）的衣物

leaflet [ˈliflɪt]　名傳單；單張印刷品　★★★★☆

The salesperson handed out leaflets that explained the wonderful qualities of his product.
該推銷員把說明他產品特點的傳單發給大家。

同義字
▶ □handbill　n.　傳單；招貼　　　□flysheet　n.　單張小廣告傳單
▶ □circular　n.　通知；公告

leisure [ˈliʒɚ]　名閒暇；空暇時間　★★★☆☆

In her leisure time, Leah enjoys cycling, reading, and playing computer games.
利亞閒暇時喜歡騎腳踏車兜風、讀書，還有玩電腦遊戲。

同義字
▶ □disengagement　n.　閒暇　　　□free time　空閒時間
▶ □spare time　空閒時間

反義字
▶ □work　n.　工作；勞動；作業　　□labor　n.　勞動；工作
▶ □toil　n.　辛苦；勞累

lenient [ˈlinjənt]　形寬大的；仁慈的；溫和的　★★★☆☆

The judge has a reputation for being lenient, and in most cases gives the minimal sentence.
該法官有仁慈的好名聲，大部分案子都判處最輕的刑罰。

同義字
▶ □kindhearted　a.　好心腸的　　　□benevolent　a.　仁慈的
▶ □merciful　a.　仁慈的；慈悲的　　□compassionate　a.　有同情心的

反義字
▶ □vicious　a.　惡意的；惡毒的　　□malicious　a.　惡意；懷恨的
▶ □venomous　a.　惡意的；惡毒的　□malevolent　a.　有惡意的

levy [ˈlɛvɪ]　動徵收（稅等）；強索　★★★★☆

The government has decided to levy a tax on blank CDs so as to prevent piracy.
為杜絕盜版，政府決定對空白 CD 片課稅。

同義字

▶ □tax　v.　向…課稅　　□ impose　v.　徵（稅）；加（負擔）於

lifelike　[ˈlaɪfˌlaɪk]　🔳栩栩如生的　★★★★★

The wax figures at Madame Tussauds are so lifelike that you wouldn't be able to tell the figure apart from the real person.
杜莎夫人蠟像館裡的蠟像，其栩栩如生的程度，讓你分不清蠟像和真人之間的區別。

同義字
▶ □vivid　a.　生動的；逼真的

lifelong　[ˈlaɪfˌlɔŋ]　🔳終身的；一輩子的　★★★★☆

Since as far back as he can remember, Gabe's lifelong dream has been to become a famous pianist.
自有記憶以來，蓋比一生的夢想就是要成為一位有名的鋼琴家。

同義字
▶ □lifetime　a.　一生的；終身的

likelihood　[ˈlaɪklɪˌhʊd]　🔳可能；可能　★★★☆☆

The future of this company is uncertain, but in all likelihood we will close down within a year.
這家公司前途渺茫，很可能一年內就會關門大吉。

同義字
▶ □possibility　n.　可能　　□probability　n.　可能

limit　[ˈlɪmɪt]　🔳限度；限制；極限　★★★☆☆

The speed limit on this road is 100km/hour. Any faster than that and you might get a ticket.
這條道路的時速限制為 100 公里，超速的話可能會接到罰單。

同義字
▶ □restriction　n.　限制；約束

linguistics　[lɪŋˈgwɪstɪks]　🔳語言學　★★★★☆

The researchers in the linguistics department are studying the origins and relationships of aboriginal languages.
語言學系的研究員正在研究土著語言的起源和相互關係。

listless　[ˈlɪstlɪs]　🔳無精打采的；倦怠的　★★★★★

Tired of the boring lecture, Bart became listless and began daydreaming about playing outside.
無聊的演講讓巴特聽得很厭倦，整個人無精打采，便開始做起到外面玩的白日夢。

同義字
▶ □tired　a.　疲倦的；厭倦的　　□lethargic　a.　不活潑的
▶ □lackadaisical　a.　懶散的　　□low-spirited　a.　無精神的

▶ □languid　a.　不感興趣的
反義字
▶ □lively　a.　精力充沛的；活潑的　　□vigorous　a.　精力充沛的
▶ □buoyant　a.　心情愉快的

literacy　[ˈlɪtərəsɪ]　名識字；讀寫能力　★★★☆☆

This non-profit group is trying to increase the literacy rate by teaching street children how to read and write.
這個非營利團體教導街頭孩童讀書寫字，希望藉此提升人民的識字率。

反義字
▶ □illiteracy　n.　不識字；文盲

literature　[ˈlɪtərətʃɚ]　名文學；文學作品　★★★★☆

In literature class today, the professor discussed the difference between poetry and prose.
教授在今天的文學課中討論了詩和散文的不同。

同義字
▶ □writing　n.　著作；文學作品

livelihood　[ˈlaɪvlɪˌhʊd]　名生活；生計　★★★★★

Jeremy was once a carpenter, but now earns his livelihood as an English teacher.
傑瑞米以前是個木匠，現在則靠英文老師的工作來謀生。

同義字
▶ □maintenance　n.　扶養；生活費　　　　□sustenance　n.　生計
▶ □subsistence　n.　生存；活命

loot　[lut]　動搶劫；洗劫；強奪　★★★☆☆

During the blackout, the mob broke windows and looted many stores.
停電期間，暴民打破窗戶，搶了很多家店。

同義字
▶ □rob　v.　搶劫；劫掠；盜取　　　□plunder　v.　掠奪；劫掠；搶劫
▶ □pillage　v.　搶劫；掠奪

lucrative　[ˈlukrətɪv]　形賺錢的；有利可圖的　★★★★☆

China is a potentially lucrative market for many companies because of its 1.3 billion consumers.
中國擁有十三億人口，對許多公司來説潛在商機相當龐大。

同義字
▶ □advantageous　a.　有利的
反義字
▶ □profitless　a.　無利的；無益的　　□gainless　a.　無利可圖的

luminous [ˈlumənəs]　　形發光的；夜光的；照亮了的　　★★★★★

The full moon in August is especially luminous.
八月的滿月特別亮。

同義字
- □bright　a.　明亮的；發亮的　　□shining　a.　光亮的；醒目的
- □beaming　a.　發光的；耀眼的

反義字
- □dark　a.　黑暗的；陰暗的　　□dim　a.　微暗的；暗淡的
- □dusky　a.　微暗的；暗淡的　　□murky　a.　黑暗的；陰鬱的

luxurious [lʌgˈʒurɪəs]　　形豪華的；非常舒適的；精選的　　★★★★★

This hotel room is so luxurious! It has two balconies, three bathrooms, and a huge hot tub.
這間旅館房間相當豪華！裡面有兩個陽臺、三間浴室，還有一個大浴盆。

同義字
- □sumptuous　a.　奢侈的；豪華的 □magnificent　a.　豪華的

反義字
- □plain　a.　簡樸的；樸素的　　□austere　a.　樸素的；無裝飾的
- □sober　a.　樸素的；樸實的

lyric [ˈlɪrɪk]　　名歌詞　　★★★★☆

Here's the microphone. Just start singing when the music starts and the lyrics flash across the screen.
麥克風拿去。聽到音樂又看到歌詞在螢光幕上閃出來時就開始唱。

同義字
- □word　n.　歌詞

以M為首的單字

5顆★：金色（860~990）證書必背
4顆★：藍色（730~855）證書必背
3顆★：綠色（470~725）證書必背

MP3-13

magnate [ˈmægnet]　　名（實業界的）巨頭、大王；要人、權貴　　★★★☆☆

Mr. Bell is an oil magnate who made his billions drilling for oil in the desert.
貝爾先生是石油界巨頭，靠著在沙漠中鑽油賺進了數十億。

同義字
- □worthy　n.　知名人士；傑出人物　　□somebody　n.　重要人物

反義字
- □nobody　n.　無足輕重的人

magnet [ˈmægnɪt]　　名磁鐵；磁石　　★★★☆☆

The magnet inside the compass keeps the needle pointed north.

這個羅盤裡面的磁鐵會讓指針指向北方。

同義字
▶ □loadstone n. 天然磁石

maintain [men'ten] 🗪維修；保養 ★★★★☆

This car is expensive to buy but cheap to maintain. It's good on gas, and rarely breaks down.

雖然買這部車很貴，但保養費卻很便宜。因為它很省油，而且很少故障。

同義字
▶ □preserve v. 保護；維護；維持 □service v. 維修；保養

malaria [mə'lɛrɪə] 🗪瘧疾 ★★★★★

To prevent malaria, wear bug spray so that infected mosquitoes won't want to bite you.

為了防範瘧疾，記得要噴防蚊液，受感染的蚊子才不會咬你。

mandatory [ˈmændəˌtorɪ] 🗪義務的；強制的 ★★★★☆

Attending school is mandatory up until age 16. After that you can do whatever you want.

十六歲前需接受義務教育，之後你就可以隨心所欲。

同義字
▶ □compulsory a. 強制的   □obligated a. 責無旁貸的
▶ □required a. 必須的   □constrained a. 被迫的
▶ □impellent a. 推動的；驅使的

反義字
▶ □volunteer a. 自願參加的   □willing a. 願意的；樂意的
▶ □volitient a. 願意的

mantel [ˈmæntl̩] 🗪壁爐架 ★★★☆☆

A picture of his grandparents sat on the mantel above the fireplace.
壁爐上面的壁爐架，放著一張他爺爺奶奶的照片。

manufacturer [ˌmænjəˈfæktʃərə] 🗪製造業者；廠商；廠主；製造公司
★★★★☆

This Chinese factory is a manufacturer on TVs. When the TVs are produced, they ship them to American wholesalers.

這間中國工廠是電視製造業者開的，電視一生產出來，就會運到美國批發商那邊。

masterpiece [ˈmæstəˌpis] 🗪傑作；名作 ★★★★★

This painting is a masterpiece of the Renaissance Era, and is worth over 50 million dollars.

這幅畫是文藝復興時期的名作，價值超過五千萬美元。

同義字
- □masterwork　n.　傑作　　　　　　　□chef d'oeuvre　（法）傑作
- □magnum opus　（拉）巨著；傑作

master　[ˈmæstɚ]　**勔**精通；掌握　　　★★★★☆

It took Leo three months to learn how to play the violin, but another thirty years to master it.
里歐只花了三個月便學會拉小提琴，但又花了三十年才精通這項樂器。

同義字
- □be proficient in　精通

maze　[mez]　**名**迷宮　　　★★★☆☆

The little white mouse took 20 seconds to run through the maze and find the cheese.
這隻小白鼠從踏進迷宮一直到發現乳酪，一共花了二十秒。
-

同義字
- □labyrinth　n.　迷宮

meager　[ˈmigɚ]　**形**粗劣的；不足的；貧乏的　　　★★★★☆

Marshall makes a meager living as a busboy, his wages are barely enough for food and rent.
馬歇爾是名餐廳雜役，生活很困苦，他賺的錢只夠勉強支付伙食費和房租。

同義字
- □destitute　a.　窮困的；貧困的　　　□poor　a.　貧窮的；貧困的
- □needy　a.　貧窮的　　　　　　　　　□impoverished　a.　窮困的

反義字
- □rich　a.　有錢的；富有的　　　　　□wealthy　a.　富裕的；豐富的
- □affluent　a.　富裕的　　　　　　　　□well-off　a.　富裕的

meander　[mɪˈændɚ]　**勔**沿…緩慢而曲折地前進；使迂迴曲折　　★★★★★

The river meanders slowly down the mountain and around the hills before finally emptying into the sea.
這條河沿著高山和小丘蜿蜒而下，最後流入大海。

同義字
- □wander　v.　（河流等）蜿蜒　　　□wind　v.　蜿蜒；迂迴

mediocre　[ˈmidɪˌokɚ]　**形**中等的；平凡的；二流的　　★★★★★

That was a mediocre movie. I give it a 5 out of 10.
那部電影普普通通，滿分十分的話我給它五分。

同義字
- □average　a.　一般的；普通的　　　□ordinary　a.　普通的；平凡的
- □second-rate　a.　二流的

反義字

▶ □first-rate　a.　第一流的　　　　□excellent　a.　出色的；傑出的
▶ □prime　a.　最好的；第一流的　　□tiptop　a.　第一流的

meditation　[ˌmɛdəˈteʃən]　　名沈思；默想；冥想　　★★★★☆

The meditation instructions are simple. Just sit up straight, close your eyes, and observe as your breath comes in and out.
冥想方法很簡單：只要坐直，閉上眼睛，然後注意吸氣吐氣即可。

同義字

▶ □rumination　n.　沈思　　□brown study　沈思；冥想

memento　[mɪˈmɛnto]　　名紀念物；引起回憶的東西　　★★★☆☆

Keep your ticket as a memento of your trip to Japan.
把你去日本旅遊的機票留下來當做紀念。

同義字

▶ □token　n.　紀念品　　　　□souvenir　n.　紀念品；紀念物
▶ □remembrance　n.　紀念品

metamorphosis　[ˌmɛtəˈmɔrfəsɪs]　　名變形；質變；完全變化　　★★★★☆

When a caterpillar comes out of a cocoon, its metamorphosis into a butterfly is complete.
毛毛蟲破繭而出時，會完全變成一隻蝴蝶。

mete　[mit]　　動分配；給予　　★★★★★

The prison guard meted out food to the prisoners.
獄守衛負責把食物分給囚犯。

同義字

▶ □distribute　v.　分發；分配　　□give　v.　給予
▶ □allot　v.　分配

metropolis　[məˈtrɑplɪs]　　名大都市；首都；首府　　★★★☆☆

When Victor turned 21, he moved from his hometown in the countryside to a huge metropolis of over 3 million people.
維克多 21 歲時，便從鄉下故居搬到三百多萬人的大都會。

同義字

▶ □megalopolis　n.　巨大都市　　□capital　n.　首都；首府；省會

反義字

▶ □countryside　n.　鄉間；農村

microscope　[ˈmaɪkrəˌskop]　　名顯微鏡　　★★★★☆

Under a microscope, a tiny bug will look like a huge monster.
把小蟲放在顯微鏡下，看起來會像一隻大怪獸。

migrate ['maɪgret]　　動遷移；移居　　★★★☆☆

Every winter, the geese migrate south to warmer habitats.
每年冬天，鵝群會遷移到南方較溫暖的棲息地。

同義字
▶ □emigrate　v.　移居外國（外地）　□expatriate　v.　使移居國外
▶ □transmigrate　v.　移居

反義字
▶ □immigrate　v.　遷移；遷入

military ['mɪlə,tɛrɪ]　　名軍隊；軍方　　★★★★☆

The government is building up its military to prepare for war.
政府正在擴建軍力，隨時備戰。

同義字
▶ □army　n.　軍隊　　　　□troop　n.　軍隊；部隊
▶ □legion　n.　軍隊；部隊

minimize ['mɪnə,maɪz]　　動使減到最少；使縮到最小　　★★★☆☆

It's too late now to prevent the crisis, but we can still try to minimize the damage.
現在要防止危機發生已經太晚了，不過我們還是可以試圖將損害降到最低。

反義字
▶ □maximize　v.　使增加至最大限度

ministry ['mɪnɪstrɪ]　　名（政府的）部（常大寫）　　★★★★★

To obtain a license to open a school, you'll need to contact the Ministry of Education.
要取得開辦學校的執照，你得和教育部聯繫才行。

同義字
▶ □department　n.　部；司；局；處　　　　□administration　n.　管理部門

minute ['mɪnɪt]　　形微小的　　★★★★☆

A mite is a minute animal, invisible to the naked eye.
蟎子是一種肉眼看不見的微小動物。

同義字
▶ □tiny　a.　極小的；微小的　　　　□wee　a.　極小的；很小的

反義字
▶ □giant　a.　巨人般的；巨大的　　　　□tremendous　a.　巨大的
▶ □huge　a.　龐大的；巨大的

mirage [mə'rɑʒ]　　名海市蜃樓　　★★★☆☆

Overcome with thirst and fatigue, Joe saw a mirage on the desert's horizon.
喬好渴好累，竟在沙漠地平線上看到了海市蜃樓。

misbehave [ˌmɪsbɪˈhev] 動 行為不禮貌；行為不端；作弊 ★★★★☆

Don't misbehave or the teacher will send you to the principal's office!

不要不規矩，否則會被老師送到校長室！

同義字
▶ □act up　調皮；任性

反義字
▶ □behave　v.　行為檢點；聽話；表現好

mischievous [ˈmɪstʃɪvəs] 形 惡作劇的；調皮的；淘氣的 ★★★★★

He's a mischievous little boy who enjoys playing tricks on others, like putting glue on seats and mud in shoes.

他是個喜歡作弄別人的淘氣小男孩，像是把膠水放在座位上或是把爛泥放進鞋子裡等等，都是他會幹的好事。

同義字
▶ □naughty　a.　頑皮的；淘氣的　　□waggish　a.　滑稽的
▶ □impish　a.　小鬼般的；頑皮的

反義字
▶ □well-mannered　a.　文雅的；有禮貌的
▶ □well-behaved　a.　行為端正的

misplace [mɪsˈples] 動 誤置；遺忘 ★★★★☆

Have you seen my keys? I seem to have misplaced them somewhere.

你看到我的鑰匙嗎？我好像把它們忘在某個地方了。

同義字
▶ □mislay　v.　把…遺忘

missile [ˈmɪsḷ] 名 飛彈；導彈 ★★★☆☆

The missile fired from the fighter plane destroyed the entire building.

戰鬥機發射的飛彈炸毀了整棟建築物。

同義字
▶ □projectile　n.　射彈（如子彈、砲彈等）

moderation [ˌmɑdəˈreʃən] 名 適度；節制 ★★★☆☆

Please drink in moderation. Too much wine will get you drunk.

喝酒要有節制，過量會醉。

同義字
▶ □moderation　n.　適度；節制　　□temperance　n.　節制；節慾
▶ □abstinence　n.　節制；戒酒　　□continence　n.　自制；節制

反義字
▶ □immoderation　n.　無節制；過度　□indulgence　n.　沈溺；放縱
▶ □intemperance　n.　不節制；過度

modernize [ˈmɑdɚnˌaɪz]　　**動**現代化　　★★★★☆

This area was once full of old shacks and warehouses, but has since been modernized with skyscrapers and condominiums.
這個地區過去蓋滿了老舊木屋和倉庫，如此已改建成摩天大樓和大廈，走上了現代化之路。

momentary [ˈmomənˌtɛrɪ]　　**形**短暫的；瞬間的　　★★★★★

You will feel a momentary pain when I put this needle in your arm. It'll be gone in a few seconds.
我把針刺進你手臂時會痛那麼一下下，不過幾秒鐘就不痛了。

同義字
- ▶ □instantaneous　a.　瞬間的　　□transient　a.　短暫的；一時的
- ▶ □transitory　a.　短暫的；瞬息的

反義字
- ▶ □permanent　a.　永久的；永恆的　□lasting　a.　持久的；持續的
- ▶ □perpetual　a.　永久的；長期的　□eternal　a.　永久的；永恆的

monarchy [ˈmɑnɚkɪ]　　**名**君主政治；君主政體　　★★★☆☆

The monarchy once ruled this country, but then the king was replaced by an elected president.
這個國家一度實行君主政體，後來國王就被民選總統給取代了。

反義字
- ▶ □republic　n.　共和國；共和政體

monitor [ˈmɑnətɚ]　　**名**監視器　　★★★★☆

This 17 inch monitor is quite big for a laptop, but not as big as the screen for your home computer.
17 吋監視器對筆記型電腦來說算是很大的尺寸，但對家用電腦的銀幕來說還差了那麼一點。

monopoly [məˈnɑplɪ]　　**名**獨佔；專賣；壟斷；完全控制　　★★★☆☆

Our company has a monopoly on selling coal, but not having any competitors has made us very inefficient.
雖然我們公司壟斷了煤市場，但也因為缺乏競爭者而變得很沒效率。

同義字
- ▶ □corner　n.　壟斷；囤積

反義字
- ▶ □competition　n.　競爭　□contention　n.　競爭

morale [məˈræl]　　**名**士氣；鬥志　　★★★☆☆

The team's morale has been low since losing ten straight games, but the coach will try to inspire them to keep trying.
該隊因為連輸十場比賽而顯得士氣低落，但教練仍設法激勵他們堅持下去。

moral [ˈmɔrəl] 形 道德的 ★★★★☆

Most religions teach the same moral rules: not to kill, not to steal, and not to lie.
大部分宗教都告誡世人同樣的道德規範：不要殺人、不要偷盜、不要說謊。

同義字
▶ □ethical a. 倫理的；道德的

反義字
▶ □immoral a. 傷風敗俗的

motto [ˈmɑto] 名 座右銘；格言；訓言；標語 ★★★★★

American Express's motto "Don't leave home without it" is on most of their advertisements.
大部分美國運通卡的廣告都有「出門不可少」這句標語。

同義字
▶ □saying n. 格言；警句；諺語 □maxim n. 格言；箴言
▶ □proverb n. 諺語；俗語；常言 □adage n. 諺語；格言；古語

mountaineer [ˌmaʊntəˈnɪr] 名 爬山能手；登山家 ★★★☆☆

Only the fittest mountaineer should attempt to scale Mount Everest.
只有最強健的登山家敢嘗試登頂聖母峰。

mundane [ˈmʌnden] 形 世俗的 ★★★★☆

I wish I could give up my mundane activities such as washing dishes and grocery shopping, and instead spend my life traveling the world to find myself.
但願我能拋下諸如洗碗、買菜等世俗活動，而把生命用在探索世界、尋找自我上。

同義字
▶ □earthly a. 塵世的；世俗的 □fleshly a. 塵世的

反義字
▶ □heavenly a. 天國的；神聖的 □supernal a. 超凡的；非凡的

以 N 為首的單字

5 顆★：金色（860~990）證書必背
4 顆★：藍色（730~855）證書必背
3 顆★：綠色（470~725）證書必背

MP3-14

narrate [næˈret] 動 講（故事）；敘述 ★★★☆☆

The storyteller began to narrate a tale about a group of friends lost in the woods.
說書人開始講述一段一群朋友在森林裡迷路的故事。

同義字
▶ □tell v. 告訴；講述；說 □recite v. 敘述；詳述
▶ □describe v. 描寫；描繪；敘述

narrow-minded [ˈnæroˈmaɪndɪd] 形 胸襟狹窄的；有偏見的 ★★★★★

He's a narrow-minded old man who dismisses any idea that he doesn't already believe in.
他是個思想偏執的老人，任何觀念除非他本來就相信，否則根本不會考慮。

同義字
▶ □petty　a.　氣量小的　　　　□contracted　a.　偏狹的
▶ □bigoted　a.　心地狹窄的　　 □intolerant　a.　不寬容的

反義字
▶ □broad-minded　a.　心胸開闊的　　□large-minded　a.　心胸開闊的
▶ □liberal　a.　心胸寬闊的；開明的

nationality　[ˌnæʃəˈnælətɪ]　名國籍　　★★★★☆

April looks like she's from Latin America, but her nationality is actually Greek.
艾普兒看似拉丁美洲人，但她的國籍其實是希臘。

naturally　[ˈnætʃərəlɪ]　副自然地；當然　　★★★☆☆

I grew up in Mexico, so naturally I speak Spanish.
我在墨西哥長大，講的自然是西班牙語。

同義字
▶ □surely　adv.　當然　　□of course　當然

nausea　[ˈnɔʃɪə]　名噁心；作嘔；暈船　　★★★☆☆

I began to feel nausea from the constant starting and stopping of the bus.
公車不斷走走停停，讓我覺得噁心起來。

navigate　[ˈnævəˌget]　動航行　　★★★★☆

Before the invention of the compass, ship captains used the stars to navigate.
指南針發明以前，船長都是靠著觀察星象來航行。

同義字
▶ □sail　v.　航行

necessitate　[nɪˈsɛsəˌtet]　動使成為必須；需要

The increased business during the busy Christmas season will necessitate hiring a few more employees.
聖誕旺季需求增加，有必要多請一些員工。

同義字
▶ □require　v.　需要　　　　□oblige　v.　使不得不；迫使

needy　[ˈnidɪ]　形貧窮的　　★★★★★

This charity collects used clothing to give to needy families.
這個慈善團體收集舊衣服來幫助貧窮家庭。

同義字
▶ □destitute　a.　窮困的；貧困的　　□poor　a.　貧窮的；貧困的

▶ □penniless　a.　身無分文的　　　　□impoverished　a.　窮困的
▶ □down-and-out　a.　窮困潦倒的

反義字
▶ □rich　a.　有錢的；富有的　　　□wealthy　a.　富裕的；豐富的
▶ □affluent　a.　富裕的　　　　　□well-off　a.　富裕的
▶ □forehanded　a.　富裕的

negotiable　[nɪˈgoʃɪəbl̩]　形可協商的　★★★★☆

The salary for that job is negotiable, so you'd better be ready to bargain for a high wage and benefits.
那分工作的薪水是可以談的，所以你要自己爭取更高的薪水和福利。

nocturnal　[nɑkˈtɜnl̩]　形夜間活動的　★★★☆☆

Nocturnal animals, like raccoons, only come out at night.
像浣熊這類夜間活動的動物只會在夜晚出沒。

同義字
▶ □moonlighting　n.　夜間活動

nominate　['nɑməˌnet]　動提名　★★★★☆

Four actors will be nominated for this award, but only one will win the Oscar for Actor of the Year.
奧斯卡年度最佳演員獎有四位演員被提名，但只有一個人可以贏得這個獎項。

同義字
▶ □propose　v.　提（名）；推薦　　　□name　v.　提名

nonchalantly　['nɑnʃələntlɪ]　副漠不關心地；冷淡地；滿不在乎地　★★★☆☆

Bored of his job, Lance spends his day daydreaming at his desk and nonchalantly walking around the office.
蘭斯厭倦了他的工作，整天不是在辦公桌前做著白日夢，就是漠然地在辦公室裡走來走去。

同義字
▶ □indifferently　adv.　漠不關心地　　　□unconcernedly　adv.　不感興趣地
▶ □apathetically　adv.　不感興趣地

反義字
▶ □enthusiastically　adv.　熱心地　　　□zealously　adv.　熱心地
▶ □passionately　adv.　熱情地　　　　　□ardently　adv.　熱心地；熱切地
▶ □fervently　adv.　熱烈地

notorious　[noˈtorɪəs]　形惡名昭彰的；聲名狼藉的　★★★★★

The notorious criminal has his name on every Most Wanted poster in the city.
這個罪犯惡名昭彰，城裡所有的「頭號通緝犯」佈告上都有他的名字。

同義字
▶ □infamous　a.　聲名狼藉的　　　□flagrant　a.　兇惡的

反義字

▶ □reputable　a.　聲譽好的　　　　　□respectable　a.　名聲好的

novice　[ˈnɑvɪs]　图新手；初學者　★★★★☆

I'm just a novice skier, so that steep hill is way too difficult for me.
我只是個滑雪新手，要滑那個陡坡對我來說太難了。

同義字
▶ □beginner　n.　初學者；新手　　　　□newcomer　n.　新手；初學者
▶ □tyro　n.　初學者；生手；新手　　　□freshman　n.　新人；新手
▶ □apprentice　n.　初學者；生手

反義字
▶ □veteran　n.　老兵；老手　　　　　□old stager　有經驗的老手
▶ □past master　有豐富經驗者

nuisance　[ˈnjusṇs]　图討厭的人（或事物）；麻煩事　★★★☆☆

My little sister is such a nuisance! She bothers me with stupid questions whenever I do my homework.
我妹真是個討厭鬼！每次我做功課時，她都會拿一些蠢問題來煩我。

同義字
▶ □annoyance　n.　使人煩惱的事　　□pest　n.　討厭的人；害人精
▶ □exasperation　n.　惹人惱怒的事

nurture　[ˈnɝtʃɚ]　動養育；培育；教養　★★★★☆

Little Karen has shown interest in music. I think we should nurture her interest by buying her a violin.
既然小凱倫對音樂有興趣，我想我們應該幫她買把小提琴來栽培她。

同義字
▶ □foster　v.　培養；促進　　　　　□breed　v.　養育；培育；教養

nutritious　[njuˈtrɪʃəs]　形有營養的；滋養的　★★★★★

Fruits and vegetables are very nutritious, whereas potato chips are totally unhealthy.
水果和蔬菜很營養，炸馬鈴薯片反而很不健康。

同義字
▶ □nourishing　a.　有營養的；滋養的　　　　□nutrimental　a.　有營養的

反義字
▶ □innutritious　a.　少養分的

● ●

以O為首的單字

5 顆★：金色（860~990）證書必背
4 顆★：藍色（730~855）證書必背
3 顆★：綠色（470~725）證書必背

MP3-15

obese　[oˈbis]　形肥胖的；過胖的　★★★☆☆

That man isn't just fat, he's obese! He's well over 400 pounds!
那個人不只是胖，簡直是過胖！他的體重居然超過 400 磅！

同義字
▶ □portly　a.　肥胖的；個頭大的　　□plump　a.　豐滿的；胖嘟嘟的
▶ □fleshy　a.　多肉的；肥胖的

反義字
▶ □lean　a.　瘦的　　　　　　　　□thin　a.　薄的；細的；瘦的
▶ □spare　a.　瘦的　　　　　　　□scrawny　a.　瘦的；骨瘦如柴的
▶ □skinny　a.　皮包骨的；極瘦的

obligated　[ˈɑblɪgetɪd]　形 責無旁貸的；有責任的；有義務的　★★★★☆

Once you become a club member, you are obligated to attend all meetings. If you miss just one, you will be kicked out.
一旦加入社團，你就有義務參加所有的集會，一次沒到就會被開除。

同義字
▶ □responsible　a.　需負責任的　　□unshirkable　a.　無法逃避的
▶ □accountable　a.　應負責任的　　□answerable　a.　有責任的

反義字
▶ □unaccountable　a.　無責任的　　□unanswerable　a.　沒有責任的

observatory　[əbˈzɝvəˌtorɪ]　名 天文臺；氣象臺；瞭望臺　★★★☆☆

There's a powerful telescope at the observatory that can see to the furthest galaxies.
天文臺上有個強力望遠鏡，可以看得到最遠的銀河系。

obsolete　[ˈɑbsəˌlit]　形 廢棄的；淘汰的；過時的　★★★★☆

Cassette tapes are almost obsolete. In a few years, they won't be produced anymore.
錄音帶幾乎快被淘汰，再過幾年就會停產。

同義字
▶ □old-fashioned　a.　過時的　　□outmoded　a.　老式的；過時的
▶ □antiquated　a.　陳舊的；過時的　□outdated　a.　舊式的；過時的

反義字
▶ □new　a.　新的；新鮮的；新型的　□current　a.　現時的；當前的
▶ □modern　a.　現代化的；時髦的　□contemporary　a.　當代的

obstruct　[əbˈstrʌkt]　動 擋住（視線）；遮住　★★★★★

No wonder the tickets for these seats were so cheap. There's a pillar obstructing our view.
我們的視野被柱子擋住了，難怪這些座位的票價那麼便宜。

同義字
▶ □block　v.　阻擋；妨礙；阻止　　□barricade　v.　阻塞；擋住

occasion [əˈkeʒən]   图 場合；時刻；重大活動；盛典   ★★★☆☆

You're all dressed up. What's the special occasion? Is it your birthday or our anniversary?

什麼大日子讓你這樣盛裝打扮？是你生日還是我們的結婚週年紀念？

同義字
▶ □instance　n.　情況；場合　　　□affair　n.　事情；事件；喜慶
▶ □occurrence　n.　事件；事變

occupied [ˈɑkjʊˌpaɪd]   形 已佔用的；在使用的；　無空閒的   ★★★★☆

I'll be occupied all weekend renovating my house, so I won't have time to come to your party.

我整個週末都會忙著整修房子，所以沒空去參加你的派對。

同義字
▶ □engaged　a.　（時間）被佔用的　　　□busy　a.　忙碌的；繁忙的
反義字
▶ □free　a.　空閒的

ominous [ˈɑmɪnəs]   形 不祥的；不吉的   ★★★☆☆

Everyone ran indoors when ominous black clouds appeared overhead.

不祥烏雲罩頂，大家都跑進室內。

同義字
▶ □inauspicious　a.　惡運的　　　□unpropitious　a.　不吉利的
▶ □ill-boding　a.　不吉利的　　　□ill-omened　a.　不吉的
反義字
▶ □auspicious　a.　吉兆的；吉利的　□propitious　a.　吉祥的；吉利的

onus [ˈonəs]   图 負擔；義務；責任   ★★★★★

I've done my part of the school project. The onus is now on you to finish it off.

我已經把我的部分的學校案子弄好了，現在你有責任把它完成。

同義字
▶ □responsibility　n.　責任　　　□duty　n.　責任；義務；本分

operation [ˌɑpəˈreʃən]   图 手術   ★★★★☆

The doctor says Blake needs to have an operation to prevent another heart attack.

醫生說布雷克需要動手術才能防止心臟病再度發作。

opinion [əˈpɪnjən]   图 意見；見解；主張   ★★★☆☆

In your opinion, should people be allowed to smoke in restaurants or not?

依你看，餐廳裡應不應該讓人吸煙？

同義字
▶ □comment　n.　批評；意見　　　□view　n.　看法；觀點
▶ □contention　n.　論點；主張

opponent [ə'ponənt]　图對手；敵手；反對者　★★★★☆

Our team has defeated every opponent we've faced except the team we play against tonight.
除了今晚遇到的這一隊，不管哪一隊都不是我們球隊的對手。

同義字
▶ □enemy　n.　敵人；仇敵　　　□contender　n.　爭奪者；競爭者
▶ □rival　n.　競爭者；對手；敵手　□foe　n.　敵人；仇敵

反義字
▶ □consociate　n.　聯合；聯盟　　□helpmate　n.　合作者；夥伴
▶ □copartner　n.　合作者；合夥人

opportunity [ɑpə'tjunətɪ]　图機會；良機　★★★★★

Spending a summer in New Zealand will be a great opportunity for you to practice your English.
去紐西蘭過暑假是你練習英語的大好機會。

同義字
▶ □chance　n.　機會；良機；際遇　□opening　n.　機會；好時機

originate [ə'rɪdʒə,net]　働發源；來自；產生　★★★☆☆

I was born in Canada, but my ancestors originated from southern China.
雖然我在加拿大出生，但我祖先來自中國南方。

同義字
▶ □spring　v.　源（於）；來（自）　□derive　v.　起源；由來
▶ □come from　來自

oscillate ['ɑsḷ,et]　働擺動　★★★★☆

The fan oscillates, but you can stop its back and forth movement by pressing this button.
風扇雖然來回擺動，但你只要按下這個鈕就可以讓它停下來。

同義字
▶ □swing　v.　搖擺；擺動　□wiggle　v.　擺動；扭動
▶ □sway　v.　搖動；搖擺

outbreak ['aʊt,brek]　图爆發　★★★☆☆

Officials tried to stop the outbreak of SARS by quarantining people infected by the disease.
政府官員把感染 SARS 的人加以隔離，試圖防止疫情爆發。

同義字
▶ □explosion　n.　爆發　　□eruption　n.　（感情等的）爆發
▶ □flare-up　n.　爆發

outdo [aʊt'du]　働勝過；超越　★★★★☆

Phyllis was sure she had the highest mark in class with 99%, but was outdone be Kylie who got 100%.

菲莉絲以為她拿 99 分是全班最高分，但凱莉比她強，拿到滿分 100 分。

同義字
- ▶ □excel   v.   突出；勝過他人；優於
- ▶ □exceed   v.   超過；勝過
- □surpass   v.   勝過；優於；大於
- □outstrip   v.   超過；勝過

outskirts   [ˈaʊtˌskɝts]   图市郊；郊區   ★★★★★

Rudy lives on the outskirts of town. Behind his house are the forest and the mountains.

魯迪住在市郊，住家後面就是森林和高山。

同義字
- ▶ □suburb   n.   近郊住宅區；郊區

overthrow   [ˈovɚˌθro]   劻打倒；推翻；廢除   ★★★☆☆

The rebels were unhappy with their ruler, and plotted to overthrow the government.

反叛者對統治者不滿意，策劃要推翻政府。

同義字
- ▶ □overturn   v.   顛覆；推翻
- ▶ □demolish   v.   推翻；打敗
- □ topple   v.   使倒塌；推翻；顛覆

以P為首的單字

5 顆★：金色（860~990）證書必背
4 顆★：藍色（730~855）證書必背
3 顆★：綠色（470~725）證書必背

MP3-16

pageant   [ˈpædʒənt]   图慶典；壯麗的場面；盛裝遊行   ★★★★☆

Of the fifty girls who entered the beauty pageant, only one will be crowned Miss California.

參加選美大會的五十名佳麗中，只有一名能得到加州小姐后冠。

同義字
- ▶ □celebration   n.   慶祝活動
- □festivity   n.   慶典；慶祝活動

palette   [ˈpælɪt]   图調色板   ★★★★★

The artist mixes his paints on the palette before beginning to paint.

畫家作畫前，先在調色板上混合顏料。

panic   [ˈpænɪk]   劻恐慌；驚慌   ★★★★☆

If the fire alarm sounds, don't panic. Walk out of the building calmly and orderly.

聽到火警時不要驚慌，要冷靜且井然有序地離開建築物。

同義字

▶ ☐scare　v.　驚嚇；使恐懼　　☐frighten　v.　驚恐
▶ ☐alarm　v.　使驚慌不安

反義字
▶ ☐calm　v.　使鎮定；使平靜　　☐compose　v.　使安定；使平靜
▶ ☐quiet　v.　使安靜；使平息　　☐soothe　v.　安慰；撫慰

parable　[ˈpærəbḷ]　🔳寓言　★★★☆☆

The teacher read a short parable to teach the children it is wrong to lie.
老師朗讀了一篇短篇寓言，教導孩子們說謊是不對的。

同義字
▶ ☐fable　n.　寓言

parallel　[ˈpærəˌlɛl]　🔳平行的　★★★☆☆

Two parallel lines will never intersect.
兩條平行線永遠不會相交。

同義字
▶ ☐collateral　a.　並行的

pedal　[ˈpɛdḷ]　🔳踏板　★★★★☆

Nicole got into a car accident because she stepped on the gas pedal instead of the brake.
妮可會出車禍是因為該踩煞車時反而踩了油門。

同義字
▶ ☐treadle　n.　踏板

peddle　[ˈpɛdḷ]　🔳叫賣；挨戶兜售　★★★★★

After losing his job, the old man is now wheeling around a cart peddling cheap t-shirts.
這個老先生失業後，便到處推著車子兜售廉價 T恤。

同義字
▶ ☐hawk　v.　叫賣；兜售　☐bawl　v.　叫賣（貨物）

pedestrian　[pəˈdɛstrɪən]　🔳行人　★★★☆☆

Slow down when those lights are flashing. There are pedestrians crossing the road.
看到燈號閃爍時要減速，因為行人要過街。

同義字
▶ ☐passer-by　n.　過路人

penalty　[ˈpɛnḷtɪ]　🔳罰款　★★★★☆

The penalty for breaking the curfew is $500 and a night in jail.
違反宵禁者將罰款 500 元並拘禁一晚。

▶ □fine　n.　罰金；罰款　　□forfeit　n.　罰金

pendant　[ˈpɛndənt]　名垂飾；掛件　★★★★★

The pendant on my necklace was a birthday gift from my cousin.
我項鍊上的墜子是表妹送的生日禮物。

penetrate　[ˈpɛnəˌtret]　動穿過；刺入；透過

The worker was not able to penetrate the concrete wall with such a small drill.
工人沒辦法用這麼小的鑽頭鑽穿水泥牆。

同義字
▶ □pierce　v.　突入；穿過；突破　　□perforate　v.　穿過；貫穿

pension　[ˈpɛnʃən]　名退休金；養老金；撫恤金　★★★★☆

Since his pension from the government was so small, Mr. Jones relied on money from his children to survive.
由於政府提供的退休金太少，瓊斯先生便靠著孩子們給的錢勉強過日子。

同義字
▶ □allowance　n.　津貼；補貼　　□annuity　n.　年金
▶ □subsidy　n.　津貼；補貼；補助金

perjury　[ˈpɝdʒərɪ]　名偽證；偽證罪　★★★☆☆

Perjury is a terrible crime, so please don't lie when you testify in court tomorrow.
做偽證是很嚴重的罪行，明天出庭作證時請千萬不要說謊。

persevere　[ˌpɝsəˈvɪr]　動堅持不懈；不屈不撓　★★★★★

Despite several major setbacks, the scientist persevered and discovered a new vaccine.
儘管經歷了好幾次重大失敗，這名科學家仍然不屈不撓，終於發明了新的疫苗。

同義字
▶ □persist　v.　堅持；固執　　□insist　v.　堅持
反義字
▶ □desist　v.　停止；打消念頭

personal　[ˈpɝsn̩l]　形個人的；私人的　★★★☆☆

Be careful when giving out personal details such as birthdates and account numbers, because identity theft is on the rise.
身分竊取犯罪層出不窮，提供生日和帳戶號碼等個人資料時務必小心。

同義字
▶ □private　a.　個人的；私人的　　□individual　a.　個人的；個體的
反義字
▶ □impersonal　a.　非個人的；客觀的

personnel [ˌpɝsn̩'ɛl] 名人事部門；人事課（或室等） ★★★★☆

If you have any questions regarding salary, please see Vicky in the personnel department.
如果你有任何薪資方面的問題，請洽詢人事部門的維琪小姐。

同義字
▶ □human resources 人事部門；人事科

perspiration [ˌpɝspə'reʃn̩] 名汗；汗水 ★★★☆☆

After hiking all afternoon, Carl's clothes were covered with perspiration.
健行一下午後，卡爾的衣服被汗水弄得濕透。

同義字
▶ □sweat n. 汗；汗水

persuade [pɚ'swed] 動說服；勸服 ★★★★★

Nancy didn't want to buy a new vacuum, but the salesman persuaded her with a convincing sales pitch.
南茜不想買新的吸塵器，但是推銷人員的三吋不爛之舌說服了她。

同義字
▶ □convince v. 使確信；使信服 □win over 說服

pertinent ['pɝtn̩ənt] 形有關的；相干的 ★★★★☆

Only include pertinent information in your summary. Don't waste the readers' time with insignificant details.
摘要裡只要記下相關資訊即可，不要讓讀者花時間在無關輕重的細節上。

同義字
▶ □relative a. 相關的 □connected a. 有關連的
▶ □relevant a. 有關的；恰當的

反義字
▶ □irrelevant a. 無關係的 □unconcerned a. 無關的

pharmacy ['fɑrməsɪ] 名藥房 ★★★★★

Where's the nearest pharmacy? I need to buy some antibiotics.
最近的藥房在哪裡？我需要買一些抗生素。

同義字
▶ □dispensary n. 診療所；藥房 □drugstore n. 藥房；雜貨店

philanthropist [fɪ'lænθrəpɪst] 名慈善家 ★★★★☆

The philanthropist set up a foundation to share his millions with non-profit community groups.
這位慈善家設立基金，將鉅額財富貢獻給非營利質的社會團體。

同義字

▶ □humanitarian　n.　人道主義者　　□philanthrope　n.　博愛的人

plagiarism [ˈpledʒəˌrɪzəm]　📙抄襲；剽竊　　★★★☆☆

If you use that author's writing in your essay, you must acknowledge that.
Otherwise it's plagiarism, and you could get expelled.
如果你把那位作者的著作用在自己文章裡，就必須承認；不然這算是剽竊行為，可能會被開除。

同義字
▶ □crib　v.　抄襲　　　　□lift　v.　偷竊；抄襲
▶ □purloin　v.　盜取　　　□pirate　v.　剽竊；非法翻印

pleasant [ˈplɛzənt]　📙令人愉快的；舒適的　　★★★☆☆

The gentle breeze is a pleasant change from the hot, dry weather we've been having.
溫和的清風為這陣子又熱又乾的氣候帶來舒適的轉變。

同義字
▶ □comfortable　a.　使人舒服的　　□agreeable　a.　令人愉快的
▶ □cheerful　a.　使人感到愉快的

反義字
▶ □unpleasant　a.　使人不愉快的　　□disagreeable　a.　不合意的
▶ □obnoxious　a.　令人非常不快的

pollen [ˈpɑlən]　📙花粉　　★★★★☆

When Steve smelled the lily, the pollen went up his nose and made him sneeze.
史蒂夫聞 合花的時候吸進花粉而打起噴嚏來。

pollute [pəˈlut]　📙污染；弄髒　　★★★★★

Don't pollute the air by driving or riding a scooter. Walk or cycle instead.
不要開車或騎摩托車來污染空氣，改成走路或騎腳踏車吧！

同義字
▶ □contaminate　v.　弄髒；污染　　□taint　v.　使感染；使腐壞
▶ □defile　v.　弄髒；損污　　　　　□foul　v.　弄髒；污染；玷污
▶ □poison　v.　污染；毒害；敗壞

portfolio [portˈfolɪˌo]　📙1.代表作選輯；代表作品　2.文件夾；卷宗夾；公事包
★★★★☆

The graphic designer opened her portfolio to show all her work, a collection of illustrations and computer graphics.
該平面設計師打開文件夾，展示她個人所有的插畫和電腦繪圖作品。

precarious [prɪˈkɛrɪəs]　📙不穩的；危險的　　★★★☆☆

Don't leave your cup of tea in such a precarious position. Anyone walking by could

easily knock it off the table.
不要把你這杯茶放在這麼危險的地方，以免有人經過把茶從桌上碰翻。

同義字
▶ □unstable　a.　不穩固的　　　□unsteady　a.　不平穩的
▶ □dangerous　a.　不安全的　　□insecure　a.　有危險的

反義字
▶ □stable　a.　穩定的；牢固的　　□steady　a.　穩固的；平穩的
▶ □safe　a.　安全的；無危險的　　□secure　a.　安全的；無危險的

predator　['prɛdətɚ]　📑食肉動物；掠奪者　　★★★☆☆

A lion is a skilled predator, and stalks his prey patiently before attacking.
獅子這種食肉動物捕食技術一流，攻擊獵物前會先耐心追蹤。

predict　[prɪ'dɪkt]　📖預言；預料　　★★★★☆

The fortune teller predicted Jim would be a successful doctor when he grew up.
算命師預言，吉姆長大後會成為一名有成就的醫生。

同義字
▶ □foresee　v.　預見；預知　　　□forecast　v.　預示；預言
▶ □foretell　v.　預言；預示　　　□prophesy　v.　預言；預告

premier　['primɪɚ]　📑首位的；首要的　　★★★★★

She is the premier tennis player in this age group. Nobody can match her skills.
她是這個年齡組的頭號網球選手，沒有人技術比她好。

同義字
▶ □chief　a.　等級最高的　　　　□principal　a.　主要的；首要的
▶ □main　a.　主要的；最重要的　□primary　a.　首要的；主要的
▶ □prime　a.　主要的；首位的

反義字
▶ □subordinate　a.　次要的；隸屬的 □ secondary　a.　次要的；從屬的
▶ □inferior　a.　（地位等）低等的

prescription　[prɪ'skrɪpʃən]　📑處方；藥方；處方上開的藥　★★★★☆

The doctor gave Jill a prescription for some strong antibiotics for the infection.
醫生針對吉爾的感染狀況，開了一些強烈的抗生素處方。

同義字
▶ □formula　n.　配方；處方　　　□medicine　n.　藥；內服藥

prevent　[prɪ'vɛnt]　📖防止；預防　　★★★☆☆

You should stretch your muscles before exercising to prevent injury.
運 前應該先伸展肌肉以免受傷。

同義字
▶ □avoid　v.　避免　　　□avert　v.　防止；避免

privilege [ˈprɪvḷɪdʒ] 名特權；優特 ★★★★☆

Club members enjoy the privilege of dining in the restaurant for half price.
俱樂部會員享有在餐廳用餐半價的優惠。

同義字
▶ □liberty   n.   特權；恩典   □peculiar   n.   特權；特有財產
▶ □concession   n.   特許；專利權

procrastinate [proˈkræstəˌnet] 動延遲；耽擱 ★★★☆☆

Although he had over a month to finish the project, Don kept on procrastinating
until he was hurrying to finish it the night before the deadline.
雖然唐有一個多月的時間來完成專案，他還是一拖再拖，直到期限前一晚才趕著完成。

同義字
▶ □wait   v.   延緩處理；耽擱   □postpone   v.   使延期；延遲
▶ □stall   v.   拖延推遲

反義字
▶ □on time   準時

productive [prəˈdʌktɪv] 形生產的；生產性的 ★★★★★

Our new factory equipment is twice as productive as the old one. It turns out the
same output in half the time.
我們新工廠設備的產能是原有設備的兩倍，同樣產量只需要花一半時間。

同義字
▶ □yielding   a.   生產的   □prolific   a.   多產的；多育的

反義字
▶ □unproductive   a.   無收益的

proficient [prəˈfɪʃənt] 形精通的；熟練的 ★★★★☆

You should be proficient at using computers, otherwise he won't be able to work in
many office settings.
你最好熟練電腦，不然很多辦公室工作你都無法勝任。

同義字
▶ □skilled   a.   熟練的；有技能的   □practiced   a.   熟練的
▶ □masterful   a.   熟練的；出色的   □neat   a.   熟練的；靈巧的

反義字
▶ □unskilled   a.   不熟練的   □inexperienced   a.   經驗不足的

prominence [ˈprɑmənəns] 名顯著；傑出；卓越；聲望 ★★★☆☆

Greg was an obscure theater actor before rising to prominence with his role on a
popular soap opera.
葛瑞格原本是沒沒無聞的劇場演員，演出熱門連續劇後聲望才越來越高。

同義字
▶ □distinction   n.   殊勳；榮譽；著名   □prestige   n.   名望；聲望；威望

propaganda [͵prɑpəˈgændə]　　图宣傳；宣傳活動　　★★★★☆

To win support for the war, the government began a propaganda campaign to increase feelings of nationalism.

為了聲援戰爭，政府進行宣傳活動來增強大眾對民族主義的情感。

同義字
▶ □advertisement　n.　廣告；宣傳　　□blurb　n.　吹捧 廣告

prototype [ˈprotəˌtaɪp]　　图原型；標準；模範　　★★★☆☆

This is a prototype of a next-generation electric automobile. If it passes all the tests, we'll begin manufacturing them next fall.

這是新一代電 汽車的原型車。只要能通過全部的測試，我們將在明年秋天量產。

同義字
▶ □ancestor　n.　原型；先驅　　□pattern　n.　模範；榜樣；典型
▶ □original　n.　原型

psychiatric [͵saɪkɪˈætrɪk]　　圈精神病的　　★★★★★

Having been diagnosed with a mental illness, she spent the next few years in the psychiatric ward of the hospital.

由於診斷出患有精神方面的疾病，她在醫院的精神病房待了好幾年。

同義字
▶ □mental　a.　精神的；心理的　　□inward　a.　內心的；精神上的
反義字
▶ □physical　a.　身體的；肉體的　　□bodily　a.　肉體的；身體的

punctuality [pʌŋktʃʊˈælətɪ]　　图守時　　★★★★☆

Our professor demands punctuality. Students who come just a minute late are not allowed into the class.

我們教授要求大家守時，任何學生即使只遲到一分鐘也不准進教室。

以Q為首的單字

5 顆★：金色（860~990）證書必背
4 顆★：藍色（730~855）證書必背
3 顆★：綠色（470~725）證書必背

MP3-17,18

quadruple [ˈkwɑdrʊpl]　　勔使成四倍　　★★★☆☆

Our profits have quadrupled in one year. Last year we made $5 million, and this year we have a $20 million profit.

我們的獲利一年成長四倍。去年才賺了五百萬，今年卻賺了兩千萬。

qualification [͵kwɑləfəˈkeʃən]　　图資格；能力　　★★★★☆

The qualifications for this job are a science degree and fluency in Spanish. People who don't have this background shouldn't apply.

有理工學位並精通西班牙文的人才有資格申請這分工作。不具相關背景的人就不用申請了。

同義字
▶ □equipment　n.　才能；素養　　　□eligibility　n.　合格

反義字
▶ □disqualification　n.　取消資格

quarrelsome　[ˈkwɔrəlsəm]　形 喜歡爭吵的；動輒吵架的　★★★☆☆

When Wayne is in a quarrelsome mood, he picks a fight with anyone who talks to him.

韋恩想找人吵架時，誰跟他說話他都會加以挑釁。

同義字
▶ □argumentative　a.　好爭論的　　□ belligerent　a.　好戰的；好鬥的
▶ □cantankerous　a.　好打架的　　　□ combative　a.　好戰的；好鬥的

反義字
▶ □friendly　a.　友好的；親切的　　□amicable　a.　友善的；友好的

quarterly　[ˈkwɔrtɚlɪ]　副 按季度；一季一次地　★★★★☆

This magazine is published quarterly, in January, April, July, and October.

這本雜誌每季出版一次，分別在一月、四月、七月和十月。

queue　[kju]　名 （人或車輛等的）行列、長隊　★★★★★

You! Don't try to sneak to the front of the line! Go to the back of the queue.

這位仁兄！別偷偷摸摸插到隊伍前面。請回去排隊。

同義字
▶ □line　n.　列；行列　　　□ procession　n.　（人或車輛）行列

以R為首的單字

5顆★：金色（860~990）證書必背
4顆★：藍色（730~855）證書必背
3顆★：綠色（470~725）證書必背

MP3-17,18

radiate　[ˈredɪˌet]　動 （光、熱等）散發、輻射　★★★★☆

The rays of the sun radiate in all directions, bringing light and warmth.

太陽的光線向各個方向散發，帶來了光明和溫暖。

同義字
▶ □glow　v.　發光；發熱　□diffuse　v.　使（氣味）四散

rebellious　[rɪˈbɛljəs]　形 叛逆的　★★★☆☆

Kirk became rebellious when he turned sixteen, and began to be disobedient towards teachers and parents.

柯克十六歲時變得叛逆起來，開始不聽老師和父母的話。

同義字
▶ □defiant　a.　違抗的；挑戰的　　□disobedient　a.　不服從的
▶ □insubordinate　a.　不順從的

反義字
▶ □obedient　a.　服從的；順從的　　□yielding　a.　聽從的；柔順的
▶ □passive　a.　順從的；順服的

recede　[rɪˋsid]　**國**後退　★★★★☆

Dad's hairline began to recede a few years ago, and now he's almost half bald.

爸爸的髮線幾年前開始後退，現在幾乎禿了一半。

同義字
▶ □retreat　v.　使後退；使往後移

反義字
▶ □advance　v.　使向前移；推進

reckless　[ˋrɛklɪs]　**國**不注意的；不在乎的；魯莽的；不顧後果的　★★★★★

Tom's a reckless driver who disregards all speed limits and traffic lights. There's no way I'm getting in the car with him.

湯姆是個魯莽的駕駛人，開車時都不太管速限和燈號。我可不想和他同車。

同義字
▶ □heedless　a.　不留心的　　□careless　a.　粗心的
▶ □headlong　a.　欠考慮的　　□inadvertent　a.　不注意的
▶ □rash　a.　輕率的；急躁的

反義字
▶ □thoughtful　a.　細心的；注意的　　□heedful　a.　深切注意的

recline　[rɪˋklaɪn]　**國**（座椅）靠背可活動後仰；使斜倚；使躺下　★★★★☆

When you pull this lever on the side of the chair, it reclines into a bed.

拉下椅子旁邊這個控制桿，椅背就會向後放下變成一張床。

同義字
▶ □lie　v.　躺；臥　　□repose　v.　躺；靠
▶ □lounge　v.　倚；靠

recollect　[͵rɛkəˋlɛkt]　**國**回憶；追憶；記起　★★★☆☆

I know you think I owe you $100, but I don't recollect ever borrowing money from you.

我知道你認為我欠你一百塊，但我不記得有跟你借過錢。

同義字
▶ □remember　v.　回憶起　　□recall　v.　回想；回憶
▶ □reminisce　v.　追憶；回想

反義字
▶ □forget　v.　忘記

recurring [rɪˈkɝɪŋ] 形 再發的；循環的 ★★★★☆

Dawn has had a recurring dream since she was very young. It's always about being chased by a wolf.

唐恩從很小開始就一直做相同的夢，老是夢到被狼追趕。

同義字
▶ □repeating   a.   反覆的；循環的

reform [rɪˈfɔrm] 動 改革；革新；改良 ★★★★★

The new government is planning to reform the health care system to allow free medicine to citizens.

新政府正在計畫改良醫療系統，讓民眾享有免費用藥的福利。

同義字
▶ □innovate   v.   革新；改革；創新

reimburse [ˌriɪmˈbɝs] 動 償還；歸還 ★★★★☆

If you buy some supplies for the company, you'll be reimbursed for your expenses at the end of the month.

如果你幫公司購買用品，公司月底就會把錢退還給你。

同義字
▶ □return   v.   歸還；退回   □repay   v.   償還；還錢
▶ □refund   v.   退還；歸還；償還

relentless [rɪˈlɛntlɪs] 形 不間斷的；持續的 ★★★☆☆

The rain was relentless, and soon caused flooding all through the valley.

雨一直下個不停，很快造成整座山谷洪水氾濫。

同義字
▶ □ceaseless   a.   不停的；不間斷的   □uninterrupted   a.   不間斷的
▶ □ongoing   a.   前進的；進行的   □continuing   a.   連續的

relinquish [rɪˈlɪŋkwɪʃ] 動 交出；讓與 ★★★★☆

Although he lost the election fairly, the president refused to relinquish control and recaptured the country using force.

總統雖然在競選中大敗，卻拒絕交出掌控權，還用武力奪回政權。

同義字
▶ □abdicate   v.   正式放棄（權力等）   □surrender   v.   交出；放棄

reluctant [rɪˈlʌktənt] 形 不情願的；勉強的 ★★★☆☆

I'm reluctant to let Jolene take care of our son because I don't trust her.

我不信任裘琳，不想讓她照顧我們兒子。

同義字
▶ □unwilling   a.   不願意的；不情願的   □grudging   a.   勉強的；吝嗇的
▶ □disinclined   a.   不願的   □loath   a.   不願意的；不喜歡的

177

反義字
▶ □willing　a.　願意的；樂意的

rendezvous [ˈrɑndəˌvu] 　動約會；會面；會合 ★★★★☆

Let's rendezvous at the City Square at noon. And don't be late.
我們中午就約在城市廣場碰面，別遲到喔！

同義字
▶ □meet　v.　集合；會合　□assemble　v.　集合；聚集

renovate [ˈrɛnəˌvet] 　動修理；改善；整修 ★★★★★

Unable to afford a new house, the Simpsons renovated their current home by putting in hardwood floors.
辛普森一家買不起新房子，便替目前的家鋪上硬木地板整修一番。

同義字
▶ □repair　v.　修理；修補　　　　□recondition　v.　修理；重建
▶ □refit　v.　整修；改裝　　　　　□do up　修理

反義字
▶ □break　v.　毀壞；弄壞；砸破　□destroy　v.　毀壞；破壞

repellent [rɪˈpɛlənt] 　名驅蟲劑 ★★★★☆

Don't forget to put on mosquito repellent, otherwise they'll eat you alive.
別忘了擦防蚊劑，不然會被叮得很慘。

同義字
▶ □vermifuge　n.　驅蟲藥　　　　□anthelmintic　n.　驅蟲劑
▶ □helminthic　n.　驅腸蟲藥

replenish [rɪˈplɛnɪʃ] 　動把…裝滿；把…再備足；補充 ★★★☆☆

We should replenish our supply of water before crossing the desert.
橫越沙漠前，我們得先補充存水才行。

同義字
▶ □supply　v.　補充；供給；供應　□recruit　v.　補充

反義字
▶ □exhaust　v.　用完；耗盡　　　　□drain　v.　耗盡

repress [rɪˈprɛs] 　動抑制；壓制；約束 ★★★★☆

Jake represses an early childhood memory of losing his mother because it's too painful to think about.
傑克一直壓抑著童年失去母親的記憶，因為一想起這件事就會令他萬分痛苦。

同義字
▶ □restrain　v.　抑制；遏制　　　□suppress　v.　抑制；忍住
▶ □curb　v.　控制；遏止　　　　　□smother　v.　忍住；抑制

反義字

▶ □incite v. 激勵；激起；煽動 □agitate v. 鼓動；煽動
▶ □ferment v. 使騷動

reprimand [ˈrɛprəˌmænd] v.訓斥；斥責；譴責 ★★★★★

Tony was reprimanded for his disgraceful behavior by having a week's wages deducted from his paycheck.
為了懲罰湯尼可恥的行為，公司扣他一個禮拜的薪水。

同義字
▶ □blame v. 責備；指責 □denounce v. 指責；譴責
▶ □censure v. 責備；譴責 □reproach v. 責備；斥責
▶ □condemn v. 責難；責備

反義字
▶ □praise v. 讚美；表揚；歌頌 □compliment v. 讚美；恭維
▶ □extol v. 讚美；頌揚 □admire v. 稱讚；誇獎

rescind [rɪˈsɪnd] v.廢止；取消；撤回 ★★★★☆

The reporter rescinded the comment he wrote yesterday because it was simply untrue.
這名記者因為昨天所寫的評論內容不實而將其撤回。

同義字
▶ □annul v. 廢除；宣告…無效 □revoke v. 撤回；撤銷；廢除
▶ □retract v. 撤銷；收回 □repeal v. 撤銷（決議等）

resemblance [rɪˈzɛmbləns] n.相似點；相似程度 ★★★☆☆

Although they are sisters, there is absolutely no resemblance between them. Perhaps one of them is adopted.
雖然她們是姐妹，彼此卻完全沒有任何相似之處。搞不好其中一個是收養來的。

同義字
▶ □likeness n. 相像；相似 □similarity n. 類似；相似
▶ □analogy n. 相似；類似

反義字
▶ □dissimilarity n. 不同；相異點 □unlikeness n. 不同；不像

retaliate [rɪˈtælɪˌet] v.報復；回敬 ★★★★☆

After being punched in the face, the soccer player retaliated by kicking his opponent in the stomach.
這名足球選手被迎面打了一拳，便踢對手肚子來報復。

同義字
▶ □retort v. 反擊；報復 □revenge v. 報仇；報復
▶ □avenge v. 報仇；報復

retrieve [rɪˈtriv] v.（獵犬）銜回（被擊中的獵物） ★★★☆☆

The hunter shot the bird, and sent his hound to retrieve it.

獵人把鳥打下來，再叫獵犬把獵物銜回來。

revise [rɪ'vaɪz] 動 修訂；校訂 ★★★★☆

This letter is just a rough draft. You'll need to revise it with the current information before sending it out.
這封信只是草稿，要根據最新資訊加以修訂才能寄出。

同義字
- ▶ □redact　v.　編輯；校訂　□amend　v.　修訂；修改；訂正
- ▶ □emend　v.　校訂；修改

rotation [ro'teʃən] 名 旋轉；自轉 ★★★★★

The Earth makes one rotation around its axis every 24 hours.
地球以地軸為中心，每二十四小時自轉一週。

同義字
- ▶ □revolution　n.　迴轉；旋轉　　□gyration　n.　旋轉；迴旋

rotten ['rɑtṇ] 形 腐爛的 ★★★★☆

Yuck! What's that smell coming from the fridge? You might have some rotten fruit in there!
噁心死了！冰箱怎麼那麼臭？可能有些水果在裡面爛掉了！

同義字
- ▶ □putrid　a.　腐敗的；放出惡臭的　□decayed　a.　爛了的；腐敗的
- ▶ □putrescent　a.　腐爛的；腐敗的

ruckus ['rʌkəs] 名 喧鬧；騷動 ★★★☆☆

The students were very quiet, but as soon as the teacher left, considerable ruckus could be heard from the classroom.
學生們原本非常安靜，但老師才一離開，教室立刻傳出不小的喧鬧聲。

同義字
- ▶ □noise　n.　聲響；喧鬧聲　　□racket　n.　喧嚷；吵鬧聲
- ▶ □hubbub　n.　吵鬧聲；騷動　　□clamor　n.　吵鬧聲；喧囂聲

反義字
- ▶ □quietness　n.　安靜；肅靜　　□calmness　n.　平靜；安寧
- ▶ □peace　n.　和平；和睦；安詳　□tranquility　n.　平靜；安靜

以S為首的單字

5 顆★：金色（860~990）證書必背
4 顆★：藍色（730~855）證書必背
3 顆★：綠色（470~725）證書必背

MP3-18

safeguard ['sef‚gɑrd] 動 保護；防衛 ★★★★☆

It's a good idea to wear a helmet while skating to safeguard against head injuries.

為保護頭部避免受傷，溜冰時戴上安全頭盔是個好方法。

同義字

▶ □defend　v.　防禦；保衛；保護　　□protect　v.　保護；防護
▶ □shield　v.　保護；保衛　　□bulwark　v.　保護；使安全

反義字

▶ □attack　v.　進攻；襲擊；抨擊　　□assault　v.　攻擊；襲擊；譴責
▶ □tilt　v.　攻擊；抨擊

salutation [ˌsæljəˈteʃən]　名招呼；致意；行禮；問候　★★★★★

A common salutation when you meet someone in India is to put your hands together and say "Namaste".
在印度要和人打招呼，一般都是雙手合十並說「Namaste」。

同義字

▶ □greeting　n.　問候；迎接　　□hail　n.　歡呼；打招呼
▶ □courtesy　n.　謙恭有禮的言辭

scarcity [ˈskɛrsətɪ]　名缺乏；不足；匱乏；蕭條（時期）；荒（年）★★★★☆

During the drought, there was a scarcity of food that affected people across the country.
旱災期間，全國各地都發生糧食匱乏的現象。

同義字

▶ □lack　n.　欠缺；不足；沒有　　□want　n.　缺乏；不足
▶ □deficiency　n.　不足；缺乏　　□shortage　n.　缺少；不足

反義字

▶ □fill　n.　充足；足夠　　□sufficiency　n.　充分；足量
▶ □plenty　n.　豐富；充足；大量

scribble [ˈskrɪbl̩]　動潦草書寫；草率創作；亂塗；亂畫　★★★☆☆

I can't read what you scribbled on this message pad. Is it "Pat 632-4883" or "Bart 883-0488"?
我看不懂你在留言條上的鬼畫符。你寫的是「派特 632-4883」還是「巴特 883-0488」啊？

同義字

▶ □scrawl　v.　潦草地寫（或畫）；亂寫　　□scratch　v.　亂劃

script [skrɪpt]　名腳本；底稿；劇本　★★★★☆

The actors memorize the lines from the script before going on stage.
演員上台前，要先把劇本裡的台詞背起來。

同義字

▶ □libretto　n.　劇本

seclusion [sɪˈkluʒən]　名隔絕；孤立；隱居；隱退　★★★★★

The monk went off into the mountains seeking seclusion, and to further his

meditation practice.
該名修道士躲進深山隱居，以便專心練習冥想。

同義字
▶ □solitude　n.　孤獨；寂寞；隱居　□privacy　n.　隱退、隱居

sedentary [ˈsɛdn̩ˌtɛrɪ]　形坐著的；需要（或慣於）久坐的　★★★★☆

Tired of his sedentary job in the office, Mick found a job leading hiking and climbing trips through the mountains.
米克受不了一天到晚坐在辦公室，便另外找了一分健行和登山嚮導的工作。

seize [siz]　動沒收；扣押；查封　★★★☆☆

The coast guard boarded the smugglers' boat and seized millions of dollars worth of illegal drugs.
海岸巡邏隊登上走私船，查扣了市價數百萬的非法毒品。

同義字
▶ □confiscate　v.　沒收；將…充公　□sequestrate　v.　扣押；沒收
▶ □distrain　v.　扣押財物　□impound　v.　扣押；沒收

seminar [ˈsɛməˌnɑr]　名研討班課程；討論會　★★★★☆

Hoping to improve her business, Maureen took a seminar that taught how to increase sales through networking.
莫琳參加了一場教人如何利用網路增加銷售的研討會，希望能讓生意更好。

同義字
▶ □forum　n.　討論會　□symposium　n.　討論會
▶ □colloquium　n.　學術報告會

sensitive [ˈsɛnsətɪv]　形敏感的；易受傷害的　★★★☆☆

You shouldn't have told Peggy her soup was bland. She's really sensitive to criticism, so I wouldn't be surprised if she's crying now.
你不該跟佩姬說她煮的湯沒味道；她對別人的批評很敏感，現在可能已經哭了。

同義字
▶ □susceptible　a.　敏感的　□impressionable　a.　敏感的
▶ □responsive　a.　易感 的；敏感的；易受影響的

反義字
▶ □insensitive　a.　感覺遲鈍的　□insusceptible　a.　無感覺的

sentence [ˈsɛntəns]　動宣判；判決　★★★★☆

The judge sentenced her to ten years in jail for robbing the bank.
她搶劫銀行，法官判她有期徒刑十年。

同義字
▶ □adjudge　v.　判決；宣判　□pronounce　v.　宣判
▶ □adjudicate　v.　判決；宣告　□decree　v.　判決；裁定

sequence [ˈsikwəns] 图 次序；順序；先後；（數）序列 ★★★★★

Which number comes next in the following sequence of numbers? 3, 4, 6, 9, 13, 18...?

從下面數列來看，接下來應該出現什麼數字？3、4、6、9、13、18…？

同義字
▶ □order n. 順序；次序　　□succession n. 一連串
▶ □series n. 連續；系列

shrink [ʃrɪŋk] 颲 收縮；縮短；皺縮；縮水 ★★★★☆

That sweater will shrink if you wash it in hot water.

那件毛衣用熱水洗會縮水。

同義字
▶ □reduce v. 減少；縮小　　□contract v. 縮小；收縮
▶ □compress v. 壓緊；壓縮

反義字
▶ □expand v. 膨脹；擴張　　□enlarge v. 擴大；擴展

shuffle [ˈʃʌfl] 颲 洗牌 ★★★☆☆

Shuffle the cards well before you deal them out.

先把牌洗乾淨再發牌。

simulate [ˈsɪmjəˌlet] 颲 模擬；模仿 ★★★★☆

The computer program will simulate the effects of an earthquake on the building to test its strength.

為測試這棟大樓的強度，電腦程式會模擬地震對它造成的影響。

同義字
▶ □impersonate v. 扮演；模仿　　□imitate v. 模仿
▶ □mimic v. 模仿　　□portray v. 扮演；表現

singe [sɪndʒ] 颲 把…微微燒焦；損傷 ★★★☆☆

Don't put your face too close to the campfire. You might singe your eyebrows!

臉不要太靠近營火，不然可能會燒到眉毛！

同義字
▶ □scorch v. 燒焦；烤焦　　□sear v. 燒焦
▶ □char v. 把…燒成炭；把…燒焦

siren [ˈsaɪrən] 图 汽笛；警報器 ★★★★☆

When I heard the police siren, I pulled my car over to the side so he could pass.

我一聽見警笛聲，就把車開到路邊讓警車通過。

同義字
▶ □alarm n. 警報；警報器　　□whistle n. 口哨；警笛；汽笛

solace [`sɑlɪs] 图 安慰；慰藉 ★★★☆☆

After the death of her husband, Mandy found solace in painting.
先生過世後，曼蒂在畫畫中找到了安慰。

同義字
▶ □comfort n. 安慰；慰藉　　□consolation n. 安慰；慰藉

souvenir [ˌsuvə`nɪr] 图 紀念品；紀念物 ★★★★☆

I picked up a little souvenir in the gift shop as I was coming home from my business trip.
出差回家途中，我在禮品店挑了一樣小紀念品。

同義字
▶ □memento n. 紀念物　　□token n. 紀念品
▶ □remembrance n. 紀念品

sparse [spɑrs] 图 稀少的；稀疏的 ★★★★★

Vegetation is very sparse in this dry region, therefore you won't find a lot of wildlife.
這個乾旱地區植物相當稀少，所以看不到太多野生動物。

同義字
▶ □rare a. 稀有的；罕見的　　□few a. 很少數的
▶ □uncommon a. 罕見的

反義字
▶ □many a. 許多的　　□numerous a. 許多的；很多的
▶ □various a. 許多的

specialty [`spɛʃəltɪ] 图 專業；專長 ★★★★☆

That lawyer can handle most cases, but his specialty is family law.
雖然那名律師大部分案件都可以處理，但家事法才是他的專長。

同義字
▶ □expertise n. 專門知識

spectator [spɛk`tetɚ] 图 觀眾 ★★★☆☆

The ten thousand spectators in the stadium began cheering when the home team ran onto the field.
地主隊上場時，運動場中的十萬名觀眾開始歡呼。

同義字
▶ □viewer n. 參觀者；觀眾　　□audience n. 聽眾；觀眾

spontaneous [spɑn`tenɪəs] 图 自發的；非出於強制的 ★★★★☆

Marvin is so spontaneous that one day he just decided to hitchhike across the country without any preparation or plan.
馬文非常隨性，有一天沒有半點準備和計劃，便突然決定要搭便車全國旅行。

同義字

▶ □voluntary a. 自發的；自決的   □vunbidden a. 未受命令的
▶ □unprompted a. 未受提示的

反義字
▶ □passive a. 被動的；消極的

squabble [ˈskwɑbl̩]   動 爭吵；口角   ★★★☆☆

The two neighbors squabbled endlessly about who was responsible for cleaning the common area.

兩位鄰居為了誰負責清掃公共區域而爭吵不休。

同義字
▶ □argue v. 爭論；辯論；爭吵   □quarrel v. 爭吵；不和
▶ □wrangle v. 爭論；爭吵   □bicker v. 吵嘴；爭吵

反義字
▶ □reconcile v. 使和解；使和好

stagnant [ˈstægnənt]   形 （水）污濁的、發臭的   ★★★★☆

In the summer, the river dries up and the water in this lake becomes stagnant.

夏天時河水乾涸，這座湖的水也跟著發臭。

同義字
▶ □dirty a. 髒的；污穢的   □foul a. 骯髒的；污濁的
▶ □muddy a. 渾濁的；模糊的

反義字
▶ □clear a. 清澈的；透明的   □limpid a. 清澈的；透明的
▶ □pellucid a. 清澄的；透明的

stationary [ˈsteʃənˌɛrɪ]   形 不動的   ★★★★★

The ceremonial guard stood stationary outside the gate, and did not move even when people made faces at him.

儀典衛兵在大門外肅立不動，即使人們對他扮鬼臉也是不動如山。

同義字
▶ □still a. 靜止的；不動的   □immovable a. 不動的
▶ □motionless a. 不動的；靜止的

stellar [ˈstɛlɚ]   形 主角的；（戲劇、電影等的）明星的   ★★★★☆

Sean's stellar performance in the movie earned him the award for Best Actor.

西恩把這部電影主角戲演得很好，一舉奪得最佳男主角獎。

stimulate [ˈstɪmjəˌlet]   動 刺激；激勵；使興奮；促使   ★★★☆☆

Life in this town is so boring! Let's go to the city and do something stimulating.

鎮上的生活無聊透了！不如進城找點刺激的活動吧！

同義字
▶ □excite v. 刺激；使興奮；使激   □irritate v. 刺激；使興奮

反義字

▶ □quiet　v.　使安靜；使平息；撫慰　　　　□allay　v.　使平靜；平息
▶ □pacify　v.　使平靜；使安靜；撫慰

stingy　['stɪndʒɪ]　形吝嗇的；小氣的　　★★★★☆

Don't be so stingy! You should give your brother more than just a card for his wedding!
別這麼小氣！你哥的婚禮總不能只送他一張卡片吧！

同義字
▶ □ungenerous　a.　不大方的　　　□mean　a.　吝嗇的；小氣的
▶ □miserly　a.　吝嗇的；貪婪的　　□niggardly　a.　吝嗇的

反義字
▶ □generous　a.　慷慨的；大方的　　□big-hearted　a.　寬大的
▶ □free-handed　a.　不吝嗇的　　　□lavish　a.　非常慷慨的
▶ □liberal　a.　慷慨的；大方的

strategy　['strætədʒɪ]　名策略；計謀；對策　　★★★☆☆

Our strategy to win the game is to neutralize their star player, and play a patient, defensive game.
為了贏得比賽，我們的策略是封鎖對方主將，準備打一場比耐力的防守戰。

同義字
▶ □tactic　n.　戰術；策略；手法　　□ploy　n.　計謀；計劃
▶ □countermeasure　n.　反抗手段

subordinate　[sə'bɔrdɪnt]　名部下；部屬　　★★★★☆

You're my subordinate, so not only should you not be giving me orders, but you should be listening to me!
你是我的屬下，不僅不應該命令我，反而更應該聽我的才對！

同義字
▶ □inferior　n.　部下；屬下

反義字
▶ □boss　n.　老板；上司；主人　　□ superior　n.　上司；長官；長輩

subside　[səb'saɪd]　動退落；消退；消失　　★★★★★

We should wait for the storm to subside before going back outside.
我們應該等暴風雨過去再回到外面。

同義字
▶ □fadeaway　n.　消退

successor　[sək'sɛsɚ]　名後繼者；繼任者；繼承人　　★★★★☆

Once the President resigned, a date was set to elect his successor.
一旦總統辭職，就會訂定推選繼任人選的日子。

同義字
▶ □heir　n.　繼承人　　　□inheritor　n.　繼承人

▶ □heiress　n.　女繼承人　□inheritress　n.　女繼承人

succumb [sə'kʌm]　動 屈服；被壓垮；死亡　★★★☆☆

After fighting the illness bravely for years, Mrs. Morris finally succumbed to cancer and died at the age of 73.
勇敢對抗病魔多年後，莫理斯太太終於因癌症而去世，享年七十三歲。

同義字
▶ □yield　v.　服從；屈服；投降　　□submit　v.　服從；屈服
▶ □knuckle　v.　屈服

反義字
▶ □resist　v.　抵抗；反抗；抗拒　　□react　v.　抗拒；反抗

summary ['sʌmərɪ]　名 總結；摘要；一覽　★★★★☆

It'll take too long to read the whole report, so I put the main points in a summary.
整分報告要很久才看得完，所以我把重點做了摘要。

同義字
▶ □abstract　n.　摘要；梗概　　□compendium　n.　概略；概要

supersede [ˌsupə'sid]　動 代替；取代　★★★★★

CDs are being superseded by MP3's, a more efficient method of storing music.
MP3 是一種更有效率的音樂儲存方式，正逐步取代 CD 當中。

同義字
▶ □replace　v.　取代；替代　　□displace　v.　取代；替代
▶ □supplant　v.　取代；替代　　□take the place of　代替

surcharge ['sɝˌtʃɑrdʒ]　名 額外費用　★★★★☆

A ten percent airport improvement surcharge will be added to the cost of your plane ticket.
機票票價中會包含一成的機場維護額外費用。

susceptible [sə'sɛptəbl]　形 1. 易受…影響的 2. 敏感的；過敏的　★★★☆☆

Mindy is very susceptible to respiratory illnesses, so she catches every cold that comes around.
敏蒂很容易感染呼吸道疾病，所以經常感冒。

同義字
▶ □sensitive　a.　敏感的　　□impressionable　a.　敏感的
▶ □accessible　a.　易受影響的

反義字
▶ □insensitive　a.　感覺遲鈍的　　□insusceptible　a.　無感覺的

sympathize ['sɪmpəˌθaɪz]　1. 同情；憐憫；吊慰 2. 體諒；諒解　★★★★☆

I can sympathize with your sadness. My dog also died recently, and it has been difficult for me too.

你難過的心情我很了解。我的狗不久前死掉時,我也是難過了好一陣子。

同義字
▶ □condole　v.　哀悼;同情;慰問　　□commiserate　v.　弔慰;同情

symphony　['sɪmfənɪ]　　图交響樂團　　★★★★★

Neil hoped the many hours of cello lessons would pay off one day, and that he could play in a professional symphony.

上了那麼久的大提琴課,尼爾希望有一天可以如願以償地進入職業交響樂團演奏。

以T為首的單字

5 顆★:金色(860~990)證書必背
4 顆★:藍色(730~855)證書必背
3 顆★:綠色(470~725)證書必背

MP3-19

tacit　['tæsɪt]　　图缄默的;不說話的;不明言的;默示的　　★★★★☆

Although we never specifically discussed it, I believe we had a tacit agreement that you wouldn't tell anyone my secret.

雖然沒有明講,但我相信我們之間有默契,你應該不會把我的秘密洩露出去才對。

同義字
▶ □assumed　a.　假定的;設想的

tactics　['tæktɪks]　　图策略;手段　　★★★☆☆

Although his tactics were considered underhanded, the politician's strategy was effective in getting the votes he needed.

雖然該政客手段卑劣,卻成功贏得需要的選票。

同義字
▶ □strategy　n.　策略;計謀　　　　□ploy　n.　計謀;計劃
▶ □countermeasure　n.　對策

tarnish　['tɑrnɪʃ]　　勔敗壞;玷污(名譽等)　　★★★★☆

His reputation as an honest accountant was tarnished when one of his clients accused him of stealing money.

這名會計師遭客戶指控污錢,原本廉潔的名聲就這樣被敗壞了。

同義字
▶ □stain　v.　玷污;敗壞　　　　□sully　v.　玷污;丟臉
▶ □dishonor　v.　使受恥辱　　　□blemish　v.　使有缺點

taut　[tɔt]　　图拉緊的;繃緊的　　★★★★★

The rope is already very taut. If we pull on it any more it will surely break.

繩索已經繃得很緊,我們再扯的話一定會斷掉。

同義字
▶ □tight　a.　拉緊的；繃緊的　　　□tense　a.　拉緊的；繃緊的
▶ □stiff　a.　（繩子等）拉緊的

反義字
▶ □loose　a.　鬆的；寬的　　　□slack　a.　鬆弛的；不緊的

teem [tim] 🔲 充滿；富於 ★★★★☆

This river used to be teeming with salmon, but now with the pollution, there's barely any fish left.

這條河一度盛產鮭魚，現在卻因為污染，魚差不多都沒了。

同義字
▶ □abound　v.　充足；充滿　　　□overflow　v.　充滿；洋溢

tempt [tɛmpt] 🔲 引誘；誘惑；勾引 ★★★☆☆

I'm on a diet! Please don't tempt me by putting that chocolate cake on the table!

我在節食耶！拜託不要把巧克力蛋糕放在桌上引誘我。

同義字
▶ □lure　v.　引誘；以誘餌吸引　　　□seduce　v.　誘惑；引誘
▶ □attract　v.　引起…的注意

反義字
▶ □repel　v.　拒絕；排斥；抵制　　　□resist　v.　抵抗；反抗；抗拒

tenacious [tɪˈneʃəs] 🔳 堅持的；頑強的；固執的 ★★★★☆

Homer has a tenacious appetite, and doesn't stop eating until the food runs out.

荷馬的胃口極佳，一定要把東西吃光才肯罷休。

同義字
▶ □persevering　a.　固執的　　　□persistent　a.　堅持不懈的

tendency [ˈtɛndənsɪ] 🔳 傾向；意向 ★★★★★

Because of your stance, you have a tendency to drive the ball to the left. Adjust the position of your feet and your golf game will improve.

你這樣站容易把球打到左邊。兩腳的位置調整一下，你的高爾夫球就會打得更好。

同義字
▶ □inclination　n.　傾向；意向　　　□leaning　n.　傾向
▶ □aptitude　n.　傾向；習性

tense [tɛns] 🔳 拉緊的；繃緊的 ★★★★☆

My shoulders are really tense from all this typing. I could really use a massage.

打字打太久，肩膀變得好緊。看來我得好好按摩一下才行。

同義字
▶ □taut　a.　拉緊的；繃緊的　　　□tight　a.　拉緊的；繃緊的

反義字

▶ □lax　a.　鬆弛的

tentatively　[ˈtɛntətɪvlɪ]　　圖 暫時地；試驗性地　　★★★☆☆

Let's tentatively schedule to meet next Friday. We can touch base again at the beginning of the week to confirm.
我們暫時先約下週五碰面，等下週一或週二再連絡一下確定時間。

同義字
▶ □temporarily　adv.　暫時地　　　□provisionally　adv.　暫時地
反義字
▶ □permanently　adv.　永久地　　　□ eternally　adv.　永恆地；不絕地
▶ □perpetually　adv.　永恆地；不斷地

terminate　[ˈtɝməˌnet]　　圖 使停止；使終止；解雇　　★★★★☆

Unfortunately, the company is going to terminate your position this month, so you'll have to look for a new job.
很遺憾，公司本月就要終止對你的雇用，所以你得另謀高就了。

同義字
▶ □end　v.　結束；終止；了結　　　□dismiss　v.　免…的職；解雇
▶ □fire　v.　解雇；開除
反義字
▶ □employ　v.　雇用　　　□hire　v.　雇用；租用

territorial　[ˌtɛrəˈtorɪəl]　　圖 領土的　　★★★★☆

Our dog Fido is very territorial. If you go into his doghouse, he just might bite you.
我們的狗狗費多領域意識很強，隨便接近它的狗屋可能會被它咬。

testimonial　[ˌtɛstəˈmonɪəl]　　圖 感謝狀　　★★★★★

Our customer gave a testimonial praising our excellent service and competitive prices.
顧客送來一張感謝狀，稱讚我們服務一流、價格公道。

theoretical　[ˌθiəˈrɛtɪkl]　　圖 理論的　　★★★★☆

Your solution to the problem sounds good, but too theoretical. I don't think it will work in real life.
你對這個問題的解決方式聽起來不錯，但是太過理論性了，我覺得在現實生活中並不可行。

同義字
▶ □abstract　a.　純理論的　　　□impractical　a.　不切實際的
反義字
▶ □practical　a.　實踐的；實際的　　　□realistic　a.　現實的

tipsy　[ˈtɪpsɪ]　　圖 喝醉的；微醉的　　★★★☆☆

Nadia felt tipsy after one glass of wine, and began to slur her speech.

娜迪亞喝了一杯酒後覺得有點醉，講話開始含糊起來。

同義字
▶ □drunk　a.　喝醉的　　　□intoxicating　a.　使醉的

tiresome [ˈtaɪrsəm]　形討厭的；煩人的　★★★★☆

Your boring jokes are getting tiresome, Harry. Please give it a rest!
哈利，你這些無聊的笑話很煩人耶，拜託別再說了！

同義字
▶ □annoying　a.　討厭的；惱人的　　□vexing　a.　引起煩惱的
▶ □unpleasant　a.　使人不愉快的　　□disagreeable　a.　不合意的

反義字
▶ □comfortable　a.　使人舒服的　　□agreeable　a.　令人愉快的
▶ □cheerful　a.　使人感到愉快的

toil [tɔɪl]　動辛苦；苦幹　★★★★☆

The farmer toils in the fields from dawn to dusk, yet never complains about the hard work.
這個農人從早到晚在田裡辛苦工作，卻從不抱怨他的辛勞。

同義字
▶ □lobor　v.　勞動；艱苦地幹活　　□grub　v.　苦幹

tolerate [ˈtɑləˌret]　動忍受；容忍；寬恕　★★★☆☆

I can't tolerate our neighbor's loud music anymore. We've put up with it all night; now I'm going to call the police.
我再也無法忍受鄰居把音樂開那麼大聲。一整晚已經受夠了，現在我要打電話報警。

同義字
▶ □endure　v.　忍耐；忍受　　　□undergo　v.　經歷；經受；忍受
▶ □bear　v.　忍受；承受　　　□stand　v.　忍受；容忍
▶ □put up with　忍受；容忍

trait [tret]　名特徵；特點；特性　★★★★★

What trait makes me so special to you? Is it my beauty, my intelligence, or my modesty?
哪些特點讓你覺得我很特別？是我的美貌、智慧，還是謙虛？

同義字
▶ □characteristic　n.　特性；特徵　　□feature　n.　特徵；特色
▶ □attribute　n.　屬性；特性；特質　□property　n.　特性；性能；屬性

tranquilizer [ˈtræŋkwɪˌlaɪzɚ]　名鎮定劑　★★★★☆

The zookeeper subdued the angry lion by shooting it with a tranquilizer dart.
物園管理員射了一發麻醉槍，把發怒的獅子給制服。

transaction [træn'zækʃən]　　名 交易；業務；買賣　　★★★★★

I'm sorry sir. I can't complete this credit card transaction because the machine is broken. You'll have to pay cash.

對不起，先生。因為機器故障，我們沒辦法進行信用卡交易，您得付現才行。

同義字
▶ □business　n.　生意；交易；商業　　　□deal　n.　交易
▶ □bargain　n.　買賣；交易

transfer [træns'fɝ]　　動 轉移；轉換；轉帳　　★★★★☆

Our bank can help you transfer money from your account to any other account in 100 countries around the world.

全球 100 個國家不管哪個帳戶，我們銀行都可以幫您從您的帳戶轉帳過去。

同義字
▶ □shift　v.　轉移；移動

transient ['trænʃənt]　　形 短暫的；一時的　　★★★☆☆

People who come to this hostel are transient. They never stay more than a few days before moving on.

這間旅館的房客都只做短暫停留，待沒幾天就會離開。

同義字
▶ instantaneous　a.　瞬間的；即時的
▶ □transitory　a.　短暫的　　　□transitory　a.　短暫的；瞬息的
▶ □transitory　a.　短暫的；瞬息的

反義字
▶ □permanent　a.　永久的；永恆的　□lasting　a.　持久的；持續的
▶ □perpetual　a.　永久的；長期的　□eternal　a.　永久的；永恆的

transplant [træns'plænt]　　名 移植　　★★★★★

During the heart transplant operation, Victor's weak heart was replaced by a younger, healthier heart.

在心臟移植手術中，維多原本衰弱的心臟被換成了較年輕健康的心臟。

同義字
▶ □graft　n.　移植物　　　□implant　n.　（醫）植入物

tremor ['trɛmɚ]　　名 震動；微動　　★★★★☆

Did you feel that tremor? Either a big truck just rumbled by or we just experienced an earthquake.

你有沒有感覺到震動？不是大卡車開過就是剛發生了地震。

同義字
▶ □shaking　n.　震動；搖動　　　□quake　n.　震動；搖晃

trepidation [ˌtrɛpə'deʃən]　　名 驚恐；慌張；不安　　★★★☆☆

The trepidation Tanya felt just before going out on stage made her sweat and tremble.
坦雅上台前因為緊張不安而發抖冒汗。

同義字
▶ □horror   n.   驚恐；震驚   □panic   n.   恐慌；驚慌
▶ □scare   n.   驚恐；驚嚇   □fright   n.   驚嚇；恐怖

反義字
▶ □calm   n.   安靜；鎮定

trio ['trio]   ⊠三重唱（或三重奏）演出小組   ★★★☆☆

There used to be four people in our band, but since Jeff left we've still been doing ok as a trio.
我們團裡本來有四個人，雖然傑夫離開後變成三重奏，不過演出還算不錯。

同義字
▶ □terzetto   n.   （義）三重唱；三重奏

tripod ['traɪpɑd]   ⊠三腳架   ★★★★☆

Professional photographers generally put their cameras on tripods to take photos, thereby reducing the likelihood of blurry photos.
專業攝影師一般會將相機置於三腳架上拍攝，以減少相片模糊的可能 。

tutelage ['tjutl̩ɪdʒ]   ⊠指導；保護；監護   ★★★★★

Students! Under my tutelage, you will learn how to defend yourself with the most effective judo techniques.
各位同學！在我的指導下，你們會學到如何用最有效的柔道技巧保護自己。

同義字
▶ □guidance   n.   指導；引導

twinge [twɪndʒ]   ⊠劇痛；刺痛；陣痛   ★★★☆☆

Nellie felt a twinge of pain as the needle entered her arm.
針刺進手臂時，奈麗感到一陣痛楚。

同義字
▶ □pain   n.   痛；疼痛；痛苦   □pang   n.   劇痛；苦痛

tyranny ['tɪrənɪ]   ⊠暴政；專制   ★★★★☆

The tyranny the dictator forced on the people finally ended when the people rose up and overthrew him.
獨裁者加諸人民的專制統治，終於在人民起而推翻他時畫上句點。

同義字
▶ □despotism   n.   專制；暴政

反義字
▶ □democracy   n.   民主政體

以U為首的單字

5 顆★：金色（860~990）證書必背
4 顆★：藍色（730~855）證書必背
3 顆★：綠色（470~725）證書必背

ubiquitous [ju'bɪkwətəs]　形 到處存在的；普遍存在的　★★★★★

IPOD MP3 players used to be quite special, by now they're ubiquitous. It seems like I'm the only one who doesn't have one!

IPOD MP3 播放機以前很特別，不過不現在到處都有。好像只有我沒有的樣子！

(同義字)
▶ □omnipresent　a.　無所不在的

ultimatum [ˌʌltə'metəm]　名 最後通牒　★★★★☆

After numerous warnings, my supervisor finally gave me an ultimatum: Show up on time or find another job!

多次警告後，我的主管終於對我下了最後通牒：準時上班，不然就另謀高就。

unanimously [juˈnænəməslɪ]　副 無異議地；全體一致地　★★★★☆

Congress voted unanimously to pass the law. It is not often that members of all parties show such accord.

國會一致表決通過這項法案。這種所有政黨成員達成高度共識的情況並不常見。

unconscious [ʌn'kɑnʃəs]　形 不省人事的；失去知覺的　★★★★★

After he hit his head, Evan blacked-out and remained unconscious for days.

伊凡撞到頭後昏了過去，很多天不省人事。

(同義字)
▶ □senseless　a.　失去知覺的　　□insensible　a.　昏迷的

(反義字)
▶ □conscious　a.　神志清醒的　　□sensible　a.　有知覺的

underhanded ['ʌndɚ'hændɪd]　形 狡詐的；可恥的；祕密的　★★★☆☆

This government is very underhanded. They carry on wars without telling the public about it, and will deny involvement if asked.

政府的行為非常卑劣。他們持續進行戰爭但秘而不宣，被外界問及時又一概否認。

(同義字)
▶ □sly　a.　狡猾的；狡詐的　　□vcunning　a.　狡猾的；奸詐的
▶ □shifty　a.　慣耍花招的；詭詐的　　□deceitful　a.　騙人的；欺詐的

(反義字)
▶ □honest　a.　誠實的；正直的　　□fair　a.　公正的；誠實的
▶ □upright　a.　正直的；誠實的

undermine [ˌʌndɚ'maɪn]　動 暗中破壞；逐漸損害　★★★★★

Francine didn't want Peter to get elected, so she spread nasty rumors about him to

undermine his campaign.
法蘭欣不希望彼得當選，便散播惡意謠言來暗中破壞他的競選。

同義字
▶ □destroy　v.　毀壞；破壞　　　　□sabotage　v.　破壞；妨害

---

underrate [ˌʌndɚˈret]　 📖低估；輕視　　　　★★★★☆

She is the most underrated actress in the world. One day she will be a superstar and everyone will realize her true talents.
她是世界上實力最被低估的女演員。有朝一日她一定會成為巨星，把真正的才華展現在世人面前。

同義字
▶ □underestimate　v.　低估　　　□undervalue　v.　低估；輕視

反義字
▶ □overrate　v.　高估　　　　　　□overestimate　v.　評價過高
▶ □overvalue　v.　對…估價過高

---

unify [ˈjunəˌfaɪ]　 📖統一；聯合　　　　★★★☆☆

The countries of East and West Germany were unified under one government on October 3, 1990.
1990 年 10 月 3 日，東西德實現統一，成為單一政府。

同義字
▶ □combine　v.　結合；聯合　　　□unite　v.　聯合；統一
▶ □consolidate　v.　合併；聯合

反義字
▶ □disunite　v.　分離；分裂　　　□disrupt　v.　使分裂；使瓦解

---

unique [juˈnik]　 📖獨特的；唯一的；獨一無二的　　　　★★★★★

Most clothing is mass produced, but this sweater is unique. It was knitted by my own grandmother.
大部分衣服都是大量製造的產品，但這件毛衣卻是獨一無二，因為這是我奶奶親手織的。

同義字
▶ □distinctive　a.　有特色的　　　□peculiar　a.　特有的；獨具的
▶ □typical　a.　特有的；獨特的

反義字
▶ □common　a.　普通的；常見的　　□general　a.　一般的；普遍的
▶ □ordinary　a.　普通的；平凡的

---

unison [ˈjunəsn̩]　 📖1. 和諧；一致　2.（音）齊唱；齊奏　　　　★★★★☆

On cue, all the members of the choir began to sing in unison.
一聲令下，所有合唱團成員開始齊聲合唱。

同義字
▶ □consensus　n.　一致　□concert　n.　一致；和諧

upheaval [ʌpˈhivḷ]　名 動亂；激變；劇變　★★★★☆

The country went through a decade of political upheaval as successive governments were overthrown and civil war broke out.

當接替的政權被推翻而爆發內戰後，這個國家經歷了十年的政治動亂。

同義字
▶ □cataclysm　n.　劇變　　□turmoil　n.　騷動；混亂
▶ □unrest　n.　動亂；動盪

反義字
▶ □peace　n.　和平；秩序

urgency [ˈɝdʒənsɪ]　名 緊急；迫切　★★★★★

I hope you understand the urgency of the situation. If something is not done right away, many people could die!

希望你明白情況已非常緊急；不馬上處理的話，可能會造成許多死傷！

同義字
▶ □emergency　n.　緊急情況　　□exigence　n.　緊急（狀態）

・・・

以 V 為首的單字

5 顆★：金色（860~990）證書必背
4 顆★：藍色（730~855）證書必背
3 顆★：綠色（470~725）證書必背

MP3-21

vacate [ˈveket]　動 搬出；空出　★★★★☆

You haven't paid the rent for three months straight. Vacate the apartment at once or I'll get the police to throw you out!

你已經連續三個月沒交房租了，立刻給我搬走，不然我就報警把你轟出去！

同義字
▶ □leave　v.　離開（某處）　　□withdraw　v.　離開；撤出
▶ □evacuate　v.　撤空；撤離

vaccinate [ˈvæksn̩et]　動 注射疫苗；種牛痘　★★★★★

The doctor vaccinated Darren against typhoid before his trip to Brazil.

達倫去巴西之前，醫生為他注射傷寒疫苗。

同義字
▶ □inoculate　v.　預防接種；給…注射預防針

vacillate [ˈvæsḷet]　動 動搖；猶豫；躊躇　★★★★☆

It was hard for Carol to decide, and she vacillated between decisions almost every day.

卡蘿很難決定，幾乎每天都在猶豫怎麼決定會比較好。

同義字
▶ □hesitate　v.　躊躇；猶豫　　□dither　v.　躊躇；猶豫

▶ □hover　v.　猶豫；徬徨　　　□falter　v.　動搖；猶豫；畏縮

反義字

▶ □dare　v.　敢於面對；敢冒（險）□determine　v.　使決定

vagabond　[ˈvægə‚bɑnd]　　图流浪漢；浪子　★★★★★

That man's not from around here. He's just a vagabond who came into town yesterday asking for food and shelter.
那個人不是這一帶的居民，只是昨天到鎮上尋找食物和住處的流浪漢。

同義字

▶ □wanderer　n.　流浪漢　　　　□tramp　n.　流浪者
▶ □vagrant　n.　流浪漢；無業遊民　□hobo　n.　遊民

variety　[vəˈraɪətɪ]　　图多樣化；變化　★★★★☆

I hate eating the same thing everyday, so I eat out for the variety.
我不喜歡每天吃一樣的東西，所以都選擇外食，這樣才有變化。

同義字

▶ □multiplicity　n.　多樣　　　□diversity　n.　多樣

反義字

▶ □monotony　n.　單調；無變化

vegetate　[ˈvɛdʒə‚tet]　　動茫茫然地過日子　★★★★★

Why don't you go out and get some exercise instead of vegetating in front of the TV all day?
出去運 運 ，不要整天窩在電視前面好嗎？

velocity　[vəˈlɑsətɪ]　　图速度　★★★★☆

The radar gun clocked the car speeding down the highway at a velocity of 150km/hour.
測速雷達槍測出那輛車，以時速 150 公里的速度在公路上超速行駛。

同義字

▶ □speed　n.　速度

vendor　[ˈvɛndɚ]　　图小販；叫賣者　★★★★★

There's a long queue of children waiting to buy ice cream from the ice cream vendor.
小孩子在冰淇淋小販前大排長龍，等著跟他買冰淇淋。

同義字

▶ □hawker　n.　叫賣小販　　　□peddler　n.　小販
▶ □pedlar　n.　（叫賣的）小販　□costermonger　n.　（叫賣）小販

venom　[ˈvɛnəm]　　图（蛇、蜘蛛等的）毒液　★★★★☆

Once the snake bites you and the venom enters your body, you have only 30

minutes to live.
一旦被毒蛇咬到而毒液又進入身體時，你便只剩下 30 分鐘的生命。

同義字
▶ □poison　n.　毒；毒藥；毒物

verbatim [vɝ'betɪm] 　副 逐字地 ★★★★★

The following is copied verbatim from a newspaper article. I have added and deleted nothing from the writer's passage.
下面內容原文取自一篇報紙新聞，我沒有增減任何原作者的文字。

同義字
▶ □literally　adv.　逐字地；照字面地

verification [ˌvɛrɪfɪ'keʃən] 　名 確認；證明；核實 ★★★★☆

You must show your ID at the security desk for verification before being given a pass into the top secret areas of the building.
你必須向安全警衛出示身分證確認身份後，才能取得通行證進入大樓最高機密區域。

同義字
▶ □confirmation　n.　確定；確證　　□validation　n.　確認

versatile ['vɝsətl] 　形 多功能的；多方面適用的 ★★★☆☆

This tool is very versatile. It can be used as a cork screw, can opener, scissors, knife, saw, and flashlight.
這個工具有很多功能，可以拿來當開瓶器、剪刀、小刀、鋸子和手電筒。

同義字
▶ □multi-function　a.　多功能的

version ['vɝʒən] 　名（同一作品的不同）版本 ★★★★★

They say there are three versions to every story: your version, my version, and the truth.
常言道所有的故事都有三個版本：你的說法、我的說法，加上真正的事實。

同義字
▶ □edition　n.　版本

veto ['vito] 　動 否決 ★★★★☆

Even if congress passes the bill, it still might not become law because the president can veto it.
即使國會通過這項法案，還是有可能不會成為法律，因為總統有否決權。

同義字
▶ □overrule　v.　否決；駁回　　□reject　v.　否決；駁回

反義字
▶ □accept　v.　接受；同意　　□approve　v.　批准；認可

vie [vaɪ]　　**動** 競爭　　★★★☆☆

After going undefeated in his first twenty bouts, Spike could finally vie for the championship belt.

史派克前面二十場比賽未嘗敗績，終於有機會爭奪最後的冠軍。

同義字
▶ □compete　v.　競爭；對抗　　　　□rival　v.　競爭
▶ □contend　v.　爭奪；競爭

vigilant [ˈvɪdʒələnt]　　**形** 警戒的；警惕的　　★★★★☆

Please be vigilant when walking home. There have been a series of muggings in this neighborhood lately.

最近這一帶搶劫事件頻傳，走路回家時請提高警覺。

同義字
▶ □watchful　a.　警惕的；戒備的　　□alert　a.　警覺的；警惕的
▶ □wide-awake　a.　機警的
反義字
▶ □absent-minded　a.　心不在焉的　　□ inattentive　a.　不注意的

vindicate [ˈvɪndəˌket]　　**動** 證明⋯無辜；為⋯辯白　　★★★★★

He was wrongly imprisoned five years ago, but was finally vindicated when the real killer confessed.

他五年前含冤入獄，直到真正的兇手坦承犯案才證明了他的清白。

同義字
▶ □acquit　v.　宣告⋯無罪

violation [ˌvaɪəˈleʃən]　　**名** 侵犯；妨害　　★★★★☆

Arresting me without cause is a violation of my rights. You'll hear from my lawyer!

無故逮捕我等於是侵犯我的人權。等我律師和你連絡吧！

同義字
▶ □infringement　n.　違反；侵犯　　□invasion　n.　侵害；侵犯

virtual [ˈvɝtʃʊəl]　　**形** 虛擬的　　★★★☆☆

If you can't make it to the hotel in person, you can take a virtual tour of the rooms on the website.

如果你不能親自走一趟旅館，可以上他們網站用虛擬的方式參觀房間。

同義字
▶ □fictitious　a.　非真實的
反義字
▶ □true　a.　真實的；確實的　　　　□real　a.　真的；真正的

visualize [ˈvɪʒʊəlˌaɪz]　　**動** 想像；設想　　★★★★☆

Close your eyes and try to visualize the childhood bedroom. Do you remember the color of the walls?

閉上眼睛試著想像小時候的臥室。你記得牆壁是什麼顏色嗎？

▶

同義字

▶ □conceive　v.　想像；設想　　　□envisage　v.　想像；設想

vogue　[vog]　留流行；風行；時髦　★★★★★

Small handbags are in vogue this season, but will probably be out of style in a few months.

這一季流行小手袋，但幾個月後可能就不流行了。

同義字

▶ □fashion　n.　流行式樣　　　□style　n.　（衣服等的）流行款式
▶ □mode　n.　流行、風尚

volatile　['vɑlət!]　留易變的；反覆無常的　★★★★★

The company's stock has been very volatile lately. Today it went up and down forty times.

公司股價最近變動得很厲害，光今天就漲跌了四十次。

同義字

▶ □capricious　a.　善變的　　　□changeful　a.　變化多端的
▶ □irregular　a.　不規則的　　　□unstable　a.　不固定的

反義字

▶ □regular　a.　規則的；有規律的　□stable　a.　穩定的；牢固的

vulnerable　['vʌlnərəb!]　留有弱點的；難防守的；易受傷的　★★★★☆

Without a strong navy, we will be vulnerable to attack by sea.

如果沒有強大的海軍，我們很難防範由海路而來的攻擊。

同義字

▶ □exposed　a.　易受攻擊的　　　□defenseless　a.　不能自衛的

以W為首的單字

5 顆★：金色（860~990）證書必背
4 顆★：藍色（730~855）證書必背
3 顆★：綠色（470~725）證書必背

MP3-22

waive　[wev]　動放棄　★★★★★

If you sign this contract, you will waive your right to sue the skydiving company if something goes wrong during your jump.

簽下這張合約就表示，跳傘過程中若發生任何意外，你願意放棄控告特技跳傘公司的權利。

同義字

▶ □resign　v.　放棄；辭去　　　□renounce　v.　聲明放棄；拋棄
▶ □relinquish　v.　放棄

wane [wen]　　動（月）虧、缺　　★★★★☆

During the first half of the month, the moon waxes or gets bigger, and during the latter part of the month it wanes.
月亮前半個月會漸圓或漸大，後半個月則會虧缺。

反義字
▶ □wax　v.　（月亮）漸圓、漸滿

warlike [ˈwɔrˌlaɪk]　　形好戰的；尚武的　　★★★★★

The President is very warlike, and starts conflicts without any regard for life.
總統非常好戰，只顧發動戰爭，完全罔顧人命。

同義字
▶ □militant　a.　富於戰鬥性的　　□martial　a.　好戰的；尚武的
▶ □belligerent　a.　好戰的；好鬥的

well-to-do [ˈwɛltəˈdu]　　形富有的；寬裕的　　★★★★☆

As you can see from all the Rolls Royces and mansions, this is a very well-to-do neighborhood.
從勞斯萊斯等名貴轎車和大廈林立便可以看出，附近住的都是有錢人家。

同義字
▶ □rich　a.　有錢的；富有的　　□wealthy　a.　富裕的；豐富的
▶ □affluent　a.　富裕的；豐富的　　□abundant　a.　豐富的；富裕的
▶ □ample　a.　大量的；充裕的

反義字
▶ □poor　a.　貧窮的；貧乏的　　□penniless　a.　身無分文的
▶ □needy　a.　貧窮的　　□destitute　a.　窮困的；貧困的

whereabouts [ˈhwɛrəˈbaʊts]　　名行蹤；下落；所在　　★★★★★

His whereabouts had been unknown for 48 hours before his friends filed a missing persons report with the police.
他行蹤不明了 48 小時，朋友才向警察報案失蹤。

同義字
▶ □track　n.　行蹤；軌道；足跡

whine [hwaɪn]　　動嘀咕；發牢騷　　★★★★☆

The children kept whining to their father until he was fed up, and took them out for ice cream.
孩子們跟爸爸嘀咕個不停，父親不勝其擾，終於帶他們出去吃冰淇淋。

同義字
▶ □whimper　v.　發抱怨聲　　□gripe　v.　訴苦；發牢騷

wield [wild]　　動揮舞（劍等）　　★★★☆☆

Be careful Sir Lancelot. The knight you are about to fight wields a very good

sword.
小心點，藍斯洛爵士。要和你決鬥的武士舞劍可是一流的。

同義字
▶ □brandish　v.　揮動；揮舞　　　□wave　v.　對…揮（手、旗等）

workmanship [ˈwɝkmənˌʃɪp]　名手藝；工藝；做工　★★★★☆

The workmanship of this table is incredible. The artwork is very intricate, the legs are virtually unbreakable.
這張桌子的做工真是完美；不僅花紋非常精細，連桌腳都異常堅固。

同義字
▶ □craft　n.　工藝；手藝　□technology　n.　工藝學；工藝

wreak [rik]　動造成（破壞）　★★★★★

The typhoon wreaked havoc on the village. All the buildings and structures were destroyed.
颱風為村子帶來一場浩劫，所有的房屋和建築物都被摧毀了。

同義字
▶ □inflict　v.　給予（打擊）

以Z為首的單字

5 顆★：金色（860~990）證書必背
4 顆★：藍色（730~855）證書必背
3 顆★：綠色（470~725）證書必背

MP3-22

zodiac [ˈzodɪˌæk]　名黃道帶；占星　★★★★☆

Which zodiac sign is that just above the horizon? Is that Pisces?
出現在地平線那頭的是哪個星座？是雙魚座嗎？

同義字
▶ □constellation　n.　星座；（占星學中的）星宿

Part 2

L&R
聽力・閱讀

共7回TEST

第一部份　句子填空

第二部份　段落填空

第三部份　閱讀理解

突破900分
L&R特訓

MP3-23

Test 1

第一部份： 句子填空

本部份共 15 題，每題有一個空格。請就下列的 A、B、C、D 四個選項，選出最適合題意的字或詞。

1. Taiwan has many _____ dogs that are left without food or *shelter.

   A. losing   B. missed

   C. abandoned   D. absent

2. Chinese New Year is the best time to shop for a _____!

   A. cheap   B. expensive

   C. sales   D. *bargain

3. Jennifer is _____ the smartest students in her senior high school.

   A. around   B. across

   C. among   D. along

4. _____ of his low test scores, Jimmy was unable to attend National Taiwan University.

   A. As a result   B. All in all

   C. In particular   D. Unexpectedly

題目中譯

1. 台灣有很多被 ____ 狗，它們被人丟在外面，沒有東西吃也沒有地方住。

   A. 遺失的　　　　　　　　　B. 遺漏的

   C. 遺棄的　　　　　　　　　D. 缺席的

2. 過年是買東西 ____ 最好的時節！

   A. 便宜　　　　　　　　　　B. 昂貴

   C. 銷售　　　　　　　　　　D. 討價還價

3. 珍妮佛 ____ 她高中算是最聰明的學生之一。

   A. 圍繞　　　　　　　　　　B. 穿過

   C. 在（……之中）　　　　　D. 沿著

4. ____ 吉米的考試成績很差，他無法唸國立台灣大學。

   A. 由於　　　　　　　　　　B. 總的來說

   C. 尤其　　　　　　　　　　D. 意外地

你答對了嗎？

(1) C　(2) D　(3) C　(4) A

5.　Taroko Gorge is one of the most _____ tourist attractions in Taiwan.

B

A.　interested
B.　interesting
C.　interest
D.　interests

6.　The _____ time of year for shopping malls in America is during Christmas.

D

A.　busy
B.　busily
C.　busier
D.　busiest

7.　Mary was very happy with the new boss because the _____ one was very strict.

B

A.　before
B.　previous
C.　next
D.　past

8.　Paula's granddaughter seemed _____ more beautiful and mature every summer she visited.

B

A.　become
B.　to become
C.　becoming
D.　to becoming

9.　Please _____ a list of your work experience with your application.

A

A.　include
B.　addition
C.　return
D.　take

5. 太魯閣峽谷是台灣最 ＿＿＿ 的觀光景點之一。

    A. 有趣   B. 有趣

    C. 有趣   D. 有趣

6. 聖誕假期是美國的購物中心每年 ＿＿＿ 的時段。

    A. 忙碌   B. 忙碌地

    C. 較忙碌   D. 最忙碌

7. 瑪麗對新老闆很滿意，因為 ＿＿＿ 那一個很嚴格。

    A. 之前   B. 先前

    C. 下一個   D. 過去的

8. 寶拉的孫女每年夏天來訪時，似乎 ＿＿＿ 越來越美麗，也越來越成熟。

    A. 變得   B. 變得

    C. 變得   D. 變得

9. 請在申請表上把你的經歷 ＿＿＿ 上去。

    A. 填（包括）   B. 附加

    C. 歸還   D. 取走

你答對了嗎？

(5) B (6) D (7) B (8) B (9) A

10. During typhoon season, you _____ to keep a raincoat in your schoolbag at all times.

    A. should   B. ought

    C. would   D. can

11. Before writing was invented, most stories were _____ by word of mouth.

    A. passed on   B. brought up

    C. fed up   D. carried to

12. Mr. Anderson was _____ for his twenty years of hard work and dedication to the company with a raise and a free trip to Italy.

    A. accepted   B. reward

    C. received   D. recognized

13. The choice to help with the *tsunami victims in Indonesia was purely _____.

    A. volunteer   B. voluntary

    C. voluntarily   D. volunteers

14. Many married couples forget why they fell in love in the first place and start _____ each other for granted.

    A. making   B. looking

    C. taking   D. wanting

10. 颱風季節時，你 ＿＿＿ 把雨衣隨時帶在書包裡。

    A. 應該   B. 應該

    C. 將   D. 可以

11. 在發明書寫文字以前，大部分故事都是口頭 ＿＿＿。

    A. 傳遞   B. 養育

    C. 養肥   D. 送到

12. 安德森先生在公司二十年來的辛苦工作與奉獻得到 ＿＿＿，公司除了替他加薪外，還送他免費到義大利旅遊。

    A. 接受   B. 酬謝

    C. 接收   D. 賞識

13. 選擇到印尼幫助海嘯受難者完全是 ＿＿＿。

    A. 志願者   B. 自願的

    C. 自願地   D. 志願者

14. 許多夫妻忘了當初他們為何相愛，開始 ＿＿＿ 彼此的一切為理所當然。

    A. 做   B. 看

    C. 視   D. 要

你答對了嗎？

(10)B (11)A (12) D (13) B (14) C

15. James was very good at _____ his ideas to his employees so they could easily be understood.

A. drawing   B. illustrating

C. speaking   D. designing

第二部份： 段落填空

本部份共 10 題， 每篇短文包括二至三個段落，每個段落各含 5 個空格。請就下列的 A、B、C、D 四個選項，選出最適合題意的字或詞。

MP3-24

Questions 16-20

When Jesse finally __16__ from his job at the post office at the age of sixty-five, he decided to take a trip around the world. It would be the first time he'd ever traveled outside of America and since he had no wife nor children, he would be traveling __17__. Jesse was a little worried, but not scared enough to stay home. The first country he visited was Japan. He loved the old traditions he found in Kyoto, and Tokyo's modern technology was unbelievable. __18__ Japan, Jesse flew to India where he discovered the beauty of the Taj Mahal and how to appreciate spicy curry.

Next, Jesse spent almost four months __19__ France, England, Germany and Italy. He learned how to drive on the opposite side of the road and how to enjoy good wine and museums. After six months, Jesse had fallen in love with traveling so much he chose to extend his stay in Europe. Now, his only worry is __20__ or not he'd ever be able to return to America!

15. 詹姆斯很善於把自己的想法 ＿＿＿ 給員工知道，所以他們很容易就懂他的意思。

　　A. 描寫　　　　　　　　　B. 說明

　　C. 說　　　　　　　　　　D. 設計

段落填空中譯

　　當傑西終於在六十五歲從郵局的工作 ＿16＿ 時，他決定要環遊世界。這是他第一次到美國以外的地方旅行，也因為他沒有太太或小孩，所以必須 ＿17＿ 旅行。傑西有點擔心，但還不至於擔心到只敢待在家裡而不敢出門。日本是他要去參觀的第一個國家。他喜歡在京都發現的古老傳統，而東京的現代科技也令人難以置信。參觀日本 ＿18＿ 傑西又飛到印度，他不僅在那裡發現了美麗的泰姬陵，也學會了如何感受辣味咖哩的樂趣。

　　接著，傑西又花了差不多四個月的時間，到法國、英國、德國和義大利＿19＿。他學到怎麼在馬路的另一邊開車，以及如何享受好酒和博物館的樂趣。六個月後，傑西深深愛上了旅行，於是決定在歐洲待久一點。現在他唯一擔心的事就是，他 ＿20＿ 還會回到美國！

你答對了嗎？
(15)B

16.

A. retiring	A. 退休
B. retired	B. 退休
C. retire	C. 退休
D. retires	D. 退休

17.

A. single	A. 單獨
B. lonely	B. 孤獨
C. alone	C. 獨自
D. one	D. 一個

18.

A. After	A. 之後
B. Before	B. 之前
C. Then	C. 那時
D. Since	D. 此後

19.

A. finding	A. 發現
B. learning	B. 學習
C. spreading	C. 延伸
D. exploring	D. 探險

20.

A. whether	A. 是否
B. neither	B. 也不
C. either	C. 或者
D. ever	D. 曾經

你答對了嗎？
(16) B (17) C (18) A (19) D (20) A

Questions 21-25

When Taipei 101 opened to the public in December of 2004, not only did it __21__ the 2world's tallest single standing building but it also became Taiwan's symbol for strength and power. Taipei 101 has a wide variety of luxury shops __22__ Gucci to Tiffany & Co., showing that wealth and prosperity has become a permanent part of Taiwanese people's lives. Martial law __23__ just lifted in the 1980's and already Taiwan has the sixteenth largest economy on earth. Taiwan's economic boom started when they __24__ producing technological equipment. Over half of the *laptops and computer screens used in the world are produced on this tiny little island. Many people attribute this rapid __25__ to an excellent educational system and the Taiwanese's dedication to hard work.

段落填空中譯

當台北 101 於 2004 年十二月，正式對外開放時，它不僅 __21__ 世界最高的獨棟建築，也是台灣實力與力量的象徵。台北 101 裡，有各式各樣的豪華商店，__22__ Gucci 到 Tiffany & Co.，在在顯示台灣人民的高所得和經濟繁榮。1980 年代剛（ __23__ ）解除戒嚴令時，台灣便已是全世界第十六大經濟國；後來台灣 __24__ 生產科技設備，經濟發展也跟著突飛猛進。全世界一半以上的手提電腦和電腦螢幕都是這個小小的島嶼所生產的。許多人都把經濟的快速 __25__ 歸功於優秀的教育體制以及台灣人在工作上的努力奉獻。

21.

- A. became
- B. become
- C. becoming
- D. because

21.

- A. 成為
- B. 成為
- C. 成為
- D. 因為

22.

- A. for
- B. include
- C. from
- D. to

22.

- A. 為了
- B. 包括
- C. 從
- D. 到

23.

- A. were
- B. is
- C. are
- D. was

23.

- A. 是
- B. 是
- C. 是
- D. 是

24.

- A. began
- B. begun
- C. beginning
- D. was beginning

24.

- A. 開始
- B. 開始
- C. 開始
- D. 開始

25.

- A. raise
- B. growth
- C. winning
- D. changes

25.

- A. 提高
- B. 成長
- C. 勝利
- D. 改變

你答對了嗎？

(21) B (22) C (23) D (24) A (25) B

第三部份：閱讀理解

本部份共 15 題，包括數段短文，每篇文章有 2-5 個相關問題，請就下列的 A、B、C、D 四個選項，選出最適合的答案。

MP3-26

Questions 26-28

Winter Sale at Lacy's Department Store

From November 1st to 8th, enjoy discount prices in every department! Don't miss this wonderful opportunity to *stock up on winter *gear from boots to jackets to blankets! Lacy's is guaranteed to have the best prices in town! If you find the same item for a lower price at another store, bring in the receipt and we'll match the price AND take off another 10%. If you are not satisfied with your purchase, just return it to the store and we'll give your money back!

閱讀理解中譯

蘭西百貨公司的冬季特賣

十一月一號到八號，每家百貨公司的折扣價一定會讓你心動！千萬不要錯過這個難得的機會，可以趁機把冬天要用的東西，如靴子、夾克和毯子等先買下來存放！蘭西百貨公司保證其價格是全鎮最低價！如果你在別家店發現同一件商品有更低價，把收據帶過來，我們不僅比照辦理，「另外」還會再打九折給你。如果你對你所購買的商品不滿意，只要拿回來退貨，我們會立刻退款給你！

Business hours will be extended during the sale:

Monday – Saturday:	9:00 AM – 11:00 PM
Sunday:	9:00 AM – 10:00 PM

Children's Department:

50% off on Girls' Winter Coats
40% off on Girls' and Boys' Boots & Shoes

Men's Department:

30% off on Sweaters
40% off on Jeans

Women's Department;

50% off on all Jackets and Coats
40% off on all Gloves and Scarves

Home Furnishing Department:

25% off on all Blankets
30% off on all Pillows and Sheets

****

26. What is half price during the sale?

    A. Girls' coats and women's gloves.
    B. Women's jackets and blankets.
    C. Men's sweaters and pillows.
    D. Girls' winter coats and women's jackets.

27. Who will get the largest discount according to this advertisement?

    A. Parents who are shopping for children's shoes.
    B. A college student looking for new bedding.
    C. A woman needing a warmer coat.
    D. A man looking for some new pants.

營業時段在特賣期間將會延長：

| 週一至週六： | 9:00 AM - 11:00 PM |
| 週日： | 9:00 AM - 10:00 PM |

兒童用品部：

女童冬季外套五折
男女童靴子和鞋子六折

男性用品部：

毛衣七折
牛仔褲六折

女性用品部：

夾克和外套五折
手套和圍巾六折

家具部：

各種毯子一律七五折
各類枕頭和床單一律七折

****

26. 特賣期間有什麼東西打對折？

    A. 女童外套和女用手套。

    B. 女用夾克和毯子。

    C. 男用毛衣和枕頭。

    D. 女童靴子和女用圍巾。

27. 根據這個廣告，誰會得到最大的折扣優惠？

    A. 幫小孩買鞋子的父母。

    B. 尋找新寢具的大學學生。

    C. 需要暖一點外套的女性。

    D. 尋找新褲子的男性。

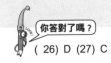

你答對了嗎？

(26) D (27) C

28. What does Lacy's Department Store promise to do during the sale?

A. Close earlier than usual.

B. Have discount prices in only a few departments.

C. Beat the prices of the competition.

D. Exchange items for unsatisfied customers.

MP3-27

Questions 29-32

Most schools in America have yearly standardized tests to show how well their students are doing compared to the rest of the students in the country. A high passing rate usually means the principals and teachers are doing their jobs well. Last week, a veteran principle was accused of giving students answers to the Pennsylvania System of School Assessment test. Principal Jane Gibbs was placed on paid leave after eighth graders at Edward E. Parry Edison Junior Academy said she had helped them during the test.

Ms. Gibbs was previously at another junior high school where students' scores on standardized tests greatly improved during the period she was principal. Between 2002 and 2003, the percentage of students passing the math section on the PSSA exam jumped from 11 percent to 71 percent.

28. 蘭西百貨公司承諾特賣期間會如何？

    A. 比平常更早關店。

    B. 只有一些部門有折扣優惠。

    C. 價格優惠沒有人比得上。

    D. 不滿意的顧客可以把商品拿來換。

閱讀理解中譯

美國大部分學校都會舉行年度統一測驗，看看他們的學生和國內其他學生相比是否更為優秀。通過的比率越高，通常也代表校長和老師們的表現很好。上個禮拜有一名退伍軍人校長被人指控在賓州學校評鑑測驗中，把答案告訴學生。當愛德華·派瑞·愛德森中小學的八年級學生說她有在測驗時幫忙測驗學生時，校長珍·吉伯斯便暫時被留薪停職。

吉伯斯太太之前在另一所初中當校長時，學生統一測驗的成績在她擔任校長那段期間突飛猛進。2002 和 2003 年間，通過 PSSA 測驗數學部分的學生比例，從 11% 跳到了 71%。

你答對了嗎？

(28) C

29. What would be a good title for this article?

    A. Students Tell Lies about Principal

    B. Principal Accused of Giving Test Answers

    C. Standardized Test is not a Useful Learning Tool

    D. Principal Receives Vacation After Good Test Scores

30. Which of the following statements about Principal Gibbs is not true?

    A. She has been a principal for a long period of time.

    B. Edward E. Parry Edison Junior Academy is her first job as principal.

    C. She had to stop coming to work after the accusations.

    D. She wants her students to perform well on the test.

31. According to the article, what is the purpose of standardized tests?

    A. To help determine what colleges the students will get into.

    B. To help determine how well the school is run.

    C. To help determine how much money each school will get from the government.

    D. To help determine the intelligence of the teachers.

32. Why did the article include Ms. Gibbs' record at the previous junior high school?

    A. To show that she may have had a similar problem before.

    B. To show that she is a great principal.

    C. To show that her students are usually very smart.

    D. To show that standardized tests are too easy.

29. 這段文章用什麼標題比較好？

   A. 學生幫校長說謊

   B. 被指控洩露測驗答案的校長。

   C. 統一測驗不是有用的學習工具。

   D. 測驗成績不錯時，校長會有假可以放。

30. 下列哪一項關於吉伯斯校長的敘述不是真的？

   A. 她已經當校長很長一段時間了。

   B. 愛德華‧派瑞‧愛德森中小學是她第一次擔任校長的學校。

   C. 被人指控後，她必須先停止校長職務。

   D. 她希望她的學生測驗成績優異。

31. 根據本文所述，統一測驗的目的是什麼？

   A. 對學生要上那一種大學提供判斷依據。

   B. 對學校運作是否良好提供判斷依據。

   C. 對每一所學校可以從政府那裡拿到多少錢提供判斷依據。

   D. 對老師的智能提供判斷依據。

32. 本文為何提及吉伯斯太太先前在初中時的前科記錄？

   A. 表示她以前也有類似的問題。

   B. 表示她是個偉大的校長。

   C. 表示她的學生通常都很聰明。

   D. 表示統一測驗太簡單了。

你答對了嗎？

(29) B (30) B (31) B (32) A

MP3-28

ATTENTION
Richland College Students

All student automobiles must be registered at the campus police station to receive a parking sticker. Parking stickers must be displayed on the rear window of your automobile, on the lower right hand corner. Students must park at the A and B parking lots only. W and Z parking lots are reserved for teachers and faculty members. Any student automobiles found in the W and Z parking lots will be towed at the owner's expense.

Please bring your student ID to the campus police station to receive your parking sticker. Stickers are $30.00 for one semester, and $70.00 for the entire year (spring, summer, and fall semesters).

The campus police station is located on the North Campus, next to the library.

Office hours: 8:00 AM – 7:00 PM
Contact: (972) 277-8980
Address: 4104 Floyd Rd., Richardson, TX 77098

問題 33-36

注意

麗晶學院的學生

　　所有學生開的車都必須向校警處登記以領取停車標籤。停車標籤必須展示在車子後車窗的右下角那裡。學生的車「只能」停在 A 區和 B 區停車場，W 區和 Z 區停車場是保留給教師和教職員用的。如果有學生的車被發現停在 W 區和 Z 區停車場，不僅會被拖吊，還要自己付錢。

　　請攜帶學生證到校警處領取停車標籤。標籤費一學期 30 塊，一學年則是 70 塊（上下學期加暑假）。

　　校警處位於北校園的圖書館旁邊。

辦公時間：8:00 AM － 7:00 PM

聯絡電話：(972) 277-8980

地址：德州 77098，李察遜市，佛洛德路 4104 號

33. What is the purpose of this notice?

A. To tell people that the parking lots will be under construction.

B. To warn teachers and faculty members that they should park in the front parking lots.

C. To inform students of parking stickers and where they should park their cars.

D. To advise students to contact the campus police if there is an emergency.

34. Which parking lots can be used by students?

A. W and Z

B. A and B

C. W and B

D. Z and A

35. What will happen if students are found parking in the teacher's parking lot?

A. They will receive a warning.

B. They will not allowed to return to school.

C. They will be arrested by the police.

D. Their cars will be taken away.

36. Which of the following is accurate?

A. Parking stickers must be displayed on the back window.

B. Students must show their driver's license to receive a parking sticker.

C. The campus police station is near the gymnasium.

D. A parking sticker for one full year cannot be used during the summer semester.

33. 這份公告的目的是什麼？

   A. 告訴大家停車場即將施工。

   B. 警告老師和教職人員他們的車要停在前面的停車場。

   C. 通知學生停車標籤的事，以及他們的車該停在哪裡。

   D. 建議學生發生緊急事故時和校警聯絡。

34. 學生可以使用哪一區的停車場？

   A. W 區和 Z 區。

   B. A 區和 B 區。

   C. W 區和 B 區。

   D. Z 區和 A 區。

35. 如果學生的車被發現停在教師專用的停車場會發生什麼事？

   A. 他們會收到警告通知。

   B. 他們將不准回來學校。

   C. 他們會被警方逮捕。

   D. 他們的車會被拖走。

36. 下列敘述何者正確？

   A. 停車標籤必須展示在後車窗。

   B. 學生必須出示駕照才能領取停車標籤。

   C. 校警處在體育館附近。

   D. 整學年的停車標籤不能在暑假使用。

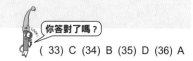

你答對了嗎？

(33) C (34) B (35) D (36) A

MP3-29

Questions 37-40

SUBJECT: Graduation Party

DATE: May 6, 2005

FROM: Sue

TO: Tim

Hi Tim!

Can you believe we'll be graduating in less than a week? I'm so excited about our trip to Europe! 31 more days and counting! Most of our friends will be traveling abroad this summer too, so let's have a big celebration before everyone leaves.

My parents agreed we could have the party at my house. They'll even go into the city that weekend and leave us kids alone. They're giving me $200 as part of my graduation present to help pay for it.

I also want The Twisted Monkeys to perform at the party. I know you don't like some of their music, but at least they're really cool guys. And yes, I still secretly like Jake. Did you know he's going to Southern University on a music scholarship?

Graduation is on the morning of May 17th so let's have the party that evening. I can get my brother to print out some invitations tonight and we can start passing them out tomorrow.

Give me a call when you get this email. I'll be at soccer practice until six.

Sue

問題 37-40

主旨：畢業派對

日期：2005 年五月六號

寄件者：蘇

收件者：提姆

嗨，提姆！

　　再不到一個禮拜我們就要畢業了，你相信嗎？要去歐洲旅行真的讓我好興奮！再數 31 天就到了！我們大部分朋友今年夏天也都會出國去玩，不如大家出發前好好慶祝一番。

　　我父母已同意可以在我家辦個派對。他們那個週末甚至會進城只留下我們這群年輕人一起玩。他們會給我 200 塊當做畢業禮物的其中一部分，可以拿來支付派對所需的費用。

　　我也想讓「滑稽猴」來派對上表演。我知道他們有些音樂你不太喜歡，不過他們幾個至少真的都很酷。對啦，我還在偷偷喜歡賈克。你知道他拿到音樂獎學金要去南方大學唸書嗎？

　　畢業典禮是在五月十七號早上，我們就當晚來辦派對吧。我會叫我弟今晚把邀請函印出來，明天就可以開始發了。

　　收到電子郵件時給我個電話，我六點前都在練足球。

蘇

37. What does the word "it" in line 6 refer to?

A. Graduation

B. The party

C. The trip to Europe

D. College

38. What does the word "them" in line 11 refer to?

A. The Twisted Monkeys

B. The party

C. The invitations

D. Sue's friends

39. What is the relationship between Sue and Tim?

A. They are boyfriend and girlfriend.

B. They are brother and sister.

C. They are best friends.

D. They are co-workers.

40. What is Sue going to be doing in June?

A. Having a big party at her house.

B. Graduating from high school.

C. Starting college.

D. Taking a trip to Europe.

37. 原文第六行的「it」指的是什麼？

　　A. 畢業典禮

　　B. 派對

　　C. 歐洲之旅

　　D. 大學

38. 原文第十一行的「them」指的是什麼？

　　A. 滑稽猴

　　B. 派對

　　C. 邀請函

　　D. 蘇的朋友

39. 蘇和提姆之間是什麼關係？

　　A. 他們是男女朋友。

　　B. 他們是兄妹。

　　C. 他們是最好的朋友。

　　D. 他們是同事。

40. 蘇六月時要做什麼？

　　A. 在她家辦個大型派對。

　　B. 高中畢業。

　　C. 開始上大學。

　　D. 到歐洲旅遊。

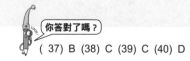

你答對了嗎？

（37）B（38）C（39）C（40）D

MP3-30

Test 2

第一部份： 句子填空

本部份共 15 題，每題有一個空格。請就下列的 A、B、C、D 四個選項，選出最適合題意的字或詞。

1. I don't like John because he _____ of people who are not as smart as him.

   A. takes care
   B. takes advantage
   C. takes a chance
   D. takes charge

2. _____ Mary would make it to her best friend's wedding even if it were on the opposite side of the world.

   A. Without question
   B. Mainly
   C. In doubt
   D. Evident

3. Henry's car accident was _____ lack of sleep.

   A. due to
   B. caused
   C. because
   D. in effect

4. As the number of car buyers _____, the owners of Riders Nissan will have to increase the amount of money they spend on advertisement.

   A. grow
   B. slide
   C. rise
   D. more

題目中譯

1. 我不喜歡約翰，因為他會 ＿＿ 聰明才智比不上他的人。

   A. 照顧　　　　　　　　　　B. 利用

   C. 冒險　　　　　　　　　　D. 掌管

2. 即使是世界的另一邊，瑪麗都 ＿＿ 會去參加她最好朋友的婚禮。

   A. 毫無疑問　　　　　　　　B. 主要地

   C. 不能肯定的　　　　　　　D. 明顯的

3. 亨利發生車禍是 ＿＿ 睡眠不足。

   A. 由於　　　　　　　　　　B. 導致

   C. 因為　　　　　　　　　　D. 實際上

4. 由於買車的人數 ＿＿，日產車商必須增加他們花在廣告上的費用。

   A. 成長　　　　　　　　　　B. 下滑

   C. 上升　　　　　　　　　　D. 更多

你答對了嗎？

(1) B (2) A (3) A (4) B

5. Increasing your daily intake of fruits and vegetables is the first _____ to enjoying a healthier lifestyle.

    A. dance   B. try
    C. step   D. effort

6. In order to avoid muscle injury, it is very important to _____ with fifteen minutes of stretching after a jog.

    A. follow up   B. chase
    C. include   D. perform

7. Oprah Winfrey had to _____ many obstacles to become the richest African American woman in history.

    A. overcame   B. overcomes
    C. overcoming   D. overcome

8. Since _____ Martin Luther King's mother knew he would grow up to do something great.

    A. beginning   B. born
    C. birth   D. start

9. The surprise birthday package _____ on the day of Mom's birthday.

    A. will be delivered   B. delivers
    C. delivering   D. is going to deliver

10. There have been _____ occasions where Mark has asked Karla for a date and she has turned him down.

    A. numerous   B. extreme
    C. dispute   D. legal

5. 要享有健康的生活方式，第一 ____ 就是要每天增加水果和蔬菜的攝取。

    A. 舞   B. 試

    C. 步   D. 努力

6. 慢跑後要 ____ 做十五分鐘的伸展運動，才能避免肌肉傷害。

    A. 接著   B. 追逐

    C. 包括   D. 執行

7. 奧普拉·溫芙蕾 ____ 了許多障礙，才成為史上最富有的非裔美國人。

    A. 克服   B. 克服

    C. 克服   D. 克服

8. 馬丁路德·金恩一 ____，他媽媽就知道他長大後會幹一番偉大的事業。

    A. 開始   B. 天生

    C. 出生   D. 開始

9. 這分驚奇生日包裹會在媽媽生日那天 ____。

    A. 送到   B. 送到

    C. 送到   D. 送到

10. 馬克在 ____ 場合中要求卡拉和他約會，但都被她拒絕了。

    A. 許多的   B. 極端的

    C. 爭論   D. 合法的

你答對了嗎？

(5) C (6) A (7) D (8) D (9) A (10) A

11. Many living creatures on Earth are so small they cannot be _____ to the naked eye.

    A. visible   B. seen

    C. detected   D. necessary

12. I'll be in the store for only a minute. _____ please keep the car doors locked.

    A. While   B. In the meantime

    C. Just in time   D. Being worthwhile

13. My father always taught me that _____ was more important than quantity.

    A. quality   B. scientific

    C. humiliate   D. generous

14. Amanda's _____ was evident when she broke her mother's favorite vase.

    A. careful   B. careless

    C. carelessness   D. carefulness

15. The _____ company picnic is held every July 4th at the California State Park.

    A. monthly   B. daily

    C. annual   D. majority

11. 地球上有許多生物因為太小，所以肉眼 ＿＿＿。

　　A. 看不到　　　　　　　　B. 看見

　　C. 察覺　　　　　　　　　D. 必要的

12. 我只會在店裡待一分鐘，＿＿＿＿ 請先把車門鎖上。

　　A. 當　　　　　　　　　　B. 這段時間

　　C. 剛好趕上　　　　　　　D. 值得的

13. 我父親總是教我要重 ＿＿＿ 不重量。

　　A. 質（品質）　　　　　　B. 科學的

　　C. 羞辱　　　　　　　　　D. 慷慨的

14. 艾曼達實在是很 ＿＿＿＿，居然把她媽媽心愛的花瓶給打破。

　　A. 小心的　　　　　　　　B. 粗心大意的

　　C. 粗心大意　　　　　　　D. 小心

15. 每年七月四號在加州公園會舉辦公司 ＿＿＿＿ 野餐。

　　A. 每月一次的　　　　　　B. 每日的

　　C. 一年一度的　　　　　　D. 大多數

你答對了嗎？

(11) A (12) B (13) A (14) C (15) C

第二部份： 段落填空

本部份共 10 題，每篇短文包括二至三個段落，每個段落各含 5 個空格。請就下列的 A、B、C、D 四個選項，選出最適合題意的字或詞。

MP3-31

Questions 16-20

A British man was coming home from work one Monday afternoon when a "strange incident" happened. He was driving his car when the offending __16__ came through his open window and hit him on the nose. The 46-year-old __17__ to stop safely before some people came to his aid. The driver decided not to go to the hospital, but lost a lot of blood and has been left with a swollen and painful nose. The man had __18__ car window down because it was such a nice afternoon.

He saw a car coming the other way and felt a shot of pain in his nose. He managed to stop his car __19__ hitting anyone else. Police said they felt very sorry for him － it must have been an incredibly lucky or unlucky shot to get the frozen *sausage __20__ a moving car window. The accident will be investigated to find the mysterious sausage thrower.

問題 16-20

　　有個英國人在週一下午下班回家時，遇到了一件「奇怪的事」。他原本開車開得好好的，突然天外飛來一個 __16__，從他打開的窗戶進來，撞到他的鼻子。這個 46 歲的英國人 __17__ 安全停車，才會有人來幫他的忙。雖然這個司機決定不去醫院，但還是留了很多血，鼻子也又腫又痛。經過情形是這樣的：一個如此美好的下午，司機搖下了 __18__ 車窗。

　　這時他看到另一輛車從對面開過來，鼻子便被東西打到痛了一下。他希望能把車子停下來而 __19__ 撞到任何人。警察說他們很替他難過，他居然會被 __20__ 移動的車窗飛進的冷凍香腸打到鼻子，不知道要算是難以置信的好運或楣運。警方會調查這起意外事故，看看這個丟香腸的神秘客到底是誰。

16.

- A. it
- B. item
- C. thing
- D. piece

16.

- A. 它
- B. 東西
- C. 東西
- D. 塊

17.

- A. managed
- B. fastened
- C. expected
- D. supposed

17.

- A. 打算
- B. 繫緊
- C. 預計
- D. 以為

18.

- A. some
- B. all
- C. his
- D. them

18.

- A. 一些
- B. 全部
- C. 他的
- D. 他們

19.

- A. without
- B. by
- C. after
- D. to

19.

- A. 不要
- B. 經由
- C. 之後
- D. 到

20.

- A. pass
- B. through
- C. under
- D. over

20.

- A. 通過
- B. 從
- C. 低於
- D. 越過

你答對了嗎？

(16) B (17) A (18) C (19) A (20) B

Questions 21-25

Someone at U.S. Airways must have gotten in big trouble. U.S. Airways became the lowset-cost carrier in history last weekend __21__ someone found the mistake in the computer. For several hours, U.S. Airways __22__ tickets to several small cities in the United States for $1.86 *round-trip plus tax. That __23__ got popular on the Internet quick. With taxes and fees, the round-trip fares were about 40 dollars each.

After finding the computer mistake Saturday afternoon, U.S. Airways __24__ it by that evening. A spokesman says the airline doesn't know how many people bought the super __25__ tickets.

問題 21-25

美國航空公司有人要倒大楣了。上個禮拜美國航空公司成為史上最廉價的客機，__21__ 被人發現電腦裡的錯誤才把問題解決。有好幾個小時的時間，美國航空公司一些飛往美國小城市的來回機票，含稅只 __22__ 1.86 美元。這個划算的 __23__ 很快在網際路上流傳開來。原本含稅的來回機票是每人 40 美元。

週末下午找到電腦錯誤後，美國航空公司當晚便把票價 __24__ 回來。一位發言人說，航空公司並不曉得到底有多少人買到這些超級 __25__ 的機票。

21.

A. firstly
B. after
C. later
D. until

21.

A. 首先
B. 之後
C. 稍後
D. 直到

22.

A. sell
B. was selling
C. are selling
D. has been sold

22.

A. 賣
B. 賣
C. 賣
D. 賣

23.

A. deal
B. debt
C. inexpensive
D. bargains

23.

A. 交易
B. 借款
C. 低廉的
D. 買賣

24.

A. hid
B. graded
C. corrected
D. check

24.

A. 隱藏
B. 分級
C. 改正
D. 檢查

25.

A. cheap
B. recent
C. population
D. ordinary

25.

A. 便宜的
B. 最近的
C. 人口
D. 平常的

你答對了嗎？

(21) D (22) B (23) A (24) C (25) A

第三部份： 閱讀理解

本部份共15題，包括數段短文，每篇文章有2~5個相關問題，請就下列的 A、B、C、D 四個選項，選出最適合的答案。

MP3-33

Everyone knows you never get a second chance at a first impression. A radiant smile is the first thing most people will notice about you! Smile Bright is the brand new toothpaste that guarantees a brighter smile within 14 days of use. It can safely remove coffee stains, *antibiotic stains, and even stubborn cigarette stains.. Smile Bright contains 5)fluoride so it can replace your regular toothpaste. It not only whitens, it's been proven effective to remove *plaque, fight against gum disease, and prevent cavities. Its *patent formula has been tested by dentists across the country.

Smile Bright cannot be found in stores anywhere. To order your first tube of Smile Bright go to www.smilebright.com. All orders come with a free battery-operated toothbrush! Your

問題 **26-29**

每個人都曉得要給人好的第一印象，永遠只有一次機會。保持容光煥發會讓大部分人一眼就注意到你！「燦爛笑容」是一種全新的牙膏，保證使用十四天後笑容會更加燦爛。它可以安全地除掉咖啡垢、菌垢，連很難去掉的煙垢也可以消除。「燦爛笑容」含有氟化物，可以代替你平常使用的牙膏。它不僅可以潔白牙齒，在去除齒菌斑、對抗牙床疾病，還有預防蛀牙方面的效果也已經過證實。它的專利配方也經過全世界牙醫師的檢測。

satisfaction is also guaranteed. If for any reason you are not happy with the results, we will happily return your money. Smile Bright is safe for all ages, but not recommended for children under the age of three.

26. Where can you buy Smile Bright toothpaste?

    A. At the grocery store.

    B. Over the telephone.

    C. On the Internet.

    D. At the dentist office.

27. Who should not use Smile Bright?

    A. An enfant with growing teeth.

    B. An elderly person who has been smoking for most of his life.

    C. A young woman that drinks black tea every day.

    D. A dentist who is taking medicine for his illness.

28. What is the message being conveyed with this advertisement?

    A. Fluoride is a good fighter against gum disease.

    B. A good smile is necessary to get a good job.

    C. Seeing the dentist once a year is important.

    D. A person gets immediately judged by their smile.

29. What does Smile Bright promise to do?

    A. Get people to like you.

    B. Give you free toothpaste.

    C. Whiten your teeth in three days.

    D. Return your money.

「燦爛笑容」不是任何一家商店都可以買得到。要訂購你第一管「燦爛笑容」，可以上 www.smilebright.com 網站。每次訂購都會附上一支免費的電池型牙刷，保證用到滿意為止。只要你不滿意，不管任何理由我們都很樂意退款。「燦爛笑容」牙膏任何年齡皆可使用，但未滿三歲的小孩則不建議。

26. 你可以在哪裡買到「燦爛笑容」牙膏？

　　A. 雜貨店。

　　B. 電話上。

　　C. 網際網路上。

　　D. 牙醫辦公室。

27. 誰不應該使用「燦爛笑容」？

　　A. 還在長牙齒的嬰兒。

　　B. 一輩子差不多都在抽煙那種上了年紀的人。

　　C. 每天喝紅茶的年輕婦女。

　　D. 因為生病而在吃藥的牙醫。

28. 這個廣告所要傳達的訊息是什麼？

　　A. 氟化物是對抗牙床疾病的剋星。

　　B. 要找到好工作，適當的笑容有其必要。

　　C. 一年看一次牙醫很重要。

　　D. 笑容直接影響你給別人的第一印象。

29. 「燦爛笑容」承諾過什麼事？

　　A. 讓別人喜歡你。

　　B. 免費送你牙膏。

　　C. 三天內讓你牙齒變得潔白。

　　D. 退款。

你答對了嗎？

(26) C (27) A (28) D (29) D

Questions 30-31

Jan Zocha, Germany's most wanted criminal, was arrested in 2003 but his trial didn't start until April of 2005 under high security measures. The 37-year-old *defendant is charged with a series of robberies and stealing $650,000.00. Zocha, who is believed to be very intelligent and known to speak six languages including Russian and Arabic ignored several questions asked by the judge and eventually pretended to be asleep during the proceedings. His lawyer criticized the security measures used by the court as inappropriate and discriminatory.

The "king of robbers" was born in Hamburg and spent his childhood in shelters and asylums after his father had shot his mother and committed suicide.

30. What is a good title for this article?

A. Germany's Most Wanted Criminal Sleeps

B. "King of Robbers" Steals $650,000

C. German "King of Robbers" on Trial

D. High Security Measures Upsets Criminal

31. What can we conclude about Jan Zocha?

A. He had an easy childhood.

B. He is a very accomplished thief.

C. He has never been caught stealing.

D. He is not a very bright person.

問題 30-31

德國頭號通緝犯賈恩‧洛洽在 2003 年被逮捕，但一直到 2005 年四月在高度保安措施下才進行審判。37 歲的被告被控一連串的搶　和竊盜罪，總金額達 650000 美金。洛洽被認為是個相當聰明的人，還以精通包括俄語和阿拉伯語在內的六國語言而聞名；他在訴訟過程中，不理會法官提出的好幾個問題，最後還假裝睡著。他的律師批評法庭使用的保安措施不僅不適當，更是一種差別待遇。

「搶劫之王」在漢堡出生，小時候父親槍殺了母親然後自殺，於是他的童年便在避難所和收容所裡度過。

30. 這段文章用什麼標題比較好？

　　A. 德國頭號通緝犯睡著了

　　B. 「搶劫之王」偷了 650000 美金

　　C. 德國「搶劫之王」接受審判

　　D. 高度保安措施讓罪犯覺得很煩

31. 我們對賈恩‧洛洽可以下什麼結論？

　　A. 他有個舒適的童年生活。

　　B. 他是個很有造詣的賊。

　　C. 他偷東西從未被逮到。

　　D. 他不是個很開朗的人。

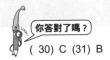

你答對了嗎？

(30) C (31) B

MP3-35

Questions 32-34

Important Notice

The Australian National Park Commission announces the reopening of Canberra Beach that was temporarily closed after the recent series of shark attacks.

In December 2004, an 18-year-old surfer was bitten in half by a 16-foot great white shark. A week earlier, a shark killed a 38-year-old diver spear-fishing on the Great *Barrier Reef. In March 2005, a 20-foot great white shark tore a man in half, killing him instantly while he was *snorkeling. Most recently, a surfer fought off a 7-foot shark with his surfboard and returned to shore unharmed.

Here are some reminders for beach users. Do not swim past unmarked waters. Adults must monitor children at all times. Be aware of shark signals and return to shore immediately when flare is fired. Canberra Beach is opened 24 hours but will be monitored by lifeguards from 9 A.M. to 8 P.M ONLY. Enter the water at your own risk.

32. What is the purpose of this notice?

A. To inform people of some new park facilities.

B. To advise the public that the beach is closed for a while.

C. To warn beach users of recent shark attacks.

D. To announce that the beach can be used now.

問題 32-34

重要公告

因近來連續鯊魚攻擊事件而暫時關閉的坎培拉海灘，澳大利亞國家公園委員會已宣佈重新開放。

2004 年十二月，一名十八歲的衝浪客被一隻十六英尺的大白鯊咬掉了一半。一個禮拜後，又有一隻鯊魚把在大堡礁捕魚的一名三十八歲浮潛客給殺死。2005 年三月，一隻二十英尺的大白鯊把一名用呼吸管潛游的人撕成兩半，讓他當場死亡。不過就在最近，一名衝浪客用他的衝浪板把七英尺的鯊魚給擊退，毫髮無傷地回到岸邊。

這裡有些事情要提醒海灘遊客。游泳時不要游到未標記的水域。大人要隨時盯緊小孩。小心鯊魚出現的信號，看到閃光要立刻回到岸邊。坎培拉海灘雖然是 24 小時開放，但只有早上九點到晚上八點才有救生員在那邊監控。其他時間下水要自行負責。

32. 這份公告的目的是什麼？

    A. 讓大家知道有哪些新的公園設施。

    B. 通知民眾海灘要關閉一會兒。

    C. 警告海灘遊客最近有鯊魚攻擊事件。

    D. 宣佈海灘現在已恢復使用。

你答對了嗎？

(32) D

33. According to this notice, when may people use the beach?

A. From 9 A.M. to 8 P.M. only.

B. Anytime they want.

C. At no time.

D. In emergency situations.

34. What can we learn from this notice?

A. Australian beaches are totally safe.

B. Australian beaches are used for many recreational activities.

C. Surfing is uncommon in Australia.

D. Children are not allowed at the beach.

MP3-36

Questions 35-37

To Whom It May Concern:

I am currently a student of Chinese at Middlebury College and will be graduating in May 2005. I spent my junior year as an exchange student in Beijing, China while also interning at Stanford and Son, a highly successful import and export company of Chinese antique furniture. As the leading salesperson of the year, I was able to increase sales by 30 percent. I have an excellent grade point average and am president of my senior class. Please refer to the attached resume for a list of my other accomplishments.

I am interested in joining your team of consultants at Bradbury Consultants. My past work experiences and high command of the Chinese language will make me a great asset

33. 根據這份公告，民眾何時可以使用海灘？

    A. 僅限上午九點到晚上八點。

    B. 任何時候想來都可以來。

    C. 任何時候都不可以來。

    D. 發生緊急狀況。

34. 我們可以從這份公告中得知什麼事？

    A. 澳大利亞的海灘全部都很安全。

    B. 澳大利亞的海灘是許多娛樂活動的最佳去處。

    C. 衝浪在澳大利亞並不常見。

    D. 小孩不准到海灘玩。

問題 35-37

敬啟者：

    我目前是米德爾布里學院的中文系學生，即將於 2005 年五月畢業。我三年級時在中國北京當交換學生，同時在相當成功的中國古董家具進出口公司「史丹佛恩桑」當實習生。身為年度最佳推銷員，我讓公司業務成長了 30%。我的平均積點分相當優異，而且是我四年級那班的班長。請參考隨信附上的履歷表，上頭有我其他方面的完整經歷。

    我想加入你們布來培里顧問公司的顧問團隊。我過去的工作經驗加上中文方面的深厚造詣，相信可以助你們台北總公司一臂之力。你們公司是某些世界頂尖電子製造商的首席顧問，名聲卓著，我有信心可以替公司開創更美好的未來。

你答對了嗎？

(33) B (34) B

to your headquarters in Taipei. I know I can make a positive contribution to your company's excellent reputation as a leading consultant for some of the top electronic manufacturers in the world.

Please contact me at your earliest convenience to set up an interview. I look forward to hearing from you soon.

Sincerely,
Jack Donovan

35. Why did Jack Donovan write this letter?

A. To get into Middlebury College.

B. To get a job.

C. To inform his friend of his accomplishments.

D. To become president of his senior class.

36. What do the employees at Bradbury Consultants do?

A. They sell furniture.

B. The make electronics.

C. They offer advice.

D. They teach Chinese.

37. Which of the following is NOT TRUE?

A. Jack Donovan wrote this letter before May 2005.

B. Stanford and Son sells new furniture.

C. Bradbury Consultants does business in Chinese.

D. Jack Donovan is a successful student.

請安排我在你們最方便的時間面試。希望很快收到你們的回覆。

敬祝商祈

傑克‧多諾凡

35. 傑克‧多諾凡為何寫這封信？

A. 為了進入米德爾布里學院。

B. 為了找工作。

C. 為了告知他朋友他的成功經歷。

D. 為了當他四年級那班的班長。

36. 布來培里顧問公司的員工都做些什麼？

A. 販賣家具。

B. 製造電子器材。

C. 提供建議。

D. 教中文。

37. 下列哪一項敘述「不是真的」？

A. 這封信是傑克‧多諾凡在 2005 年五月前寫的。

B. 「史丹佛恩桑」販賣新家具。

C. 布來培里顧問公司談生意時都用中文。

D. 傑克‧多諾凡是個成功的學生。

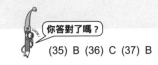

你答對了嗎？

(35) B (36) C (37) B

MP3-37

Questions 38-40

A Romanian man who invited women for romantic meals at expensive restaurants before running off was finally arrested after several months of serial dating. Police say that 23-year-old George Hodoroaba lured dozens of women in the town of Suceava in eastern Romania. He was finally caught after restaurant owners were given a photo of his face. In May 2005, five women came forward to register a complaint against Hodoroaba, who was well dressed with expensive suits when he approached them in bars and clubs to invite them for a "romantic meal."

During the dates, he was always generous with the order and asked for the best wines. He would also urge his female guest to have whatever she wanted. In every case, he would then say he had to make an important phone call and needed to go outside where the mobile phone reception was better. After a few minutes, he would then vanish, leaving the women to pay the bill. Sometimes he would borrow the women's phone to make the call and disappear with the phone as well.

Hodoroaba faces two years in jail if he is convicted. The police believe the number of victims is far larger than the complaints they have received, but most women would probably be too embarrassed to come forward.

問題 38-40

　　有個羅馬尼亞人專門邀請女性到昂貴餐廳共進浪漫晚餐然後消失，經過幾個月的連續約會後，終於被警方逮捕。警方說 23 歲的喬治‧霍多洛巴在東羅馬尼亞的蘇恰瓦鎮引誘多名女性，經過餐廳老闆提供他臉部的照片後，才終於將他繩之以法。2005 年五月時，有五名婦女站出來對霍多洛巴提出控訴，說他穿著體面，一身昂貴的西裝出現在酒吧和俱樂部裡向她們搭訕，邀請她們共進「浪漫晚餐」。

　　約會時他總是慷慨地點餐，酒也是點最好的來喝。他也會慫恿女伴想點什麼就點什麼。每一回他都會藉口說要打個重要電話，而且需要到外面打，手機的收訊才會比較好。沒幾分鐘他人就會落跑不見，留下女伴一個人結帳。有時候他還會向女伴借手機打電話，然後帶著手機一起消失。

　　霍多洛巴如果被定罪，就要吃兩年的牢飯。警方認為受害人數遠超過目前的控訴案件，但大部分婦女可能因為覺得很尷尬而不敢前來報案。

38. Why is George Hodoroaba facing two years in jail?

   A. Because he dated too many women.

   B. Because he ran away from the police.

   C. Because he got into a fight with the restaurant owners.

   D. Because he did not pay his restaurant bill.

39. What can we assume about George Hodoroaba?

   A. He is attractive.

   B. He doesn't eat at expensive restaurants.

   C. He hasn't dated many women.

   D. He is an American.

40. How was George Hodoroaba finally caught?

   A. The five women went searching for him.

   B. The police saw him on the street.

   C. The restaurant owners recognized his photo.

   D. The telephone company traced his call.

38. 喬治・霍多洛巴為何要吃兩年牢飯？

    A. 因為他和太多婦女約會。

    B. 因為他從警方那裡逃跑。

    C. 因為他和餐廳老闆發生衝突。

    D. 因為他在餐廳吃飯都沒有結帳。

39. 我們可以如何設想喬治・霍多洛巴？

    A. 他很有吸引力。

    B. 他不在昂貴餐廳吃飯。

    C. 他沒有和很多婦女約會。

    D. 他是美國人。

40. 喬治・霍多洛巴最後是怎麼被抓到的？

    A. 五名婦人把他給找出來的。

    B. 警方在馬路上看到他。

    C. 餐廳老闆認出他的照片。

    D. 電話公司追蹤他打的電話。

你答對了嗎？

(38) D (39) A (40) C

MP3-38

Test 3

第一部份： 句子填空

本部份共 15 題，每題有一個空格。請就下列的 A、B、C、D 四個選項，選出最適合題意的字或詞。

1. Jon rushed out of the house not knowing he had put his shirt on _____.

   A. inside out
   B. over
   C. upside down
   D. forward

2. Everything the weatherman predicted today _____ true.

   A. came
   B. come
   C. coming
   D. comes

3. Why did the soldiers _____ the bridge after the war was won?

   A. destruction
   B. blow up
   C. pollution
   D. execute

4. Does your friend live by _____ in that huge apartment?

   A. yourself
   B. his
   C. himself
   D. themselves

5. Jenny was too _____ by the scary movie to sleep alone last night.

   A. disturb
   B. disturbing
   C. disturbs
   D. disturbed

題目中譯

1. 約拿趕著出門，不知道自己把襯衫穿 ＿＿＿ 了。

   A. 反　　　　　　　　　　　B. 超過

   C. 顛倒　　　　　　　　　　D. 向前

2. 氣象預報員今天預報的每件事都 ＿＿＿ 真了。

   A. 成　　　　　　　　　　　B. 成

   C. 成　　　　　　　　　　　D. 成

3. 士兵為何要在打勝仗後把橋給 ＿＿＿ ？

   A. 破壞　　　　　　　　　　B. 炸毀

   C. 污染　　　　　　　　　　D. 執行

4. 你朋友 ＿＿＿ 住在那棟大公寓裡嗎？

   A. 你自己　　　　　　　　　B. 他的

   C. 他自己（獨自）　　　　　D. 他們自己

5. 珍妮被那部恐怖電影弄得很 ＿＿＿，害她昨晚不敢一個人睡覺。

   A. 不安　　　　　　　　　　B. 不安

   C. 不安　　　　　　　　　　D. 不安

你答對了嗎？

(1) A　(2) A　(3) B　(4) C　(5) D

6. _____ Elvis was a little boy, he wanted to become a rock star.

    A. Because   B. Before

    C. Since   D. Whether

7. The average _____ for most Americans is one of the highest in the world.

    A. increase   B. income

    C. industry   D. insurance

8. Rita likes every kind of music _____ country music.

    A. according to   B. except for

    C. next to   D. addition to

9. The students waited nervously _____ their test results.

    A. for   B. over

    C. among   D. past

10. Jon was determined to keep the relationship going _____how far his girlfriend moved.

    A. doesn't matter   B. no matter

    C. don't matter   D. the matter

6. 艾維斯 ____ 小就希望成為搖滾巨星。

    A. 因為   B. 之前

    C. 從   D. 是否

7. 大部分美國人的平均 ____ 是全世界數一數二的。

    A. 增加   B. 所得

    C. 工業   D. 保險

8. ____ 鄉村音樂，其他的每種音樂，莉塔都喜歡。

    A. 根據   B. 除了

    C. 緊鄰   D. 附加

9. 學生緊張地等待（____）考試結果。

    A. 為了   B. 超過

    C. 之中   D. 經過

10. 喬恩決定 ____ 他女朋友搬到多遠的地方，他都要繼續維持這段關係。

    A. 沒關係   B. 無論

    C. 沒關係   D. 事件

你答對了嗎？

(6) C (7) B (8) B (9) A (10) B

11. The business failed because the partners _____ each other.

    A. distrusted   B. lied

    C. disappointment   D. trusted

12. After Mark got married, he only would drink beer _____.

    A. numerous   B. occasionally

    C. never   D. a few

13. I _____ gone to the movies on a school night! Now, I won't have enough time to study!

    A. couldn't have   B. shouldn't have

    C. might have   D. wouldn't have

14. Please _____ all that broken glass!

    A. watch out for   B. walk up

    C. take after   D. be careful

15. Jennifer visits her grandmother _____ she is in town

    A. whatever   B. whenever

    C. whether   D. where

11. 生意會失敗是因為合夥人之間互相 ＿＿＿ 。

    A. 懷疑   B. 說謊

    C. 失望   D. 信任

12. 馬克婚後只會 ＿＿＿ 喝啤酒。

    A. 許多的   B. 偶爾

    C. 從不   D. 一些

13. 我 ＿＿＿ 在平常上課日晚上去看電影的！現在讀書時間不夠用了！

    A. 無法   B. 不應該

    C. 或許   D. 沒有

14. 請 ＿＿＿ 那些碎玻璃！

    A. 小心   B. 走近

    C. 相像   D. 小心

15. (＿＿＿) 珍妮佛只要進城，都會去探望她奶奶。

    A. 不管什麼   B. 無論何時

    C. 是否   D. 哪裡

你答對了嗎？

(11) A (12) B (13) B (14) A (15) B

第二部份： 段落填空

本部份共 10 題，每篇短文包括二至三個段落，每個段落各含 5 個空格。請就下列的 A、B、C、D 四個選項，選出最適合題意的字或詞。

`MP3-39`

Questions 16-20

In the year 2000, Stuart Murray fell fifteen feet from the *ledge of his first floor apartment and broke his neck and back. Doctors told him he __16__ never walk again. His family was told he would be confined to a wheelchair for the rest of his life. Yet, Murray __17__ to give up. Inspired by Christopher Reeves, the former Superman star who became paralyzed from the neck down after a horse riding accident, Murray was walking on crutches __18__ four months. Murray's doctors have all been amazed by his progress.

Now five years later at the age of 29, he __19__ to run in the London Marathon, one of the world's toughest races, to __20__ money for spinal research. He wants to dedicate his life to helping other people who have found themselves in the same predicament as himself and Superman.

段落填空中譯

西元 2000 年時，史都華·莫瑞從他公寓二樓十五英尺的窗台上掉下來，摔斷了頸子和背脊。醫生告訴他他 __16__ 永遠都不能走路了，還通知他家人他一輩子都要坐在輪椅上。但是莫瑞 __17__ 放棄。過去飾演「超人」的明星克里斯多夫·李維在一次騎馬意外中，不幸頸部以下全部癱瘓；在他的激勵下，莫瑞 __18__ 四個月內都用枴杖走路。莫瑞的醫生們對他的進步都感到很驚訝。

現在五年過去了，莫瑞 29 歲這一年正 __19__ 參加全世界最困難的比賽之一－－倫敦馬拉松大賽，希望能為脊髓研究 __20__ 到研究經費。他要一生致力於幫助其他那些陷入和他自己及超人一樣困境的人們。

16.

    A. should

    B. would

    C. couldn't

    D. cannot

16.

    A. 應該

    B. 將

    C. 無法

    D. 無法

17.

    A. excused

    B. sought

    C. grateful

    D. refused

17.

    A. 原諒

    B. 尋找

    C. 感激的

    D. 拒絕

18.

    A. almost

    B. within

    C. near

    D. close to

18.

    A. 幾乎

    B. 在

    C. 接近

    D. 接近

19.

    A. is preparing

    B. was prepared

    C. prepared

    D. won't prepare

19.

    A. 準備

    B. 準備

    C. 準備

    D. 沒準備

20.

    A. come up

    B. share

    C. raise

    D. take

20.

    A. 發生

    B. 分享

    C. 籌

    D. 拿

你答對了嗎？

(16) B (17) D (18) B (19) A (20) C

MP3-40

Questions 21-25

The Guangdu Bikeway around the Taipei area has become a haven for cyclists and nature enthusiasts. Different sections of the 100km trail __21__ its own unique attractions such as temples, waterfalls, and a wonderful mix of natural wonders. __22__, biking along Keelung River was too dangerous because of the pollution and traffic. The Guangdu Bikeway __23__ the shores of Keelung River and parts of Danshui River far away from the chaos of Taipei. It winds through and around the area's Aquatic Bird Marshlands, as well as Guangdu Nature Park -- a preserve with 58 hectares of grass, mangroves, saltwater marsh, and freshwater ponds. More than 100 species of birds, 150 species of plants, and 800 species of animals call the park home.

At the Guandu end of the trail is Guandu Wharf\, a busy area full of colorful shops, food stands __24__ delicious seafood, old men discussing the day's issues on benches, and people simply enjoying the scene. For many years to come, the bikeway will give the residents of Taiwan a chance to __25__ Taipei's beautiful scenery in a very special way.

問題 21-25

喜歡騎單車和熱愛大自然的人，台北附近的關渡單車專用道已成為最佳去處。100 公里長的各個不同區段裡，__21__ 著它獨特的魅力景點，如寺廟、瀑布、還有各類混合式的自然奇景。__22__，沿著基隆河騎單車由於污染和交通狀況仍然相當危險。關渡單車專用道 __23__ 基隆河岸和部分遠離台北塵囂的淡水河前進，它沿著該區的水生鳥類沼澤區和關渡自然公園迂迴而行。關渡自然公園是一塊面積達 58 公頃的保護區，裡頭有草地、紅樹林、鹽水沼澤，以及淡水池。100 種以上的鳥類、150 種植物，還有 800 種動物都以這座公園為家。

專用道的盡頭是關渡碼頭。這裡非常熱鬧，除了有各式各樣的商店、各類打著美味海產 __24__ 的小吃攤，還可以看到老人們在長椅上閒話家常，或是單純來這裡觀賞景色的人潮。相信在未來幾年，這條單車專用道可以讓台北居民有機會用一種非常特殊的方式 __25__ 台北的美景。

21.		21.	
A.	give	A.	給予
B.	offer	B.	展示
C.	lack	C.	缺乏
D.	balance	D.	平衡

22.		22.	
A.	After	A.	之後
B.	Past	B.	經過
C.	Until now	C.	直到現在
D.	Upon now	D.	接近現在

23.		23.	
A.	is following	A.	沿著
B.	followed	B.	沿著
C.	has followed	C.	沿著
D.	follows	D.	沿著

24.		24.	
A.	eating	A.	吃
B.	featuring	B.	招牌（特色）
C.	entertaining	C.	娛樂
D.	deserving	D.	應得

25.		25.	
A.	experience	A.	體驗
B.	create	B.	創造
C.	support	C.	支持
D.	recognize	D.	識別

你答對了嗎？

(21) B (22) C (23) D (24) B (25) A

第三部份：閱讀理解

本部份共 15 題，包括數段短文，每段短文後有 2~5 個相關問題，請就下列的 A、B、C、D 四個選項，選出最適合的答案。

MP3-41

Questions 26-28

Undoubtedly, students in America have a much easier time during test days than the students in Taiwan. Across America, educators are trying a variety of methods including beach days, barbecues, flute music, and fun hats to help ease student test anxiety as schools face increased pressure to improve their scores under the federal No Child Left Behind Act.

In Pennsylvania, Asia Pearson and her fifth-grade classmates enjoyed a taste of summer as a reward for enduring a string of state math and reading tests. After their exams, the students changed into sunglasses, tank tops, and sandals — clothing normally not allowed under the school's dress code — and had a make-believe "beach day."

Brent Swartzmiller, principal of Wayne Trail Elementary School in Ohio wants to take the stress off the kids and make the test-taking days as normal as possible. At his school, one teacher leads her students through mental and physical exercises before Ohio's state tests. In an exercise to increase blood flow to the brain, the students touch their chests with their thumbs and index fingers just below the collarbone. Swartzmiller admits it sounds strange, but he also thinks it works.

閱讀理解中譯

　　毫無疑問地，美國學生在考試期間，會比台灣學生輕鬆許多。由於聯邦政府推行「不讓任何一個孩子落後」的方案，為了提升學生成績，學校面臨的壓力日益增加；於是美國各地的教育人員都會嘗試各式各樣的方法來幫助學生減輕考試焦慮，例如海灘日、烤肉、長笛音樂，還有趣味戴帽等等。

　　賓夕法尼亞州的愛莎·派爾森和她十五年級的班上同學在忍受一連串州立數學和閱讀測驗後，享受到夏日趣味的回報。考試完後，學生們換上平常學校規定不准穿戴的太陽眼鏡、背心裝和涼鞋等，度過了一個假扮的「海灘日」。

　　俄亥俄州韋恩小道小學的校長布蘭特·史華茲密勒，希望能消除孩童的壓力，讓他們考試的日子能儘可能和平常一樣。在他的學校裡，有老師帶著學生在俄亥俄州州立考試前進行一種心理和生理上的運動。這項運動是為了增加腦中血液的流動，學生們必須用拇指和食指碰觸自己的胸膛鎖骨下方的部分。史華茲密勒承認這個方法聽起來有點怪，但他個人覺得倒是蠻有效的。

26. What is the purpose of "beach day" at Asia Pearson's elementary school?

   A. To celebrate the beginning of summer.

   B. To relieve stress.

   C. To prove that the school's dress code is useless.

   D. To help ease the summer's heat.

27. What does the word "their" in the second paragraph refer to?

   A. The government's

   B. The student's

   C. The school's

   D. The teacher's

28. What does the exercise at Swartzmiller's school supposedly do?

   A. Prevents students from failing the test.

   B. Increases blood flow to the brain.

   C. Increases the student's ability to think.

   D. Makes the student's heart healthier.

MP3-42

Questions 29-30

Soong Mayling was one of the most important figures of the 20th century in the struggle between the Nationalists and the Communists. She was western educated, shrewd in politics, and charming as could be. Married to Chiang Kai-shek in 1927, Madame Chiang rose to importance during World War II. In 1943

26. 愛莎・派爾森的小學假扮「海灘日」的目的是什麼？

  A. 為了慶祝夏天的到來。

  B. 為了減輕壓力。

  C. 為了證明學校的服裝規定沒有用。

  D. 為了幫助減輕盛夏酷暑。

27. 原文第二段裡的「their」指的是什麼？

  A. 政府

  B. 學生

  C. 學校

  D. 老師

28. 史華茲密勒的學校裡所做的運動據稱可以發揮什麼效果？

  A. 讓學生不會考試不及格。

  B. 增加腦中血液的流動。

  C. 增加學生的思考能力。

  D. 讓學生的心臟更健康。

問題 29-30

　　宋美齡是二十世紀民族主義和共產主義的鬥爭史中，最重要的人物之一。
她在西方接受教育，精通政治，人也很有魅力。她在 1927 年嫁給了蔣中正，
第二次世界大戰期間，蔣夫人的地位可謂舉足輕重。她在 1943 年成為在美國
國會上發表聯合演說的第一個中國人和第二個女性。她那些年在華府的影響

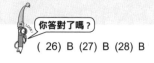

你答對了嗎？

(26) B (27) B (28) B

she became the first Chinese and the second woman to address a joint session of the U.S. Congress. Her influence in Washington during those years played a big part in the close relationship that exists today between Taiwan and the United States. After her husband's death in 1975, Madame Chiang moved to New York. She remained in seclusion in New York until her death at the age of 106 in October 2003.

29. What is the purpose of this article?

   A. To describe the relationship between Taiwan and the United States.

   B. To tell a short history of Soong Mayling.

   C. To show how the U.S. Congress gets addressed by only a few women.

   D. To make known that Chiang Kai-shek and his wife had a successful marriage.

30. According to the article, which of the following is a FALSE statement?

   A. Madame Chiang and her husband lived in New York together.

   B. Madame Chiang is an important part of Taiwan's history.

   C. Madame Chiang was very skilled in politics.

   D. Madame Chiang lived an extremely long life.

力，在今天台灣和美國的密切關係上扮演了重要的角色。先生於 1975 年去世後，蔣夫人便搬到紐約。她在紐約過著隱居的生活，2003 年十月以 106 歲的高齡駕鶴西歸。

29. 這篇文章的目的何在？

　　A. 描述台灣和美國的關係。

　　B. 簡單介紹宋美齡。

　　C. 説明美國國會如何僅由一些女性來發表演説。

　　D. 讓大家知道蔣中正和他夫人婚姻美滿。

30. 根據本文所述，下列敘述可者為「假」？

　　A. 蔣夫人和她先生一起住在紐約。

　　B. 蔣夫人是台灣歷史上的重要人物。

　　C. 蔣夫人非常精通政治。

　　D. 蔣夫人相當長壽。

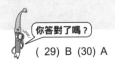

你答對了嗎？
(29) B (30) A

Questions 31-33

Early one morning in November of 2003, Bethany Hamilton did something she regularly did -- she went to Makua Beach in Hawaii to go surfing. A 13-year-old professional surfer, Hamilton often went surfing with her best friend and fellow competitor, Alana Blanchard. On this morning, Holt and Byron, Alana's dad and brother, joined Bethany and Alana. At about 7:30 a.m., a tiger shark 12 to 15 feet in length suddenly bit off Hamilton's left arm below the shoulder.

"Nobody saw the shark," said Bethany's 21-year-old brother, Noah, who also said that it was a calm day with clear water. After Hamilton was bitten, instead of *panicking and possibly drowning, she *paddled over to her friends with only one arm. Along the way, she even made sure to warn other surfers and swimmers nearby by shouting that there was a shark. Many of Hamilton's friends and family *attest to her quiet strength, pointing out that she has never cried about the incident. Even her doctors were surprised at her determination.

Fortunately, the loss of Hamilton's arm has not stopped her from dreaming, she has simply changed her focus. Hamilton plans to pursue a career in photography, standing on the other side of the camera when an accident happens.

問題 31-33

2003 年十一月某個大清早，貝瑟妮・漢米敦和平常一樣到她經常去的夏威夷馬夸海灘衝浪。她是一名年僅十三歲的專業衝浪客，常常和她最好的朋友兼同伴競賽者阿拉那・布蘭佳一起衝浪。這天早上，阿拉那的父親霍爾特和弟弟拜倫也一起加入貝瑟妮和阿拉那的行列。到了早上七點半左右，突然出現一隻 12 到 15 英尺長的虎鯊，把漢米敦的左手臂從肩膀上給咬了下來。

「沒人看到那隻鯊魚。」貝瑟妮二十一歲的弟弟諾亞說道。他還說那天風平浪靜，水面清澈。漢米敦被咬掉手臂後，她並沒有驚慌失措讓自己陷入可能淹死的處境，反而用一隻手向她朋友們划去。她甚至沿途不忘大喊鯊魚出現了，以警告附近的其他衝浪客和游泳者。許多漢米敦的朋友和家人都可以見證她這種保持鎮定的能力，並指出她沒有因這件意外而哭泣。連她醫生都對她的堅定感到很驚訝。

漢米敦雖然失去手臂，但幸運的是她並未因此而放棄夢想，只不過把重心稍加轉移而已。漢米敦打算往攝影界發展，一旦再有意外事故發生，她要站在一旁用相機做見證。.

31. What is the relationship between Bethany and Alana?

A. They are sister and brother.

B. They are friends.

C. They are daughter and father.

D. They are sisters.

32. What did Bethany do after the shark bite?

A. She drowned.

B. She stayed still.

C. She called for help.

D. She went to her friends.

33. According to the story, what lesson can we learn from Bethany?

A. Surfing is too dangerous a sport to try.

B. When difficulties arise, give up!

C. Family is more important than friends.

D. Never stop dreaming!

MP3-44

Questions 34-36

Bad-mouthing your neighbors can *land you in jail in one Colombian town after the Mayor banned gossip. Ignacio Jimenez, mayor of Icononzo, told El Tiempo newspaper he announced the ban because rumors can cost lives in Colombia, which is in the grips of a *guerrilla war involving Marxist rebels and far-right *paramilitary *outlaws. Justifying his decision, the mayor said at least eight people were in the local prison accused "purely by gossip" of being members of the outlawed, Marxist-inspired

31. 貝瑟妮和阿拉那之間是什麼關係？

    A. 他們是姐弟。

    B. 他們是朋友。

    C. 他們是父女。

    D. 他們是姐妹。

32. 貝瑟妮被鯊魚咬到後做了什麼事？

    A. 她淹死了。

    B. 她靜止不動。

    C. 她呼救。

    D. 她划向朋友那邊。

33. 根據本文所述，我們可以從貝瑟妮身上學到什麼？

    A. 嘗試衝浪這項運動相當危險。

    B. 碰到困難時便放棄！

    C. 家人比朋友重要。

    D. 永遠不要放棄夢想！

問題 34-36

    當哥倫比亞伊果南羅鎮的鎮長伊格那西歐・吉姆奈茲宣佈禁止流言蜚語後，說你鄰居的閒話可能會帶來牢獄之災。鎮長告知艾爾・提安波報他之所以宣佈這項禁令，是因為哥倫比亞目前正面臨馬克斯主義反叛軍和極右派反叛軍的游擊戰中，任何謠言都可能讓人無端喪生。為了證明他這項決定是對的，鎮長說至少有八個人單純因為他們是哥倫比亞的馬克斯派革命軍這項「小道消息」便被人指控而關進當地監獄。人們也可能因為贊成其中一支反叛軍的立場

你答對了嗎？

(31) B (32) D (33) D

Revolutionary Armed Forces of Colombia. People could also be killed just due to rumors that they agree with one of the illegal armed groups.

He and other backers of the new law, which went into effect this week, say people need to think hard before making accusations without real proof. Failing to do so in Icononzo can now result in fines or up to four years in jail.

34. What would be a good title for this article?
    A. The Mayor of Icononzo Goes to Jail
    B. Talking to Neighbors Becomes Illegal
    C. Marxist Rebels Gain New Members
    D. Gossip Puts You In Jail

35. What will happen to someone who makes a false accusation against another person?
    A. He will receive a written warning.
    B. He will have to move to another city.
    C. He will have to join the Marxist rebels.
    D. He will have to pay a fine.

36. Why is the mayor banning people from telling rumors?
    A. Because innocent people are being jailed or killed.
    B. Because the Marxist rebels are gaining new members.
    C. Because neighbors are stealing from each other.
    D. Because telling a lie is a sin.

這種謠言而被殺害。

　　新法將於本週生效，市長和其他新法的支持者告訴大家，如果沒有確實的證據，指控別人之前請三思。在伊果南羅鎮如果違反規定，現在會處以罰金或判處最高四年的有期徒刑。

34. 這段文章用什麼標題比較好？
　　A. 伊果南羅鎮鎮長入獄
　　B. 和鄰居講話變成違法
　　C. 馬克斯主義反叛軍獲得新成員
　　D. 說閒話帶來牢獄之災

35. 如果有人對別人進行不實的指控會發生什麼事？
　　A. 他會收到書面警告。
　　B. 他必須搬到別的城市。
　　C. 他必須加入馬克斯反叛軍。
　　D. 他必須繳納罰金。

36. 鎮長為何禁止人們散播謠言？
　　A. 因為會有無辜的人因而入獄或被殺。
　　B. 因為馬克斯反叛軍正在吸收新成員。
　　C. 因為鄰居互相偷東西。
　　D. 因為說謊是一種罪惡。

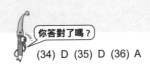

你答對了嗎？

(34) D (35) D (36) A

Questions 37-40

Dear Mr. Cruise,

My wife and I were at Cruise Cars earlier this week trying to purchase our third Nissan truck. Disappointed, we were unable to buy the car as planned because our salesperson, Mr. Holmes, was very unhelpful. We requested to be shown only your selection of trucks, but Mr. Holmes persistently kept taking us to the more expensive sports car section. After wasting our time for half an hour, he finally agreed to show us a few trucks.

My wife and I were very interested in the Nissan Tacoma and proceeded to sit down with Mr. Holmes to talk about prices. He quoted fifteen thousand dollars, which was much higher than the price you had printed in the newspaper. When we began to explain that to Mr. Holmes, he became very angry and threw his pencil at my wife. At this point, we had become very irritated and tired of Mr. Holmes lack of help and hostility. When I requested to see the general manager, he became very upset and used a string of *foul language towards my wife and I. We hope Mr. Holmes is no longer an employee of yours. He has caused your dealership two very valuable customers.

Sincerely,
Stan Johnson

問題 37-40

親愛的克魯斯先生：

　　我太太和我本週稍早曾到克魯斯汽車公司，想要購買我們第三部日產卡車。令人失望的是，我們無法按照計畫買到我們所要的車，因為銷售員霍姆斯先生相當不合作。我們本來只想看你們的卡車種類，但是霍姆斯先生堅持帶我們去看較昂貴的跑車。他浪費了我們半小時後，終於同意讓我們看卡車。

　　我太太和我對日產 Tacoma 這款卡車很有興趣，便坐下來要和霍姆斯先生談談價錢。他開價一萬五千塊，比你們在報紙上所刊登的價格還要高很多。我們向霍姆斯說明此事時，他竟然勃然大怒，還用鉛筆丟我太太。當下我們相當惱怒，對霍姆斯先生幫不上忙又充滿敵意感到很厭煩。結果我要求見總經理時，他不僅變得很煩，還對我太太和我罵了一連串的髒話。我們不希望看到你們公司有像霍姆斯先生這樣的員工，他已經讓你們公司付出了損失兩名重要顧客的代價。

　　祝安好

　　史坦・詹森

37. What is the purpose of this letter?

    A. To ask for a refund

    B. To criticize a salesperson

    C. To inquire about a price of a Nissan truck

    D. To complain about the General Manager

38. How would you describe Mr. Holme's attitude?

    A. Professional

    B. Curious

    C. Affectionate

    D. Rude

39. Who is this letter addressed to?

    A. The general manager

    B. The salesperson

    C. The owner

    D. The assistant manager

40. Which of the following would most likely happen next?

    A. Mr. Holmes will get a raise.

    B. Stan Johnson will return to Cruise Cars.

    C. Mr. Cruise will ignore the letter.

    D. Mr. Holmes will get fired.

37. 這封信的目的為何？

　　A. 要求退款

　　B. 批評某個銷售員

　　C. 詢問日產卡車的價格

　　D. 抱怨總經理

38. 你會如何形容霍姆斯先生的態度？

　　A. 專業

　　B. 好奇

　　C. 溫柔親切

　　D. 無禮

39. 這封信是寄給誰的？

　　A. 總經理

　　B. 該銷售員

　　C. 老闆

　　D. 助理經理

40. 下列何者最像接下來會發生的事？

　　A. 霍姆斯先生得到加薪。

　　B. 史坦‧詹森會回到克魯斯汽車公司。

　　C. 克魯斯先生不會理睬這封信。

　　D. 霍姆斯先生被炒魷魚。

你答對了嗎？

(37) B　(38) D　(39) C　(40) D

MP3-46

Test 4

第一部份： 句子填空

本部份共 15 題，每題有一個空格。請就下列的 A、B、C、D 四個選項，選出最適合題意的字或詞。

1. Children in the United States love to _____ during Halloween.

   A. get dress
   B. dress
   C. dress up
   D. wear dress

2. You should brush your teeth _____ two times a day.

   A. at once
   B. at last
   C. at times
   D. at least

3. Mike was very good at _____ his mother to give him anything he wanted.

   A. persuade
   B. persuaded
   C. persuading
   D. persuades

4. Danny _____ two times for not paying his speeding tickets.

   A. has been arrested
   B. have been arrested
   C. is arrested
   D. arrested

題目中譯

1. 美國小孩喜歡在萬聖節前夕 ____。

    A. 穿衣服　　　　　　　　B. 穿衣服

    C. 裝扮自己　　　　　　　D. 穿衣服

2. 你一天 ____ 應該刷兩次牙。

    A. 馬上　　　　　　　　　B. 最後

    C. 有時　　　　　　　　　D. 至少

3. 麥克很善於 ____ 他媽媽給他任何他想要的東西。

    A. 説服　　　　　　　　　B. 説服

    C. 説服　　　　　　　　　D. 説服

4. 丹尼被 ____ 兩次沒有繳超速罰單。

    A. 抓到　　　　　　　　　B. 抓到

    C. 抓到　　　　　　　　　D. 抓到

你答對了嗎？

(1) C　(2) D　(3) C　(4) A

5. Rebecca wanted to _____ the plans first before they bought the tickets to Hong Kong.

   A. talk over   B. take up

   C. turn off   D. try on

6. Can you _____ a nice hotel in Tokyo that isn't too expensive?

   A. suggest   B. recognize

   C. occupy   D. charge

7. When Helen was younger, she _____ play with dolls. Now, she only likes sports.

   A. use up   B. used to

   C. used before   D. use again

8. The party is _____ at Mary's new house in New York City.

   A. take place   B. took place

   C. taking place   D. takes place

9. NASA sends astronauts to the moon to _____ for aliens.

   A. explore   B. explored

   C. are exploring   D. were exploring

10. Your waist has _____ before the tailor can make you the pants.

   A. to measure   B. to be measured

   C. measuring   D. been measured

5. 瑞貝卡希望先 _____ 一下計畫，再決定是否購買到香港的機票。

    A. 討論   B. 占用

    C. 關掉   D. 試穿

6. 你可以 _____ 東京有哪家好旅館不太貴的嗎？

    A. 建議   B. 識別

    C. 占據   D. 索價

7. 海倫過去年輕時 _____ 喜歡玩洋娃娃。如今她只喜歡運動。

    A. 用完   B. 一向

    C. 之前使用   D. 再度使用

8. 派對在瑪麗位於紐約市的新居 _____。

    A. 舉行   B. 舉行

    C. 舉行   D. 舉行

9. NASA 送太空人到月球 _____ 外星人的蹤跡。

    A. 探索   B. 探索

    C. 探索   D. 探索

10. 裁縫師要先 _____ 你的腰才能幫你做褲子。

    A. 量   B. 量

    C. 量   D. 量

你答對了嗎？

(5) A (6) A (7) B (8) C (9) A (10) B

11. Ballet dancers are very good at _____ on their toes.

    A. nominating   B. balancing

    C. seizing   D. maintaining

12. At the next meeting the landlord's daughter _____ since her father does not speak English.

    A. translate   B. translated

    C. will translate   D. have translated

13. William _____ a bad fever today so he couldn't come to school.

    A. have got   B. has got

    C. gotten   D. to get

14. I want to invite the neighbors over for a barbeque, _____ we don't have a grill.

    A. except   B. because

    C. so   D. since

15. You can always count _____ your family during difficult times.

    A. over   B. on

    C. up   D. off

11. 芭蕾舞者非常善於用腳尖取得 _____。

    A. 提名   B. 平衡

    C. 抓住   D. 維持

12. 由於房東不會講英文，所以下回碰面時他女兒會擔任 _____。

    A. 翻譯   B. 翻譯

    C. 翻譯   D. 翻譯

13. 威廉今天 ___ 高燒，所以無法上學。

    A. 發   B. 發

    C. 發   D. 發

14. _____ 我們沒有烤肉架，所以我想邀請鄰居過來一起烤肉。

    A. 除了   B. 因為

    C. 所以   D. 自從

15. 遇到困難時，家人永遠可以讓你 _____。

    A. 依靠   B. 依靠

    C. 依靠   D. 依靠

你答對了嗎？

(11) B (12) C (13) B (14) A (15) B

第二部份： 段落填空

本部份共 10 題，每篇短文包括二至三個段落，每個段落各含 5 個空格。請就下列的 A、B、C、D 四個選項，選出最適合題意的字或詞。

MP3-47

Questions 16-20

Chris and Terrence __16__ for several months before they began their bicycling trip around Taiwan. They started in Taipei and wanted to save money __17__ camping along the way. Chris tied the tent to his bike, and Terrence carried the food supplies.

On rainy days, they stayed inside the tent reading and playing chess. On sunny days, they rode for __18__ 50 kilometers. Their favorite section was Taiwan's east coast. The scenery __19__ Suao and Hualien was one of the most beautiful they had ever seen. Before they had even finished the trip around the island, they were already planning their next bicycling trip! __20__, the boys haven't traveled any other way. Traveling on a bicycle is a great way to intimately explore a country and a great way to keep healthy!

段落填空中譯

克里斯和泰倫斯先 __16__ 了幾個月，才踏上他們的單車環島之旅。他們由台北出發，希望沿路 __17__ 露營的方式把錢省下來。克里斯把帳篷捆在單車上，泰倫斯則負責攜帶食物。

如果遇到雨天，他們就待在帳篷裡看書下棋；如果遇到晴天，他們會 __18__ 騎五十公里的路。他們最喜歡的地方是台灣的東海岸，蘇澳和花蓮 __19__ 的景色是他們看過最美麗的景色之一。他們還沒完成環島之旅以前，就

已經計畫好下一次單車之旅了！ __20__，這兩個男生就一直用這種方法旅行。
單車旅行可以說是最棒的旅行方式，既可以在國內做一趟深度之旅，又可以保持
身體健康！

16.

A. participated
B. reached
C. trained
D. handled

16.

A. 參加
B. 抵達
C. 訓練
D. 處理

17.

A. to
B. by
C. if
D. as

17.

A. 到
B. 以
C. 如果
D. 如同

18.

A. at least
B. as many
C. for example
D. just for

18.

A. 至少
B. 一樣多
C. 例如
D. 只是為了

19.

A. between
B. because
C. among
D. against

19.

A. 之間
B. 因為
C. 之中
D. 反對

20.

A. Because of
B. Again
C. Due to
D. Since then

20.

A. 因為
B. 再度
C. 由於
D. 從那時起

你答對了嗎？

(16) C (17) B (18) A (19) A (20) D

Questions 21-25

Taiwan's National Museum of Prehistory takes visitors __21__ to witness the ways of life in the distant past. The museum has a __22__ and accidental origin. Sometime in 1980, a group of laborers who were then working on the construction of the Peinan Railway Station, now the Taitung Station, accidentally dug into a major prehistoric archaeological site.

This accidental discovery sent archaeologists, anthropologists and researchers from the National Taiwan University to Taitung. They further __23__ more interesting relics that were several hundred years old. From these relics, it was concluded that the stone slab burials are the __24__ in its form in East Asia and the Pacific Rim. The museum has just opened to the public in 2001, but has already __25__ a popular reputation as Taiwan's first world-class museum of archaeology.

問題 21-25

台灣史前文化博物館把參觀者 __21__，目睹遠古時代的生活方式。該博物館是在一種 __22__ 又偶然的情況下產生的。時間是在 1980 年，當時有一群勞工在卑南火車站那裡工作，也就是現在的台東火車站；他們意外挖到了一個重要的史前考古學遺跡。

這項偶然發現吸引了台灣大學的考古學家、人類學家和研究人員前往台東一探究竟。他們進一步 __23__ 了一些更有趣的遺跡，已有幾百年歷史之久。從這些遺跡中可以推論出，這種石板墓地乃是東亞和太平洋沿岸地區 __24__ 石板墓地。雖然該博物館在 2001 年才剛對外開放，但它早已 __25__ 台灣第一間世界級考古學博物館的名聲。

21.

A. backward
B. previous
C. back in time
D. before

21.

A. 向後的
B. 先前的
C. 帶回過去
D. 之前

22.

A. simple
B. fortune
C. convenient
D. quantity

22.

A. 簡單
B. 幸運
C. 方便
D. 數量

23.

A. been uncovering
B. uncover
C. were uncovering
D. uncovered

23.

A. 發現
B. 發現
C. 發現
D. 發現

24.

A. oldest
B. ancient
C. exotic
D. interesting

24.

A. 最古老的
B. 古代的
C. 奇特的
D. 有趣的

25.

A. earns
B. earned
C. to earn
D. will earn

25.

A. 贏得
B. 贏得
C. 贏得
D. 贏得

你答對了嗎？

(21) C (22) A (23) D (24) A (25) B

第三部份：閱讀理解

本部份共 15 題，包括數段短文，每篇文章有 2~5 個相關問題，請就下列的 A、B、C、D 四個選項，選出最適合的答案。

MP3-49

Questions 26-30

Michael Zinn was born in 1993 with a disease that damages his kidneys and made him deaf. Before his second birthday, he received his first kidney transplant. The new kidney lasted for seven years, but then it stopped working. For the next year and a half, Michael was hooked up to a dialysis machine to clean out his blood every day. He could not eat pizza and hamburgers like other children; he had to be in bed hooked up to the machine by 7 pm so it could be finished in time for school in the morning.

Jennifer Beltz is a 29 year-old marathon runner. She has run 28 marathons, one for almost every year of her life. She describes herself as a "very healthy woman." Belz has donated blood every eight weeks since she was in high school. One day it struck her that she could do more. She researched kidney donation on Sentara Healthcare's Web site and decided to become a donor. Her parents and her boyfriend worried. Any surgery is risky, even for healthy people. Being left with one kidney meant any pregnancy would be high-risk. On May 3, 2004, doctors took Beltz's kidney at Sentara Norfolk General Hospital through laparoscopic surgery. The kidney was transferred to the Children's Hospital of The Kings Daughters, where it was transplanted into Michael.

A year after the surgery on May 24, 2005, Beltz and Michael finally met. Beltz told herself she wouldn't cry. "Obviously, that didn't happen," she said. Michael showed up with a bright smile and a picture frame he had made for her. It held a photo of him the day after the transplant, looking so much healthier with the new kidney. It showed the sign language for "I love you."

閱讀理解中譯

　　麥克・秦恩生於 1993 年，由於一場大病弄壞了腎臟，讓他變成了聾子。他在第二年生日前接受了生平第一次腎臟移植。新腎臟持續用了七年便失去功用。接下來的一年半，麥克每天都必須用洗腎機來清洗血液。他不能像其他小孩那樣吃披薩或漢堡，而且必須在晚上七點以前上床用洗腎機洗腎，才能趕在第二天早上上學前做完療程。

　　珍妮佛・貝爾茲是名 29 歲的馬拉松長跑健將。她跑了 28 年的馬拉松，一生中幾乎每年都會跑一次。她形容自己是個「非常健康的女人」。貝爾茲從高中開始，每八週會捐一次血。有一天她突然覺得她可以做得更多。她開始上山塔拉保健網站研究腎臟捐贈，並決定成為一名捐贈者。她父母和男朋友都很擔心，因為即使對健康的人來說，任何手術都一樣有危險，而且只剩一顆腎臟也意味著將來如果懷孕危險性會很高。2004 年五月三號，醫生透用內視鏡手術在山塔拉的諾福克大眾醫院取下了貝爾茲的腎臟，這顆腎臟被轉往「國王女兒」兒童醫院，在那裡移植到了麥克身上。

　　手術後一年的 2005 年五月二十四號，貝爾茲和麥克終於碰面了。貝爾茲告訴自己不能哭。「顯然沒有發生。」她說。麥克帶著愉快的笑容出現，還拿著他為貝爾茲所做的相框，上面有一張他自己接受腎臟移植後的照片，看起來因為新腎臟而健康許多。他用手語表達了「我愛你」的訊息。

The Zinns tried to help Michael understand who Beltz was, tried to explain about the transplant and why he no longer uses the dialysis machine. Finally Michael's teacher, a woman who can interpret a roomful of conversation into sign language, got through. She said, "It's because of this woman that you can eat," Dawn Zinn said, "Cheeseburgers, pizza, whatever you want."

26. How has the disease affected Michael?

    A. It has made him unable to walk.

    B. It has made him unable to hear.

    C. It has made him unable to eat.

    D. It has made him unable to go to school.

27. Why did Jennifer Beltz decide to donate her kidney?

    A. Because she didn't want to get pregnant.

    B. Because her family persuaded her.

    C. Because she wanted to save a life.

    D. Because she liked to donate blood.

28. What is the relationship between Jennifer and Michael?

    A. They are girlfriend and boyfriend.

    B. They are strangers.

    C. They are cousins.

    D. They are sister and brother.

29. According to the story, which of the following is FALSE?

    A. Jennifer was not excited to see Michael.

    B. Michael has a liver disease.

    C. Jennifer had saved Michael's life.

    D. Michael communicates through sign language.

　　秦恩家人試著讓麥克明白貝爾茲是誰，也試著解釋腎臟移植和他為什麼不必再使用洗腎機的事。由於麥克的女老師可以將整屋的談話翻成手語，終於建立了溝通橋樑。她說：「你可以吃東西全是這位女性的功勞。」唐恩・秦恩接著說：「漢堡、披薩，想吃什麼就可以吃什麼。」

26. 生病如何影響到麥克？

　　A. 讓他無法走路。

　　B. 讓他聽不到。

　　C. 讓他無法吃東西。

　　D. 讓他無法上學。

27. 珍妮佛・貝爾茲為何決定捐贈自己的腎臟？

　　A. 因為她不想懷孕。

　　B. 因為她家人勸她這麼做。

　　C. 因為她想解救別人的生命。

　　D. 因為她喜歡捐血。

28. 珍妮佛和麥克之間有什麼關係？

　　A. 他們是男女朋友。

　　B. 他們是陌生人。

　　C. 他們是表姐弟。

　　D. 他們是姐弟。

29. 根據本文所述，下列敘述何者為「假」？

　　A. 珍妮佛要見麥克並沒有很興奮。

　　B. 麥克患有肝病。

　　C. 珍妮佛救了麥克的命。

　　D. 麥克用手語溝通。

你答對了嗎？

(26) B (27) C (28) B (29) A

30. How old was Michael when he received the kidney from Jennifer?

A. He was 2 years old.   B. He was 11 years old.

C. He was 9 years old.   D. He was 7 years old.

MP3-50

Questions 31-33

The story began when the sheep, called Helen, was sent with the rest of her flock up to the mountains in the summer of 2001. It's common for Norwegian sheep ranchers to release their flocks for open summer grazing. The rest of Helen's flock was eventually rounded up at the end of that summer, but she wasn't found.

On Saturday, sheep rancher Andy Manger spotted her in Stordalen, western Norway. Her wool had grown to a length of around 40 centimeters. "With all that grey wool, the sheep looked mostly like a large grey rock," said Manger. With the help of his sheepdog Iris, Manger whistled to the sheep and eventually got her roped up. Suddenly, however, he slipped on a stone and fell into a river. He kept hanging on to the rope, and the sheep stood steadfast, so Manger didn't disappear downstream himself. When he finally got back on his feet, Manger then redelivered the sheep to her owners, Tommy and Mary Appleton. "This is like winning the lottery," they told newspapers.

The sheep ended up well off, too. The Appletons decided that after surviving three years on her own in the wild, and then saving Manger, she deserved to avoid the slaughterhouse.

30. 麥克從珍妮佛那裡得到腎臟時是幾歲？

A. 兩歲。

B. 十一歲。

C. 九歲。

D. 七歲。

問題 31-33

　　這個故事是從一隻名叫海倫的綿羊開始的。牠和其他羊群一起在 2001 年的夏天被帶到山上。對挪威綿羊牧場經營者來說，夏天時帶羊群到山上進行開放式放牧是很常見的事。後來，那年夏天結束時，海倫其他伙伴都被牧場主人聚集在一塊，但他卻找不到海倫。

　　禮拜六那天，牧場主人安迪・曼澤在挪威西部的史托達倫發現了海倫。牠的毛已經長到 40 公分那麼長。「全身灰色羊毛讓那隻綿羊看起來好像一塊巨大的灰色石頭。」曼澤如此說道。靠著牧羊犬艾利斯的幫忙，曼澤向綿羊吹口哨，終於把牠用繩子給綁住；不過他這時卻突然在石頭上滑倒並掉進河裡。由於他一直緊握著繩索，加上綿羊海倫又紋風不動，讓曼澤沒有順著水流被沖走。最後他平安無事歸來，把綿羊重新交給飼主湯米和瑪麗・愛波頓時，他們對報社說：「這好像中了彩券一樣。」

　　綿羊海倫最後也有好的結局。由於牠獨自在野地裡生活了三年，最後還救了曼澤，愛波頓一家人於是決定牠不應該被送到屠宰場。

你答對了嗎？

（30）B

31. What would be a good title for this story?

  A. Sheepdog Saves Lost Sheep B.
  A Sheep's Life is Saved

  C. Lost Sheep Saves Farmer's Life

  D. Farmer Saves Sheep

32. How did the sheep rescue Manger?

  A. She called for help.

  B. She jumped into the river.

  C. She did not move.

  D. She whistled to the dog.

33. What will most likely happen next?

  A. Manger will keep the sheep.

  B. The Appletons will kill the sheep.

  C. The sheep will live a long life.

  D. Manger will stop rescuing sheep.

MP3-51

Questions 34-37

Dear Mr. Benjamin,

Thank you for your inquiry into the position of assistant editor at the London Times. The position will not be available until September, but we are holding interviews from June 10th - June 15th. Please inform us of which day would be most convenient for you.

31. 這個故事用什麼標題比較好？

    A. 牧羊犬救了走失的綿羊

    B. 綿羊的生命獲得解救

    C. 走失的綿羊救了農場主人的命

    D. 農場主人救了綿羊

32. 綿羊是如何營救曼澤的？

    A. 它大聲呼救。

    B. 它跳進河裡。

    C. 它一動也不動。

    D. 它對狗狗吹口哨。

33. 接下來最可能發生什麼事？

    A. 曼澤會把綿羊留在身邊。

    B. 愛波頓會殺了綿羊。

    C. 綿羊會活很久。

    D. 曼澤不再營救綿羊。

問題 34-37

親愛的班傑明先生：

    謝謝你詢問有關倫敦時報的助理編輯一職。該職位九月才有職缺，但我們會先在六月十號到十五號進行相關面試。請通知我們你哪一天最方便前來面試。

你答對了嗎？

(31) C (32) C (33) C

Please keep in mind that we also have other positions available. We are currently looking for reporters for the Sports section and Editorial section. Please let us know if you would also like to interview for these positions.

Please bring all necessary documents including your resume, driver's license, and college diploma. The position also requires that you pass a drug test, a criminal background check, and a financial stability check. We look forward to meeting you.

Sincerely,

Jack Daniels

Editor-in-Chief

34. What is the purpose of this letter?

A. To inquire about a job position.

B. To offer a job interview.

C. To ask about what jobs are available.

D. To turn down a job interview.

35. Which job position is Benjamin most interested in?

A. Editor-in-Chief B. Assistant Editor

C. Sports Reporter D. Editorial Reporter

36. Which of the following is NOT a requirement for the job?

A. A driver's license B. A college education

C. A drug test D. A criminal record

我們也有其他職缺，這點請記在心上。我們目前要找運動部門和社論部門的記者，如果你也想參加這些職缺的面試，請一併通知。

請攜帶所有必要文件，包括履歷表、駕照，以及大學文憑。你也必須通過藥檢、犯罪背景調查及財務穩定性調查，才能擔任此一職位。我們期待與你會面。

祝安好

主編傑克・丹尼爾

34. 這封信的目的為何？

    A. 詢問工作職缺。

    B. 安排工作面試。

    C. 查詢有哪些職缺。

    D. 拒絕工作面試。

35. 班傑明對哪個工作職缺最感興趣？

    A. 主編   B. 助理編輯

    C. 運動記者   D. 社論記者

36. 下列哪一項「不是」工作職缺的必備要件？

    A. 駕照   B. 受過大學教育

    C. 藥檢   D. 犯罪記錄

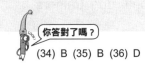

你答對了嗎？

(34) B (35) B (36) D

37. What kind of business is the London Times?

A. A TV news station

B. A newspaper company

C. A book publishing company

D. A woman's magazine

MP3-52

Questions 38-40

"We make bad dogs good and good dogs better!"

The Academy of Canine Education is dedicated to educating both people and dogs. Our dog-training programs include everything from housebreaking, etiquette, and behavior modification, through obedience training and protection training services.

We accept all types and ages of dogs. So whether your pooch is 8 weeks old or a full-grown adult dog, we have the training programs to suit your companion. We are confident that our dog training programs will provide you with an enjoyable experience and a well-trained dog. If you are not satisfied with the results, we will be happy to return your money.

Using the latest and most effective training techniques, the Academy of Canine Education is the only dog training academy that provides not only dog obedience programs but also provides Trainer Programs for individuals who wish to become certified professional dog trainers.

37. 倫敦時報是哪一種企業？

A. 新聞電視台

B. 報社

C. 出版社

D. 女性雜誌

問題 38-40

「我們讓壞狗變好，好狗變得更好！」

「狗狗教育學院」致力於教育主人和狗。我們的狗狗訓練計畫透過服從訓練和 protection training 服務，從住宅入侵、禮儀和行為改正等項目通通包括在內。

我們接受各式各樣的狗，年齡亦無限制。所以不管你的雜種狗是八週大還是發育完全的成年狗，我們都有適合你伙伴的訓練計畫。你一定可以快樂地體驗這分訓練計畫，狗狗也會變得訓練有素，這點我們很有信心。如果你對結果不滿意，我們會很樂意退款。

「狗狗教育學院」使用的是最新又最有效率的訓練技巧，除了提供狗狗服從計畫之外，也提供想成為公認的專業訓狗師的人合適的訓練計畫。這方面「狗狗教育學院」乃狗狗訓練學院中唯一的選擇。

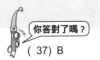

你答對了嗎？

（37）B

38. Who is most likely going to respond to this ad?

    A.   Someone who wants to buy a well-trained dog.

    B.   Someone who wants to be a dog trainer.

    C.   Someone who wants to sell her puppies.

    D.   Someone who has lost his dog.

39. Which of the following services does the Academy of Canine Education NOT offer?

    A.   Teach your dog how to protect the house.

    B.   Teach your puppy where to use the bathroom.

    C.   Teach you how to train old dogs.   D.

Teach you how to run a dog-training academy.

40. In paragraph 2, what does the word "confident" mean?

    A.   certain

    B.   trusting

    C.   unsure

    D.   guarantee

38. 誰最有可能回應這則廣告？

    A. 想要買隻訓練有素的狗的人。

    B. 想成為訓狗師的人。

    C. 想要賣自家小狗的人。

    D. 狗狗走失的人。

39. 「狗狗教育學院」「不」提供哪項服務？

    A. 教你的狗如何保護房子。

    B. 教你的小狗上廁所。

    C. 教你如何訓練老狗。

    D. 教你如何經營一家狗狗訓練學院。

40. 在原文第二段中，「confident」這個字是什麼意思？

    A. 確信

    B. 信任

    C. 無把握

    D. 保證

你答對了嗎？

(38) B (39) D (40) A

MP3-53

Test 5

第一部份: 句子填空

本部份共 15 題,每題有一個空格。請就下列的 A、B、C、D 四個選項,選出最適合題意的字或詞。

1. The other kids don't like Mandy because she likes to show _____ and talk about herself.

   A. off   B. for

   C. in   D. on

2. Tell mom we ran _____ milk before she goes to the supermarket.

   A. out of   B. away from

   C. over   D. up to

3. The Cherokee Indians are _____ to North America.

   A. population   B. belonging

   C. native   D. local

4. Dr. Johnson is a _____ in eye surgery and other matters concerning vision.

   A. contemporary   B. nuisance

   C. recognition   D. specialist

題目中譯

1. 其他孩子都不喜歡曼蒂，因為她愛 ____ 又老是談她自己。

   A. 賣弄
   B. 賣弄
   C. 賣弄
   D. 賣弄

2. 媽媽去超級市場前，告訴她我們牛奶 ____ 了。

   A. 喝完
   B. 喝完
   C. 喝完
   D. 喝完

3. 卻洛奇族印第安人是北美洲的 ____。

   A. 人口
   B. 親密關係
   C. 土著
   D. 當地居民

4. 詹森醫生是眼科手術和其他與視力領域有關的 ____。

   A. 同時代的人
   B. 討厭鬼
   C. 識別
   D. 專家

你答對了嗎？

(1) A (2) A (3) C (4) D

5. It was Justin's job to _____ the workers while the manager was at lunch.

    A. enforce   B. permit

    C. supervise   D. reverse

6. Peter Pan is one of the most loved _____ in the history of story telling.

    A. members   B. mysteries

    C. politics   D. characters

7. Becoming a rock star was not a _____ goal for Betty because she had a terrible singing voice.

    A. difficult   B. realistic

    C. parallel   D. honor

8. Will you be able _____ this delicious soup since you have a cold?

    A. taste   B. to taste

    C. tasting   D. to tasting

9. Janet _____ from the contest after she discovered her best friend was competing against her.

    A. withdrew   B. withdraw

    C. was withdrew   D. will withdraw

10. The pants were so tight, they _____ Adam from walking normally.

    A. were restricted   B. restrict

    C. will restrict   D. restricted

5. 經理吃午飯時幫忙 ＿＿＿ 員工並不是賈斯汀的工作。

    A. 實施　　　　　　　　　　B. 允許

    C. 監督　　　　　　　　　　D. 顛倒

6. 彼得潘是歷久不衰的故事裡最受人喜愛的 ＿＿＿ 之一。

    A. 成員　　　　　　　　　　B. 秘密

    C. 政治　　　　　　　　　　D. 角色

7. 成為搖滾明星對貝蒂而言並不是個 ＿＿＿ 可行的目標，因為她的歌聲很難聽。

    A. 困難　　　　　　　　　　B. 實際

    C. 平行　　　　　　　　　　D. 名譽

8. 你感冒了還 ＿＿＿ 得出來這道美味的湯嗎？

    A. 嚐　　　　　　　　　　　B. 嚐

    C. 嚐　　　　　　　　　　　D. 嚐

9. 珍妮特發現她最好的朋友竟是她競爭對手時，便 ＿＿＿ 了比賽。

    A. 退出　　　　　　　　　　B. 退出

    C. 退出　　　　　　　　　　D. 退出

10. 亞當穿的褲子太緊，如果要正常走路會受到 ＿＿＿。

    A. 限制　　　　　　　　　　B. 限制

    C. 限制　　　　　　　　　　D. 限制

你答對了嗎？

(5) C (6) D (7) B (8) B (9) A (10) D

11. Would you _____ your life for your children?

    A. sacrifice   B. sacrificed

    C. had sacrificed   D. sacrificing

12. Paula wants _____ wild flowers for her mother's birthday.

    A. to gather   B. gather

    C. gathering   D. to gathering

13. When Jason was younger, he _____ on the piano everyday before school.

    A. practiced   B. practice

    C. practices   D. practicing

14. His heart attack was brought _____ by too much work.

    A. on   B. up

    C. after   D. over

15. John is going to take Kathy _____ for a nice dinner and movie.

    A. out   B. around

    C. down   D. in

11. 你會 ____ 生命來救你的孩子嗎？

    A. 犧牲   B. 犧牲

    C. 犧牲   D. 犧牲

12. 寶拉想 ____ 野花給她媽媽當生日禮物。

    A. 摘   B. 摘

    C. 摘   D. 摘

13. 傑森年輕時，每天上學前都會 ____ 鋼琴。

    A. 練   B. 練

    C. 練   D. 練

14. 他的心臟病是因為工作太繁忙所 ____ 的。

    A. 引起   B. 引起

    C. 引起   D. 引起

15. 約翰要帶凱西 ____ 好好吃一頓晚餐，然後去看電影。

    A. 出去   B. 出去

    C. 出去   D. 出去

你答對了嗎？

(11) A (12) A (13) A (14) A (15) A

第二部份：段落填空

本部份共 10 題，每篇短文包括二至三個段落，每個段落各含 5 個空格。請就下列的 A、B、C、D 四個選項，選出最適合題意的字或詞。

MP3-54

Questions 16-20

The first fireworks were hollowed-out bamboo stalks stuffed with black powder. The Chinese called __16__ "arrows of flying fire" and shot them into the air during religious occasions and __17__ to *ward off imaginary dragons.

__18__ legend, the essential *ingredient – black powder – was first discovered in a Chinese kitchen in the 10th century A.D. A cook __19__ potassium nitrate (a *pickling agent and preservative) over a *charcoal fire laced with sulfur. Somehow the three chemicals – potassium nitrate, *charcoal, and *sulfur – combined, caused an explosion. The meal was destroyed, but the powder, later __20__ as *gunpowder, was born.

段落填空中譯

最初的煙火是把竹子的莖挖空，然後在裡面填入火藥。中國人稱 __16__ 為「飛焰之箭」，宗教慶典或 __17__ 時會用來放射到天空，以避開想像中的龍。

__18__ 傳說，一開始發現火藥這項必要原料是在西元十世紀時的一個中國廚房裡。有個廚子在正在添加硫磺的木炭上 __19__ 鉀硝酸鹽（一種醃漬用防腐劑）。結果不知怎麼的，這三種化學製品－鉀硝酸鹽、木炭和硫磺混在一起後就爆炸了。這一餐當然是毀掉了，但這種粉末，也就是後來大家 __20__ 的火藥，就這樣誕生了。

16.

A. it
B. they
C. them
D. the

16.

A. 它
B. 它們
C. 它們
D. 那個

17.

A. holidays
B. organizations
C. industries
D. fortunes

17.

A. 節日
B. 組織
C. 工業
D. 財富

18.

A. Even though
B. Because of
C. So that
D. According to

18.

A. 即使
B. 因為
C. 以便
D. 根據

19.

A. prepares
B. was preparing
C. prepared
D. has prepared

19.

A. 準備
B. 準備
C. 準備
D. 準備

20.

A. known
B. knows
C. know
D. knew

20.

A. 已知的
B. 知道
C. 知道
D. 知道

你答對了嗎？

(16) C (17) A (18) D (19) B (20) A

Questions 21-25

In the 1800s, women did not wear underwear made from cotton or silk. __21__ underwear was made out of iron because they wanted to have tiny little waists. __22__ get an *hourglass shape, they wore *corsets that were __23__ with iron *rods. Some were stiffened with *whalebones! But whatever was used, it hurt!

Corsets were laced so tight that some women's ribs __24__ broke. Women often couldn't get enough air into their lungs, so fainting was common. __25__ inventing looser underwear, they invented "fainting couches." This way a woman with too tight a corset had a soft place to land when she passed out from lack of oxygen.

問題 21-25

1800 年代的婦女穿的不是綿製或絲製內衣。因為希望自己有個小蠻腰，所以 __21__ 內衣是鐵製的。__22__ 擁有沙漏型的好身材，她們穿的是用鐵棒撐 __23__ 的束腹。有些甚至還用鯨鬚撐挺的！但不管用什麼，都會對婦女造成傷害！

束腹繫得太緊，有些婦人的肋骨 __24__ 都已經斷了。由於婦女往往無法把足夠的空氣吸進肺裡，昏倒於是成為家常便飯。當時的人沒有發明更為寬鬆的內衣，__25__ 發明了「昏厥沙發」。這樣一來，一旦婦女因為所穿的束腹太緊而缺氧昏倒時，便有柔軟地方可以倒下來了。

21.

A. Their
B. They're
C. They
D. Them

21.

A. 他們的
B. 他們是
C. 他們
D. 他們

22.

A. In order to
B. As if
C. Unless
D. So that

22.

A. 為了
B. 好似
C. 除非
D. 以便

23.

A. stiffened
B. stiff
C. stiffs
D. stiffening

23.

A. 挺
B. 挺
C. 挺
D. 挺

24.

A. thought of
B. were going to
C. decided to
D. actually

24.

A. 想到
B. 即將
C. 決定
D. 事實上

25.

A. As to
B. Instead of
C. Because of
D. Inside of

25.

A. 關於
B. 代替
C. 因為
D. 少於

你答對了嗎？

(21) A (22) A (23) A (24) D (25) B

第三部份：閱讀理解

本部份共 15 題，包括數段短文，每篇文章有 2~5 個相關問題，請就下列的 A、B、C、
D 四個選項，選出最適合的答案。

MP3-56

Questions 26-29

The stock market crash of 1929 put millions of Americans out of work. One of them was Charles Darrow. He and his friends often sat around the kitchen table, dreaming about what they would do if they had lots of money. That gave Charles an idea. Why not invent a game where people could pretend to be millionaires?

He made a game board using the street names of his favorite town, Atlantic City, New Jersey, cut out *cardboard houses and hotels, and typed up title cards for the different "properties." He called this new game Monopoly and invited some friends to play it. Soon they were making (and losing) fortunes in pretend real estate just like the millionaires they read about in the newspapers. His friends loved the game so much that they asked for their own copies so they could play at home. Charles couldn't *keep up with the demand. Finally he asked the Parker Brothers game company to sell it. Monopoly soon became the most successful board game in history, and Charles Darrow retired at the age of 46, a genuine millionaire at last.

閱讀理解中譯

1929 年的股市大崩盤讓數百萬美國人面臨失業的窘境。查理斯‧達洛也是失業人口之一。他和他朋友常常坐在廚房餐桌前夢想著如果他們有很多錢要做什麼。查理斯因此有個想法：何不發明一種遊戲，讓人們可以假裝自己是百萬富翁呢？

他用他最喜歡的城鎮－新澤西州大西洋城的街道名稱製作了一種遊戲盤，再用硬紙板剪成房屋和旅館，然後把不同的「房地產」卡片加以分類。他把這項新遊戲稱為「大富翁」，並邀請一些朋友一起來玩。很快地，他們就像自己在報紙上看過的那些百萬富翁一樣，在假想的不動產中賺進（或損失）財富。他的朋友太喜歡這款遊戲了，紛紛向查理斯要求帶個複製品回家自己玩。查理斯後來無法繼續答應這項請求，最後請帕克兄弟公司代理銷售。「大富翁」很快成為史上最成功的棋盤遊戲，而查理斯‧達洛也終於在 46 歲退休時，成了一名真正的百萬富翁。

26. What happened in **1929**?

    A. Many people became millionaires.

    B. A lot of people were out of jobs.

    C. Charles Darrow quit his job at the stock market.

    D. Charles Darrow retired.

27. According to the story, why did Charles Darrow invent Monopoly?

    A. His friends asked him to.

    B. The Parker Brothers needed a new game.

    C. He wanted to pretend to be a millionaire.

    D. He was tired of his old games.

28. How can you win at Monopoly?

    A. By owning a lot of hotels and houses.

    B. By reading the newspapers.

    C. By retiring at an early age.

    D. By moving to Atlantic City.

29. In the second paragraph, what do the words "keep up" mean?

    A. to take away

    B. to not give back

    C. to carry on

    D. to stay away from

26. 1929 年發生了什麼事？

    A. 許多人成為百萬富翁。

    B. 很多人失業。

    C. 查理斯‧達洛辭掉他股市的工作。

    D. 查理斯‧達洛退休了。

27. 根據本文所述，查理斯‧達洛為何會發明大富翁遊戲？

    A. 他朋友叫他發明的。

    B. 帕克兄弟公司需要新遊戲。

    C. 他想要假裝自己是百萬富翁。

    D. 他厭倦了自己的舊遊戲。

28. 大富翁要怎樣玩才會贏？

    A. 擁有很多旅館和房屋。

    B. 看報紙。

    C. 早點退休。

    D. 搬到大西洋城。

29. 在原文第二段中，「keep up」這個詞是什麼意思？

    A. 拿走

    B. 沒有恢復

    C. 繼續

    D. 離開

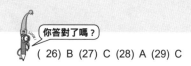

你答對了嗎？

(26) B (27) C (28) A (29) C

Questions 30-33

Tornadoes can *pop up almost anywhere, but about 800 of them *whirl through the U.S. every year. That's more than any country in the world! Tornadoes are usually created by strong thunderstorms. When a large mass of warm air meets a large mass of cold air, you've got the ingredients for a twister. They can be a few feet wide and 10 feet tall or nearly five miles tall and a mile wide. But they're always destructive and dangerous.

Tornado winds blow the hardest of any winds on Earth — more than 300 miles an hour! In 1931 a Minnesota tornado *hoisted an 83-ton passenger train filled with 117 people into the air and threw it down 80 feet from the tracks! Some people say a tornado sounds like a jet *taking off; others say it sounds like the buzzing of a million bees. Some have compared it to the sound of a speeding train.

30. How are tornados formed?

    A. In the United States.

    B. When a large amount of cold air meets hot air.

    C. When there are weak thunderstorms.

    D. When they are dangerous and destructive.

31. What is another name for a tornado?

    A. A thunderstorm   B. A buzzing

    C. A twister   D. A jet taking off

問題 30-33

雖然龍捲風幾乎在任何地方都可能突然出現，但全美國每年大約會出現 800 個龍捲風，比世界上任何國家都還要多！龍捲風通常是由強烈的大雷雨所形成。當一大團暖空氣遇到一大團冷空氣時，便構成旋風形成的條件。它們可能幾英尺寬、十英尺高，大一點甚至差不多五英里高、一英里寬。但不管規模大小，它們永遠都具有破懷性和危險性。

龍捲風可以說是地球上最猛烈的風－每小時風速達 300 英里以上！1931 年在美國明尼蘇達州的龍捲風把一輛載有 117 名乘客、重達 83 噸的火車吹到空中，然後在離鐵軌 80 英尺高的地方把它扔了下來！有些人說龍捲風的聲音聽起來像是噴射機起飛，也有人說像是一百萬隻蜜蜂一起發出嗡嗡聲。還有些人把它的聲音拿來和高速行駛的火車聲音相比較。

30. 龍捲風是如何形成的？

    A. 在美國。

    B. 當大量冷空氣遇到熱空氣時。

    C. 當出現不強的大雷雨時。

    D. 當它們具有危險性和破壞性時。

31. 龍捲風另外一個名稱是什麼？

    A. 大雷雨   B. 嗡嗡聲

    C. 旋風   D. 噴射機起飛

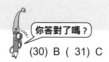

你答對了嗎？

(30) B (31) C

32. According to the story, how fast can a tornado wind blow?

    A. 300 miles per hour   B. 117 miles per hour

    C. 1931 miles per hour   D. 83 miles per hour

33. Which of the following is NOT TRUE about a tornado?

    A. It sounds like an airplane.

    B. Its wind speed is stronger than a typhoon's.

    C. It can lift trains into the air.

    D. They only occur in the United States.

`MP3-58`

Questions 34-38

Stainless Carpet Cleaning
Annual Sale

Fifty years of reliable service, consistent quality and attention to detail, Stainless has earned the trust of millions of homeowners and has become the undisputed leader in the carpet cleaning industry. Our trained technicians are professionals you'll feel comfortable having in your home. We take great pride in our people, and we hire only the best and brightest employees. Stainless' *exclusive hot water *extraction method uses powerful equipment to remove the toughest spots and odors, from carpet and furniture, safely and gently. No other method can provide a deeper clean that lasts so long.

When you choose Stainless, you'll get a team of experts dedicated to giving you the most thorough carpet and furniture cleaning possible - with no hidden charges. Any pre-treating, spot

32. 根據本文所述，龍捲風的風速有多快？

    A. 每小時 300 英里   B. 每小時 117 英里

    C. 每小時 1931 英里   D. 每小時 83 英里

33. 下列關於龍捲風的敘述哪一項「不是真的」？

    A. 它的聲音聽起來像飛機。   B. 它的風速比颱風還快。

    C. 它可以把火車吹到空中。   D. 它們只會出現在美國。

問題 34-38

「無污」地毯清潔公司
年度大優惠

    「無污」公司五十年來以可信賴的服務、一貫的優良品質和鉅細靡遺的工作態度，贏得無數屋主的信任，毫無疑問是地毯清潔業界的龍頭老大。我們訓練有素的技術人員都是這一行的專家，到府工作時保證您可以完全放心。我們深深以自己的員工為榮，而且公司僅雇用最優秀最聰明的員工。「無污」的熱水抽洗法利用強大的配備，安全而小心地將您府上地毯和家具上最難除去的污點和臭味一次搞定。沒有其他方法可以清潔得那麼徹底，效果又可以持續那麼久。

    您選擇「無污」公司便等於請到一個專家團隊，來替您的地毯和家具儘可能進行最徹底的去污，而且費用不會另計。任何前期處理、去污，或是我們可能使用的特定清潔劑，都包括在原始報價內，不會再另外收費。

你答對了嗎？

(32) A (33) D

removal, or special cleaning agents we may use are included in the initial quote, not as an added charge.

We are currently having our yearly sale!! All carpet cleaning comes with FREE furniture cleaning, including couches and dining room chairs!

Sample Prices (prices are per room):
Living Room: $50.00
Bedroom: $35.00
Dining Room: $45.00
Hallway: $20.00
Furniture: Free!!

34. How has Stainless Carpet Cleaning become the leader in the carpet cleaning industry?
    A. By earning the trust of millions of people.
    B. By removing tough spots from furniture and carpet.
    C. By having hidden charges.
    D. By giving initial quotes.

35. Who is most likely going to respond to this ad?
    A. Pet owners   B. College students
    C. Computer engineers   D. Single businessmen

我們目前正舉辦年度大優惠活動！所有的地毯清潔都贈送「免費」的家具清潔，連沙發和餐廳的椅子都包括在內！

樣本價（每間房間的價格）：

客廳：$50.00

臥房：$35.00

餐廳：$45.00

走廊：$20.00

家具：免費！！

34. 「無污」地毯清潔公司如何成為地毯清潔業界的龍頭老大？

    A. 贏得無數人的信任。

    B. 將家具和地毯上難以去除的污點給除掉。

    C. 另外收費。

    D. 提供原始報價。

35. 誰最有可能回應這則廣告？

    A. 寵物飼主   B. 大學學生

    C. 電腦工程師   D. 單身商人

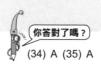

你答對了嗎？

(34) A (35) A

36. What offer is not given by Stainless Carpet Cleaning?

A. Furniture cleaning without charge.

B. Special hot water extraction methods.

C. Do-it-yourself home kits.

D. Well-trained professionals.

37. How much would it cost to have an apartment with 3 bedrooms, 1 living room, 1 hallway, 1 couch, but no dining room cleaned?

A. $ 225.00

B. $ 185.00

C. $ 220.00

D. $ 175.00

38. This ad would most likely appear in:

A. a teen magazine

B. a daily newspaper

C. a tourist brochure

D. a shop window

36. 「無污」地毯清潔公司不提供什麼？

    A. 不另外收費的家具清潔服務。

    B. 特殊的熱水抽洗法。

    C. 自助式家庭工具箱

    D. 訓練有的素的專業人員。

37. 一棟三間臥房、一間客廳、一個走廊、一張沙發，但沒有餐廳的公寓，
    如果全部清潔要多少錢？

    A. $ 225.00

    B. $ 185.00

    C. $ 220.00

    D. $ 175.00

38. 這則廣告最有可能出現在：

    A. 青少年雜誌

    B. 日報

    C. 觀光小手冊

    D. 櫥窗

你答對了嗎？

(36) C (37) D (38) B

Questions 39-40

Dear Oliver,

Kate and I are getting married soon after we return to the United States on June 20th. We are currently spending the spring traveling Europe. We would like to invite you to the wedding. It will be at my parents' house in New York, probably at 2:30pm, and there will be a party afterwards, starting at about 8pm. You are welcome to stay the night as there is plenty of room, though it would help if you could let me know in advance. I could also help you find some nice hotels located close to the area. Hope to see you then!

Best wishes,

Giorgio

39. Where was Giorgio when he wrote this letter?

    A. In the United States

    B. In New York

    C. In Europe

    D. At his parent's house

40. What kind of event is Oliver getting invited to?

    A. A wedding

    B. A graduation ceremony

    C. A house warming party

    D. A New Years celebration

問題 39-40

親愛的奧利佛：

　　凱特和我回美國不久後，將於六月二十號結婚。我們目前趁著春季，正在歐洲旅遊中。我們想邀請你來參加婚禮，地點在紐約我父母家中，時間則是下午兩點半；婚禮結束後會有一場派對，大概八點左右開始。家裡房間很多，所以歡迎你過夜，有意願的話先通知我一聲會更好安排。或者我也可以幫你找一間附近不錯的旅館。期待那天能見到你！

祝安好

喬治

39. 喬治寫這封信時人在哪裡？

　　A. 美國

　　B. 紐約

　　C. 歐洲

　　D. 他父母家裡

40. 奧利佛被邀請參加什麼活動？

　　A. 婚禮

　　B. 畢業典禮

　　C. 喬遷慶宴

　　D. 新年慶祝活動

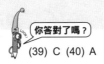
你答對了嗎？
(39) C (40) A

MP3-60

Test 6

第一部份： 句子填空

本部份共 15 題，每題有一個空格。請就下列的 A、B、C、D 四個選項，選出最適合題意的字或詞。

1. Have you _____ what you want to do after college?
   - A. heard of
   - B. saw
   - C. thought
   - D. figured out

2. When you fill out the job application, please do not _____ your date of birth.
   - A. leave out
   - B. make sure
   - C. put on
   - D. never mind

3. It is very _____ of Tim to think he is better than everybody else.
   - A. acknowledge
   - B. arrogant
   - C. academic
   - D. ashamed

4. Kelly showed only a small amount of _____ when the doctor gave her the shot.
   - A. uneasy
   - B. comfortable
   - C. discomfort
   - D. painful

題目中譯

1. 你有 _____ 大學畢業後要做什麼嗎？

    A. 聽説

    B. 看見

    C. 想過

    D. 想好

2. 填工作申請表時，請不要 _____ 你的生日。

    A. 漏掉

    B. 確定

    C. 穿上

    D. 沒有關係

3. 提姆覺得自己比其他每個人都要優秀，實在很 _____。

    A. 承認

    B. 自大

    C. 學術

    D. 羞愧

4. 醫生替凱莉打針時，她只表現出些微的 _____。

    A. 不舒服

    B. 舒服

    C. 不適

    D. 痛苦

你答對了嗎？
(1)D (2)A (3)B (4)C

5. Lisa's little brother always likes to _____ when she is talking on the phone with her boyfriend.

    A. interfere   B. bother

    C. *nuisance   D. annoy

6. Willie takes great _____ in being able to speak five different languages.

    A. fond   B. glorious

    C. happiness   D. pride

7. Sam hates gossip, so she keeps her love life _____.

    A. safety   B. national

    C. private   D. public

8. My mother always told me to not _____ people by their looks.

    A. judge   B. judging

    C. judges   D. to judge

9. Since Rita was a child, she was taught to _____ God.

    A. worshipping   B. worships

    C. worship   D. worshipped

10. Nicky called _____ you of tomorrow's basketball practice after school.

    A. remind   B. to remind

    C. to reminding   D. reminding

5. 麗莎的小弟總是喜歡在麗莎跟她男友講電話時 ____。

    A. 插嘴   B. 打擾

    C. 討厭鬼   D. 惹惱

6. 威利因為可以說五種不同語言而覺得很 ____。

    A. 喜歡   B. 光榮

    C. 幸福   D. 驕傲

7. 山姆討厭流言蜚語，所以 ____ 自己的感情生活。

    A. 安全   B. 全國性的

    C. 不愛談論   D. 公開

8. 我媽媽老是告訴我不要以貌 ____ 人。

    A. 取（判斷）   B. 判斷

    C. 判斷   D. 判斷

9. 莉塔從小被教導要 ____ 上帝。

    A. 信奉   B. 信奉

    C. 信奉   D. 信奉

10. 尼奇打電話來 ____ 你明天放學後要練習籃球。

    A. 提醒   B. 提醒

    C. 提醒   D. 提醒

你答對了嗎？

(5)A   (6)D   (7)C   (8)A (9)C (10)B

11. Scientists _____ outer space since the invention of the telescope.

    A. have been observing   B. are observing

    C. have observe   D. observing

12. I don't want to go out because I have no money and hate _____ people money.

    A. owing   B. will owe

    C. have owed   D. is owing

13. _____ history, men's average salary has always been higher than women's.

    A. Toward   B. In between

    C. Underneath   D. Throughout

14. Once _____ a time, Cinderella was a poor woman living with her stepmother.

    A. up   B. upon

    C. on   D. in

15. Please come back home _____ a reasonable amount of time.

    A. within   B. without

    C. with   D. while

11. 自從發明望遠鏡後，科學家便一直用它來 ＿＿＿ 外太空。

    A. 觀察　　　　　　　　　　B. 觀察

    C. 觀察　　　　　　　　　　D. 觀察

12. 我不想出門是因為我沒有錢，也不喜歡 ＿＿＿ 別人錢。

    A. 欠　　　　　　　　　　　B. 欠

    C. 欠　　　　　　　　　　　D. 欠

13. 有史以來（＿＿＿ 整個歷史），男性的平均薪資一直都比女性來得高。

    A. 朝向　　　　　　　　　　B. 之間

    C. 在下面　　　　　　　　　D. 遍及

14. 灰姑娘 ＿＿＿ 是個和繼母住在一起的窮苦女孩。

    A. 從前　　　　　　　　　　B. 從前

    C. 從前　　　　　　　　　　D. 從前

15. 請你（＿＿＿）時間差不多了就回來。

    A. 在　　　　　　　　　　　B. 沒有

    C. 和　　　　　　　　　　　D. 當

你答對了嗎？

(11) A　(12) A　(13) D　(14) B　(15) A

第二部份： 段落填空

本部份共 10 題，每篇短文包括二至三個段落，每個段落各含 5 個空格。請就下列的 A、B、C、D 四個選項，選出最適合題意的字或詞。

MP3-61

Questions 16-20

On May 8, 1936, horse racer Ralph Neves was thrown to the ground after his horse tripped. The 19-year-old jockey was stepped on __16__ his own horse and then four other horses. An ambulance rushed him to a hospital where doctors tried everything they could to bring him back, including a shot of adrenaline directly into his heart. But nothing brought him __17__ life. Finally, they __18__ him with a sheet, tagged his toe, and sent his body to the morgue.

Minutes after he reached the morgue, Ralphe Neves sat up. He was cold, bloody, shirtless, and wearing only one boot. He didn't know where he was, but he __19__ ran outside to catch a taxi back to the racetrack. Once he arrived, he ran straight for the jockey room, still wearing his toe tag! Neves assured track officials that he didn't feel dead and was perfectly able to ride in the next race, but they wisely convinced him to take the day __20__. The next day, Neves came back to the track and rode five winners!

段落填空中譯

1936 年五月八號，賽馬師雷夫·那維斯從馬上摔下來跌到地上。這名十九歲的騎士 __16__ 他自己的馬和其他四匹馬從他身上踏過去。救護車趕來送他去醫院後，醫生盡一切努力要救他回來，甚至直接把腎上腺素注射到他心臟裡面。但無論怎麼努力都無法將他 __17__。最後，他們用床單把他 __18__ 上，腳趾加上標籤，然後把他的遺體送到陳屍間。

抵達陳屍間沒幾分鐘後，雷夫·那維斯坐了起來。他覺得很冷，全身到處是血又沒穿衣服，腳上只穿著一支靴子。雖然他不知道自己身在何處，但 __19__ 跑到外面叫了輛計程車回到賽馬場；抵達後便直接衝到騎師間，腳上的標籤都還戴著！那維斯向賽馬場人員保證自己一點都不累，完全可以在下一場比賽中出賽，不過他們很明智地說服他那一天最好 __20__ 個假。那維斯隔天便回到賽馬場，而且還拿下了五項冠軍！

16.

    A. so

    B. by

    C. for

    D. with

16.

    A. 所以

    B. 被

    C. 為了

    D. 和

17.

    A. back to

    B. away from

    C. around

    D. beyond

17.

    A. 救活

    B. 離開

    C. 周圍

    D. 越過

18.

    A. recycled

    B. covered

    C. spread

    D. included

18.

    A. 再利用

    B. 蓋

    C. 延伸

    D. 被包括的

19.

    A. possibly

    B. originally

    C. immediately

    D. realistically

19.

    A. 可能

    B. 原來

    C. 立刻

    D. 寫實地

20.

    A. over

    B. on

    C. off

    D. up

20.

    A. 休

    B. 休

    C. 休

    D. 休

你答對了嗎？

(16)B (17)A (18)B (19)C (20)C

Questions **21-25**.

Over three hundred different kinds of butterflies live in Taiwan. The best place to see the butterflies is at Yangming National Park, __21__ just 45 minutes from the center of Taipei. A hundred and fifty different kinds of butterflies are at full play in the park __22__ the months of April and May. A protected area called the "Butterfly Zone" retains and maintains a natural environment __23__ by the butterflies. Lepidopterists (butterfly experts) agree that butterflies are most numerous in the mountains as flowers at higher climates __24__ better, richer nutrition. A specially paved 3 km trail called the "Butterfly *Corridor" is a favorite __25__ visitors. The path is *strewn with wild flowers and large trees to provide the perfect amount of shade and scenery.

問題 **21-25**

台灣的蝴蝶種類超過三百種。要觀賞蝴蝶，最好的地方就是陽明山國家公園，它的所在 __21__ 僅離台北市中心 45 分鐘。四五月 __22__，公園裡有一百五十種不同的蝴蝶到處飛來飛去。公園裡有保留一塊名為「蝴蝶區」的受保護區域，裡頭維護的是蝴蝶 __23__ 的自然環境。鱗翅類昆蟲學家（蝴蝶專家）都同意蝴蝶在山上之所以數量最多，是因為高山氣候下生長的花能 __24__ 更好、更豐富的養分。遊客（__25__）最喜歡的是一條經過特別鋪設、長達三公里的步道，稱為「蝴蝶走廊」。這條小徑鋪滿了野花和大樹，以提供遊客最佳的林蔭和景色。

21.

    A. maintained

    B. located

    C. built

    D. placed

21.

    A. 維持

    B. 位置

    C. 建造

    D. 放置

22.

    A. during

    B. besides

    C. close by

    D. concerning

22.

    A. 期間

    B. 此外

    C. 在旁邊

    D. 關於

23.

    A. are preferring

    B. preferred

    C. have been preferred

    D. have preferred

23.

    A. 偏愛

    B. 偏愛

    C. 偏愛

    D. 偏愛

24.

    A. provide

    B. provided

    C. providing

    D. to provide

24.

    A. 提供

    B. 提供

    C. 提供

    D. 提供

25.

    A. among

    B. with

    C. on top of

    D. including

25.

    A. 之中

    B. 和

    C. 在頂端

    D. 包括

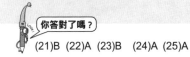

你答對了嗎？

(21)B (22)A (23)B (24)A (25)A

第三部份：閱讀理解

本部份共 15 題，包括數段短文，每篇文章有 2~5 個相關問題，請就就下列的 A、B、C、D 四個選項，選出最適合的答案。

MP3-63

Questions 26-28

Chino is a nine-year-old Golden Retriever with fuzzy paws. Falstaff is a freshwater fish that likes to nibble on fuzzy paws. The two have been friends for three years according to Mary and Dan Heath of Medford, Oregon. They say that as soon as Chino discovered the fishpond in the backyard of their new house, he began lying on the rocks, watching the fish. Chino's favorite fish is Falstaff, a 15-inch orange-and-black koi, and the feeling is mutual. When Chino lies down with his nose an inch from the water, Falstaff swims up to the surface and playfully *nibbles on the dog's paw.

閱讀理解中譯

奇諾是隻九歲大、有著毛爪的金黃拾獚。福斯塔夫則是喜歡啃毛爪的淡水魚。根據美國奧勒崗州梅德福德的「瑪麗與唐」健康中心的說法，牠們兩個變成朋友已經三年了。他們說奇諾一發現他們新家後院的養魚塘後，便開始躺在石頭上看魚。奇諾最喜歡的魚是一隻名叫福斯塔夫的橘黑色錦鯉，而福斯塔夫似乎也很喜歡它。每當奇諾躺下，鼻子離水面很近時，福斯塔夫就會游到水面，好玩地啃著那隻狗的爪子。

26. What is a Golden Retriever?

    A. A fish

    B. A dog

    C. A paw

    D. A koi

26. 金黃拾獴是什麼？

    A. 魚

    B. 狗

    C. 爪子

    D. 錦鯉

27. How long has Chino and Falstaff been friends?

    A. For fifteen years

    B. For two years

    C. For three years

    D. For nine years

27. 奇諾和福斯塔夫變成朋友已經幾年了？

    A. 十五年

    B. 兩年

    C. 三年

    D. 九年

28. What does the word "mutual" mean in line 6?

    A. shared

    B. understand

    C. similar

    D. together

28. 原文第六行中的「mutual」這個字是什麼意思？

    A. 共享的

    B. 了解

    C. 類似的

    D. 一起

`MP3-64`

Questions 29-32

    In 1996 fifth-grader Richie Stachowski was snorkeling with his dad in Hawaii when he spotted some sea turtles. Richie was so amazed to see them that he shouted for his dad to look. But his dad couldn't hear Richie because they were underwater.

你答對了嗎？

(26)B (27)C (28)A

That night Richie began thinking about inventing a way that people could talk to each other underwater. He drew out some designs of an underwater megaphone in his hotel room and when he returned to California researched underwater acoustics on the Internet. Then Richie built a model of his idea, using the $267 he had in his savings account. It looked something like a megaphone attached to a snorkel mouthpiece.

Richie tested his underwater megaphone in every bathtub and swimming pool he could find. Three months later he had perfected his new invention: Water Talkies. Soon Richie was selling his Water Talkies through Wal-Mart, K-Mart, and Toys R' Us.

問題 29-32

1996 年時，一名五年級生理奇・史塔柯烏斯基和他父親在夏威夷進行呼吸管潛水時，發現了一些海龜。理奇看到它們很驚訝，便向父親大叫要他也過來看；不過因為他們當時在水面下，所以他父親聽不到理奇的叫喊。

那天晚上，里奇開始想要發明一種可以讓人在水面下互相通話的方法。他在旅館房間裡畫了一些擴音器的設計圖，回到加州後，便立刻上網研究水中聲響方面的資料。接著理奇花了他帳戶裡頭的 267 塊錢，依自己的想法製作出一種模型。它看起來像是一個和換氣裝置送話口連接的擴音器。

理奇在每個他找得到的浴缸和游泳池裡測試他的水中擴音器。三個月後，他的新發明已經改良得很完美了，他把它叫做「水中對講機」。不久之後，理奇便透過沃爾瑪、凱爾特和玩具反斗城來販售他的水中對講機。

29. What is snorkeling?

    A. It's a water sport.

    B. It's a swimming technique.

    C. It's a type of turtle.

    D. It's an animal found in Hawaii.

30. Where does Richie live?

    A. In a hotel

    B. In California

    C. In Hawaii

    D. In Wal-Mart

31. Which of the following did Richie NOT need for his invention?

    A. A telephone

    B. A swimming pool

    C. Snorkeling gear

    D. A creative mind

32. According to the story, why did Richie invent the Walkie Talkies?

    A. Because he wanted to become rich.

    B. Because he had a lot of free time.

    C. Because he loved to snorkel.

    D. Because he couldn't communicate underwater.

29. 呼吸管潛游是什麼？

    A. 一種水中運動。

    B. 一項游泳技巧。

    C. 一種海龜類型。

    D. 一種在夏威夷發現的動物。

30. 理奇住在哪裡？

    A. 旅館裡

    B. 加州

    C. 夏威夷

    D. 沃爾瑪

31. 下列哪一樣「不是」理奇的新發明所需要的東西？

    A. 電話

    B. 游泳池

    C. 呼吸管潛水設備

    D. 有創意的心靈

32. 根據本文所述，理奇為何會發明水中對講機？

    A. 因為他想要致富。

    B. 因為他空閒時間很多。

    C. 因為他喜歡呼吸管潛水。

    D. 因為他無法在水中和別人通話。

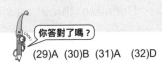

你答對了嗎？

(29)A　(30)B　(31)A　(32)D

Questions 33-34

Baseball has a long history in Taiwan. The Japanese taught the game to the Taiwanese in the early 1900's, and the locals then turned around and beat their colonial masters in a landmark tournament in 1930. The game surged in popularity in the 1960's when Taiwan's Little League team won the first of an eventual 17 world titles. The Chinese Professional Baseball League was launched in 1990, and two years later, Taiwan's national team won a silver medal at the Barcelona Olympics.

Baseball fever in Taiwan peaked in 1996. That year, more than 1.3 million fans poured into ballparks around the island, and television ratings soared. A *high-profile gambling scandal in the late 1990s caused the eventual collapse of several teams, and attendance began dropping. But by 2002, the game had regained its former popularity, as three new baseball parks opened, two near Taipei and a third in Kaohsiung.

33. When did the popularity of baseball in Taiwan start to decline?

    A. After 1996   B. In 1996
    C. Before 1990   D. In the 1960's

34. Why does the author think baseball has become popular again in 2002?

    A. Because Taiwan's Little League team won the world title.

    B. Because the television ratings were really high.

    C. Because Taiwan's national team won a silver medal in the Olympics.

    D. Because three new baseball parks were opened.

問題 33-34

　　棒球在台灣歷史相當悠久。日本人在 1900 年代初期把這項運動教給台灣人後，當地居民回過頭來在 1930 年代的一次重大錦標賽中擊敗他們的殖民地主國。當台灣的小聯盟球隊在 1960 年代贏得第一次世界冠軍時（最後拿了十七次冠軍），這項運動一時大為流行。中華職棒聯盟於 1990 年成立，兩年後，台灣的國家代表隊又在巴塞隆納奧運會中拿到了銀牌。

　　棒球熱在 1996 年達到最高峰。那一年有一百三十萬以上來自台灣各地的球迷湧進棒球場，電視收視率也不斷往上竄升。後來爆發了一時廣受矚目的簽賭醜聞，最後導致一些球隊解散，棒球觀眾也開始下降。不過到了 2002 年，棒球又和以前一樣流行，同時國內也成立了三座新的棒球場，兩座在台北附近，另一座則在高雄。

33. 棒球在台灣流行的程度何時開始減退？

　　A. 1996 年以後　　　　　　B. 1996 年

　　C. 1996 年以前　　　　　　D. 1960 年代

34. 本文作者為何認為棒球在 2002 年又重新流行起來？

　　A. 因為台灣的小聯盟球隊贏得世界冠軍。

　　B. 因為電視收視率確實很高。

　　C. 因為台灣的國家代表隊在奧運會中拿到銀牌。

　　D. 因為國內成立了三座新的棒球場。

你答對了嗎？

(33)A　(34)D

Questions 35-37

IMPORTANT NOTICE
TO ALL EMPLOYEES

1. Effective May 27, 2005, all members from the current Med Life Health plan will be switched to Cigna Healthcare. New forms will be handed out in April. Please have your forms turned into the Human Resources office by May 1, 2005. If you fail to do so, your health insurance will be cancelled. The next enrollment period will not be until November 1, 2005. If you need help filling out the forms, please contact Mary at extension 566.

2. The company dress code will be strictly enforced beginning in April. Everyone should dress in business casual. Men will need to wear a shirt and tie. Previous regulations about female employees wearing revealing clothing have been ignored. Jeans, sneakers, and T-shirts are not allowed for any employee. Please be professional.

3. Renovations to the east wing of the building will begin next week, March 25, 2005. The construction is planned to end by May 1, 2005. Please excuse the noise.

Management apologizes for the inconvenience.

35. Which of the following is NOT a purpose of this notice?

    A. To tell people that they cannot wear strange hairstyles to work.

    B. To inform employees of a new health insurance plan.

    C. To apologize for the noise of the building construction.

    D. To tell people that jeans are not allowed at work.

問題 35-37

重要公告
致全體員工

　1. 自 2005 年五月二十七號生效日開始，所有目前參加梅德健康計畫的員工將轉到西格納保健中心。四月會發給各位新的表格，請在 2005 年五月一號前將表格交到人事部辦公室，否則你的健康保險將會被取消。下次登記時間要等到 2005 年十一月一號。如果對於表格的填寫有任何問題，請撥分機 566 給瑪麗。

　2. 公司的服裝規定將於四月開始嚴格執行。每位員工均需穿著工作休閒服。男生要穿襯衫打領帶。之前關於女性員工穿著較暴露服裝的規定已經取消。任何員工均不准穿著牛仔褲、運動鞋和短袖圓領運動衫。請大家保持專業形象。

　3. 建築物東側的修建工程將於下週－ 2005 年三月二十五號開始進行。該工程預計於 2005 年五月一號完工。這段期間帶來的噪音請多加包涵。

　若造成任何不便，經理部門在這裡向各位致歉。

35. 下列敘述何者「不是」這項公告的目的？

　A. 告訴大家公司不准員工留奇怪的髮型。

　B. 通知員工新的健康保險計畫。

　C. 為建築物的整修工程所帶來的噪音致歉。

　D. 告訴員工上班不准穿牛仔褲。

你答對了嗎？
(35)A

36. When was this notice written?

    A. On May 27, 2005   B. Before March 25, 2005

    C. In November   D. At the beginning of April

37. According to the notice, what did some employees not pay attention to in the past?

    A. The employee's notice   B. The manager's request

    C. The original dress code   D. The boss' advice

MP3-67

Questions 38-40

Dear Tara:

    I'm looking for some advice and counsel from people I know and trust.Rocky Mountain Bank, the company I worked for the last five years, was sold at year-end and joined with another financial institution. As a result, my job was eliminated. The Federal Savings and Loan Insurance Corporation, receiver for Rocky Mountain Bank, asked me to remain and assist in managing the real estate loan/asset portfolio. The position was temporary, as a move to California would be required to make it permanent. I've completed that assignment and I'm ready to move forward with something more long-lasting.

    I'd like to continue to be a manager in a financial services company (bank, savings and loan, credit union, insurance company, etc.) I'm good at managing people and other resources to attain

36. 這項公告何時寫好的？

   A. 2005 年五月二十七號　　　B. 2005 年三月二十五號以前

   C. 十一月　　　　　　　　　　D. 四月初

37. 根據這項公告，哪件事是有些員工過去沒有注意到的？

   A. 給員工的公告　　　　　　　B. 經理的要求

   C. 原來的服裝規定　　　　　　D. 老闆的建議

問題 38-40

親愛的塔拉：

　　我希望能從我認識並且信任的人那裡獲得一些建議和忠告。

　　我過去五年工作的洛基山銀行要在年底賣給別家金融機構，結果工作就沒了。接手的聯邦儲蓄與信貸保險公司要我留下來幫忙處理不動產借貸／資產投資方案。這個職位只是暫時的，因為要一直待下來便需搬到加州才行。手上工作目前已完成，我準備朝更長遠的道路去走。

　　我希望能繼續擔任金融機構的經理職務（銀行、儲蓄與信貸機構、信用合作社、保險公司等等）。我很善於處理客戶問題，對各類可以幫公司賺錢的方案也很有一套。我正在尋找下一個這樣的機會。

你答對了嗎？

(36)B　(37)C

corporate profits. I am looking for that next opportunity.

You're a successful person with friends who are also successful. Perhaps you, or someone you know, are aware of a firm that needs someone with my capabilities. If so, I'd appreciate your giving them a copy of the enclosed resume, and I'd like their name so that I can contact them personally.

I'd appreciate your thoughts and ideas. Please contact me at (303) 755-8880. Thanks for your help.

Best regards,

John H. Norris

38. What is the main reason Norris wrote this letter?

    A. To ask for advice   B. To ask for money

    C. To ask for a raise   D. To ask for a resume

39. What kind of job is Norris looking for?

    A. An insurance salesperson   B. A bank teller

    C. A mountain climber   D. A bank manager

40. What is the relationship between John Norris and Tara?

    A. They are brother and sister.

    B. They are business partners.

    C. They are trusted friends.

    D. They are boyfriend and girlfriend.

　　你不僅是位成功人士，周遭朋友亦為成功典範。或許你個人或是一些你認識的人，有注意到什麼機構需要借重我的專才。如果有的話，要是你能替我把附上的履歷表副本拿給他們，我會感激不盡。方便的話也請把他們的名字給我，以便我私下與他們聯繫。

　　感謝你的費心。請撥 (303) 755-8880 與我聯絡。謝謝你的幫忙。

祝好

約翰・諾瑞斯

38. 諾瑞斯寫這封信的主要理由是什麼？

　　A. 要求建議　　　　　　　　B. 要錢

　　C. 要求加薪　　　　　　　　D. 要履歷表

39. 諾瑞斯在找什麼樣的工作？

　　A. 保險推銷員　　　　　　　B. 銀行出納員

　　C. 登山者　　　　　　　　　D. 銀行經理

40. 約翰・諾瑞斯和塔拉之間是什麼關係？

　　A. 他們是兄妹。

　　B. 他們是生意伙伴。

　　C. 他們是彼此信任的朋友。

　　D. 他們是男女朋友。

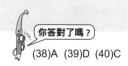

你答對了嗎？

(38)A　(39)D　(40)C

MP3-68

Test 7

第一部份： 句子填空

本部份共 15 題，每題有一個空格。請就下列的 A、B、C、D 四個選項，選出最適合題意的字或詞。

Questions 1-15

1. Brandy is really _____ spending next summer studying Spanish in Mexico.

   A. making sure
   B. looking forward to
   C. making clear
   D. paying attention

2. How has the rapid growth in the technology field affected Taiwanese _____?

   A. population
   B. society
   C. realistic
   D. justice

3. I don't think I could _____ your decision if you had chosen to not attend college.

   A. have respected
   B. respected
   C. respects
   D. been respected

4. Please do not hold his opinions _____ him; he is only a child.

   A. after
   B. for
   C. on
   D. against

題目中譯

1. 布蘭迪很 ____ 下個暑假到墨西哥唸西班牙語。

   A. 確定
   B. 期待
   C. 顯示
   D. 注意

2. 技術領域的快速成長對台灣 ____ 造成了什麼影響？

   A. 人口
   B. 社會
   C. 實際的
   D. 公平

3. 如果你當初選擇不唸大學，我想我無法 ____ 你的決定。

   A. 尊重
   B. 尊重
   C. 尊重
   D. 尊重

4. 他不過是個小孩，請不要和他唱 ____ 調。

   A. 之後
   B. 為了
   C. 在
   D. 反

你答對了嗎？
(1) B　(2)B　(3) A　(4)D

5. Joshua _____ in love with his girlfriend the first time they met.
   A. fell
   B. went
   C. got
   D. made

6. Eve's lie was so _____; her mother knew she was lying as soon as she walked in the door.
   A. splendid
   B. reluctance
   C. reveal
   D. transparent

7. The police officer was _____ the situation well until the thief pulled out a gun.
   A. handled
   B. to handle
   C. to handling
   D. handling

8. _____ today, Mr. Johnson is retiring and will no longer be the principal of our school.
   A. Until
   B. As to
   C. In
   D. As of

9. You must get written _____ from your parents before you can go on the field trip.
   A. counselor
   B. advice
   C. permission
   D. permanent

10. Rita likes _____ before she speaks because it allows her to think more clearly.
    A. paused
    B. to pause
    C. to pausing
    D. pauses

5. 約書亞對他女友一見鐘情（ ____ 他女友）。

    A. 愛上　　　　　　　　　　　B. 愛上

    C. 愛上　　　　　　　　　　　D. 愛上

6. 伊芙說謊太 ____ 了；她一走進門她媽媽就知道她在說謊。

    A. 顯著　　　　　　　　　　　B. 勉強

    C. 顯露　　　　　　　　　　　D. 明顯

7. 竊賊拔槍以前，該名警察一直都把情況 ____ 得很好。

    A. 處理　　　　　　　　　　　B. 處理

    C. 處理　　　　　　　　　　　D. 處理

8. 詹森先生 ____ 今天開始退休，不再是我們學校的校長。

    A. 直到　　　　　　　　　　　B. 至於

    C. 在　　　　　　　　　　　　D. 從

9. 你必須得到父母的書面 ____ 才能參加實地考察。

    A. 顧問　　　　　　　　　　　B. 建議

    C. 同意　　　　　　　　　　　D. 永久的

10. 莉塔喜歡在說話前 ____ 一下，因為這樣可以讓她想得更清楚。

    A. 暫停　　　　　　　　　　　B. 暫停

    C. 暫停　　　　　　　　　　　D. 暫停

你答對了嗎？

(5) A　(6) D　(7) D　(8) D　(9) C　(10) B

11. I think I _____ eating at that new Indian restaurant tonight. How about you?

 A. figure out   B. feel like

 C. look for   D. want to

12. _____ path you choose in life, make sure it leads to a lot of love and happiness.

 A. What   B. Wherever

 C. Whichever   D. Whenever

13. It took Elle at least six months _____ to her new life in Taiwan.

 A. to adjust   B. adjusted

 C. adjusting   D. will adjust

14. Megan was very _____ as a child so she grew up crying a lot.

 A. loveable   B. independent

 C. sensitive   D. confident

15. Life is a long _____ of hellos and goodbyes.

 A. series   B. continue

 C. general   D. profile

11. 我覺得我今晚 ＿＿＿ 在那家新的印度餐廳吃飯。你呢？

    A. 想出　　　　　　　　　B. 想要

    C. 尋找　　　　　　　　　D. 希望

12. ＿＿＿ 你選擇那一條人生道路，務必讓它通往愛和幸福。

    A. 什麼　　　　　　　　　B. 無論在哪裡

    C. 無論（哪一個）　　　　D. 無論何時

13. 艾莉至少花了六個月才 ＿＿＿ 台灣的新生活。

    A. 適應　　　　　　　　　B. 適應

    C. 適應　　　　　　　　　D. 適應

14. 梅根小時候很 ＿＿＿，於是長大後變得很愛哭。

    A. 可愛　　　　　　　　　B. 獨立

    C. 敏感　　　　　　　　　D. 自信

15. 生命乃一長 ＿＿＿ 的聚散過程。

    A. 串（系列）　　　　　　B. 繼續

    C. 一般的　　　　　　　　D. 輪廓

你答對了嗎？

(11)B　(12)C　(13)A　(14)C　(15)A

第二部份： 段落填空

本部份共 10 題，每篇短文包括二至三個段落，每個段落各含 5 個空格。請就下列的 A、B、C、D 四個選項，選出最適合題意的字或詞。

`MP3-69`

Regular polo is played __16__ teams of horses; elephant polo is played with two teams of four elephants. Each elephant carries a polo player and a mahout, or driver. The mahout sits directly behind the elephant's ears and directs the beast using his voice, hands, and feet. The player sits behind the mahout and hangs __17__ the elephant while striking at the ball with a long-handled mallet. The umpire watches the play from a wooden platform seat on the back of another elephant. Not only does the umpire need to stop the game every __18__ to bring out a giant poo-poo scooper, but he also has to make sure the elephants don't __19__ – something they love to do. Elephants are not allowed to pick up the ball with their trunks and just toss it into the goal. Nor are they allowed to __20__ down in front of the goal.

段落填空中譯

一般的馬球是 __16__ 馬組成隊伍來比賽，而大象馬球是分兩隊四隻象來比賽。每隻大象背上都有一名馬球選手和一名象夫，即管象人。象夫直接坐在大象耳朵後面，用他的聲音和手腳來指揮大象。選手則坐在象夫後面緊 __17__ 著大象，然後用長手柄的球棍來擊球。裁判則坐在另一隻大象背上的木製平台座位來觀看比賽，不僅要 __18__ 暫停比賽把一大勺巨大大便運走，還要確保

大象不會 __19__ －它們很愛這麼做。大象不准用鼻子把球拿起來直接扔進球門，也不准在球門前 __20__ 下來。

16.

A. use
B. uses
C. using
D. used

16.

A. 用
B. 用
C. 用
D. 用

17.

A. up on
B. around
C. onto
D. with

17.

A. 抓
B. 抓
C. 抓
D. 抓

18.

A. often
B. now and then
C. this and that
D. again

18.

A. 時常
B. 偶爾
C. 有的沒的
D. 再次

19.

A. excuse
B. cheat
C. play
D. fun

19.

A. 原諒
B. 作弊
C. 玩耍
D. 樂趣

20.

A. laid
B. lies
C. lie
D. lay

20.

A. 躺
B. 躺
C. 躺
D. 躺

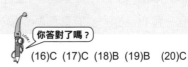

你答對了嗎？

(16)C (17)C (18)B (19)B (20)C

MP3-70

Questions 21-25

The Japanese were given Formosa in 1895 after the end of the Sino-Japanese War to __21__ for fifty years. The only obvious signs of their occupation that __22__ today are the lunchboxes, the sharp green wasabi that is eaten with sashimi, and a language that some older Taiwanese speak. The only signs of Japanese architecture that still stands intact can be found in Ilan.

Three houses __23__ in 1906 to house the Ilan County magistrate; the chief of general affairs, the second in command to the magistrate; and the president of the Taipei Provincial Ilan School of Agriculture and Forestry, what is today National Ilan University. The three homes represent the __24__ of the former resident's positions. The magistrate's house is the largest, the chief of general affairs is the second largest, and the Taipei Provincial School of Agriculture and Forestry president's house is the smallest. Admission to the magistrate's house and __25__ museum is NT$30 for adults, NT$20 for students, and NT$15 for children. There is no fee to view the School of Agriculture and Forestry President's House or to visit the coffee shop.

問題 21-25

1895 年中日戰爭結束後，日本交還 __21__ 了五十年的台灣。日本曾占領台灣到今天所 __22__ 的唯一明顯跡象，除了配生魚片一起吃那種辛辣綠色芥末的午餐飯盒外，就是有些老一輩台灣人會説日本話。至於留下的完整日式建築則可以在宜蘭看到。

1906 年曾 __23__ 了三棟房子給宜蘭縣官員居住，他們分別是總務長、地方法官，還有台北州立宜蘭農林學校的校長，也就是今天的國立宜蘭大學。

這三棟建築代表了先前住在裡面的人 __24__ 各有不同。法官的房子最大，其次是總務長的房子，最小的是台北州立宜蘭農林學校校長的房子。參觀法官房子及 __25__ 博物館的費用是全票 30 塊、學生票 20 塊、兒童票 15 塊。參觀台北州立宜蘭農林學校校長的房子或是那裡的咖啡店則不用門票。

21.

A. rule   A. 統治
B. ruler   B. 統治者
C. ruling   C. 統治
D. rules   D. 統治

22.

A. functions   A. 功能
B. remain   B. 留下
C. evident   C. 明顯的
D. left behind   D. 忘了帶

23.

A. built   A. 蓋
B. were built   B. 蓋
C. are building   C. 蓋
D. have been building   D. 蓋

24.

A. experiment   A. 實驗
B. financial   B. 財政的
C. importance   C. 重要性
D. significant   D. 重要的

25.

A. a few   A. 幾個
B. they   B. 他們
C. its   C. 其
D. some   D. 一些

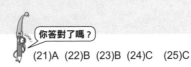

你答對了嗎？

(21)A (22)B (23)B (24)C (25)C

第三部份：閱讀理解

本部份共15題，包括數段短文，每篇文章有 2~5 個相關問題，請就下列的 A、B、C、D 四個選項，選出最適合的答案。

MP3-71

Questions 26-28

The United States *Bullion *Depository is one of the most secret places in the world. The nation's entire gold reserve is kept there in a two-story underground valut surrounded by a super-secret fortress. The *vault's walls are made of *granite, *concrete, and steel. The door alone weighs 60,000 pounds!

The Depository has its own Treasury Department defense force, but it's also protected by the next-door neighbor, the U.S. Army. For obvious reasons, details of its security system are kept secret from the public. No one person knows the entire combination to the vault door; many people each know little pieces of it. What's inside? About 368,000 gold bars, each weighing 400 ounces (11kg). That's 147 million ounces of gold, which, at the current price of about $400 per ounce, would be worth roughly $58.8 billion! That's enough money for one large pizza, one half-gallon of ice cream, and two CDs for you and five friends, every day for more than a million years!

閱讀理解中譯

美國金塊貯藏所是世界上最神秘的地方之一。整個國家的黃金儲藏量都存放在一棟地下兩層樓、由極機密的堡壘所包圍的金庫裡。這個金庫的牆壁是花崗岩、混凝土和鋼做的，光是大門就重達 60000 磅！

該貯藏所有自己金庫部門所屬的防衛軍，但也同時受到它的鄰居－美軍的保護。它的安全系統保密不對外開放是可以理解的。沒有人知道金庫大門全部的密碼，很多人都只知道其中一小段。金庫裡面放的是什麼？大約有 368000 塊金條，每條重 400 盎司（11 公斤）。所以總共有一億四千七百萬盎司的黃金，以目前市價每盎司 400 元美金計算，總值大約五千八百八十億美金！如果你和你五個朋友每天吃一塊大披薩、半加侖冰淇淋，另外再買兩張 CD，這些錢足足可以這樣過一百萬年！

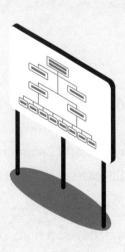

26. According to the article, why is the Depository one of the most secret places in the world?

   A. Because it was built by a king.

   B. Because it holds a lot of important documents.

   C. Because the door is 60,000 pounds.

   D. Because it holds a lot of gold.

27. Who knows the whole combination to the lock?

   A. The president

   B. The U.S. Navy

   C. The Depository's defense force

   D. No one

28. What is the value of one bar of gold?

   A. $368,000.00   B. $580,000.00

   C. $400.00   D. $160,000.00

MP3-72

Questions 29-31

Green Grass Lawn Care

Green Grass Lawn Care is the world's largest lawn and landscape company. We started as a small private company in 1974 and now serve more than 3.4 million residential and commercial customers across the U.S. with lawn care, tree and shrub care, and landscaping services.

For many years, Green Grass has been the industry leader in the development of new technology for lawn care. Green Grass

26. 根據本文所述，該貯藏所為何是世界上最神秘的地方之一？

    A. 因為它是某個國王建造的。

    B. 因為裡頭有很多重要文件。

    C. 因為大門重達 60,000 磅。

    D. 因為裡頭有很多黃金。

27. 誰知道密碼鎖全部的密碼？

    A. 總統

    B. 美國海軍

    C. 貯藏所的防衛軍

    D. 沒有人

28. 一塊金條價值多少？

    A. $368,000.00　　　　　　B. $580,000.00

    C. $400.00　　　　　　　　D. $160,000.00

問題 29-31

綠色草坪保養公司

　　「綠色草坪保養」公司是全世界最大的草坪和造園公司。我們從 1974 年時的一家私人公司起家，目前所提供的草坪保養、樹木及灌木保養，以及造園服務，服務對象包括全美三百四十萬以上的住宅區和 commercial 商業區的客戶。

　　「綠色草坪」多年來在草坪保養的新技術方面，一直是業界的龍頭老大。「綠色草坪保養」公司花費龐大資本持續評估新式產品及各項設備，致力於發展更好的方法進行草地、樹木及灌木的保養工作。另外，我們所有的草坪專家

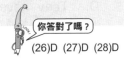

你答對了嗎？

(26)D　(27)D　(28)D

devotes substantial resources to continually evaluate new products and equipment and to develop better methods for taking care of grass, trees, and shrubs. Further, all of our lawn specialists are full-time employees who must complete an intensive training program before they can be certified by Green Grass Lawn Care.

Additionally, we have taken an active leadership role in both developing and supporting sound environmental practices and regulatory policies. Green Grass is committed to environmentally responsible practices and products, and we have established our own set of environmentally friendly principles.

Receive $30 worth of lawn care FREE every time you refer a friend who becomes a Green Grass Lawn Care customer!!

29. Which of the following services is NOT offered by Green Grass Lawn Care?

A. Plant flowers   B. Cut grass

C. Grow trees   D. Build fences

30. What has helped Green Grass Lawn Care become successful?

A. They do not use environmentally friendly methods.

B. They offer services to private homes only.

C. They are always developing new technology for lawn care.

D. They have an easy training program for their employees.

都是全職員工，他們都必須通過密集的訓練課程，才能拿到「綠色草坪保養」的合格證明。

此外，我們在發展與支援聲音環境實踐及管理政策上，也扮演積極的龍頭角色。「綠色草坪」不僅負起重要的環境實踐和產品的責任，也建立了自己的一套環保原則。

你每介紹一位朋友成為「綠色草坪保養」公司的客戶，就可以省下 30 元的草坪保養費用！！

29. 「綠色草坪保養」公司「不」提供下列哪一項服務？

    A. 種花   B. 割草

    C. 種樹   D. 建籬笆

30. 什麼幫助了「綠色草坪保養」公司成功？

    A. 他們不使用環保方法。

    B. 他們只服務私人家庭。

    C. 他們不斷發展草坪保養的新技術。

    D. 他們給員工的訓練課程很容易。

你答對了嗎？
(29)D (30)C

31. Who will get a discount according to this information?

    A. A new customer who got referred by an old customer.

    B. A loyal customer that gets her neighbor to hire Green Grass.

    C. A satisfied customer of Green Grass.D. Someone who often uses the services of Green Grass.

`MP3-73`

Questions 32-33

Lone Star Volkswagen
Celebrating our GRAND OPENING in Garland!
0% interest for 72 months for those who qualify on used or new cars!
The new 2005 Jetta is here and ready for immediate delivery!

The New Jetta. It's an icon, it's an emotion, it's just pure Volkswagen.

It's gotten bigger. It's all grown up, sort of. What you expect from a Jetta you'll get from this new Jetta. What you don't realize is this car is so much better than the outgoing model. There have been tremendous refinements in it's drive and levels of fit and finish that rival much more expensive cars. There is even a new steering system that doesn't even use a steering pump, so no more fluid to replace and check. There's even a new choice of color to choose from! The purple Jetta is simply amazing! And the back seat, whoa, there's WAY more room now.

This is an all new car that completely rewrites what makes a Volkswagen a Volkswagen.

The New Jetta. Expect the unexpected. Really.

31. 根據這項消息，誰可以得折扣？

A. 舊客戶介紹的新客戶。　　B. 介紹鄰居給「綠色草坪」的忠實客戶。

C. 滿意「綠色草坪」的客戶。　　D. 經常請「綠色草坪」來服務的人。

問題 32-34

孤星福斯汽車
慶祝佳園隆重開幕！
無論二手或新車，一律 72 個月零利率！
2005 年新款車捷達 (Jetta) 問世，準備立即送到府上！

新款捷達是一種圖像、一種情感，更是道地的大眾汽車。

這款新車大多了，也差不多更接近完美。新款捷達絕對能滿足任何你對捷達的期待。你可能不知道這款車比現有的模型車好太多了。它在駕駛及舒適度上做了重大的精細改變，那些更高價位的同級車種根本無法相比。甚至連駕駛系統都不需要動力轉向幫浦，所以也不用換油和檢查。此外還有不同的顏色可以選擇！紫色捷達簡直令人驚奇！還有後座，哇，現在的空間可是大多了。

這款全新車種完全改寫了大眾的歷史，保證顛覆你對大眾的既定印象。

全新的捷達，將帶給你意外的驚喜。不要懷疑。

你答對了嗎？

(31) B

32. What is Lone Star Volkswagen celebrating?

    A.   The immediate delivery of the Jetta.

    B.   The arrival of the new Jetta.

    C.   The opening of a new store.

    D.   The closing of an old store.

33. Which of the following is not an improvement of the new Jetta?

    A.   More color choices   B.   Bigger tires

    C.   More space   D.   A new steering system

`MP3-74`

Questions 34-36

Outdoor Sports Store
Father's Day Sale
June 4th-19th
Give Dad what he really wants!!

Outdoor Sports Store wants to help you celebrate Father's Day the right way.

Dad doesn't want a tie or another pair of socks. What he really wants is a brand new fishing rod or a bigger bar-b-que grill! We have everything Dad would ever need for his outdoor adventures. We are guaranteed to have the biggest selection of equipment for water sports, fishing, camping, cycling, and MORE!

We are also extending our return policy for this Father's Day

32. 「孤星福斯汽車」公司在慶祝什麼？

    A. 立即運送捷達。

    B. 新款捷達已到貨。

    C. 新店開幕。

    D. 舊店結束營業。

33. 下列哪一項不在新款捷達車的改進項目之內？

    A. 更多種顏色可以選擇   B. 更大的輪胎

    C. 更多空間   D. 新式駕駛系統

問題 34-36

戶外運動商店
父親節特賣
六月四號至十九號
送父親一分他真正需要的禮物！！

「戶外運動商店」想幫你用對方式慶祝父親節。

父親要的不是領帶或另一雙襪子，他「真正」要的是一支全新的釣竿或大一點的烤肉架！父親戶外探險活動可能需要的東西，我們這裡應有盡有。無論是水上運動、釣魚、露營、騎單車，還是其他各類戶外活動，我們保證提供最多樣化的配備選擇！

為了慶祝父親節，我們的退款期限也會延長。父親不只有一個月的時間可以試用禮物再決定要不要，而是兩個月！

你答對了嗎？

(32)C (33)B

373

celebration. Instead of having a month to decide if he wants to keep his gift, Dad will have 2 months!

Free delivery provided! All purchases over $100.00 come with a FREE Father's Day T-shirt!

Men's Waterproof Jackets 50% off	Water *Skis $25.00 off
Fishing Rods 75% off	Bicycles $50.00 off
Tents 25% off	Underwater Watches $20.00 off

34. What will Outdoor Sports Store do during the sale?

A. Reduce prices in all departments

B. Stay open longer than usual

C. Give free gifts to all customers

D. Offer a longer return period to unhappy customers

35. What is a quarter of its original price during the sale?

A. Fishing rods

B. Water skis

C. Jackets

D. Tents

36. According to the advertisement, what is Outdoor Sports Store offering its customers?

A. The largest selection of ties

B. A *non-refundable, exchange only policy

C. Delivery without being charged

D. A discount in every department

不另外收取運費！購物超過一百塊美金則「免費」贈送一件父親節短袖圓

領運動衫！

男用防水夾克五折	滑水橇七五折
釣竿二點五折	腳踏車五折
帳蓬七五折	水用錶八折

34. 「戶外運動商店」會在特賣期間做什麼事？

    A. 每個部門全面降價

    B. 比平常營業時間晚

    C. 贈送免費禮物給所有顧客

    D. 提供不滿意的顧客更長的退款期限。

35. 特賣期間，什麼東西只賣原來價格的四分之一？

    A. 釣竿

    B. 滑水橇

    C. 夾克

    D. 帳蓬

36. 根據這則廣告，「戶外運動商店」會提供顧客什麼服務？

    A. 種類最多的領帶

    B. 只換不退的規定

    C. 免運費

    D. 每個部門都提供折扣

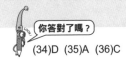

你答對了嗎？

(34)D (35)A (36)C

Questions 37-40

After 35 years in prison for stealing a black-and-white television set, Junior Allen is finally a free man. Allen, 65, walked out of prison on May 29, 2005, ending a case that attracted widespread attention because he remained in jail while other inmates convicted of murder, rape or child molestation were released.

Allen was a 30-year-old migrant farm worker from Georgia with a criminal history that included burglaries and a violent assault when he sneaked into an unlocked house and stole a 19-inch black-and-white television worth $140. He was sentenced in 1970 to life in prison for second-degree burglary. The penalty for the offense has since been changed to a maximum of three years in prison.

The state Parole Commission decided last year to release Allen if he behaved and completed a transitional work-release program. He worked at a restaurant washing dishes and floors and had no prison infractions during the past three years. He did so well he was released several months early — on his 26th try at *parole. His parole could last up to five years, meaning he could gain complete freedom by age 70.

The parole commission hasn't been able to give a reason why Allen wasn't released earlier. "He wasn't the best prisoner, but he also wasn't the worst," they told reporters.

Enoch Hasberry, the programs director at Carteret Correctional Center in Newport where Allen went through work-release, said he worries Allen might not adjust well to life on the outside. "For a black-and-white TV, how much do you have to pay?" Hasberry said. "We've got an in-house joke here: How much time would he have gotten if he had stolen a color TV?"

問題 37-40

由於偷了一台黑白電視而入獄 35 年的小艾倫終於重獲自由。由於艾倫監禁期間，其他因謀殺、強姦或孩童性騷擾罪名而入獄的囚犯都已被釋放，故艾倫的案件一時引起了廣泛注意；等到 65 歲的艾倫於 2005 年五月二十九號離開監獄時，這個案件總算告了一段落。

艾倫當年 30 歲，是名來自喬治亞州的移民農場工人；他當時偷偷溜進一間未上鎖的房子裡偷了一台十九吋、價值 140 塊美金的黑白電視，便多了竊盜和暴力攻擊的犯罪前科。他在 1970 年以二級竊盜罪被判終身監禁。這項罪名的徒刑從那時起便被改成最高三年有期徒刑。

州立假釋委員會去年決定，只要艾倫表現良好，能完成過渡期的監外就業，便要將他釋放。艾倫在一家餐廳做清洗碗盤和地板的工作，過去三年都沒有違法入獄情事發生。由於他表現相當良好，便在他第二十六次申請假釋時，提早幾個月被釋放。他的假釋最多可以持續五年，也就是說他七十歲以前都享有完全的自由。

假釋委員會一直沒有說明為何艾倫不能早點被釋放的理由。委員會告訴記者：「他不是最好的囚犯，但也不是最壞的囚犯。」

艾倫通過監外就業的紐波特那裡的卡特里特懲治中心監外就業主任愛諾克·漢斯貝瑞說，他擔心艾倫無法適應外面的生活。「為了一台黑白電視，究竟要付出多少代價？」他說：「我們內部有個笑話是，如果他偷的是彩色電視機，那他到底要關多久？」

37. What was Allen convicted for in **1970?**

  A. For stealing a color television set

  B. For not finishing his work-release program

  C. For committing murder

  D. For being a thief

38. Why has Allen's case attracted media attention?

  A. He completed the work-release program.

  B. He will gain complete freedom by the age of 70.

  C. He stole a television set.

  D. He has been in jail longer than worse criminals.

39. Why has Allen been kept in jail for so long?

  A. Because he did not listen to the rules of the Parole Commission

  B. Because he stole something that was worth a lot of money

  C. Because he murdered another inmate

  D. The Parole Commission doesn't really know the reason

40. Which of the following best describes Enoch Hasberry's opinion on Allen's case?

  A. He thinks Allen was the worst criminal they have ever had.

  B. He thinks Allen should have stolen a color TV instead.

  C. He thinks Allen shouldn't have been kept in jail for that long.

  D. He thinks Allen deserves harsher punishment.

37. 艾倫在 1970 年被判什麼罪？

　　A. 偷了一台彩色電視

　　B. 未完成他的監外就業

　　C. 謀殺

　　D. 當小偷

38. 艾倫案為何吸引媒體的注意？

　　A. 他完成了監外就業。

　　B. 他會在七十歲前得到完全的自由。

　　C. 他偷了一台電視機。

　　D. 他比其他更壞的罪犯關得更久。

39. 艾倫為何坐那麼久的牢？

　　A. 因為他沒有聽從假釋委員會的規定

　　B. 因為他偷了很值錢的東西

　　C. 因為他謀殺了另一名囚犯

　　D. 假釋委員會其實不太清楚原因

40. 下列哪一項敘述最能貼切形容愛諾克‧漢斯貝瑞對艾倫案的看法？

　　A. 他認為艾倫是有史以來最壞的罪犯。

　　B. 他認為艾倫應該偷彩色電視機才對。

　　C. 他認為艾倫不應該坐那麼久的牢。

　　D. 他認為艾倫應受到更嚴厲的懲罰。

你答對了嗎？

(37) D　(38) D　(39) D　(40) C

MP3-76

[Test 1]

shelter [ˈʃɛltɚ]n. 避難所

bargain [ˈbɑrgɪn]n. 廉價買賣

tsunami [tsuˈnɑmɪ]n. 海嘯

illustrate [ˈɪləstret]v. 說明

laptop [ˈlæptɑp]n. 手提電腦

stock up 貯存

gear [gɪr]n. 用具

[Test 2]

sausage [ˈsɔsɪdʒ]n. 香腸、臘腸

round trip 來回旅行

fare [fɛr]n. 車費、船費

antibiotic [ˌæntɪaɪˈɑtɪk]a. 抗菌的、制菌的

fluoride [ˈflɔraɪd]n. 氟化物

plaque [plæk]n. 疫病

patent [ˈpætn̩t]n. 專利

defendant [dɪˈfɛndənt]n. 被告

Hamburg [ˈhæmbɝg]n. 漢堡〈西德的港市〉

discriminatory [dɪˈskrɪmənəˌtɔrɪ]a. 歧視的

asylum [əˈsaɪləm]n. 避難所

barrier [ˈbærɪɚ]n. 國境的碉堡

snorkel [ˈsnɔrkl̩]n. 潛水艇通氣管

convict [kənˈvɪkt]v. 宣判有罪

[Test 3]

Elvis (搖滾歌手) 貓王名

ledge [lɛdʒ]n. 從牆壁突出的檯

tank tops 背心裝

sandal [ˈsændl̩]n. 涼鞋

panic[ˈpænɪk]n.v. 恐慌

(過去式和進行式分別為 panicked, panicking.)

paddle[ˈpædl̩]n.v. 槳、用槳划行

attest [əˈtɛst]v. 證實、見證

land sb. in sth. 使某人陷入困境

guerrilla [gəˈrɪlə]n. 游擊隊隊員

paramilitary [ˌpærəˈmɪlɪˌtɛrɪ]a. 輔助軍隊的

outlaw [ˈaʊtˌlɔ]n. 不法之徒

foul [faʊl]a. 骯髒的

dealership [ˈdilɚˌʃɪp]n. 經銷權

[Test 4]

archeological [ˌɑrkɪəˈlɑdʒɪkl̩]a. 考古學的

archaeologist [ˌɑrkɪˈɑlədʒɪst]n. 考古學家

anthropologist [ˌænθrəˈpɑlədʒɪst] n. 人類學家

kidney [ˈkɪdnɪ]n. 腎臟

dialysis [daɪˈæləsɪs]n.(醫學) 滲析、透析

rancher [ˈræntʃɚ]n. 牧場 (農園) 主人

sheepdog [ˈʃip͵dɒg]n. 牧羊犬

slaughterhouse [ˈslɔtɚ͵haʊs]n. 屠宰場

etiquette [ˈɛtɪkɛt]n. 禮節

pooch[putʃ]n.(俚、謔) 狗

certify [ˈsɝtə͵faɪ]v. 認證

[Test 5]

ward off 避開

ingredient [ɪnˈgridɪənt]n. 成分、原素

pickle [ˈpɪkl]n. 醃汁

charcoal [ˈtʃɑr͵kol]n. 木炭

sulfur [ˈsʌlfɚ]n. 硫磺

gunpowder [ˈgʌn͵paʊdɚ]n. 火藥

hourglass [ˈaʊr͵glæs]n. 沙漏

corset [ˈkɔrsɪt]n. 整形內衣、緊身褡

rod [rɑd]n. 棒

whalebone [ˈhwel͵bon]n. 鯨鬚

cardboard [ˈkɑrd͵bord]n. 厚紙

keep up 持續不停

pop up 出乎意料的發生

whirl [hwɝl]v. 捲成漩渦

hoist [hɔɪst]v. 捲起、吊起

take off (飛機) 起飛

exclusive [ɪkˈsklusɪv]a. 獨家的、獨有的

extraction [ɪkˈstrækʃən]n. 抽出

[Test 6]

nuisance [ˈnjusn̩s]n. 討厭鬼、討厭的東西

jockey [ˈdʒɑkɪ]n. 騎師

adrenaline [æˈdrɛlɪn]n. 腎上腺素

morgue [mɔrg]n. 陳屍所

corridor[ˈkɔrɪdɚ]n. 走廊

strewn [strun]v. 散播 (strew 的過去分詞)

nibble [ˈnɪbl̩]v. 一點一點地啃

snorkel [ˈsnɔrkl̩]n.(潛水用的) 呼吸管

megaphone [ˈmɛgə͵fon]n. 擴音器

high-profile 引人矚目的

extension [ɪkˈstɛnʃən]n. 分機

[Test 7]

polo [ˈpolo]n. 馬球

mahout [məˈhaʊt]n. 象奴、馭象者

poo-poo [ˈpu͵pu]n. 大便

toss [tɔs]v.n. 丟擲

bullion [ˈbʊljən]n. 金塊

depository [dɪˈpɑzə͵torɪ]n. 貯藏所

vault [vɔlt]n. 金庫

granite [ˈgrænɪt]n. 花崗岩

concrete [ˈkɑnkrit]n. 混凝土

ski [ski]n. 滑水板

non-refundable 不予退還的

parole [pəˈrol]n. 假釋

國家圖書館出版品預行編目資料

NEW TOEIC突破900分必考單字.聽力.閱讀/
張小怡, Johnson Mo合著. – 新北市：布可
屋文化, 2023.02

面； 公分. –(多益系列；6)
ISBN 978-626-7203-25-5(平裝)
1.CST: 多益測驗
805.1895   111021751

免費下載QR Code音檔
行動學習，即刷即聽

NEW TOEIC 突破 900 分必考單字 . 聽力 . 閱讀
（附 QR Code 線上學習音檔）

作者 / 張小怡 · Jonson Mo
出版單位 / 布可屋文化
總編輯 / 沈瑋鑫
責任編輯 / Francis Wu
封面設計 / 李秀英
內文排版 / lin lin
行銷企劃 / 高廷榮
業務經理 / 王笠宇
行政助理 / 楊婷雅
出版公司 / 六六八企業有限公司
地址 / 新北市淡水區民族路 148 號 4 樓

email ／ bookhouse68@Gmail.com
電話／（02）2808-4587
傳真／（02）2808-4587
出版日期／ 2023 年 2 月　再版二刷／ 2023 年 4 月
台幣定價／ 449 元（附 MP3 線上音檔）
港幣定價／ 150 元（附 MP3 線上音檔）
郵政劃撥／ 31598840
戶名／哈福企業有限公司

總代理／易可數位行銷股份有限公司
地址／新北市新店區寶橋路 235 巷 6 弄 3 號 5 樓
電話／（02）8911-0825
傳真／（02）8911-0801